CRUEL THORNE

AVA HARRISON

Cruel Throne
Published by AH Publishing

Cruel Throne
Cover Design: Hang Le
Editor: Editing4Indies
Content Editor: Readers Together
Proofreader: Virginia Carey

AUTHOR NOTE

This is Lorenzo Amante's villain origin story. This story takes place before the Corrupt Empire Series.

You do not have to read those books to read this and this won't spoil the other books.

Enjoy!

For a full list of triggers, please head to

THE BEGINNING

CHAPTER 1

Lorenzo

MOM KEEPS HER HAND CLAMPED AROUND MY WRIST LIKE she thinks I'll bolt.

To be fair, I might.

The Danforth family estate rises in front of us—if you can even call it an estate. Estates are lawns and fences and maybe a fountain if the owners want to brag. This? This is . . . obscene. A peninsula jutting into the Long Island Sound, like a giant hand reaching out to strangle the ocean.

The mansion looks less like a house and more like something ripped out of a documentary about robber barons. White stone columns, glass walls that catch the morning sun, balconies stacked like gold. Every inch of it screams money. Old money. The kind that buys influence, hides sins, and buries bodies beneath a philanthropic foundation.

My naive mother beams anyway. I don't have the heart to tell her there's probably a room in her new place of employment reserved for sacrificing the poor.

Mom—sweet, sweet Angela, bless her heart—squeezes my wrist as if that might extract enthusiasm from me like juice from a lemon. "Isn't it beautiful, Enzo?"

"It's big," I mutter.

The sigh she gives me, like she gave birth to a disappointment but still loves me enough to endure it, earns her an eye roll.

She swats my hand away when I try to pull her luggage out of the popped trunk of our car. "Be on your best behavior. We need this job. This could pay for—"

"Don't," I cut in. "Don't say college."

This pipe dream of hers is laughable at best.

Her eyes soften in that way that always makes my chest tighten. "You're smart enough."

"People like me don't end up in colleges." I tilt my head, pausing to correct, "We clean them. Maybe."

Not my fault that I spent the past eighteen years as a proud delinquent. Who told the illustrious public school system of Middlesex to make a lazy lifestyle so appealing? Or Kent County. Or Somerset. Or any of the other billion hellholes I've hopped in and out of.

Mom swats my arm. "Stop it. You're going to work hard, keep your head down, and not get into any trouble. You hear me?"

I grunt, which she generously interprets as agreement.

A sleek black golf cart hums toward us. A man in a white uniform hops out, sunglasses cutting half his face.

He doesn't even glance at me, just nods to my mother. "You must be Mrs. Rossi."

"Miss," Mom gently corrects. "Miss Rossi."

The dude continues without pausing, "The kitchen manager said to bring you straight to staff housing."

Mom smiles politely. "And my son?"

"Oh. Right. He'll be in staff housing, too." The man gestures to me like I'm extra luggage.

Mom nudges me. "Say thank you."

I don't. I climb into the back of the golf cart and stare at the mansion as it looms closer, swallowing us whole.

The path curves through gardens that look like they require daily worship. Flowers I can't name. Bushes trimmed into shapes I didn't know bushes could be. Marble statues of people who probably never lifted anything heavier than a gold spoon.

The golf cart stops in front of a wing of the estate tucked behind a line of trees. A corridor connects it to the main house, but it's still far enough away that the staff is out of sight. It's still nicer than any place I've ever lived—clean brick, fresh paint, windows without cracks. Staff housing, I assume.

"Your room is 2B," the man tells me. "Don't touch anything outside the servant wing. Don't wander. Don't—" He pauses, as if trying to find the right words to avoid calling me what he's thinking. "Just . . . keep to your lane."

I smirk. "I wasn't planning on graduating to yours."

He doesn't laugh. Figures. I have very little faith in the sense of humor of the people who walk these obsessively manicured grounds. "Angela, your room is this one." He points to the door across the hall from mine.

My mother nods at him, and then the stranger is gone after giving both us our keys. We never even got his name.

My room is small—seven feet by seven feet, with just a dresser and a twin bed that stretches from wall to wall. But that's not the point. The point is it's safe.

Which is more than I can say about anywhere we've lived in the past thirteen years.

Mom pretends not to notice the way I pause in the doorway or how my chest tightens at the sight of a bed that doesn't sag, a window without bars, and clean sheets.

"We'll be fine working here," she tells herself more than me.

I don't say anything, just toss my backpack onto the bed and nod in satisfaction when the frame doesn't collapse into a heap of rotten wood like my last one.

"Go keep yourself busy. I'll check out my room." Mom pushes me out the open door. "Maybe go for a walk? Just stay away from the main part of the house unless someone asks for you."

"Trust me." I slide my phone into my pocket and back away from our room. "Buttering up to rich people isn't my hobby."

To be fair, her warning is warranted. My only concern for as long as I can remember—hell, probably for my whole life—has been making sure Mom and I had enough money to eat.

We're poor *poor.* Walk-to-work-in-the-snow poor. No-new-shoes-even-when-my-feet-grow poor. The only three shirts I own were scrounged from the stained discards of our local Salvation Army and bleached to unsightly hues, courtesy of the dish bleach from Mom's last job as a busser.

"I need this job, Lorenzo."

Not sure who she's trying to reassure—her or me.

I edge backward, dragging my feet. "You've said that seven times."

"I mean it. We're lucky to be here. This job pays well." Mom sighs, brushing invisible lint off her blouse. She's always obsessed with keeping up appearances as if cleanliness can hide the stench of poverty on us. "Keep your head down. Be polite. Work hard. No trouble. And for God's sake, don't talk back to anyone."

I hear it then. It's not the warning or the worry. She's scared, and it's more than just about the job and the house. It's about me.

The possibility that I might fuck up my life beyond repair downright terrifies her. Hence, her banging on my door this morning at the ass crack of dawn and demanding that I pack. Within two hours, out of nowhere, my life was uprooted. All because I got into a bit of trouble.

Or . . . I guess, a lot of trouble. Depends on who you ask.

"Okay." My voice dips. "I'll behave."

It's my fault we're here, after all. I might as well play nice.

Mom shakes her head, smiling the way she does when she worries I'm turning into my father—cold, distant, and mysteriously absent.

I don't want to be him.

Especially since that's basically all the info I know about my dad, and I managed to scrounge it all up on my own with some subtle clues.

Ditched his kid for eighteen years? Distant.

Not even a Christmas card? Cold AF.

Not a phone call, either, by the way—absent.

So, no, I don't want to be like my deadbeat dad.

But I don't want to be a charity case either.

I escape before Mom can keep lecturing me.

The estate—correction: summer home. Apparently, these are a thing—is quiet in that expensive way. It's the type of silence that feels purchased. Even the ocean breeze seems trained, brushing the hedges like it's been ordered not to rustle them too loudly.

I wander along a stone path, hands shoved deep in my pockets. The air smells like salt and lemon trees, a natural scent that could be bottled and sold as perfume, costing more than my mother's old car.

A gardener kneels near a row of rose bushes, trimming them with surgical precision. When I pass, he nods without looking up. Staff recognize staff. Or at least, they recognize the defeated slouch of someone who can't afford to quit.

I keep walking until the mansion rises across a long sweep of lawn. It looks different from this angle. More glass, more light, more angles to see everything I'm not supposed to touch.

I should turn around.

I don't.

Because of her.

The girl standing on the balcony.

She's leaning forward, elbows propped against the railing, staring out at the ocean, her brows furrowed like she's trying to memorize the horizon. The wind lifts her hair—light blonde, glossy, long enough to whip across her face. She tucks it behind her ear in a motion so smooth it looks trained.

She wears white.

Not a simple white dress or some casual rich-girl outfit. No, this thing is made of silk that probably costs more than the entire staff earns in a month. It drips off her frame, soft and light, like it was carved out of air.

She looks . . . untouchable.

And bored.

Painfully, devastatingly bored.

Her eyes flick down. Land on me.

For a second—just one—her expression cracks.

Not disdain. Not superiority.

Curiosity.

The dangerous kind.

I immediately look away.

The last thing I need is to get noticed by someone who can ruin our lives with one complaint.

I head back toward the path.

"Hey."

Her voice drops from above like a coin tossed into a wishing well.

I freeze.

God-fucking-dammit.

I pause but don't say anything until she repeats herself in that same detached tone.

Finally, I turn. She's still on the balcony, leaning over the rail more now, studying me the way kids study animals at the zoo. Except she doesn't have that smug, tight-lipped smile I usually see on rich people. She looks . . . fascinated.

And fascinated is worse.

Fascinated pays attention.

She rests her elbow on the railing and her chin on her open palm to better stare at me. "Who are you?"

"Staff."

"That's not a name."

I shrug.

She tilts her head like she's evaluating artwork. "Are you new?"

"Obviously."

Not to be egotistical, but most people who see me remember me . . . even at a glance. It is what it is.

A slow, amused curve forms on her mouth. It seems she's not used to someone answering her without bending a little.

"What's your name?"

"Don't worry about it."

She laughs softly, but the wind carries the gentle sound to my ears. "Wow. Incredible bedside manner. I'm Victoria."

Of course she is.

The Danforth heiress herself. The sole one. Seventeen. Rumored to be beautiful, prim, polite, homeschooled, and one stuffy, flawless day away from calcifying into another statue decorating these grounds.

I don't look at her again. "Good for you."

She leans even farther over the railing. "You always this friendly?"

"Friendliness isn't in my job description."

"What *is* in your job description?"

"Not talking to you."

Her smile widens like I've just given her a gift.

Rich girls.

They just love to run toward the one person walking away.

Before she can respond, a voice snaps from inside the house. Sharp, irritated, older than the marble columns holding this place up.

"Victoria! Come inside. Now."

Victoria's eyes flick toward the open balcony doors, then back to me. Something mischievous sparks there. Something rebellious and reckless.

It strikes me that she's different than the rumors suggest. So different that I'm shocked that no one has noticed it before.

Victoria ignores the call, still focused on me. "Are you going to be here all summer?"

"No."

"You sound very sure."

"I don't plan on sticking around longer than I have to."

"A shame." Her voice drops into something almost . . . disappointed. "It's boring here."

"Sounds like a personal problem."

She laughs again, and it's soft but bright. Like the satisfying *whoosh* that comes from striking a match.

The voice inside grows louder. "Victoria!"

She pushes off the railing. "You should tell me your name."

"Not happening."

"Why not?"

"Because you're trouble."

Her smile tells me she agrees. "Maybe."

Without another word, she disappears inside, the silk dress drifting behind her like a wave.

I stand there longer than I should.

Long enough for annoyance to prick at my spine.

She shouldn't fascinate me.

She's rich. She's sheltered. She's everything I swore I'd never waste time thinking about.

But I can still hear her laughter brushing the back of my neck like a warm breath.

CHAPTER 2

Victoria

THEY SAY GIRLS LIKE ME ARE BORN LUCKY.

Wrapped in silk. Schooled in etiquette. Raised in homes where the paintings are real and the smiles are not. We grow up knowing which fork to use, when to laugh, and how to fold grief into polite conversation.

But I don't feel lucky . . .

I feel caged.

The kind of cage that has a beautiful view, but it's still a prison, nonetheless.

From the second-floor balcony, I watched them arrive. Now I'm watching as they go back to grab their belongings out of an old, battered sedan that looks like it's seen better days. For a second, when they first pulled up to the house, I didn't even think it would make it up the driveway, but in the end, it did.

It sputtered the whole way, but now it's safely parked in the loading dock. The woman opens the trunk. If the chatter I heard near the kitchen is true, her name is Angela, and she's starting with the kitchen staff today. She seems calm and capable as she rummages through the trunk. Next up is the boy from before—correction, a man, or maybe somewhere in between. Hard to tell from this angle.

He heads over to where the woman, whom I assume is his

mother is, then grabs the bag from her hand before slamming the trunk in anger.

There is something dark about him, an anger I can see even from where I'm hiding in the shadows.

He leans against the car with a chip on his shoulder and a patch of hair falling in his eyes.

He's tall. Broad-shouldered. The kind of handsome you don't see on magazine covers because it's too raw, too real.

He doesn't belong here. Not just because of the car or the clothes, but because he's looking at the estate like he wants to burn it to the ground.

Good.

I'm tired of people who submit.

It's hard enough being Victoria Danforth, but when people suck up to me, it's even worse.

I'm no one special, despite what my parents think, and even then, they consider me a prize and possession, not a living, breathing teen with real feelings and thoughts.

The stranger steps away from the car and heads toward the door. With each step he takes, the arm muscles visible in his T-shirt flex. My cheeks warm. I might not know this guy, but *wow*.

He's going to make it hard not to want to.

There is no question that he is the best-looking person I have ever seen.

With dark eyes and a chiseled jaw, I want to head downstairs and get a better look at him, but I can't, of course. That would not be acceptable behavior for a girl like me.

Instead, I step forward, crossing my arms over the balcony and looking down.

I'm torn between wanting him to see me again and hoping he doesn't.

But when his gaze catches mine, and my heart threatens to burst from my chest, I realize getting caught staring is the least of my problems.

This boy is dangerous.

And I don't just mean that figuratively. He's the type of guy who will break my heart if I let him, and seeing how my pulse won't slow down, if given the chance, I will.

"Still need your name."

He doesn't answer.

With eyes locked, we're at a standstill, and I wonder who will break the connection first.

He chooses to.

And when he strides away, it feels like this was all a dream.

Like I imagined the connection.

I must stand there for a few moments, but eventually, when a soft breeze tickles my skin, thoughts of having to speak to my parents hit me like a freight train.

This summer is going to suck.

Or . . .

Maybe it won't.

This new guy could help.

CHAPTER 3

Lorenzo

MY MOTHER FINDS ME AT LUNCH IN THE STAFF DINING quarters, which is nicer than any restaurant I've ever eaten in. Everything smells like rosemary and butter.

I'm in the corner by myself since I'm not sure what the protocol is on taking the food, and I promised Mom I'd behave for now.

She places a plate in front of me. "Eat."

I poke the roasted chicken. "We can't afford this."

"It's free, Enzo." She joins me with a plate of her own. "They feed staff well."

"Because they can."

"Because they should."

I don't argue.

But in my heart, I realize for the first time that some people are just fucking blessed. While Mom and I toil with skin and blood for every little thing we have, others are born into wealth and privilege.

Mid-bite, Mom glances around and lowers her voice. "Have you seen her?"

On instinct, my stomach tightens. "Who?"

"Victoria Danforth."

Oh hell no.

"She's your age," my normally oblivious mother continues,

eyes shining with some maternal fantasy that she immediately crushes. "I hear she's pretty, but remember to stay away—"

"Obviously."

"But," she continues, ignoring my attitude, "there might be other kids around this place from the staff. Maybe you could make a friend."

"No." I cut off her delusions. "Absolutely not."

"You haven't even met any of them."

We don't even know they exist, I want to say.

I stab the chicken with a fork. "I don't need to."

Mom sighs dramatically. "Enzo, you're eighteen, not eighty. Don't spend the summer moping. Make a friend."

"Mother," I enunciate, voice flat, "this is a mansion that could buy a small nation."

"So?"

"So we both know what trouble the type of friends I like to make tends to stir up." I shovel the rest of the plate into my mouth at top speed. "Trash begets trash."

My mother gives me that look, the pitying one. "You need to stop believing that."

"I don't believe it." I wipe my mouth and drop my fork. "I know it."

After lunch, I help my mother carry boxes into the kitchen. It's not the highlight of my day, that's for sure. It smells of garlic and sweat. Not a good combo if you ask me.

The cooks move with military efficiency—knives flashing, pans sizzling, orders shouted.

My mother looks happy. Really happy. It settles something in me, and I feel a tiny, *tiny* bit less pissed off to be woken at an ungodly hour and relocated here.

Then Chef Arthur storms past us.

"We have a problem with the ice delivery," he bellows. "Someone fetch more from the auxiliary freezer. You—" He pauses to snap at me. "Boy!"

I freeze.

Oh, great.

Being an errand boy wasn't on my summer bingo card, but here we are.

"Yes, you." He points at me with a knife, which feels like an HR violation. "Freezer. Now. And hurry. The Danforths have been waiting for their lunch for three minutes."

"Wow. Three whole minutes. How will they ever survive?" I want to say, but Mom's face pleads with me to behave.

So I nod and head toward the hallway.

Meryl—the fifty-something lead housekeeper—gives me half-assed directions and rushes away with a warning to stay out of sight when not working. Next, Elise, the mid-thirties-ish sous chef, repeats the same directions more palatably before continuing to chop vegetables with an intensity wasted on a casual summer lunch.

Then, I'm off, thinking about what I heard while eating.

Apparently, the Danforths are a nouveau riche steel family, desperate to be accepted by the upper echelon. Before they managed to snag this place after the old owner croaked, they lived in a gaudy mansion made entirely of gold, down to the toilets.

Their sense of style—or lack thereof—caused such a spectacle that every interior designer in the region refused to work with them.

My footsteps echo along the corridor. The auxiliary freezer is somewhere near the north wing of the mansion, past the wine cellar and too many doors. When I finally push into the cold, the air hits me hard, icy fingers crawling down my neck.

I grab two bags of ice, sling them over my shoulder, and turn—

And nearly slam into someone.

Victoria.

Because of course.

She stands in the doorway wearing a thin cardigan over that

silk dress, cheeks flushed from the cold. Her hair is damp, like she just got out of the pool.

"Well." She greets me with a nonchalant grin. "If it isn't the mysterious staff boy."

I grit my teeth, adjusting my grip on the ice so the cold touches less of my back. "I'm busy."

"Doing what? Ice delivery?" Her eyes sparkle with amusement. "Very impressive."

"Move."

She does not move.

She steps closer.

The cold air shifts between us.

She stops the door with her back just centimeters before it closes on us. "You didn't tell me your name earlier."

"Still not going to."

She studies me with interest. Genuine interest. Like she's flipping through a book she can't put down.

"Most people tell me their names before I even have to ask."

Truly, it's a wonder how no one has read this bored rich girl like the open book that she is. Prim and proper, my ass.

I finally set down the ice bags, resigned to this conversation, lest I lay hands on this heiress and physically move her myself. "It must be tiring avoiding all the bent spines sprawled around your feet."

It occurs to me that this is precisely the behavior my mother begged me not to engage in. Giving attitude to the bosses' precious daughter. Yet my instinct tells me that Victoria Danforth isn't a narc. Or rather, she enjoys toying with me, just like I don't exactly hate snarking back at her.

She bites back a smile. "You're really committed to this whole 'I don't care' act, aren't you?"

"It's not an act."

"Hmm." She tilts her head. "Feels like one."

I hike the bags back over my shoulder and move past her,

forcing her to step aside with the frosted edge of an icy cold bag. She inhales sharply, surprised—not by my rudeness, but by the fact that I didn't pause, didn't give her the reverence she's used to.

"Are you always like this?" she calls as I walk away.

"Only with people who don't listen," I toss over my shoulder.

Her laugh is so soft I barely hear it. "You're interesting."

"I'm not."

"You are."

I don't look back.

But I feel her gaze burning between my shoulder blades like sunlight through a magnifying glass.

And I hate how aware of her I suddenly am.

Her scent—something faint like citrus and saltwater.

Her voice—smooth but edged with rebellion.

Her presence—impossible to ignore.

This is exactly why my mother warned me.

Exactly why I keep walls higher than this mansion's ceilings.

Girls like Victoria Danforth don't get tired.

They get what they want.

And me?

I can't afford to be anything anyone wants.

By the time I return to the kitchen, Chef Arthur is screaming about something else, and the cooks are pretending not to hear him. My mother mouths *thank you* to me, and I nod, pretending the encounter with Victoria hasn't rattled me.

It has.

More than I'd like.

Meryl returns to the kitchen in time to curl her nose at the sight of me drenched in sweat from the trek with forty pounds of ice.

She nods at a roll of paper towels, the unspoken order clear, and pivots to my mom. "You'll be given a weekly menu from Mrs. Danforth. Breakfast at seven. Lunch at one. Dinner at eight sharp. You prep, plate, and disappear. Any deviation and I hear about it."

Mom nods. "Understood."

Meryl turns to Elise. "Assign the boy the pantry and prep. Nothing to do with knives, though."

Elise smirks at me, whispering under her breath so only I can hear, "Aw. They don't trust you with sharp objects?"

"Not unsupervised." I grin. "I wouldn't either."

And I mean that. I've always been a little dark. The thrill I get from violence has danced beneath my skin for as long as I can remember. I've tried to ignore it, but apparently not hard enough. Seeing as it's the reason Mom had to take this job.

Stabbing someone will do that.

Granted, only the families involved know, and I'm lucky enough not to be shipped off to juvie or now that I'm eighteen . . . jail, but Mom's scared my luck will run out, so we moved. No forwarding address, just got up and left, and here we are.

Kind of dramatic if you ask me.

With a shake of my head, I try to pay attention to what everyone is talking about. Whatever I miss, I'm sure my mother will fill me in on, so I'm not that concerned.

After the lunch rush, I escape to the staff hallway, lean against the wall, and let out a heavy breath I've been holding in the pit of my stomach. The entire time in the kitchen, the staff kept going on and on about Victoria. It's clear how much everyone here adores the girl.

I should avoid her.

No, you dumb fuck, you will *avoid her.*

The Danforth girl is a silky storm.

The kind that destroys everything in its path.

But as I head back toward my room, something catches my eye. A flutter of white near the corner of the corridor.

A small square of paper.

I bend down. Pick it up.

A note.
In delicate handwriting:
You still owe me your name.
—V.
My pulse does something stupid.
Dangerous.
I crumple the note immediately.
But I don't throw it away.

CHAPTER 4

Lorenzo

MY HANDS FEEL RAW. THE SKIN SPLIT AT THE KNUCKLES, SOAP getting into every scrape. I've been here for hours.

Rinsing. Scrubbing. Stacking.

Repeating the same motion for so long that I'm not sure if I'm alive or if I'm dead, and this is hell. Maybe this is what my penance looks like. An endless cycle of dishes.

At least I'm alive.

And Mom and I have a roof over our heads.

Not that we've ever been homeless, but there have been times when shit got rough. Most recently because of me.

"Stop daydreaming." Elise cuts through my thoughts, bringing me back to the here and now. "Concentrate on your job."

I turn over my shoulder and find her leaning against the counter beside me. Elise is small and sharp. She's the kind of woman who could charm the devil and then sell his secrets when all is said and done. She's not one to fuck with, but also, she's a good one to have on your side.

I flick a handful of suds at her. "Maybe I'm waiting for the dishes to talk back."

She laughs, a quick, bright sound that doesn't belong in this place. "I have a feeling you're waiting on something else entirely."

My brow rises. "What does that mean?"

"It means you've got that look again. The one that says you're thinking about something you shouldn't be."

"Maybe I am." A certain blonde that I shouldn't be thinking about.

Her grin widens. "Let me guess . . . a certain girl."

I turn my eyes back to the sink. "I have no idea what you're talking about."

"Sure, you don't. So . . . you're not daydreaming about the princess?" Elise's tone changes to a tease.

"Princess? Didn't know this house had one?"

"Cute." She scoffs. "Victoria is practically sainted. Pretty, polite, rarely speaks. Says thank you to the staff and means it. She's the perfect accessory for her parents to tote around."

I'm not sure why what she says irritates me so much, but it does. What *Victoria* does, or what people think of her, shouldn't bother me.

She means nothing to me.

Nor I to her.

So then why have my hands formed fists under the warm suds?

I've hardly spoken to her, and I already feel protective.

Not a good sign.

This won't bode well for me.

A flash of her pale skin and soft laughter plays through my mind. The way the light spills through her hair is like an angel.

Shit.

Head in the game.

No thinking about your boss's daughter like this.

"Same age as you, I think." Elise bumps my shoulder. "It would be quite the scandal."

"Scandal?" I arch a brow. "You make it sound like I'm plotting something."

"Please." She laughs from beside me. "You have that look. The one people get before they ruin themselves."

Before I can answer, a low voice cuts through the noise of the sink.

"Don't encourage him, Elise." I turn in the direction of the man's voice. "I'm Rob, work here too." He's tall and broad with grease on his hands and shadows under his eyes. He looks like he's been around a long time, or at least longer than Elise and certainly longer than me.

He wipes his hands on a rag, eyes flicking over me. "If you're smart, kid, you'll stay away from her."

Elise groans. "Here we go."

"I mean it," Rob says, his voice calm but edged. "You're new here. You don't know how this place works. The family's bad news. Especially for people like us."

"People like us," I echo. "You mean the help?"

He doesn't deny it. "We clean up their messes, pretend not to see the blood, and they keep the world spinning. That's the deal."

Elise rolls her eyes. "You make it sound like we work for vampires."

Rob's gaze doesn't flinch. "You think I'm exaggerating? These people will eat you alive. Money and privilege don't play by the same rules."

I lean against the counter, watching him. "Yet you're still here."

He gives a humorless shrug. "Some of us don't have anywhere else to go." His eyes linger on me, measuring. "Don't get ideas about the girl. She's not for you."

That strikes a nerve. Not because I want her—hell, I barely know her—but because of how easily people decide who belongs where. I'm already marked, and I haven't even been here that long.

Before I can say anything else, Mary, one of the housekeepers, steps into the kitchen. "Can someone help me move the linens to the west wing?" she calls out to no one in particular.

"I'll do it," I say way too fast, making Elise snort.

"Volunteering for laundry now? You must really be bored." Elise is clearly enjoying my pain.

"Better than dishes." I grin, wiping my hands on my apron. "Just trying to earn my keep."

Rob mutters something under his breath that sounds a lot like *idiot*, but I ignore him as I walk past him and follow Mary.

The estate stretches for what seems like forever, with endless corridors of polished wood and chandeliers that glow as if lit from beneath. Every step echoes beneath my shoes, and the air smells faintly of lemon polish.

I tell myself that I'm not looking for her. That I'm here just to do the damn linens.

But when I turn the corner and see her—everything in me stills.

Victoria stands by a tall window, sunlight slipping through the sheer curtains, turning her hair to gold. She's laughing. It's soft, real, and unguarded. It fills me with a sensation I haven't felt in years.

Warmth.

She turns her head slightly, and our eyes meet.

The world goes silent.

For a heartbeat, it's just her and me.

Two unlikely friends caught in each other's orbits, staring at the other like we've known each other for a lifetime. Her expression is curious and cautious, but there's a spark there, too. A flicker that shouldn't be there at all. Not for a man like me.

And then she smiles.

It's small. Hesitant. But it hits harder than it should.

Knocking the wind right out of my lungs. Something about her makes my chest tighten, makes me suddenly aware of every wrong thing about this moment.

I don't smile back. I can't. Not with Mary so close.

More footsteps sound down the hallway, and with that, the spell is broken.

Rob again. *Of course.*

He strides past, surveying me, and leans in close so only I can hear him. "I told you," he says under his breath. "Stay away."

"I'm not doing anything."

He drills me with a stare that says I'm not fooling anyone. "You're looking. That's enough."

I clench my jaw. "You sound like her bodyguard."

"I'm trying to keep you alive."

He grabs one end of the linens, forcing me to pick up the other. I follow him down the hall, though my eyes still linger back toward her.

Victoria raises a hand in a soft wave—half shy, half brave.

But I turn away before she can finish it.

Not out of pride. Out of survival.

I know that look in her eyes. The kind that can ruin a man like me.

A few minutes later, and no longer holding the linens, I make it back into the kitchen. Elise waits by the door, smirking. "So?" She crosses her arms. "Did you see her?"

"Briefly."

"And?"

"She looked . . . normal."

She barks out a laugh. "You're the worst liar I've ever met."

I don't answer. I just head back to the sink. To the new pile of dishes stacked on the counter. The water is still hot enough to sting. I let it run and watch as the suds swirl down the drain, trying not to think about the way she looked when I didn't acknowledge her.

A tight feeling spreads in my chest.

I shouldn't seek her out. And I certainly shouldn't want her.

But the lie sits heavy on my chest.

And I can't decide if that scares me or thrills me more.

CHAPTER 5

Victoria

TIME FOR DINNER . . .

Great.

To me, this is the worst hour of my life.

It's not that I hate my parents; it's just that I can't stand them. The constant judgment. Condescending tone, and the conversations they have . . .

How self-important can two people be?

That doesn't matter, though, because they have summoned me, so that's where I'll be.

Once dressed, I head downstairs and take a seat.

Dinner is exactly what you'd expect from a family who puts more effort into optics than affection.

A table that seats twelve. Only four places are set.

Father at the head, Mother two seats down, and me across from no one. The symmetry is part of the performance. The silence, too.

All this bullshit makes me want to gag.

Why keep up the false pretense? No one cares. It doesn't matter how hard we try to pretend. No one on the staff cares if we are just another dysfunctional, wealthy family who hates each other. Why do we have to go through all this trouble?

"Victoria, sit up straight," my mother says gently, eyes flicking to my elbows.

I adjust my posture and resist the urge to mutter something about Victorian torture devices. Pretty sure that wouldn't go over well.

Death or anything controversial like that is not a "proper" subject for the table.

Father clears his throat. "Tell me about the new staff."

My mother sits up, perfecting her posture. She's not used to Father making conversation. She's practically starved for attention, so this is her moment to shine. "I've hired on new summer staff. With all the entertaining we have planned, I thought it would be best to bring on a few more people to help around the house. Angela will be working in the kitchen. Her son will assist."

Son.

No name. No identity. Just a category.

This woman is so pretentious it's almost comical.

Father nods. "What does the boy do?"

My father runs his dinner table like his boardroom: with precision, condescension, and an unshakable belief in his own superiority. Why she married him is beyond me.

Mother dabs the corner of her mouth with a cloth napkin she hasn't dirtied. "He's there to help. Chop vegetables. Carry groceries. Nothing complicated."

My father turns to me. "Stay out of the kitchen."

"Because my presence might contaminate the produce?" I counter.

His eyes flicker. "Because you're a distraction. And you're a Danforth."

I almost laugh. Being a Danforth is a title worth defending.

"Angela comes highly recommended," Mother adds, placating. "Margret recommended her."

"And who is Margret?"

"You remember, she was the head of the household for the Winslows."

Father's head bobs up and down. "Yes. Good. They are old money. Discreet."

There it is again. That word.

Discreet.

My father worships discretion the way some people worship God. Preferably a god with a tight-lipped lawyer and offshore accounts.

He cuts into his filet mignon with precision.

"If this goes well, I might offer her a long-term contract," Mother adds, trying desperately to engage him in more conversation.

"How generous," I say. "And her son?"

He pauses, sips his wine. "Help is help. He'll take what he's given and be grateful."

I push my small, chopped asparagus pieces into a line. "Maybe he has a name."

My father doesn't answer. He never does when he's decided the conversation is over.

After dinner, which should probably be referred to as torture, I slip away before coffee is served.

I know the routine. The adults, a.k.a. the parentals, will stay and discuss estate finances and upcoming fundraisers. My mother will pretend to be interested in business. My father will pretend to value her input. It's all so exhausting.

Instead, I head toward the back staircase, the one that leads to the servants' wing. I don't usually take this path, but I'm dying to bump into the son.

The estate is quiet this time of night. The kind of silence that echoes. Polished hardwood. Dim lighting. Hallways lined with portraits of long-dead relatives who were probably awful people.

I don't know why I'm looking for him.

Curiosity, maybe. Or guilt that he was the subject of dinner conversation, but not important enough to be named.

Maybe I just want to see the look on his face when I give him a preemptive *sorry*. Followed by, *my father will most likely treat you like garbage.*

But I don't find him. I do hear him, though. Low voices through a cracked pantry door.

"Don't get any ideas, Lorenzo." Meryl's voice sounds sharp and tired.

Lorenzo. So that's his name. It's fitting. Sexy. Like him. Oh, jeez . . . head out of the gutter.

I wait for a beat to see if they say anything else, but all I hear is silence.

Then a cough. "She's not for you. You're just the help. Her father would skin you alive for even thinking about it." Elise speaks this time. She's closer to my age and has no filter. Or at least that's what I've gathered over the years when I have eavesdropped on the staff.

There's not a lot to do around here when your parents forbid you from socializing with people whom they deem less than . . .

And seeing as everyone has their opinion. I have grown up all alone in this hellhole.

My heart stutters.

I step back into the shadows, out of instinct. Not wanting to be caught, but still not wanting to leave. I want to hear what he says and how he says it.

Oh, who am I trying to kid? I want to hear his voice.

Lorenzo doesn't reply. Not at first. "Good thing I wasn't thinking." His voice is flat. Controlled. But something else is there as well. It doesn't sound like defeat. It sounds like a dare.

I hope it is.

Because as I take a step back and leave my hiding place and head to my room, I can't stop thinking about his voice. The perfect amount of danger in his tone. But I also can't stop hearing what was said, by everyone . . .

"Just the help."

They say it like it's a sin.

Like breathing the same air as us is some kind of offense. But what if the air down there is cleaner? What if the helper sees more than the helped?

What if the boy they tried to put in a box doesn't stay in it?

I want to know what happens when he breaks out. I think I want to be the one watching when he does.

Because I'm done being stuck behind glass.

Maybe he's the one with the key.

CHAPTER 6

Victoria

The Danforth gardens were designed to impress people.

Not people like Lorenzo and his mom, of course. No, in my parents' minds, this is above their pay grades.

Endless rows of roses.

A fountain shaped like a cherub. A bit ridiculous if you ask me, but it probably costs more than most people's mortgages.

Which is the look my family is going for.

The whole thing disgusts me.

Not because it isn't beautiful. It is, obviously. For the cost, I'd expect no less, but it's obnoxious. In that curated, restrained kind of way. A floral museum that forgot real things grow wild.

Normally, I don't come out here very often, not unless I stop on my way down to the beach, but today, I'm here for a different reason.

I saw him . . .

Near the stone archway. Alone. Wearing a plain gray T-shirt and jeans. Even from a distance, I could see that his forearms were tan from the sun.

It looked like he was heading toward the herb garden, and well, curiosity killed the cat. I needed to get an up close look.

So here I am, stalking.

From what I can make out in the distance, he has a small

paring knife in one hand and a sprig of rosemary in the other. He lifts it to his face, inspecting it. Does he think it will tell him what plant it is?

And because I'm curious—and a little reckless—I walk toward him.

He doesn't see me at first. His focus is on the little plant in his hand. Studying.

"It's rosemary."

At the sound of my voice, his head turns, and his gaze meets mine. Bottomless chocolate-brown eyes, full of emotions I can't even comprehend, stare back at me.

My words get clogged in my throat. I'm thankful I spoke before he saw me, or I'd be stumbling over my words. Instead, now I wait for him to respond.

"I know that."

"Didn't look that way from here," I point out. Tact apparently isn't my strong suit. I'll chalk it up to nerves and not knowing how to shut up.

"This is what the help does on break." That shuts me up. "I'd bow," he continues, sarcasm etched in his voice, "but I might stab myself with this knife and bleed on your heirloom sage."

"A tragedy." I cross my arms. "We'd have to bury you under the hydrangeas. My father would insist."

He arches a brow. "Nice to know I'd be memorialized with seasonal color."

There's a beat of silence, and then he cocks his head, looking me over once. At his perusal, my cheeks warm, and I'm sure I'm blushing. Hopefully, he thinks it's from the heat, but when a smirk spreads across his face, I know I've been caught.

"Victoria, right?"

"Yep," I pop the p. "But you already knew that. I told you the other day . . ."

"True."

I tilt my head. "And you're Lorenzo. What's your deal?"

That earns me the twitch of a full smile. "You trying to spy on me, Little Bird?"

My heart flinches at the nickname, but I smile instead. "And pray tell, why am I a *bird*?"

"You watch from high above the ground."

"Which would make you what?"

His eyes narrow. Sharp. Measured. Waiting for the insult that he thinks will roll off my lips.

It won't. I'm not like my parents.

"So"—I step closer—"where are you from?"

He shrugs. "Everywhere. Nowhere. Pick up a map of the East Coast and then throw a dart."

"That's vague and suspicious. You could've just said Jersey."

"Why lie?" he says, looking at me sideways. "I like disappointing people the honest way."

I laugh before I can stop it. I like him. He's dry and sarcastic. He practically speaks my language.

He looks away quickly. Like he didn't expect me to find him funny, but I see his lip twitch again. He wants to smile, but doesn't often let himself.

"You live here year-round?" he asks, deflecting.

I shrug. "Until summer ends. Then I leave for college."

He doesn't react at first. Just nods, tossing the rosemary into the basket beside him.

"Where?"

"Stanford."

That got a flicker of something. Surprise? Approval? Disappointment?

He quickly covers up his interest, grabbing another herb and inspecting it.

"Thyme," I tell him as he throws it into the basket.

"Let me guess," he says. "Botany major? Minor in pretending to be interested in charity work."

"Close, but wrong."

"Was I close with the botany?"

That makes me laugh. I shake my head.

"Art history, then?"

"Still wrong."

He narrows his eyes. "You're not a math girl."

"How do you know?"

"You'd have corrected me by now."

I grin. "Okay, fine. Philosophy and literature. Double major. With a minor in disappointment, courtesy of my father."

That wins me a full smile, and my stomach flutters. "Let me guess. He wants a legacy, and you give him metaphors."

"Exactly."

We are quiet for a moment, and the wind shifts. Carrying with it the smell of thyme and saltwater.

"Do you always work with your mom?" I ask.

He looks down at his hands before picking up another leaf from the garden.

"My mom needed work, and I came with. Figured she could use the company, and I could use the money."

It was a simple answer. Deceptively so.

"That's oddly noble for someone who glares at everything around here like you want to burn the place to the ground."

"Takes one to know one."

"Very true. Is it the house? Did it personally insult you, or do you just not like rich people?"

"Depends on the people."

"And me?"

He glances at me. "The jury is still out on you."

"And why is that?"

"You haven't decided what kind of rich girl you want to be yet."

I blink. "That's . . . not wrong."

He looks back at the garden.

"Most of the people here are trying so hard to belong. You look like you're trying to fly away."

My throat feels tight.

He doesn't say it like a compliment. He says it like the truth.

And still, it rattles something deep inside me. Something small and trapped. I turn away before he can see my face.

"Don't psychoanalyze me, Lorenzo. I'm delicate."

"You're not delicate, Little Bird. You're just bored."

He's right. Again.

I pick up a fallen petal from the path and twist it between my fingers.

"*Little Bird*. Shouldn't it be Rapunzel if I'm watching from a tower?"

He looks at me for a long time.

"You might be perched in glass towers, but you act like your wings are broken."

"Aren't they?" I whisper under my breath.

"No. They're not. You just haven't figured out where to fly yet."

Silence. The kind that fills all the spaces words fail to reach.

I drop the petal. It floats down like something surrendering.

"I should go," I say softly.

"You should."

I don't, not right away, because I want to stay. I want to ask more questions. Push past the guard-dog glare and dig until I find whatever fire burns beneath that skin.

But I don't.

Because I'm not stupid.

And if I stay, I will burn too.

So I leave.

But I don't fly.

Not yet.

CHAPTER 7

Victoria

NO MATTER HOW HARD I TELL MYSELF I SHOULDN'T BE walking this way, I can't stop my feet from carrying me in the direction I'm heading.

The old boathouse sits at the far edge of the estate. A forgotten structure that has long been left abandoned and replaced by a new building closer to the house.

No one comes here.

Which is why when I saw him walking in this direction, I couldn't help but follow.

The first thing I see as I round the path is peeling white paint. Ivy also crawls up one side as if trying to reclaim it for nature.

The next thing I notice is him.

My heart sputters in my chest with excitement. I knew he would be here, of course, but his presence still takes my breath away.

You got it bad, Victoria.

I blame my sheltered life.

In all my seventeen years on this planet, stuck in this gilded cage, I've never met a boy like him. One who awakens feelings inside me that I've never had before.

Speaking of the devil . . .

There he is.

Lorenzo is currently crouched near the door. One hand braces the splintered frame, and the other grips a screwdriver with the kind of focus I usually reserve for surviving dinner with my parents.

"What are you doing?" I ask, slipping past him.

"Trying not to lose a finger," he mutters. "Door sticks. Figured I'd fix it before it caves in and takes someone with it."

"What a hero," I say. "Next, you'll be rescuing cats from trees and winning humanitarian awards."

He doesn't look up. "That was the original plan."

"Bet you love it."

He looks up then. Eyes dark and unreadable. "Maybe . . . Do you?"

"You know that no one comes in here, right? You're wasting your time."

His shoulders lift into a shrug. "I got nothing else to do on my day off, so I might as well keep busy."

"You're fixing a door on your day off?"

"Not everyone is allowed to use the pool."

I'm not even sure how to respond to that, so I don't. Instead, I drop onto the dusty bench near the back window. Sunlight filters through warped panes, bringing a strange dimension to the space. It's almost cinematic how the light bounces around, making his silhouette dance across the floor in shadows.

Not wanting to be caught staring, I reach into the bag I brought when I thought I was heading to the beach and pull out a book.

"*Wuthering Heights*?" Lorenzo asks, and I lift my gaze to find him squinting at the book cover.

"Have you read it?"

"No."

"Then don't knock it. It's not all corsets and rain."

"I didn't say anything."

"You made a face."

He takes the book from my hands and turns it over to examine it. "This is what you think I want to read? Doomed love?"

"I think you're broody enough to qualify as a Brontë character." I shrug. "Besides, it's not about love. It's about obsession. And consequence. And class." The moment the words pour from my mouth, his eyes narrow. Shit. What did I say? Oh . . . I want to bury myself in a hole for speaking about class. *Way to put your foot in your mouth.*

"Is this supposed to be relevant?"

"Relevant?" Smart, Victoria . . . play dumb.

"Relevant as in, talking to you . . . or the fact that I'm not supposed to."

"Who said that?"

"Everyone."

My eyes widen. Did my parents say something? Shit. "Calm down. Just other members of the staff. Your secret is safe for now."

"My secret?"

"That you don't mind talking to the staff."

I open and then shut my mouth, not really knowing what to say. "Who would I be in this story . . . since it's so relevant."

"I never said it was relevant. You did."

"Heathcliff?"

"Again . . . you said that. Not me."

"Just answer."

I hesitate, then sigh. "That depends on how you end it."

He tilts his head. "You think I'm going to destroy everything and haunt the girl?"

"I think you could," I respond quietly. "But I don't think you will."

That shuts him up for once.

He finishes fixing the door.

I lean back on the bench until my back hits the wall behind me, arms crossed, watching him like he's a puzzle I want to solve. *If only there were a cheat code.*

"Do you read?" I ask.

"Of course I read," he huffs.

Is it possible for me to sound like a bigger bitch? I keep saying shit I don't mean and look like an idiot. I chalk it up to nerves. Lorenzo has me wrapped in knots, but jeez, I need to think before I speak. "I meant for pleasure. Not everyone does."

"When I can steal the time."

I stretch my arm out to place the book in his hand. "You could read this."

He flips to the first page. His gaze drifts over the words before he closes it and hands it back. "Or you could read it to me."

That catches me off guard. "Seriously?"

He nods. "You brought it. Might as well commit."

I stare at him for a long second, then open the book.

"Chapter one," I start. "1801. I have just returned from a visit to my landlord—the solitary neighbor that I shall be troubled with."

He chuckles. "Sounds familiar."

Lorenzo stands, then does something that takes me completely by surprise. He plops down on the bench next to me.

"You haven't even met my neighbors."

"I meant you." He laughs. The sound does crazy things to my belly, but rather than focus on that, I playfully roll my eyes. "Well, what are you waiting for? Keep reading."

So I do.

We sit there for almost an hour. Each word hangs in the air, heavy and weighted. The longer I read, the closer he gets, and at some point, he's right beside me. Only a breath away. Our bodies almost touch, and I want desperately to cross the space.

I don't, though. I read. He listens.

Occasionally, he asks questions. Most are dry and sarcastic. "Why is everyone in this book miserable?" or "Has anyone ever made a good decision on the moors?"

It's easy. Too easy. And I like it. Which is probably why I start to feel something close to nervous. Not because I don't know what I'm doing. But because, for once, I don't care. I'm playing with fire being here with Lorenzo, but I don't care.

"Why did you come here today?" His voice is soft, and it takes me a moment to realize he's talking to me.

I look up from the book and at him. "Here?"

"The boathouse that is clearly abandoned, as you pointed out earlier."

I consider what to say. To be honest? Or not? I opt for a half-truth.

"Because this place is real. And you're not boring." I don't say I followed him, but it's implied.

He snorts, having the courtesy of not calling me out. "High praise from the glass tower."

"Don't mock me, Lorenzo."

"I'm not." He looks at me. Really looks. "I like that you read books and talk back and don't flinch when someone tells you no."

"Is that a compliment?"

He shrugs. "Don't let it go to your head."

"Too late. You ever think we're just the background to someone else's story?" I ask.

"Everyday. Especially when I'm working in the kitchen," he says. "But otherwise, when I'm not in this house, I'm the main character."

"Of course you are."

He smirks. "So are you, Little Bird."

"You keep calling me that like you think it's charming."

"Not charming." He lifts his brows. "But true."

I don't have a comeback. So instead, I open the book again.

Because it's easier to lose myself in someone else's storm than admit I'm standing in the middle of my own.

CHAPTER 8

Lorenzo

THE FIRST TIME SHE READ TO ME, I DIDN'T EXPECT TO GIVE a damn. The idea that she would even want to spend time with me was so foreign that my brain could barely process the words coming out of her mouth.

I just watched her . . .

Completely enthralled. The whole moment felt loaded.

A turning point I had no hope of controlling.

Her voice, her words, they crawled under my skin, and days later, they're still there, whispering things I don't want to hear.

Because Victoria Danforth read them to me.

Because she put her voice to this famous tragedy and somehow made it feel like a prophecy. But underneath all of it, despite how much I want to listen, I can't help but wonder . . .

Did she pick that book on purpose?

Is there a deeper meaning to why she reads it to me daily? Or am I just imagining things when it's only a coincidence?

Other than the fact she's rich and I'm not, we have nothing to do with these characters. Not one damn thing.

If she picks up *Gatsby* next, then yeah . . . *I might start spiraling.*

But for now, I tell myself it's just time spent with her. Nothing more. Nothing less.

Today, we're in our usual spot. Her spot, technically. This is her domain, after all.

The boathouse is too warm and humid. Sunlight streaks through the glass roof in thick rays.

She walks in like she owns the place, which is fitting because she does. The book is tucked under her arm, and her hair is pulled back. Where most people would look like a mess, she looks perfect, as always.

Man, you have it bad.

She sits next to me on the bench that's seen better days, crossing her legs at the ankle like she's posing for a portrait somewhere fancier than this boathouse that's falling apart.

Her floral fragrance floats toward me, subtle yet mouthwatering.

I want to dip my head down and inhale her, drag the scent into my lungs. I don't, because that would be insane. Just because the girl reads to you doesn't mean she wants more.

I'm pretending to work on a leaf blower for the gardener. Its guts are in my lap, wires exposed, screws scattered, but I'm not fixing shit.

She cracks the spine of that damn book with delicate, confident fingers and begins to read.

Never one to enjoy being read to, it's weird how much I love it when she does it.

She reads with emotion I can barely comprehend. Like she's fully immersed in the plot, as the story flows through her bloodstream. Each word leaves her lips, and the passion behind it hits me like a punch to the sternum.

She reads like she's trying to impress me. Not like she's showing off, but like the words belong to her, and I sit here silent, pretending the blower is important while she dismantles me with every sentence.

When the words become too real, too pointed, too much like

confessions disguised as literature, I hop up from the bench and move to the door.

I tighten bolts . . . *every bolt.* Then the hinge. Then the other hinge.

All of it a way to remind myself that she isn't mine. And won't be.

She's from another world. A world I can view but never enter. If that weren't enough, she's leaving soon. College. A future with rich boys who quote philosophers between lacrosse practice and legacy luncheons.

Greek life. Secret societies. Generational wealth.

And me? I'll go back to the kitchen. Side jobs. Looking over my shoulder, waiting for the next man in a suit to tell me I don't belong.

She's a Danforth. I am the help.

But when she reads, none of that matters. Not for a moment. Not to me.

"Heathcliff doesn't actually love Catherine." She flips a page. The sound echoes through the glass, ricocheting straight into my ribs. "He loves the idea of her and what she means to him. The obsession becomes more important than the person."

"That's the tragedy," I reply instantly, faster than I mean to, masking the hit that line just delivered. "And the warning."

Her eyes stay on the page, but I feel them. Like a spotlight cutting straight to the parts of me I avoid.

"Yeah," she whispers, voice soft, dangerous.

My breath leaves my body. She tilts her head, slow, searching, and then looks right at me.

Like she knows exactly what I am. And dares me to be different.

I shouldn't care. Not about her. Not about her metaphors, her mouth, her thoughts, her voice.

But she makes caring feel like inevitability. A gravity that I'm stupid enough to think I can fight.

She reads for another minute or two, then stops abruptly. She closes the book halfway, thumb marking her place.

Her eyes lift. They find mine and hold my gaze.

"You're staring." Her voice is soft but laced with warmth.

"So?" I answer, stepping closer.

"It's distracting," she whispers, lips curling into a challenge.

"Stop being interesting, then."

Her grin is immediate. Dangerous. "Stop being dramatic."

"Impossible." I lean in just slightly. "I read Brontë now."

She shoves my arm with a laugh, and I let her. I always let her.

The worst part? She makes all of this feel real.

The connection. The ease of it. The possibility we could be more.

It doesn't matter that her father looks at me like I'm a stray dog they're debating calling animal control on. It doesn't matter that her world is stitched together with money and privilege while mine is duct tape and survival.

When she's happy, it feels like a rebellion. One I'm desperate to partake in.

This whole thing feels like a secret.

The air shifts. Thickens. I rise from the bench, and she follows. Slowly, almost nervously. Walks toward me. One step. Another.

Her breath catches when we end up inches apart. I can smell spearmint on her lips. I can see the pulse fluttering in her throat. Her fingers twitch at her side—like she's fighting the urge to touch me.

"Don't look at me like that," she whispers, voice trembling.

"Like what?" I lean down without thinking, drawn like a magnet, despite knowing I shouldn't.

"Like I'm . . . something," she breathes, eyes flicking to my mouth. "Like this matters."

"It does." The words slip out of me before I can stop them.

Raw. Unfiltered. Stupid.

Her breath stumbles. She leans in.

Just enough that her nose brushes mine.

Just enough that if either of us moves an inch, it's happening.

Her lips part. My heart does something violent. And then, she freezes.

She pulls back fast like she burned her fingers on the moment. Clutches the book to her chest, like a shield. As if that will save either of us.

"We shouldn't," she whispers, stepping away, eyes shining with something I don't dare name. "I shouldn't."

It breaks something in me. Quietly, efficiently.

I force a smirk, armor sliding back into place. "Relax, princess. I wasn't going to kiss you."

She flinches, most likely from my comment and what I just called her. Or maybe she knows I'm lying.

"You don't have to pretend." Her fingers tremble around the book's spine. "Not with me."

She sees me.

All of me.

No matter how hard I try.

And that . . . that destroys me more than the retreat.

I look away, jaw clenching.

Words slip out before I can cage them.

"You're the only thing in this damn house that feels real."

Her lips part. Her eyes soften. Too much. Too close. I want to swallow the words back down.

"Forget it," I shove a hand through my hair.

"Lorenzo . . ." she whispers, stepping forward again.

I lift a hand between us. Not touching her, just holding distance. "Don't."

"Why not?" she breathes.

Because if you touch me, I'll never let you go. Because if you ask one more time, I'll ruin everything. Because you're leaving, and I'm not good enough for you.

I give her the safe version. The lie she can live with.

"Because your world doesn't have room for someone like me," I rasp, swallowing hard. "And because I can't afford to want something I can't keep."

Her breath trembles. She nods, barely. Pain flickers across her face like she's trying to hide it.

She backs away slowly, steps soft, careful. *Deliberate*. She slips out the boathouse door, sunlight wrapping around her.

When she's gone, the quiet caves in around me. I let my guard fall, punching the wall.

I would've kissed her. Should have . . .

Fuck the consequences.

CHAPTER 9

Victoria

It happens in passing. The way most dangerous things do.

A hallway. A breath. A brush of fingers.

One second, I'm walking through the east wing with a book in one hand and an iced tea in the other, pretending I'm not already bored enough to consider flinging myself out a window, and the next, *he's* there.

Moving through the corridor as if he belongs, even though we both know he doesn't. Toolbox in hand, smelling faintly of cedar, sweat, and something else. Something warm and masculine. It should be criminal how good he always smells.

We pass each other like strangers. Except we're not. *Not anymore.*

Our hands touch. Just barely.

His fingers graze the back of mine like a secret being slipped under a door. Like a signature he shouldn't be leaving on me at all.

My breath stutters, and my heart races at a clip that can't be healthy.

It's not thumping in my chest because I'm surprised, but because I'm not. Because some traitorous part of me has been waiting for something to happen. *Anything.* Even this. It's not a lot, but at this moment, when I'm so desperate to be with him, this is enough.

I look up. He's already looking at me.

Eyes dark.

Intent. Like he's reading the thoughts I pretend I don't have.

He doesn't speak. Doesn't need to.

His lips move in silent words. "Meet me later."

The iced tea nearly slips from my hand.

I nod, but barely. But he sees it. He sees everything.

He keeps walking. And so do I. Even though my pulse stays with him.

Hours later, I can't stop thinking about him. I wish he were here with me right now.

He's not, of course, and I swear because of that, the house feels heavier.

There are too many voices. Too much pretending.

My father talks about business like it's a war strategy, and people are pawns he can afford to sacrifice. My mother smiles through casualties, as if she's practicing for the next charity gala.

I eat half a peach. Taste nothing.

"I have a headache." I touch my temple. No one acknowledges me. *Perfect.*

If no one is going to acknowledge me, then I don't even need to be here. They won't even notice if I leave.

So that's what I do. While my mother drones on about something, I slip out of my seat and head toward the back door barefoot, heels dangling from my fingers, heart racing ahead of me like it knows exactly where I'm going.

It doesn't take long to be far enough away from the house that the lights are no longer visible.

The garden path is slick with moonlight, silvering every leaf and making the hydrangeas glow. I don't go to the boathouse this time. He isn't there.

But I know where he is.

The beach on the far-right side of the estate isn't really a beach. It's not where my family or I would ever go swimming. No, this isn't the glamorous kind of beach with striped umbrellas and cocktails garnished with fruit. That's on the left side of the property where the beach forms a cove. This part is something altogether different.

It's raw. The sand is coarse and full of broken shells that scratch your feet if you're not careful.

It's where I often see Lorenzo going when he thinks no one is watching. Which makes sense. This place has rough edges. All beauty you have to bleed for.

As I turn the corner, I spot him near the waterline.

Worn jeans. Shirt rolled at the sleeves; forearms inked with the moonlight.

His hands are shoved in his pockets as he stares at the ocean.

"You always this dramatic?" I call out, voice threading through the wind.

He doesn't turn. Not right away. Just tilts his head. "Only when I know you'll show up to witness it."

Heat blooms under my ribs. I close the distance slowly, letting the wind whip my hair behind me, the hem of my dress brushing against salt-damp sand.

When I stop beside him, he finally looks at me.

His gaze sweeps over me. Slow and unhurried. It's like he's trying to memorize me.

"Took you long enough." His smirk tugging on one side like he's in on a joke I'm not privy to.

"I had to pretend to care about dessert," I drawl, lifting my abandoned heels in a lazy gesture.

His brow arches. "Did you succeed?"

"Barely," I confess with a shrug. "I almost believed myself."

His smirk widens, but not for long.

The silence between us settles again. It's heavy and charged.

It's full of things that vibrate under the skin. It's never empty with him. Never simple.

We start walking along the shore. Not touching. But not apart either. Close enough that the space between us feels like temptation. A forbidden fruit. One I want to taste.

Too bad it might be catastrophic . . .

But something tells me it would be so in the best possible way.

The waves crash against the shore as we walk. He stays quiet. While I try unsuccessfully to keep the wind from tangling my hair. I probably look like a mess. Mother would be horrified. *I'm always a disappointment.* My stomach bottoms out at the thought, shoulders tensing.

"Do you ever feel like you're . . . in a cage?" I ask, toes sinking into cold sand.

His brow lifts as he glances sidelong at me. "That sounds like a metaphor. Is this because I call you Little Bird?"

"No." I let my fingers trail through the salty air. "I know I have everything. I know I'm lucky. I know people would kill for this life. But sometimes I wake up, and it feels like the walls are closing in. Like I'm this perfectly bred little creature on a silk perch, and if I sing too loudly, someone will cover the cage and tell me to shut up."

He's silent. Long enough that I think maybe I scared him off.

"What happens if you fly?" he asks, jaw flexing.

I shake my head. "I don't know. I think the cage follows."

No laugh. No teasing. Just a quiet storm building in his eyes.

He keeps walking beside me, fists now buried in his pockets like he's holding back the urge to reach for something he shouldn't want.

"You're not soft." His voice is low and rough, like gravel under tires.

"Who said I was?" I counter, chin lifting.

"Everyone who sees your name before they *see* you."

I stop breathing for a second because he's right. Yet no one has ever said it out loud. Not like that. Not with that kind of knowing.

We drift toward the rocks. Jagged silhouettes jutting toward the sky.

The waves crash hard enough to send mist onto our skin.

It's almost cinematic. Too perfect. *Too doomed.*

He turns to me, and I turn to him.

The air shifts. Tightens. Draws us close, like magnets.

He looks at me like I'm something he's not supposed to want. Something forbidden. I like it more than I should.

I look back like I don't care about rules, like I don't care about anything but this.

Then his hand brushes mine, and there is a whisper of heat.

I don't move.

"Do you ever stop thinking?" he asks, voice dropping to something that curls low in my stomach.

"No," I whisper, my breath catching in my chest.

"Do you want to?" He steps just close enough that I feel his warmth.

I nod, but it comes off shaky.

I'm already undone.

He leans in.

Slow. Careful.

He's giving me time to run.

I won't.

I don't.

Instead, I lean in too. Heart pounding so loudly I'm sure he hears it.

Our lips hover. Close enough that we are a single breath away . . .

"Victoria!"

My mother's shrill voice slices through the night like a crack.

We stop, but we don't jerk apart. Instead, we both move slowly, neither of us happy that we have to.

I want to cry out.

Curse the fates and my mother.

It physically hurts to create distance.

He steps back a single pace. I exhale; the moment now lost.

"Another time." His eyes linger.

"Maybe," I whisper, even though it's a lie. We both know it. It's not maybe at all.

It's already happening . . .

The cage. The door.

And the crazy part, I'm not afraid to fly.

CHAPTER 10

Lorenzo

I'M NOT TRYING TO LISTEN. I'M JUST WALKING THE BACK corridor with my head down and toolbox in hand, mentally cataloging every broken thing at this estate. The sink drips. The busted dumbwaiter (that I still don't understand the point of). The east hallway that creaks like it needs an oil change.

I'm halfway through the study when I hear someone say the name Victoria. I don't slow at first. But my body reacts before my brain can catch up.

Her father's voice cuts through the crack in the door. He speaks in a low and controlled tone. In the way the rich speak, to make every sentence feel like it's the law.

"You are not to associate with the help. Do you understand me?"

My feet stop. I don't mean for them to. They just do.

Silence.

He's talking to her.

To Victoria.

"He is beneath you, Victoria. This summer fantasy you're entertaining is over. I won't allow it to ruin everything we've built."

My grip on the toolbox tightens. The metal digs into my palm.

Another beat. Then I faintly hear the sound of her voice.

"That's not what this is." Her words come out like a whisper, and it feels like something punches me in the ribs.

"Oh, please. Don't be naive." Her father's tone shifts into that special brand of refined disgust only dynasties can perfect. "You think he wants your mind? He wants what every man wants. And once he gets it, you'll be the one left embarrassed."

My jaw locks so hard I think it might snap.

"You don't know him," she fires back, the sentence taut and trembling like a violin string pulled too tight.

"I don't need to." His voice drips with boredom. "I've seen boys like him my entire life. They want what they can't have. They crawl their way into pretty girls' lives with sad stories and bad intentions, hoping to rise one social rung at a time. They take and leave. But mark my words, Victoria, they always leave."

I stop breathing.

"You're being cruel," she breathes.

"I'm being realistic. He's not your equal, not in breeding, not in ambition, and certainly not in the future. He is nothing, Victoria. He comes from nothing. Look at his mother . . . She's nothing too. And I will not have you lowering yourself for someone who isn't worth the dirt on your shoes."

Nothing. It echoes. Repeats. I can't stop hearing it.

Silence hangs between them. Then, finally, her voice, barely a whisper. "You don't get to decide who I care about."

"I get to protect what's mine."

That's it. That's my breaking point.

I turn and walk the other way before I go in there and ruin something I can't un-ruin.

The word follows me down the hall.

I avoid her that night. Don't go to her. I can't.

The next day, I'm still mentally cold.

I scrub the back patio until the sponge tears in half. I fix the wine cellar door and slam it just to hear it crack. My fists ache from gripping the screwdriver like a weapon instead of a tool.

I don't talk to anyone. Not that anyone tries. Well, except Elise.

She watches me scrub the same countertop twice, eyebrows arching slowly in amusement. "What's with you today?" She blows a bubble with her gum and pops it loudly.

"Nothing," I clip out, wiping the counter harder.

"You look like you murdered someone in your head," she teases, leaning her hip against the sink and studying me.

I don't answer. Because answering means talking about it.

And I won't do that. Especially not her.

Then she walks in.

Victoria.

She's wearing something soft and white again. The dress floats around her thighs with each step she takes. It's a temptation.

I love it and hate it in equal measure.

She stops walking and stands in the doorway of the kitchen. Waiting. Watching me like she's trying to read my thoughts.

Good luck, Little Bird, even I can't decipher what I'm feeling.

I keep scrubbing. Ignoring her, I shove the rag against the counter so hard the muscles in my forearm strain.

My body feels like it's been through a war zone. Everything burning.

She says my name quietly but sharply, like she's poking the bruise. I put the rag down and then walk past her. Like I'm immune. Like the other night didn't almost end with me kissing her senseless in the moonlight.

Because if I stop, if I look, I'll forget what I heard.

And I can't afford that.

I head to where I think best.

The boathouse is the only place on this estate that doesn't try to pretend it's something it's not. It's openly a piece of shit. It smells like dirt and is falling apart. But despite how gross it is, it reminds me of Victoria.

Once inside, I sit on the bench, fists tight, breathing through my teeth as the word pounds through me. *Nothing. Nothing. Nothing.*

No matter how much time has passed, no matter how many hours, it doesn't lessen the pain.

The door creaks. I don't turn. I don't have to.

She walks in.

The sound of her footsteps echoes around me until she's standing in front of me.

Now, I look up.

Her jaw is set. She doesn't look the same today.

She looks pissed.

"Why are you avoiding me?" she snaps, storming closer, chin lifted in challenge.

"I'm working." Except I'm not. I'm sitting empty-handed on a damn bench.

"You walked right past me." Her voice hits me like a punch to the gut.

"Congratulations. You're observant."

Her eyes flash. "What the hell is your problem?" she demands, stepping closer into my space, like she wants to start a war.

"You, Little Bird," I growl, heat rising. "You're my problem."

She freezes. Chest rising, falling. Eyes wide, bright, furious.

I don't stop. Can't.

"You walk around tossing scraps of attention like it's a favor," I bite out, stepping into her space. "Like I should be grateful you looked at me. Like I'm a toy you'll outgrow the second your daddy pulls up in his private jet and whisks you back to your designer future."

Her breath hitches. But I'm not done.

"News flash—" I move closer. Close enough to feel her inhale. "I'm not one of your manicured boys in polos. I don't fetch. I don't kneel. And I sure as hell don't need a rich girl slumming it for a little summer entertainment."

The slap comes fast. Sharp. Loud. Honest.

My head snaps to the side. The sting blooms across my cheek.

And I deserve it. All of it.

But then, before I can breathe . . .

She grabs my shirt. Fists it. Yanks me toward her with a sound that's half sob, half fury.

And kisses me.

Hard and furious.

Desperate in the way only suppressed things can be.

It steals my breath.

My thoughts. My restraint.

And I kiss her back. I kiss her like she's oxygen. Like I've been denied air for years. Like I mean to set her on fire. Because I do. Because she already lit the match.

And I'm nothing. Not to her. Not anymore.

CHAPTER 11

Victoria

DAYS HAVE PASSED SINCE THE KISS, AND I KEEP WAITING FOR something to happen. Anything.

And then it does.

The note is slipped to me.

One minute, Lorenzo is just passing by in the hall, and the next thing I know, something small and folded is tucked beneath the book I'm pretending to read on the couch.

He doesn't speak. Doesn't even glance my way. He just keeps walking like he didn't light my entire chest on fire with one motion of his hand.

I wait a beat. Two. Long enough to pretend I'm not dying to open it.

Then I slip my finger under the fold.

Meet me on the roof.

Five words.

I stare at it intently. It feels like a challenge.

I don't even know how to get to the roof. Of course, he would choose somewhere unreachable. Somewhere forbidden.

Am I up for the challenge?

I stare at the note, heart thudding against my ribs.

Yes.

Later, I'm in my room brushing my hair and trying not to overthink my pajama choice (and doing a horrible job at that).

Because who overthinks pajamas for a rooftop rendezvous? Apparently, me. That's who.

I'm mid–internal argument with myself when a soft scrape breaks across the floorboards. A slip of paper slides under my door.

I freeze mid-brush. Then stand from my vanity to go pick it up.

Another note.

I open it. This time, a tiny pebble falls out. *Weird.* I place it in my pocket and continue to read what he wrote.

Servants' stairwell. Midnight.

My pulse jumps so fast it's almost embarrassing. Seventeen years in this house and I've only used the servants' staircase a handful of times.

Midnight.

When the time comes, I head toward the meeting spot.

The hallway is dark. Colder.

We aren't in Kansas anymore.

I feel like I'm living a double life. Right now I'm the Victoria no one sees. Not the polished or perfect one. No, this version is rebellious. This Victoria doesn't care if she gets caught sneaking around in the wrong part of the house.

I take each step carefully.

When I reach the bottom of the servants' stairs, I pause . . . and that's when someone grabs me. A hand slips over my mouth. It's strong and calloused. But it's familiar. My back hits a solid chest, and I almost scream, but I don't.

Because I know it's him. Of course, it's *him.*

A giddy, inappropriate giggle escapes against his palm.

He exhales softly against the shell of my ear, sending heat down my spine. "You weren't supposed to enjoy that."

I turn my head just enough to meet his shadowed gaze.

"You're not as scary as you think," I whisper back, my lips brushing the edge of his palm.

"You're not as careful as you should be."

His hand leaves my mouth, only to catch my fingers instead. He holds me firmly and leads me up the narrow stairwell.

The air is dusty, and it's hard to see, but regardless of that, I follow him.

We climb two stories, and duck through a freaking hatch I didn't know existed.

Next thing I know, we're outside.

He lets go of my hand. But only barely. His fingers linger like he's reluctant to lose the connection.

"This is where the staff comes in the fall to clean leaves." He rolls his sleeves higher. "There's a locked door on the north side. No one uses it in the summer."

I look at him, heart knocking on my ribs like it wants to escape. "How did you know I'd come?" I ask, letting the question tilt upward like a dare.

He shrugs, but there's nothing casual about the way his eyes hold mine. "I didn't," he admits, his voice softly. "I just knew I'd wait."

Heat blooms under my skin.

I sit first.

Probably should have brought a blanket, because the stone is super cold.

I don't mention it though, don't want to ruin the mood. Or seem high maintenance.

Lorenzo sits beside me.

The silence is different up here. Not heavy. Not sharp. Just . . . full.

"Tell me something true," I breathe, drawing my knees up like him, resting my chin on them.

He exhales, slow and steady. "That's a dangerous game." He glances at me from beneath his lashes.

"Then play it," I challenge, nudging his knee with mine.

He doesn't look at me. Just at the stars, like they're easier to confess to.

"It's always just been my mom and me," he starts, voice low, words dragging. "She never talked about my dad. Ever. Not even when I asked."

I nod slowly, something softening in my chest. "That's hard." My fingers curling against the stone.

He shrugs, but it's stiff. "It was normal to me. Until it wasn't."

"Why did you move here?" I ask, watching his throat work as he swallows.

He hesitates. It's a long pause. Drawn out.

"We had to leave where we were," he admits, rubbing his thumb across his knee. "I got in some trouble. Nothing huge, just . . . enough. Then one day, she packed everything in the car and said we were going east."

"Just like that?" I whisper, leaning closer.

He nods once, jaw tightening. "Just like that. Like she was running. Or hiding. I didn't ask too many questions. She looked scared, and I don't like seeing her scared."

I look at him now. Really look.

Something is beneath the anger. Beneath the sharp edges and the sarcasm.

There's history. And hurt. But most importantly . . . loyalty.

"She's your mom. You love her," I breathe, the truth shaping itself without my permission.

He nods. "She's all I had. All I have."

"You're lucky," I whisper, blinking hard. "To have someone like that. Someone who sees you. Fights for you."

He looks over then. But I don't meet his gaze. It's too much. Too raw.

I stare at the sky because it's easier than saying the rest out loud.

"I'm not a daughter to them," I say, voice cracking. "Not really.

I'm a possession. Something to show off, polish, and control. A bargaining chip for legacy. A name in a marriage contract."

My throat tightens, and I swear a tear threatens to fall. I try to bite it back, but one escapes anyway. It slides down my cheek in perfect, humiliating silence.

He catches it with the tip of his finger.

"You're not a possession to me," he whispers, each word a vow. "You're everything."

A sound escapes me, half laugh, or maybe half scoff. I have no idea what I'm doing or thinking. It feels like everything is spinning, and I shake my head to right myself.

"You don't even know me," I whisper. "Not really."

He leans in. "I don't need to know you to know this." His eyes locked on mine. "Anyone with eyes can see it. You're kind. And sweet. And beautiful. And you look at me like I mean something."

My voice breaks. "No one has ever looked at me like that, Lorenzo."

His jaw flexes. It looks like he might break. "I do."

"Why?"

"Because you do mean something." His voice cracks, and then he kisses me.

No hesitation. No warning. Just fire and stars and every broken piece of us fitting together like this moment was carved into fate long ago.

It's gentle. Then desperate. Then everything.

And I kiss him back like I finally found the part of me I've been missing all along.

CHAPTER 12

Lorenzo

ALL I CAN THINK ABOUT ALL DAY LONG IS WHEN I CAN SEE her next.

I'm obsessed and not in a good way.

She occupies my every thought. I don't even understand why.

Sure, she's gorgeous, but I barely recognize the person I've become around her.

Fighting on street corners is a distant thought. In its place are images of her. Thoughts of her.

Take this moment. It's two in the morning, and I've been waiting for one hour before she finally slips into the library.

The sound is soft. Her bare feet pad lightly on the polished hardwood.

I haven't looked up to see if it's her yet, but I don't need to. I know it is.

I've been waiting long enough. Sitting on the floor between two shelves with a flashlight balanced on a stack of leather-bound history books, pretending to read something I can't remember the title of.

The door clicks shut behind her, and that's when I tilt my head up to look.

Her hair is a little messy, like she ran a hand through it too many times. Her robe is tied too loosely, slipping off one shoulder. She looks like perfection.

"You're late." I drag my thumb across the edge of the page.

"You're early," she counters, stepping closer, her tone light but her eyes still ring with exhaustion.

"I don't sleep." I lean back against the wall behind me.

She raises a brow, climbing over my leg to sit beside me. "Ever?" she teases, tapping my knee with her foot.

"Not well," I admit, trying not to look at the slip of bare thigh peeking through her robe.

She steps over me fully, lowering herself into the space by my hip like the floor was built to fit the shape of her. She doesn't ask permission. She never does. She just molds her body as close to me as possible.

She pulls the book from her robe pocket. *Wuthering Heights.* The damn thing again.

She opens it, flipping a page with the kind of reverence people reserve for hymns.

"Read me something." I let my head fall back. "Even though I won't admit I missed your voice more than I missed the words."

She smirks. It's small and secretive, then she's flipping through a few pages. "Okay. Listen to this," she whispers, clearing her throat, soft but serious.

"'He shall never know how I love him: and that, not because he's handsome, Nelly, but because he's more myself than I am. Whatever our souls are made of, his and mine are the same.'"

Silence drops between us like a wall. Thick. Charged. Too heavy to breathe through.

I swallow hard. "That's the part you picked?" My voice dips lower than I intend.

"It's where I left off."

"And what is this part about?"

"It's the important part," She drags her fingertip along the page. "It's the part about how love can wreck things."

I nod slowly, the corner of my mouth twitching. "Still sounds more like obsession than love."

She tilts her head, eyes sharp. "What's the difference?"

That stops me, my gaze taking her in.

Her knees are tucked beneath her, and her fingers rest lightly on the open pages. Her whole posture is calm, but her eyes? She's wound tight. Something is sitting behind them tonight. Something she hasn't said yet. Something that's not the book.

"You ever wish you weren't born into it?" I ask quietly. "The name. The family. The *cage*."

She lets out a soft, bitter laugh. "Every day."

"Then why not leave?"

She exhales.

I watch as she pulls her robe tighter around herself even though the room isn't cold. "Because they trained me to stay," she says, voice cracking like a glass under too much pressure. "Trained me to smile. Trained me to be perfect. Because they told me love is conditional, and legacy is not. Because if I run—"

"They lose a daughter."

She laughs once. The sound through us is dry and humorless. "No, they lose an asset."

My jaw clenches hard enough to ache. "That's insane," I bite out through my teeth.

"It's normal here," she whispers, staring down at the book like it's safer than looking at me.

"It doesn't have to be."

Her head snaps up, eyes flashing hot. "Then what does it have to be?" Her voice slices the air. "A runaway story? A scandal? A headline? You don't get it, Lorenzo. You weren't born with a chain around your ankle."

Her words hit me. It feels like a knife under my ribs. I flinch. I don't mean to, but I do.

My mouth opens. Closes. Nothing comes out.

She sees the damage. Regret flashes across her face.

"I didn't mean that," she breathes, rubbing her temples, pulling her knees closer up to her chest. "I just . . . "

She presses her palms to her eyes, shoulders shaking just once. "It's suffocating."

I nod slowly, letting the quiet settle thicker between us. The room feels smaller now. The space between us is hotter. More fragile.

"None of that matters to me," she whispers suddenly, dropping her hands and looking at me. "Not when I'm with you. Not your job. Not my name. Not what anyone thinks. I don't care."

For some reason, one I can't even understand, I believe her.

I lean closer. My movements are slow. I'm careful not to scare her off.

She doesn't pull away.

"You shouldn't care," I whisper, brushing a strand of hair behind her ear. "But I'm glad you do."

She tilts her head, leaning forward until her lips are only inches from mine. "I do," her voice trembles. "More than I should."

I kiss her. Because there's nothing else left to do. Because if I don't, I'll lose my mind. Because she looks at me like I'm worth saving, and I'm selfish enough to want the lie.

The kiss starts quietly. Her lips part against mine, and I wrap my arms around her and pull her close to my body.

The kiss builds fast.

Her hands slide up my chest, fingers curling into my shirt.

Mine slip into her hair, tugging her closer until I'm not sure where she ends, and I begin.

The library disappears. The books. The names. The rules.

All gone.

Until it's just her. And me. And a kiss that tastes like the beginning of something we're not ready to name, but already can't stop.

CHAPTER 13

Victoria

All day, I imagine where the note will be.

Lorenzo has been leaving me notes every day since the roof.

When I finally head back to my room, after a day in the sun, I find it.

The note is folded and sitting on my desk. Each time I get a note from him, a tiny stone accompanies it. I don't understand the rocks, but I keep each one regardless.

Now at dinner, I stare at my mother's vacant smile, and I almost laugh.

But I don't. I just smile into my wine water goblet, like I'm hiding something scandalous. Because I am.

Under the table, I unfold it, heart already racing.

Boathouse. Midnight.

No greeting. No name.

And it thrills me.

Sneaking out of the house has become a strange kind of art. I love it.

Love the feeling when I tiptoe through the house and out the door.

It feels illicit. Addictive. Romantic in a way none of my books ever prepared me for.

And tonight, after dinner, when I slip out the back door with socks on, and a hoodie pulled tight over my nightgown, I feel . . . alive.

The night air wraps around me like a robe, and my socks grow damp from the wet grass. I hurry toward the old boathouse. The house lights vanish behind me, swallowed by trees and distance.

With every step I take, I leave my world behind. The expectations. The suffocation. The girl I'm supposed to be.

Out here, I get to be someone else. Someone reckless. Someone his.

The boathouse is quiet. The black ocean glimmers in the distance.

He's already there. *Of course he is.*

Leaning against a beam, he has his hands in his pockets and his hair a mess. He is already wearing that smug little smile that drives me insane.

"You're late." He pushes off the beam with one lazy step, his voice dripping with amused accusation.

"You're early," I counter, stepping inside and letting the door swing shut behind me with a soft thud.

"You say that every time," he drawls, trailing his gaze down my hoodie, my bare legs, the hem of my nightgown peeking out, and then at my wet socks.

At his stare, I lean down and peel them off, placing them down on the floor beside the door.

"Then maybe stop being so damn punctual," I shoot back, standing before brushing a strand of hair out of my face.

"I like being here before you," he admits with a shrug, pacing a slow arc toward me. "Gives me time to pace."

"How charming," I tease, lifting an eyebrow.

"I do my best." He crosses the space between us until he's standing in front of me. He reaches his hand out and pulls lightly at the drawstring of my hoodie. "It's not easy being this neurotic."

The corner of my mouth lifts because seeing him nervous feels wickedly intoxicating. It means I'm not the only one undone.

He continues to stand in front of me, and I wait for him to do something. Maybe kiss me? He doesn't, though, and it feels intentional. Like he's giving me time to run if I want to.

Which I don't.

The air between us crackles like a struck match.

"You wore the hoodie." His eyes drop, and they turn dark and satisfied.

"It's your hoodie," I remind him, twisting the fabric between my fingers.

He smirks, low and hungry. "It's better on you."

I roll my eyes even though heat curls low in my stomach. "Talk about a line."

"Line?" he asks, closing the space until I can feel the warmth of his breath. "Then why do you keep coming back if I'm only giving you lines?"

I reach for his collar, fist it, and tug him toward me until our chests almost brush. "Because you leave notes in my books."

"So this is your kink? Stationery or does it have to be in a book?" he teases, grin crooked and sinful.

"Don't make it weird," I warn, tightening my grip on his shirt.

"Oh, Little Bird," he breathes against my mouth, "it was always weird."

And then he kisses me. It's soft at first, but not for long.

His hands slide to my waist, fingers digging into the fabric. My fingers thread into his hair, tugging just enough to make him groan.

We press together like we're trying to escape our own skins.

Like there's no world outside this old wooden shack.

He groans against my mouth when I tug his hair harder. The sound shoots straight through me.

And I feel it. All of it. The ache. The want. The overwhelming relief of finally having something that feels like mine.

After a few more moments, we pull apart—barely.

His forehead rests against mine. His breath is hot. His chest rises hard and fast against mine.

"Jesus." He brushes his thumb against my lip. "You're going to be the death of me."

"You like it," I whisper, nudging my nose against his.

"That's not the point," he breathes, his eyes dropping to my mouth again like he's fighting himself.

"Then what is?" I ask, fingers curling into his shirt, pulling him impossibly closer and begging to be kissed again.

He hesitates long enough to make my pulse trip, and then his voice drops, raw and unguarded.

"No one's ever wanted me like this before. Sure, I've had girls, but this—this is different."

The words hit me like a punch, and all the air leaves my lungs. I pull back just enough to look at him. Really look at him.

His eyes are serious. Dark. A little afraid. And I realize he means it.

Not just physically. Not in the shallow, temporary way people want something pretty or dangerous.

He means no one's ever chosen him. No one ever thought he was worth sneaking out for. Worth breaking rules for. Worth fighting for.

"I want you," I whisper, lifting his chin with my hand so he has to hear it.

His brows furrow, his breath shaking. "You shouldn't."

"But I do."

He swallows, the muscles in his throat working hard. "Why?" he asks, voice cracking open.

"Because you see me," I say, letting my fingers slide down his jaw. "Because you talk to me like I'm not fragile or foolish. Because you don't want me quiet or perfect or still." My voice trembles, but I don't stop. "Because when you kiss me, I feel like I matter."

His hand flies to my face.

Urgent.

Rough.

Almost desperate.

"You do matter, Little Bird," he growls. "To me. You have no idea how much."

I lean in. He meets me halfway.

Our mouths crash together again. It's harder this time, hungrier, like we're trying to memorize the shape of something doomed. We know the clock is ticking. And the notes won't be enough for much longer.

His hands slide under the hem of my hoodie, finding the bare skin of my waist. I gasp into his mouth. He swallows the sound.

I press closer, chest to chest, heartbeat to heartbeat.

We move together like a storm. Crazy and relentless.

Fierce and breathless.

We are want and need.

Built-up passion simmering to explode.

It's dangerous yet . . . perfect.

Then—suddenly—he pulls back. Just enough to break the kiss.

Why did he stop?

His forehead drops to mine, breath shaking. "We can't," he whispers, voice rough.

"Why?" I breathe, reaching up and sliding my fingers down the column of his throat.

"Because once I start wanting more with you"—his eyes close like the thought hurts—"I won't be able to stop."

I take his hand. Lift it. Place it flat against my racing heart.

"Then don't stop."

His eyes widen.

It looks like he has something more to say, but instead, he shakes his head and kisses me again.

Slower and deeper this time.

A kiss that says all the things he can't say.

A kiss that says *everything.*

CHAPTER 14

Lorenzo

I KNOW THE LOOK ON MY MOTHER'S FACE BEFORE SHE SPEAKS. It's the one she used to wear when I was ten and coming home with bruised knuckles and a chipped tooth.

The look that says . . . *You don't have to tell me what you did. I already know.*

But more importantly, at this very moment, it clearly states, *You are not one of them. Know your place.*

We're in the staff kitchen. She's elbow-deep in dough for tomorrow's breakfast rolls, her hands moving with the kind of practiced calm only someone who's lived an entire lifetime serving others can maintain.

The overhead light flickers as I brace for a lecture.

It's coming . . . that much I know for sure.

If my mother is one thing it's predictable with how she reacts when she thinks I'm fucking up.

I lean against the counter, waiting. I wish she would just spit it out already so I can go on with my day.

She coughs once, clearing her throat.

Be careful what you wish for.

"You keep staring at that girl, and we are going to have a problem, Enzo."

My shoulders tense. Just slightly. But enough for her to notice because she always notices.

"What girl?" I ask, but it comes out more like a deadpan because with my mother, I'm a terrible liar and an even worse actor. With everyone else, I'm fantastic, but Mom is my kryptonite.

She gives me a look that is so sharp it could slice through bone. "I didn't raise an idiot. Don't pretend to be one now."

I lean back harder, crossing my arms like that might protect me. "What if I am?"

She slams the dough against the marble, the crack echoing through the room. "Then you're being reckless."

There's a long beat. The only sound in the air is the dough being rolled and turned.

Actually, if you strain real hard, you can hear the hum of the refrigerator, but other than that, you could drop a pin, and it would echo.

My heartbeat pounds in my chest.

"If someone else notices," she continues, voice tightening as she punches the dough, over and over again, "we're both gone. Out. No job. No place to go. No second chances. You understand?"

I nod, jaw tight. "So we just pretend nothing's happening? Pretend I don't feel—"

"Yes." She finally lifts her gaze.

Her eyes land on mine with a force that makes my back go ramrod straight.

"That's exactly what you do. Because this isn't a fairy tale, Lorenzo. And you're not a prince."

That lands hard. Too hard. Like a fist between the ribs.

I swallow the hurt down, but I swear it feels like I've just consumed needles by how hard it burns.

Then I ask quietly, "Why can't we just go home?"

Her brows tighten. A small movement, but a tell, nonetheless, and certainly big enough for me to notice.

She looks away, wiping her hands on a towel that's already clean. "It's not that simple,".

"Why?" I push, taking a step toward her.

She grabs a bowl from the cabinet with more force than necessary. "Because it isn't."

I wait for her to say more, but she doesn't give me anything else.

I file the silence away. Add it to the growing list of secrets we pretend aren't secrets.

Another thing to unpack later.

For now, I'll concentrate on getting my work done, because despite what my mother says, I have no intention of staying away from Victoria.

An hour later, I do what I always do when I can't get her out of my head. Which is every night. Every hour. Every damn breath.

I find the worn copy of *Wuthering Heights* that she's been reading in the library, and slide a note and pebble inside.

Same time.

I don't sign it. There's no need. She knows it's from me.

The rest of the day, I keep my head down.

Ever since I walked past Mr. Danforth's office and heard him call me a fucking idiot, and then saying my mother wasn't good enough to work in his house, I've needed a distraction so I don't kill the man.

I fix a busted pipe under the main sink. Oil a squeaky hinge in the foyer closet.

Reattach a loose banister rail that's been threatening to send someone to the ER . . .

I pretend everything is normal.

Then I see her, and two things happen after that . . .

One: I'm no longer thinking of gutting Victoria's father.

Two: She's the only thought I'm now able to have.

I pretend I'm not thinking of her smile, her mouth, her laugh that hits me underneath my ribs like a fishhook.

But mentally, I'm like a ticking time bomb. Waiting.

And by midnight, I'm already at the meet spot.

She steps into the hallway with that same spark in her eyes, and it makes my pulse accelerate.

She's the match, and I'm the gasoline.

"Come on," she whispers, grabbing my hand before I can say a word. "I want to show you something."

"Can you give me a hint?" I tease, letting her pull me along. "Or are we playing hide-and-seek?"

She squeezes my fingers, smirking over her shoulder. "It's better if I show you."

Her steps are faster than normal, which excites me.

We sneak past the grand stairwell. Up two levels. Down a narrow hallway.

She leads me into a corner of the house I've never seen. Which says a lot, since I was sure I'd seen everything in this place. Guess not.

She pushes aside an antique mirror. It's the biggest mirror I've ever seen.

It flings over easily despite its size. My eyes go wider when I see what's behind it. There's a small wooden door.

She pulls out a key from her pocket—silver and old—and slips it into the lock.

"Victoria," I whisper, leaning close, my breath ghosting her ear. "Are you about to murder me in a hidden hallway?"

"Don't tempt me," she jokes as she slips inside first.

I follow. She closes the door behind us with a quiet click.

The room is dusty but quiet, and the air smells like the room hasn't been aired out in decades.

It probably hasn't, by the looks of things.

"What is this place?" I ask, running my fingers over the peeling wallpaper.

"It was added during Prohibition." She drags her hand along a wood-paneled wall. "My great-grandfather used it to make and store bootleg booze. It's been boarded up for decades, but I found the key in an old ledger."

She glances back at me, eyes gleaming in the low light. "No one knows I come here."

"You're full of surprises, Little Bird." I step closer.

Despite how small the room is, it's still wide enough to hold a faded green velvet couch and a vintage record player perched on an old crate.

She walks over to the record player, gently dusting off the top with her sleeve.

"Does it work?" I lean over the crate beside her.

She glances over her shoulder, smiling. "Yeah, it still works. It's just a little dusty."

I nod toward it. "Then turn it on."

She raises a brow, teasing, "You trying to dance with me?"

I shrug, stepping closer until our arms almost brush. "You trying to get out of it?"

She laughs under her breath, the sound warm and dangerous. Then she crouches beside the crate of vinyls.

"You realize I have to pick the right mood." She flips through records. "Jazz? Blues? Cheesy '60s love songs?"

"Surprise me," I challenge, watching her.

She pulls out a vinyl, holds it up to the low light, then slips it from its sleeve.

She sets it on the turntable. The needle scratches before melting into a slow, old-school tune.

The soft tune settles over us in no time.

I hold out my hand, and she takes it, her fingers threading through mine.

We start to dance. If you can call it that.

It's awkward at first.

Too close, then not close enough.

But somewhere between the second verse and the lazy sax solo, she sinks into me.

Her head finds my chest, and my hand slides to her lower back.

We move as one. Like the world outside this hidden room no longer exists.

"What happens in the fall?" I ask quietly, barely above the music.

She exhales.

The thought of her leaving physically pains me.

Fall isn't that far away.

Fuck.

Just the thought of it makes me want to vomit.

She looks up at me then, like she already knows what I'm thinking. I feel like she always knows.

"It's not that far," she whispers. "A few hours, tops. We'll make it work."

I want to believe her. But my mother's voice echoes in my head. *You're not a prince.*

"What are you thinking about?" she asks, tipping her chin up to study me.

I shake my head, forcing a small smile. "Nothing."

She squints at me. "Liar."

I just kiss her temple because it's easier than explaining. Instead, the unspoken words settle in my chest.

We dance a little longer. She hums along to the music. Off-key but perfect.

Eventually, we collapse onto the couch..

"You planning anything big for school?" I ask, tilting my head toward her.

She shrugs, the movement brushing her shoulder against

mine. "A few things. I want to intern at a paper. Maybe join a writing group. You?"

"Avoid jail," I joke.

"That sounds perfect," she giggles.

The record finishes its song, but neither of us moves to change it.

I let the moment take me in.

Because she's next to me. And everything else can wait.

CHAPTER 15

Victoria

THE STAFF NEVER SPEAKS TO ME DIRECTLY UNLESS IT'S TO pass along something dumb. A menu change. Sometimes staffing issues, but that's about it.

So when Helen, one of the longtime housekeepers, stops me in the hall with her hands clutched tightly in front of her apron, my stomach goes cold.

"Your father wishes to see you in his office." Her voice is tight, and it sounds almost scared.

I look down and see that her fingers twist the fabric. Yep. She's terrified of my dad.

You and me both.

It would be great if we could both feign ignorance, and I can go about my day, like she didn't just drop an explosive device on my lap. And by explosive device, I mean some annoying lecture by my father that I'm sure is about to come.

My mouth goes dry thinking about what he wants to talk to me about.

It's not like his lecturing me isn't a regular occurrence, but after last night, I'm worried.

The hidden room. The dancing. Falling asleep wrapped in Lorenzo.

He must know.

He has to know.

"Thank you." I manage a nod.

Helen doesn't meet my eyes. Instead, she turns and hurries back the way she came.

The hallway shifts as I walk, my balance off because I'm so nervous.

Up ahead, I see the closed door. I don't want to go in, but I have no choice.

Taking a breath, I then knock.

"Come in," he calls, his voice as sharp as a blade.

I step inside. It feels like I've just entered the gates of hell. Dark wood. Heavy doors. The scent of scotch clings to everything.

He's seated behind the enormous mahogany desk.

I hate it in here. It's always cold and dark. And honestly scary.

A chill runs down my spine.

He doesn't need to gesture, because I know the drill.

Not my first rodeo . . .

Like the obedient daughter I am, I sit.

Back straight. Hands folded.

The perfect daughter. Or whatever version of that he's rewritten in his head.

He eyes me for a long moment, sipping from his glass, gaze moving over me.

"There's an important dinner tonight," he says.

My spine tightens. "Yes, sir."

He nods once. Slowly. Too slow for my liking.

"Not just important. Pivotal."

I stay quiet. My pulse doesn't.

He leans back in his chair, swirling the amber liquid.

"You're old enough now to understand the pressure this family is under. The world is changing. Markets are unpredictable. And the competition is more cutthroat than ever."

Translation: Profits are down, and the empire is crumbling.

"Yes, sir," I say again, quieter.

He sets the glass down with a dull thud.

"Our biggest competitor is arriving tonight for dinner. Jameson & Company. We've danced around each other for years, but now . . . we may need to lie in bed with them."

I blink.

"Lie in bed?" I echo, my brows lifting.

He gives a humorless smile.

"It's a metaphor. Though, in this case, not entirely."

Something in my stomach twists.

"Their son will be attending," he adds, casual, like he's inviting me to tea with a dead man.

I say nothing. My silence does the screaming for me.

"He's older. Polished. Runs the financial side of their business. Doesn't suffer from your generation's sensitivity issues."

"Meaning?" I ask, throat dry, voice steady only because I've been trained to make it so.

"Meaning he's not afraid of hard work. Or difficult women."

I flinch.

Just slightly.

He clocks it. Of course he does.

"You're going to be seated next to him. I expect you to smile. Be gracious. Charming. The future of this business may very well rest on your ability to be likable."

My nails dig into my palms.

So that's what this is.

A trade.

My freedom for the business.

"Of course," I manage, voice calm despite the way my insides scream.

He stands and moves toward the bar in the corner, refilling his glass like it's water. Ice clinks. His shoulders stay relaxed, like he didn't just seal my fate.

"Don't give me that look," he says.

"What look?" I tilt my head, letting my hair fall over one shoulder.

"Like you have thoughts."

"I do have thoughts."

He laughs. "You're a Danforth, Victoria. It's time you started acting like it. Stop thinking."

I rise slowly from the chair.

My knees shake beneath my skirt, but I don't let it show.

He returns to his desk, already dismissing me with the tilt of his head.

"Wear the blue dress. The one that makes you look softer."

"Yes, sir."

I walk out before I say something that burns the whole house down.

My hands are trembling as I close the door behind me.

But my back stays straight.

Because tonight, I will smile.

And tomorrow, I will find a way to never need this man again.

The day turns into night way too fast.

And before I know it, I'm sitting at the long formal table, hands in my lap, pretending to be something I don't want to be. The dining room has never felt more like a courtroom.

I sit at the long, polished table, blue silk clinging to my skin like a bribe. My father's voice echoes through the vaulted ceiling as he laughs.

The sound bounces off every surface of the room. Vibrating off chandeliers and dishes like he's the most important person in the world.

The guest of honor tonight is Richard Jameson, the man my father has spent years calling an arrogant, shortsighted bastard. Now he's grinning like they're old college roommates.

Next to Mr. Jameson sits his son.

Grant.

Grant Jameson is all teeth and entitlement. A few years older than me. Impeccably dressed. Expensive watch. Dead eyes.

He's seated to my right, of course.

Where else would the future bargaining chip go?

Dinner starts with wine. Grant pours one for me before I can protest, leaning in so his cologne almost suffocates me.

"You clean up nice," he says, smirking, eyes dragging slowly over my dress. "Your father said you were pretty. He undersold it."

I grip the stem of my glass. Smile. Don't scream.

"How generous of him," I say, voice sweet as poisoned honey, turning my head just enough to slice him with a look.

"I always appreciate an obedient daughter," he adds, loud enough for both fathers to hear, his tone smug and performative.

My father lets out a chuckle.

"She can be a handful," he says.

My skin crawls.

Luckily for me, the conversation is cut short when the first course is served.

However, it's fleeting as Grant shifts closer. His knee brushes mine.

I move. He follows.

"So," Grant says, voice casual as his hand lands on my thigh beneath the tablecloth, "you planning to work for the family empire, or just marry into one that can keep up?"

My hand drops to his. I pry his fingers off. Quietly. Firmly. My nails bite his knuckles.

"As if I'll tell you," I whisper, lips curved in a smile that doesn't reach my eyes.

He grins. "Spicy."

Of course, he likes that. Of course, he thinks it's a performance for him.

The main course arrives. The wine keeps flowing. The fathers talk shop.

Margins. Assets. Consolidation.

I might as well be a side dish.

"It's all about the merger now," Mr. Jameson says. "We need to find ways to integrate."

My father raises his glass. "Shared goals. Shared futures."

Grant's hand returns. Higher this time. Fingers trailing up my thigh like a silent agreement.

My leg jerks, knocking him off me.

I stand abruptly. "Excuse me." My voice is tight. "I need the restroom."

I don't wait for permission. I walk fast, jetting toward somewhere far from here.

With each step I take, it feels like I can't breathe.

I reach the powder room, and shove open the door. I'm about to close it, when Lorenzo slips in behind me, and then he closes it behind him.

"Jesus," I breathe. "You scared the hell out of me."

He locks the door. Leans against it. His jaw is tight. His eyes burn.

"I saw everything," he growls.

"You shouldn't be here," I whisper, wiping at the corner of my eye even though I'm not crying. Not yet.

He steps forward. "You're shaking."

"I'm fine."

"You're not."

His hand cups my face.

I close my eyes.

"He touched you like he owned you."

"He thinks he does."

Lorenzo's voice is low, lethal. "He doesn't."

"And what say do you have?" I ask, eyes snapping open.

His thumb grazes my cheekbone. "I don't care who I am. Or what your father thinks of me. I won't let him have you."

"You can't stop them."

"Watch me."

And then he kisses me.

Hard.

Fierce.

Like he's branding a vow into my mouth.

I kiss him back like I believe it.

Because for one second, I do.

We break apart, both breathless. My fingers curl around his wrist.

"Thank you," I whisper.

He nods, jaw still clenched. "You go in there with your head high, Little Bird. Let the bastard see what real fire looks like."

I square my shoulders.

And step out of the bathroom.

Back toward the flames.

CHAPTER 16

Victoria

I make it back to my room after dinner before I fall apart. *Barely.*

The door clicks shut behind me.

The silence feels suffocating, and my skin still burns where Grant touched me.

I move to the edge of my bed, grabbing a handful of my skirt and clenching until the silk wrinkles between my fingers.

In. Out. In.

It doesn't work.

The walls feel too close. And my hands shake.

"You're fine," I whisper to myself, pacing now. My bare feet thud softly against the plush rug like I'm trying to stomp down the panic. "You're fine. You're fine. You made it through dinner. You're in your room. He's not here. He can't touch you now."

But the tremble won't stop.

My chest stutters with every breath.

I rub my hands up and down my arms, whispering anything.

Nonsense, comfort, lies . . .

Anything to drown out the sound of my pulse.

And then I see it.

A slip of paper on my desk. With a pebble sitting on top of it.

I blink. Step closer, heart tripping.

The small pebble is smooth and gray. It looks like it doesn't belong anywhere near me.

I lift it slowly.

Lorenzo. Of course.

A laugh breaks out of me. It sounds thin and shaky.

I tuck the pebble into the small wooden box on my desk, where I've been storing them. The one I keep for earrings. Somehow, these little stones feel more precious than all of them.

I unfold the note.

Are you okay? Just that, scribbled in dark pen.

Underneath, it says ***Meet me outside. Same place***.

While the panic continues to buzz inside my veins, something inside me loosens its grip seeing his note.

I strip off the silk dress, the fabric whispering as it hits the floor. I throw on my softest pajama shorts and a hoodie two sizes too big. The one I stole from Lorenzo.

I crawl onto the window seat and sit there, knees to my chest, watching. Waiting.

The estate lights go out one by one.

By the time the last lamp flickers out in the west wing, my hand is already on the doorknob.

I move silently out of my room and down the hall until I'm walking out the back door and into the summer night.

The grass is cool against my toes, and the air smells like fresh rain. I'm all the way to the beach when I see him.

A towel is laid out on the sand with Lorenzo sitting there like he's been waiting a lifetime for me.

His knees are bent, and his forearms are resting casually on top. He's so cute when he doesn't know I'm watching, and it's just him and his thoughts. I take another step closer, and his gaze snaps to mine.

He smiles as he hops up, and I walk straight into his arms.

No words.

He wraps his arms around me instantly, holding tight, but not too tight, just enough. My cheek presses against his chest, and I listen to his heart beat a steady rhythm. The sound is my anchor.

Then, together, still entwined, we sink onto the towel.

We lie back, his arm under my shoulders, my hand pressed to his chest. The stars stretch across the sky.

Bright and infinite. It feels like right here and now, anything is possible.

"That one," I say softly, pointing.

He turns his head, his cheek brushing my hair. "Which one?"

"Cassiopeia," I tell him. "The queen. She was punished for being vain. Hung upside down in the sky forever."

He huffs a laugh, brushing his thumb along my arm. "Sounds familiar."

I smile, small but real.

"She thought her daughter was the most beautiful woman alive. The gods didn't like that," I continue.

He glances at me from the corner of his eye. "You sure it wasn't because she got caught dancing with a boy on a beach?"

"That's not technically in the myth."

"Should be," he says, nudging me lightly with his shoulder.

We go quiet again. The stars pulse overhead. The ocean crashes against the shore.

"Sometimes I wish I could disappear into them," I whisper. "Just float up and be done with all of it."

He rolls onto his side, facing me, his body warm in the cool night air.

"What would you leave behind?" he asks, voice low, threaded with something fragile.

"Everything."

His eyes search mine. Not judging. Just seeing.

He runs his fingers down my arm, slow, gentle, like he's memorizing the shape of me.

"Even me?" he whispers.

I pause. My throat tightens.

Then I shake my head. "You're the only thing I'd bring with me."

His expression flickers. Almost like my words hurt. Or heal. Maybe both.

I help him. I take his hand and thread our fingers together, squeezing once.

"Do you feel trapped?" I ask.

"Every day." His thumb brushes the back of my hand at his confession.

"Tell me," I urge.

He swallows hard. "My mom acts like we're here by choice. But it doesn't feel like a choice. It feels like exile."

"You asked her about it?"

He nods, jaw flexing. "She shut me down. Said we have no family. But I remember . . . I swear I remember someone. A boy, a little older than me, but he was my friend. It just doesn't make sense."

"What if she's protecting you?" I whisper.

"From what?" he asks, voice rough.

"I don't know," I admit softly. "Something worse than this."

He sighs and lies back on his side again, the sand shifting beneath us.

"She keeps saying we have nowhere else to go. But I think we had somewhere. And someone took it away."

My chest tightens. I know that feeling. The slow rot of being treated like property.

A pawn. A possession.

"Maybe we are both caged," I say.

He reaches up and brushes a piece of hair behind my ear, his fingers lingering on my jaw. "But at least now we're in the same cage."

I laugh, but it cracks in the middle.

He hears it. I feel it.

He pulls me into his arms, and I melt into him, curling against his chest like we've done a thousand times.

Maybe in another life, we did.

We talk for a long time. About nothing. About everything.

I tell him about how I used to pretend to be a spy and hide in the attic, eavesdropping on dinner parties—my childhood rebellion.

He tells me about stealing comic books from gas stations and giving fake names to mall security—his childhood survival.

He tells me he used to be angry all the time.

"What changed?" I ask, tracing small circles on his shirt.

He lifts my hand to his mouth. Kisses my knuckles.

"You," he whispers against my skin.

My throat closes. Tears prick. But I don't cry. Instead, I press my mouth to his shoulder, breathing him in.

For tonight. For this single, dangerous, precious sliver of time . . .

We stay right here. And for tonight, that's enough.

CHAPTER 17

Victoria

I WAKE TO THE SOUND OF MY MOTHER HUMMING.

That's the first sign something is wrong.

The second is the garment bag hanging from the armoire.

"Happy birthday, darling," she sings, sweeping into my room with her hair perfectly curled and her lipstick already in place.

What the hell is happening? And why is she singing?

She hates me . . .

I squint at her. "It's barely nine."

"Exactly," she chirps, smoothing imaginary wrinkles from her silk blouse. "We have a schedule."

"Do I get a say in this schedule?" I push myself upright, letting the sheets tangle around my legs.

"Don't be difficult, Victoria Danforth."

That's the third sign. Because when she uses my full name, a disaster is guaranteed.

She claps her hands, and suddenly, I'm surrounded.

A makeup artist and a hairstylist, wielding enough hot tools to power a small city, have appeared out of nowhere.

If that's not bad enough, a woman with a clipboard who looks like she organizes royal weddings for sport stands beside them.

Great, just fucking great.

I'm ushered out of my bed, in a whirlwind, and the next thing

I know, I'm being thrust into the bathroom to brush my teeth, followed by being practically slung into a makeup chair.

I'm in a complete daze as foundation is buffed into my skin.

"Any particular look you'd like?" the stylist asks, holding up a palette like she's offering me the gift of self-expression. Who is she kidding? If I tell her what I want, Mother would never allow it.

"Freedom," I mumble under my breath.

She blinks, probably wondering if I really said that. *Yes, sweetheart, I did.*

"A soft smoky eye it is."

Of course. The universal translation for your mother already told me what you are to look like.

Thanks for the false pretense, though.

For the next hour, I feel like a pincushion, and then my mother returns, making this moment even worse.

She holds out the garment bag. "Put this on," she says.

I do as I'm told, unzipping it slowly.

It's a gown. Midnight blue and strapless with a boned bodice. It's pretty in a way that's perfect for a princess, with layers of tulle that look like storm clouds.

She crosses over to me as she clasps her hands. "You'll look divine."

"I'll look like a very expensive one, that's for sure," I mumble under my breath.

She doesn't respond. Just waits, arms folded like an executioner with a schedule.

So I change. Because today is about pretending.

The zipper bites my skin, and then, when I put on my shoes, the heels make my feet scream.

The last straw is the damn necklace that clasps onto my skin like a collar.

But when I step out, my mother beams like she's sculpted me herself.

"Perfect," she says.

The door opens again.

And in walks my father.

He takes one long look at me . . . up, down, across. It's like he's inspecting a piece of merchandise that someone might return.

"You'll do," he says. "Now remember, the Jamesons will be here. You know what that means."

I smile. Sweet and lethal. A sugar-coated blade.

"Be charming. Be silent. Be traded like a stock option."

"Don't test me tonight, Victoria."

"Wouldn't dream of it."

He leaves without another word.

I stare at the mirror. The girl staring back doesn't look like me.

She looks like the silent and obedient daughter they always wanted.

A puppet carved from stone.

With a giant sigh, I head toward the party.

The ballroom is drenched in opulence. Gold-trimmed everything and floral arrangements that cost more than most people's rent.

A string quartet is currently playing something delicate, and soulless if you ask me.

Can this get anymore ridiculous?

I'm eighteen, not the queen of England.

Guests arrive in waves. All the same . . . Pretentious and people I just don't want to associate with.

I stand at the top of the stairs like some tragic debutante, waiting to descend into the snake pit.

They clap when they see me, and my mother beams. My father, on the other hand, isn't one to gush, so instead, he clinks glasses with a senator.

And I can't stop scanning the room.

I know what I'm searching and hoping for, but it's pointless.

Lorenzo isn't here. Mother would never allow it.

In her mind, he doesn't belong in a castle.

Even if he's the only thing that makes me feel real.

It doesn't take long for the one person I hope will not find me to find me. My life is a comedy of errors. I definitely pissed off a god because there he is. Grant Jameson stands by the champagne tower, naturally.

"Birthday girl." He steps too close, his grin stretched thin. If my life were a book, he would be the villain. Actually, so would my father . . . Can a story have two villains?

"Unfortunately," I reply, lifting my glass and wishing it were poison.

He smirks. "You look exquisite," he says, eyes raking down my dress. "Your father must be proud."

"He is. Of the stock value I'm projected to bring in."

Grant laughs. I don't.

He hands me another glass of champagne when mine is empty, one I didn't ask for, then places his hand on the small of my back like he's claiming me.

I'm already taken.

"You know, when we get married, we should honeymoon somewhere with fewer clothes."

I recoil, my voice sharp enough to cut him. "We?"

"Come on," he drawls, tapping the rim of his glass. "Don't act shy. Your father practically handed you over on a platter. I'm just here to enjoy the meal."

I go cold. Glacial, in fact.

"Don't talk to me like that." I step into his space.

He laughs like I'm adorable. Then he touches my hip. Because he doesn't care what I think or how I feel. I'm an object. Something to possess. Nothing more. Nothing less.

That's it. I need out. Now.

"Excuse me," I say brightly, smiling the way women smile when they're two seconds from committing arson. "Bathroom."

I walk. Fast. Heartbeat roaring. Stomach twisting. Vision tunneling.

I turn a corner, and a hand grabs mine, pulling me into a side corridor.

"Jesus," I gasp, slamming into the wall of his chest.

He's in black. No tie. Hair slightly messy, but it's his eyes that make me gasp. They burn like he's Orpheus, and he's walked through hell to reach me.

"Hi." His hands still hold my arms to steady me.

"What are you doing here?" I whisper, breath hitching.

"You really thought I wouldn't show up on your birthday?" He brushes his thumb over my wrist like he's soothing sparks under my skin.

I want to cry.

Instead, I pull him down and kiss him like drowning people grab air.

He grins against my mouth. "Come on."

"Where are we going?" I let him tug me along the hallway.

"Away from here."

We sneak through the kitchen, then make our way through the staff doors. The next hallway we walk through is dim and narrow, but it's not long before we are outside. We dash across the garden, then across the lawn. My dress whips around my ankles, but I don't care. I'm desperate to be far away from that damn party.

The tightness in my chest doesn't dissipate until we reach the boathouse.

Lorenzo flings the door open, then walks over to the corner, grabbing the blanket I stored there, and lays it down.

I stride over to him and don't wait for permission, no. I throw my arms around him, and he holds me like he's never letting go.

We sink to the floor, bodies pressed together, breaths tangled.

Then his lips brush my temple. "You looked like you were suffocating in there."

"I was," I breathe.

He presses his mouth against my skin. "You're not alone, Little Bird. Not anymore."

I kiss him again. Like this is the one place I still belong.

For a second, I forget how to breathe.

The moonlight streaming in through the dirty window casts a glow across his handsome face.

I shift closer to him, needing there to be no distance between us.

Lorenzo's eyes seem darker than usual, intense and bottomless.

Something shifts in the air between us.

"Little Bird, you can't look at me like that."

"Why not?" I whisper.

"Because I'm not sure I won't die if I can't touch you."

"Who says I won't let you touch me?"

"Will you let me touch you, Victoria?"

My body shivers at his words. "Yes."

His lip tips up into a sexy smirk. "Good to know . . . "

I lean in, closing the space between us slowly, telling him with my body that I'm serious. I want this. I want him.

He leans in, too.

"You sure?"

"Yes." And before he can ask again, I brush my lips against his, it's soft at first—tentative. But then he presses closer. Sealing his mouth to mine.

I open to him, and he takes the moment to slip his tongue into my mouth.

Lifting my hands, I grab onto his shirt.

He kisses me like I'm everything, and when I'm in his arms I feel like I am.

He cups my face in his hands, deepening the kiss.

I swear the world around us fades away.

There is no party.

No parents.

No Grant.

It's just us.

With each passing second, the kiss grows hungrier.

More frantic.

Until we are all tongue and teeth.

I tug his shirt up, pulling away from his mouth for a brief second.

"Your turn," Lorenzo practically growls.

His hands find the back of my dress and pull the string.

"You can't do it like that."

"Show me."

I stand, and then once I'm standing, he follows suit, turning me around and loosening the strings.

The dress falls away from my frame. I'm left standing in front of him in only a small pair of white panties.

"Turn around." His voice is rough and gravelly.

I follow his order, turning to face him, hands now covering my breasts.

He shakes his head. "Lower your hands."

I do.

My nipples pebble instantly.

His gaze meets mine, and he breaks eye contact to look at me.

Down my face, over my collarbone, and then it drifts down farther.

"You're perfect." He moves closer, hands reaching out, trailing across by jaw, down my neck, until his palms cup my breasts. "So perfect."

I feel needy, my body tingling with built-up tension.

"I need you," I admit, making his eyes darken.

"Where do you need me?"

I lick my lips. "Everywhere."

Lorenzo nods, drops his hands, and strips off his own clothes. Then he takes my hand in his and helps me down to the ground and lies beside me.

Only a second passes before we're crashing back together.

Kissing.

Biting.

Claiming each other with our mouths.

His hands roam all over me.

Fingers caressing. Touching. When his hands find my breasts again, he pulls and teases my nipples.

It's like there is a line that runs straight down to my core. I squirm against him, and he must notice because his hands leave my breasts and trail lower.

"Is this what you need?" His hands part my thighs. Then I feel him, one finger finding my clit.

I'm hot and wet. And desperate for more.

He gives me what I want.

Rubbing furiously until I'm lifting my hips and begging for more.

"Touch me," he rasps. I reach my hand out and grip his hardness at the base. Tugging upward, I draw a groan from him. "Fuck. That feels so good. I need to fuck you."

"Okay."

"Okay?" he asks, and I nod. "You're going to let me fuck you?"

I nod again, and he shakes his head. "I need words, Victoria."

"Please fuck me."

He smirks at that, and it's nearly my undoing.

He's so damn handsome that I can barely take it.

I watch as he reaches into the pocket of his pants on the floor beside us and grabs a condom.

Lorenzo wastes no time slipping it on.

Then he's back beside me, parting my legs, but instead of placing his cock there, he lines his face with my core.

His mouth moves to latch onto my clit.

I squirm beneath him, loving the sensation, but it's so intense I can't help but move.

"Shh," he coos. "I got you. Let me take care of you."

His tongue continues to devour me, as his finger slips inside me until he's fucking me with his hand.

"I love how wet you are."

I moan at his filthy words. Loving them. Needing them.

My head rolls back while Lorenzo strokes a spot inside me that drives me crazy. Before I know it, my vision is spotty, and it feels like a rubber band is pulled so tight it's going to snap. "I want you to come on my dick."

Before I can ask what he means, Lorenzo pulls his finger out and crawls on top of me. The tip of his cock is poised right outside my entrance.

"Are you sure you want this, Little Bird?"

I wiggle, lifting my hips so that the tip slips inside me.

"Someone is impatient."

"Please," I beg.

"Okay, but this is going to hurt," he warns as he moves his hips. The tip of his cock slips farther inside me.

It feels so tight.

So snug.

It's hard to breathe as he moves another inch. The feeling is weird but not unwelcome.

"I'm almost there," he tells me, and I move my hips again. Another inch.

God, I feel so full.

"You ready?"

"Yes."

Lorenzo pulls his hips back and then pushes forward. A snap of pain blurs my vision as he breaks through my resistance, but it's not as bad as I thought it would be.

"Fuck," Lorenzo grits through clenched teeth. "You feel so fucking good."

For a moment, he doesn't move his body, his lips finding mine and kissing me senseless.

I swirl my hips, testing the feeling of him inside me.

A groan escapes his mouth. "Patience."

"I don't want to be."

"I don't want to hurt you."

"You won't. I trust you."

"As you wish." He pulls his dick out, then pushes back in.

My eyes widen at the sensation, but I love it. I love every single second of it.

He pulls out again, then pushes forward.

"I've never felt anything this good." He groans against my lips as his dick slips in and out of me. A moan escapes my mouth, which must signal to him that he can give me more because he starts to thrust faster and harder. "So good."

"Are you going to come?" I ask, reaching around and pulling him closer to me.

"Not until you do." I lift my brow in question when he reaches his hand between our bodies. His finger finds my clit again. "Be a good girl, Victoria, and come for me."

I'm about to say I don't know if I can, when his fingers begin to rub me again. This time, they match the pace of his hips.

"Oh god," I moan.

He picks up his pace.

His thrusts come faster and harder.

"I'm coming," I pant as my pussy tightens and begins to flutter around his dick.

Lorenzo pulls back, his gaze leaving mine and looking at where we're joined.

I look down to follow his gaze and see what he's looking at.

He's watching himself fuck me. Watching as his dick pulls out, glistening before he thrusts back in.

It's the most erotic thing I have ever seen and throws me over the edge.

Heart pounding.

Body trembling.

"That's right. Come all over my cock." And I do. Just like he tells me to.

Lorenzo fucks me harder through my orgasm, his cock jerking inside me as he comes too. We lie on the floor after, tangled together. My head on his chest, his fingers tracing lazy, reverent patterns on my bare shoulder.

The silence between us is full . . .

Full of everything we haven't said, yet everything we're terrified to admit.

But I say one thing. The one thing I need to.

"I love you."

He exhales sharply, like he's been holding that breath since the day we met.

His hand slides into my hair, pulling me closer.

"I love you too."

I lift my head. "What happens now?"

He looks up at the ceiling as if it might offer a map out of this place. "We figure it out," he whispers. "I'll wait for you. However long it takes."

Tears prick my eyes, but I smile. Because for the first time in years, maybe ever, I believe something might actually be mine.

CHAPTER 18

Lorenzo

SHE'S STILL CURLED INTO MY CHEST WHEN A SOUND JERKS US both upright.

What was that?

We both must have heard it, or she wouldn't be up too, right?

Maybe a creak.

I lift my finger to my mouth to make sure she doesn't make a sound, and then I listen.

A noise echoes through the silence. It sounds almost like a door hinge.

Someone is trying to open it without being heard.

My hand drops from my mouth and touches Victoria's arm, my fingers curling instinctively around her skin.

Victoria tenses, her body going still against mine, as her breath catches.

One thing is for sure. We're both wide awake now.

Another footstep.

Heavy. Deliberate.

"Shit," I whisper, lips brushing her temple.

I move to a standing position as quietly as I can, and then I pull her up with me.

Together, we move fast, hiding behind a few crates.

The door opens wider.

This time a light spills in.

Shit.

We are so fucked if they come in.

I wrap my arm around her shoulders, pulling her in close.

"Anyone in here?" a voice calls out. Male. Not Grant. Not staff either. Must be estate security? One of the night guards who patrols the grounds.

He lingers for beat, waiting. Then the door clicks shut.

Thank fuck.

We stay frozen for a full minute, just in case

Victoria lifts her face toward me, wide-eyed. "That was too close."

I nod, wiping a bead of sweat from my brow. "You okay?"

"I think I forgot how to breathe for like five minutes," she whispers, brushing hair out of her face with trembling fingers.

"You didn't even flinch." I try to keep the moment light, my thumb brushing the back of her shoulder. "You're practically a professional."

She cracks a grin. It's adorable.

"Please." She flicks my knee with her finger. "I was three seconds from confessing everything and fainting dramatically just to buy us time."

I laugh under my breath. God, I love her. I love the way she jokes only moments after almost being caught.

She sits, brushing dust off herself.

"I should go," she says, voice soft but steady.

I hate it. Every second without her feels like someone thinning out the oxygen around me. But she's right.

I help her up. Our fingers linger far too long in that charged space between holding and letting go.

"I'll wait a few minutes before I head in," I say, brushing my thumb across her knuckles.

She nods.

Then she steps forward and presses a kiss to my lips.

"Be careful," she whispers.

"Always," I respond, even though it's the biggest lie I've ever told.

She slips out into the night, and I wait until the faint sound of her steps disappears until I leave and head toward the back entrance of the staff wing.

Once inside, everything seems too quiet.

I walk fast, head down, body angled with purpose. If I can just get back to my room, clean up, change, pretend I've been in bed all night . . . maybe, just maybe . . .

"Lorenzo," my mother says, her voice sharp as a knife. I should've known better.

I freeze.

She steps out from the shadows at the edge of the staff hallway, arms folded tightly across her chest. But she's not alone. Standing next to her is Helen, the senior maid.

Great. Just perfect.

"Evening." I stuff my hands in my pockets.

Helen crosses her arms tighter. "Why are you out so late?" she says, her voice high and disapproving.

I shrug, leaning one shoulder against the wall. "I was fixing a lock in the east wing. Took longer than expected."

"Funny," she says, narrowing her eyes. "I could've sworn I saw you sneaking off through the garden with Miss Victoria."

My heart slams against my ribs, but I don't flinch. I don't blink. I won't give her the satisfaction.

"You're mistaken," I say, as casual as I can manage.

She lifts a brow so high it's practically an accusation. "You calling me a liar?"

"I'm saying maybe you saw someone else," I reply, forcing a lazy shrug. "Lots of guys on staff with dark hair."

Helen turns to my mom. "You believe this?"

My mother presses her lips into a severe line. "I'll speak to him."

Helen huffs, loud and theatrical. "I have no interest in cleaning up after a scandal. If he ruins this for the rest of us—"

"He won't," my mom says, tone firm enough to end the conversation.

Helen gives me one last glare—the kind that says I have eyes everywhere—then turns and disappears down the hall, mumbling about kids and consequences.

The moment she's gone, my mom rounds on me.

"What the hell are you doing?" she hisses, stepping so close I can see the fury flickering in her pupils.

I fold my arms. "Nothing she said is true."

"Don't insult me," she grabs the bridge of her nose. "You think I can't see it? The way you look at her? The way she looks at you?"

I stay quiet.

Because she's right. Because every truth I want to say is dangerous. Because my feelings for Victoria are the one thing I'm terrified to confess out loud.

She steps closer, lowering her voice. "You're going to get us both thrown out."

"So what?" I snap, louder than I should, chest heaving. "Why are we even here? Why are we hiding? You never give me real answers."

"Because they don't concern you."

"That's bullshit."

"Language," she snaps.

"No," I fire back. "I'm done pretending we're not in some kind of exile. I'm done walking on eggshells. Tell me the truth."

She exhales and closes her eyes for a long second.

When she opens them again, there's something older in her face. She looks tired.

Honestly, she looks afraid.

"The truth is," she says slowly, "you don't know what these people are capable of. What will they do if you ruffle the wrong feathers?"

"Feathers?" I scoff, stepping forward. "You think I give a damn about their feathers?"

"You should, because we need this job. Because this is the only roof over our heads. Because the moment we stop being useful, we disappear."

I stare at her.

And I see it. Fear. Not anger. Not frustration. Fear of something bigger. Something behind her eyes she refuses to name.

"Why did we really come here?" I ask, voice softer now.

She presses her fingers to her temple like she's holding in a scream.

"We came here because it was safe," she finally says.

"Safe from what?"

She looks at me. And then, maddeningly, she shakes her head. "It doesn't matter."

"It matters to me."

"Well, it shouldn't," she fires back. "Because what you did tonight? That kind of recklessness? That's the kind of thing that gets people like us erased."

The word hits harder than a fist. *Erased.* Erased like we never existed. Erased like the boy I vaguely remember from childhood.

I flinch. She sees it.

"Go to bed," she says, turning away.

I don't move. Not at first.

Then anger floods my body, tensing my muscles until I feel I might break.

I slam the door behind me as I storm down the hall toward my room.

Because I'd rather be reckless than invisible. I'd rather burn down this whole estate than spend one more night pretending.

For the first time in my life, I have something worth losing, and I'm not letting it go.

CHAPTER 19

Victoria

I SNEAK BACK INTO THE HOUSE LIKE I'M FLOATING. MY FEET barely touch the ground. It's like I'm gliding over the surface.

My body aches as I move, but it's the most amazing ache I have ever felt.

I've never been so happy. Which is funny because the night started off as the worst of my life, but now, with my hair a mess and my lips still tingling from his kiss, all I can do is smile, because Lorenzo is amazing.

I should be worried.

Hell, I should be more cautious, but I'm not. I have no desire to play the perfect daughter anymore.

How could I when my whole body is still warm and weightless from everything that happened tonight?

Lorenzo's scent still clings to my skin, sweet and real and maddeningly sexy. His voice echoes through me, making me feel weak in the best way. *I'll wait for you.*

I can't stop smiling. It's reckless.

Dangerous. Treasonous.

Which, apparently, is my new personality trait.

I turn the corner, and everything goes cold.

My father waits for me at the top of the stairs, arms folded, jaw tight, posture carved from marble.

My stomach turns.

Fear coils inside me.

The chandelier spills gold light over his shoulders, spotlighting every hard angle of his expression.

He looks like an evil king in exile. One who is about to send me to my death.

"Where the hell have you been?"

My heart stutters, catching like a misfired engine. "I was—"

"Spare me the lie," He cuts in. "You think I didn't notice? Half the fucking staff saw you sneak out like some rebellious little brat."

My stomach twists. "I went for air. That's not a crime."

He laughs. The sound is strange and not normal.

"Air? Is that what we're calling it now? Because what I saw was you sneaking off with that boy."

"His name is Lorenzo," I hiss.

"You are going to destroy everything," he snarls. "Do you understand that? Do you have any idea what your little rebellion costs this family?"

"Costs you," I bite back, heat rising under my skin. "Not me. You. Because you see me as a bargaining chip, not a daughter."

He storms down the stairs toward me, voice rising with every step. "You are seventeen—"

"Eighteen," I snap. "Today, remember?"

"You are a child," he spits, "who is about to ruin a billion-dollar deal because she got wet over a boy who fixes the goddamn gutters!"

His words slap me across the face. Tilting my world until my ears begin to ring. I want to hit him. I want to scream. I want to disappear. But my voice comes out cold. Steady. Lethal.

"I love him."

He stops.

And laughs again. This time it's sharper. Crueler.

"Love?" he echoes. "You don't know the first thing about love. But let me tell you something about reality. That boy is a liability.

And if you think for one second that I'll let you throw away your future—our future—for a fling, then you're more foolish than I thought."

I take a step forward, the marble cold beneath my bare feet. "You don't get to decide who I love."

He leans in close. I smell scotch. I smell smoke. I smell the ruin of everything I should have been but never wanted to be.

"You think this is about love?" His voice drops to a whisper sharp enough to cut. "No. This is about power. About reputation. And you . . . you are my daughter. Which means your heart isn't yours to give away."

I shake my head, whispering, "I won't let you control me."

He grabs my wrist hard, and I yelp out in pain.

"You won't have to," he says. "Because you're leaving. Your bags are already packed. The car will be here in twenty minutes."

My mouth falls open. "What? No. You can't do that."

"I can, and I have."

I yank my wrist back like his touch burns. "You're insane."

He gives me the kind of smile men give seconds before they break something fragile.

"You think this is insane? If you don't cooperate, I'll make sure that boy and his mother are on a bus to nowhere by sunrise. Better yet"—he pauses, savoring it—"I'll let the people who are looking for them know exactly where they are."

Everything inside me freezes.

"What . . . what do you mean?" My voice cracks as my heart slams against my ribs.

He just shrugs. Casual as hell. It's infuriating.

We aren't discussing the damn weather.

"You really thought she just wound up here? She's hiding from people who don't like to be disrespected. Dangerous people."

My breath leaves my lungs like it's been punched out. "Who?"

"Does it matter?"

"Yes," I snap. "It matters. Lorenzo said things . . . stories. About how she always ran. Always looked over her shoulder. Are you saying you know who she's running from?"

He checks his watch.

"You've got nineteen minutes left," he says. "Use them however you like."

He spins on his heel and walks off.

Just like that.

Like I'm disposable.

And to him, I am.

My legs almost give out. I grip the wall until the spinning slows.

Then I run.

I check the servant wing—empty. The kitchen is silent. It's barely dawn.

Shit. What do I do? I need to tell Lorenzo.

I check the staff stairwell and even behind the laundry room. My heart pounds so violently that it shakes my ribs.

Then I see her.

Angela. Holding a tray. Her eyes widen when she sees me.

"Miss Victoria—"

"I need you to give him this." My voice breaks, splintering in the middle. I snatch a notecard from the counter and scribble something on the back, my hands shaking hard enough to smear the ink.

They're sending me away. I don't want to leave you. I love you.

I press it into her hand. "Please. Tell him I'm sorry. Tell him I didn't want to leave."

Her eyes go glassy. She nods slowly. "I'll make sure he gets it."

I turn and run again.

Because if I stop, I'll break into pieces too small to ever glue back together.

By the time I reach the front entrance, the car is already waiting—sleek and black. It's still dark out. How is this happening?

My suitcase sits beside the door. This was planned. I'm a foregone conclusion.

We never stood a chance. I just need him to find me.

The driver opens the door.

I climb in, trembling.

The engine rumbles. The estate gates groan open.

And as the mansion shrinks behind me, my heart shatters with every inch of road we put between us.

Lorenzo will wake to a note. He'll find me.

CHAPTER 20

Lorenzo

THE FIRST MOMENT I HAVE A FREE SECOND, I HEAD TO THE boathouse to see if she's there.

It still smells like her.

Roses and something else I can't name.

The blanket we lay on is folded neatly in the corner. Like it never happened.

I hate it.

Because it did, and I never want to forget that it did. I need to see her. *Now.* I move faster, cutting through the trees toward the estate.

Branches slap against my arms, but I don't care. I'd happily take a beating if it brings me to her.

Man, I sound like a pussy.

I'm definitely not the kid who came here only a month ago. If my friends saw me now, they'd ask what the fuck happened to me?

Only a month ago, I stabbed someone and was sent away. Now . . .

Yeah. Fuck. I changed a lot. All because of *her.*

She makes me want to be a better man.

The halls are quiet as I head to her room. I spot my mother in the staff corridor and jog toward her.

"Have you seen Victoria?" I step into her space before she

can pretend she didn't hear me. After the scolding last night, I'm sure she would go the opposite direction if she thought she could keep me from Victoria.

She looks up from a basket of folded towels, her face smoothed into something neutral. Too neutral. She doesn't answer.

But she knows something . . . Her eyes flick to the left before she drops her gaze again.

"I need to talk to her," I say, trying to keep the panic out of my voice. "It's important."

She presses her lips together, tightening them into a thin, resigned line.

"What the fuck, Mom. Speak."

Her eyes go wide at the tone in my voice. "Don't talk to me that way."

My stomach twists. Something is wrong. And I can't wait for tell me what. So I don't. I take the service stairs two at a time, my heart pounding like a warning bell. I don't care if I'm caught. I don't care if I'm fired. I just have to get to her.

Her hallway is deserted, but the door is slightly open.

"Victoria?" My voice cracks. I push the door. Nobody answers.

I step inside, and my whole world rips open. Her vanity is cleared. Jewelry gone. Hell, her closet is even empty. The only thing left behind is the pile of pebbles on the dresser.

"No." My voice comes out raw. "Where—"

"She's gone."

I spin around so fast I almost lose my balance.

Her father stands in the doorway, arms crossed, wearing a smile so smug it makes me want to put my fist through his perfect mahogany paneling.

"What?" I breathe.

"She left this morning," he says, stepping into the room like he owns the entire universe and is bored with the view.

"Left?" The word hits like a punch.

He nods and laughs under his breath. "Didn't she tell you?"

He tilts his head. "Of course she didn't. Why would she? You're nothing. No one important. Just the help."

My fists clench so tight my nails dig into my palms. "She wouldn't—"

"Oh, but she did." He smirks. "College, then after that . . . marriage to someone worthy. Actually, you must have seen him around. Grant Jameson. She will be marrying him once she gets her degree . . . You didn't really think a girl like her would give up her future for someone like you?"

"Shut up."

"She used you," he continues. "That's what girls like her do. Get bored. Play pretend. Then move on. You were a summer game. Nothing more."

I storm past him before I do something stupid like murder him.

"I'd worry more about your job than your broken heart," he calls after me.

I shove through the staff doors, ignoring the sting in my chest, and find my mom in the kitchen now.

"Where is she?" I demand, my voice cracking.

She doesn't look up. "She's gone, Lorenzo."

"You knew." The betrayal tastes bitter in my mouth.

"I saw her leave," she continues to chop the vegetable in front of her. "But maybe it's for the best."

"The best?" I echo, stepping closer. "The best for who?"

She finally meets my eyes. "You're from two different worlds," she whispers. "You always have been. And we need this job. We have nowhere else to go."

I step back as if she slapped me. "You don't believe that," I whisper.

"I do," she says softly. "And one day, so will you."

Before I can respond, I hear soft footsteps echo behind me.

I turn.

Victoria's mother stands in the doorway.

Her expression is . . . unreadable. Not cruel. Not kind. Just composed in that expensive way, only money teaches.

"I thought you might want this," she says, holding out an envelope. My pulse stops.

My throat closes.

I wipe my palms on my jeans and take the envelope from her fingers. She gives me a small, practiced smile.

"Take care of yourself, Lorenzo." She turns and walks away, heels clicking on the wood floors.

My hands shake as I break the seal.

Then the words.

Lorenzo, I'm leaving. I should've said goodbye in person, but that would've made this harder.

My stomach drops.

This summer was exactly what it needed to be—an escape. A moment out of time. Something sweet before life becomes real again. But that's all it can ever be. A summer. A moment. Not a life.

My vision blurs.

I have my world, and you have yours. Please don't come after me. Please don't wait for me. We were never meant to last.

The last line cuts cleanest.

Thank you for the memories.

—V

It doesn't say she loved me. It doesn't say she'll miss me. It doesn't say one thing that could anchor me.

It's tidy.

And most importantly . . .

Final.

This can't really be from her? Can it?

"No. This is bullshit. Victoria would never—"

"She did, Enzo."

It feels like I've been stabbed in the gut.

"I'm sorry," my mother says, but I hardly hear her. Because all at once, there's a knock on the front door of the estate.

A heavy one.

We both freeze.

It isn't polite or rhythmic. It's deliberate. The kind of knock that means business. The violent kind.

My mother drops the knife, the clang echoing through the kitchen.

She hurries down the hall to peer out the nearest window. The rest of the staff follow.

Hell, I follow.

From the window, I see the SUV. Black. Expensive. Tinted windows.

Three men get out.

One stands by the car. One heads toward the front door. The third is older. He looks mean with cold eyes.

He looks like me.

My mother does something I never expected and walks to the door and opens it. Her face drains of color.

The older man smiles faintly at her. "It's time, Angela."

Her throat works. Her hands tremble. "I knew it would be you."

I step out from behind her. "What the hell is going on?"

My mom turns slowly, like she's about to confess a crime.

"Lorenzo . . ." Her voice shakes. "This is your uncle."

I blink. "What?"

The man steps forward, hands clasped behind his back. "Your father's brother."

The world tilts. My ears ring.

My mother turns to me, eyes wet—not with soft tears but terrified ones.

"Your father . . ." she breathes, "he was part of a powerful family. After he died, I ran. And then ran some more. I didn't want that life for you."

"What life?"

"A criminal one," she whispers. "Your father was in deep. But then, when he was gone, I knew they'd come for you eventually. I ran, and we've been running ever since."

My blood goes ice cold.

"You lied to me."

"I protected you."

"No," I choke out. "You hid me. You made me feel like nothing, when I was something all along."

The back door of the SUV opens.

A young man around my age steps out. Tall. Sharp. Familiar.

The moment I see him, something inside me cracks open. A memory crashes in—a backyard, dirt bikes, a boy shouting, *Come on, Lorenzo!*

"You're him," I breathe.

He grins. "You remember."

He strides toward me and pulls me into a hug.

"Matteo," he says. "Your cousin. Brother, really. We've been searching for you for years."

I stagger back, staring.

I turn to my mother, betrayal scorching under my skin.

"You said I didn't have any family," I whisper.

Her face crumples. "I was trying to protect you."

"All this time—"

"I thought I could keep you safe!"

My uncle steps forward. "Your boss made it easy. He ran a background check. DNA. Everything. Once he realized you were going to be a problem, he called us."

A sick twist hits my gut.

Of course he did.

My uncle extends his hand. "It's time you came with us, Lorenzo. Where you belong."

My chest twists.

I look at my mother. She shakes her head, desperate. "Please. Don't go. We can run again. We'll figure it out."

Run again? Hide again? Pretend again?

No.

I look at Matteo. He watches me with real hope.

"There's nothing left for me here," I say quietly.

"Lorenzo, please—"

But I'm already moving.

Toward the car. Toward the truth. Toward an unknown future.

I don't look back.

Because if I do, I might not be able to leave.

CHAPTER 21

Lorenzo

THE CAR RIDE STRETCHES ON. A STRANGE SILENCE SITS between us. It hovers, filling the air. It's heavy but not unwelcome.

I sit in the back seat, boxed in by the two people who just turned my entire life inside out.

My cousin, Matteo, grins. And my uncle is stone-faced.

I lean my head back against the seat, fingers drumming against my thigh.

She's gone. Victoria.

Gone.

And maybe I should be crushed, but I'm not.

All I feel right now is numb.

Fuck that . . .

I feel angry.

The fucking bitch left me.

She didn't give a fuck about me.

I gave her everything. And she shits on me.

Left like I was nothing because, as it turns out, to her, I was.

It was all a lie.

A painful truth I should have seen, but I was pussy-whipped and blind.

Now I'm not.

But I won't mourn. Not now. Not ever.

Especially with my new family watching me like I'm a puzzle piece they've finally snapped into place.

"We looked everywhere for you," Matteo says, his voice cutting through my thoughts.

I glance over. He's leaning forward, elbows on his knees, watching me like he still can't believe I'm real and that this is happening.

"You were like a brother to me," he says, his grin softening. "My mom said we were inseparable. Then you were just . . . gone."

I nod slowly, a memory surfacing. "You had the red bike."

His eyes widen. "You remember that?"

"Yeah." I shift in my seat. "You always wiped out trying to do wheelies."

Matteo laughs. "God, I did. I have this scar right here"—he jabs at his elbow—"from that one summer we built a ramp out of plywood. You dared me to jump the fountain."

"That was your idea."

"You dared me."

I almost smile. Almost.

It feels unfamiliar but not unwelcome.

"You were my best friend," Matteo says, quieter now. Something raw flickers in his voice. "And then . . ." He shakes his head. "It's fine, you're here now."

"Only because my boss sold me out," I mutter.

My uncle glances at me, his voice as dry as bone. "Which worked in your favor. You're lucky we found you when we did."

"Lucky?" I echo. "For who?"

"For all of us," he says. "Including you."

He turns slightly, his gaze sharp as steel cutting open old truths. "We need you, Lorenzo."

"Why?" I ask, even though something in me already knows.

"War is coming," he says simply. "The other side of the family has cozied up to your father's enemies in Boston. We think they're going to make a play. We've managed so far to keep them down, but we need you."

"Why?"

"Because your name matters. Your blood matters. It carries weight. And if what we think is coming . . . we're going to need you with us. Not acting as a servant in a mansion." His eyes narrow. "You're an Amante. And you need to live like one."

The name hits me like a door slamming. Amante. Sharp. Heavy. Dangerous.

A name people fear. A name people follow.

It tastes strange on my tongue, like something belonging to someone else.

Someone harder. Someone colder.

Someone who doesn't waste his time getting into fights over stupid shit.

And most importantly, someone who doesn't fall in love.

"I'm supposed to just . . . what?" I ask. "Pick up a gun and join the cause?"

"We'll train you," Matteo says quickly, leaning forward like he's afraid I'll bolt. "No one's expecting miracles. But you belong here. You're family. And we protect our own."

Family.

The word hits something in me I didn't know survived the years of running. Years of hiding. Years of pretending I didn't need anyone.

I look out the window.

The world blurs past. Forests and fences. Miles of private land. A security checkpoint with men with rifles standing at attention.

This is power.

The kind Victoria's world only pretended to have.

"Still," I say quietly, more to myself than to them, "fuck it, why not? She left anyway."

Matteo glances at me, sympathy flickering across his features. "Victoria?"

I don't answer. I don't need to.

He seems to get it anyway. "She's an idiot."

My jaw clenches so hard I taste iron.

The car slows as we round a corner, and then I see it.

Massive steel gates rise ahead of us, taller than anything I've ever seen. Surveillance towers on either side. Armed guards are on patrol.

Where the fuck are we?

Is this how they live?

Past the gates, I see a sprawling estate.

Holy shit.

"Home sweet home," Matteo says.

My uncle speaks without looking at me. "Welcome to your new life. The life you never should've left."

The gates begin to open. I grip the edge of my seat as the SUV rolls forward. I'm not the same person I was this morning. That boy is gone, buried beneath betrayal.

Everything is about to change.

This is the beginning of something else.

Something darker.

THE MIDDLE

CHAPTER 22

Lorenzo

Five Years Later . . .

THE AIR INSIDE THE WAREHOUSE STINKS OF SWEAT AND STALE cigars.

I prefer to conduct my business elsewhere, but I have no choice tonight.

It's payday from our last collection run, and I have to be here to oversee my men.

The dim overhead lights flicker, casting a faint glow over the tables where the bags sit. The four men standing in front of me look like they'd rather be anywhere else. Probably with strippers at the club. Work first, fucking later.

My boots echo across the concrete as I approach the center of the floor.

"Are we missing something?" I ask, voice low and controlled. I'm known as being a loose cannon, so whenever I'm the opposite, people take notice.

Vin nods once, flipping open the metal case on the folding table beside him.

Cash. Which is not surprising. There are stacks of it, but right away, I know something is off. There's a lot less than there should be.

"Light," Vin responds, his jaw grinding. "By almost fifty grand."

"Fifty?" I arch a brow, slow and mocking. "What, did we forget to collect from half the city? Or did someone suddenly develop a gambling habit and a death wish?"

"Every venue reported," Deeks says from across the room, arms crossed. "Bars, lounges, private rooms. Every single one of our books came back clean. Which means . . ."

"Which means someone's skimming," I finish for him, tapping two fingers against the edge of the table.

Rafe leans against the wall, picking dirt from under his nails. "Always the same story. Someone gets greedy, thinks we won't notice."

"News flash," Vin adds, sarcasm thick, "we notice."

"Barely." I drag a hand down my jaw. "They've been shaving off the top for a while. Quiet. Careful. Now they're getting cocky."

Deeks grunts his approval. "I say we cut off a few fingers."

I glance at him, unimpressed. "Cute. Normally, I'm all for chopping limbs, but I'd rather get names before we start a trim job."

"Shame." Rafe (aka Raffaello) smirks.

I like him.

Besides Matteo, he's the only one in my uncle's organization I'd consider a friend. He reminds me a lot of myself. We both have a taste for killing.

"I just sharpened the bone saw."

"And I promise, once we find out who's responsible, I'll let you take a turn . . . after me." I let my lip lift into a mischievous grin. "But first, bring me whoever was in charge of picking up the money this week. Let's ask him why he thinks math is optional."

Rafe straightens. "You got it."

The men scatter, and then I'm finally met with silence.

I roll my shoulders, trying to shake it off. Doesn't work. My pulse is already shifting. Beating faster. Uneven.

I reach for my phone out of habit.

No missed calls.

Just one notification.

A flagged alert. From a contact I haven't heard from in over a year.

No message. No subject. Just a photo.

I tap it open, and the moment I do, the world tilts on its axis.

Victoria.

She's older, yet still stunning. It's almost painful how beautiful she is.

The only problem with this picture is that she's not alone.

There's a man next to her, hand resting on the small of her back like he has the right.

Grant Jameson.

The same bastard from five years ago. He still looks like a douchebag.

My jaw locks so tight it aches. I zoom in, searching for something, anything. A flinch. A crack. A sign she hates this.

Nothing.

She looks fucking fine. Content even.

Like she never once thought about the boy she left without a word.

Me.

A headline screams across the top of the photo:

Danforth Enterprises and Jameson Group hint at a more permanent merger. Maybe the heirs to the empire will finally seal the deal.

I laugh—it's short and bitter. Of course they're getting married. I was just the summer distraction after all.

Old feelings rush back. Suddenly I'm transported to that day . . .

The day that changed my life.

I throw my phone across the room. It hits concrete and clatters, but doesn't shatter.

Fuck.

I drag a hand through my hair, pacing the length of the warehouse because if I stand still, I'll put my hand through the wall. I should've known. Should've guessed she wouldn't stay frozen like I did. That she'd move on. Thrive. *Forget.*

But with him?

It was always going to be him. Her father fucking told me it would be.

What the fuck did I expect?

I stalk across the room and punch the wall. It dents, and my knuckles crack and bleed.

It still doesn't help.

I breathe in. Out. I'm still not calm. I grab my phone from where I threw it and then dial. "Rafe. Now."

Ten seconds later, the door creaks open. Rafe steps inside, eyebrow raised like he's already planning which exit to sprint toward if I go feral.

"What's up?"

I shove my phone with the photo in his face.

He squints, then whistles low. "Well, shit."

"Exactly."

"Did she always have a taste for suits?"

"She had a taste for me," I snap, heat flaring in my chest. "This? This is a downgrade."

He shrugs. "Looks more like a power play."

I turn away, because if I keep looking at that screen, I might crack the earth open.

"Call Cyrus Reed."

"Cyrus?"

"Yeah, you know, he has that poker game? He told me if I ever needed any help with anything . . . "

"Got it. And what help are we looking for?"

"I want everything on Danforth Enterprises. Financials.

Current deals. Press leaks. Private holdings. If her name is on it, I want it. Tell him I'll owe him one."

Rafe nods slowly, expression sharpening. "You want a hit too?"

I consider it. Feel the weight of it in my blood. Then shake my head. "A takeover. But first, we make them bleed in places they won't see coming."

"Once you got everything on them, I want you to strip their leverage. Corner them. Then we make our move."

Rafe smirks. "Going for the slow choke, huh?"

"Exactly." My smile is razor-thin. "I want her to feel it. I want the family to beg."

Rafe snorts. "Damn. Remind me never to break your heart."

"You're not my type."

He claps the doorframe twice. "I'll get started," he shouts over his shoulder as he leaves.

Five years.

Five years of working for my uncle and building a name for myself within the organization. Five years turning myself into someone no one could crush. Five years of killing the man I was, the man I once thought I needed to be . . . for her.

He's dead now.

All because she never looked back.

Soon, she'll see how much she fucked up.

I sit down at the table that sits in the middle of the open space, fingers pressed to my temples, when my phone rings. Matteo. *Of course.*

"If this is about the fifty grand, I don't need to hear your shit. I'm doing a damn fucking good job. If your dad has a problem with it . . ."

"Want to continue that sentence? Pretty sure Pops wouldn't appreciate it."

I sigh because he's right. My uncle loves me in his own way, but he'd also not lose a minute of sleep if he killed me. At this point, the only reason he doesn't is because of his son. Matteo considers me a brother, so for now . . . I'm safe.

"Get off my dick, cuz. I already know who I'm killing, so make it quick."

"Jesus Christ." Matteo laughs into the receiver. "You've become quite unhinged in your old age."

"You called to compliment me?"

"I'm actually calling because I saw an interesting article in the paper." His voice softens just a fraction.

I stare at a distant wall. "You mean the one about the Danforths? Yeah. I saw it."

Matteo exhales sharply. "You good?"

"Oh yeah," I say, sarcasm dripping like venom. "Fantastic. Thinking about sending her a fruit basket. Maybe with a note that says, 'Congrats on the engagement, make sure to have a bomb squad at your wedding.' Or maybe something like, 'Can't wait to make you a widow.'"

He laughs hard, and then the sound stops abruptly. "You're kidding, right?"

"Maybe. If she's lucky."

"You've really turned into an angry bastard."

"Life will do that to you."

"Life," he repeats. "Or a girl?"

My smile goes dark. "Don't worry. I'm currently sharpening my knives. I might as well put this sadistic energy to good use."

Matteo whistles low. "I remember the boy who got into the car all those years ago. Sweet. Ridiculous. Terrible at lying."

"He died."

"You . . . okay?"

"Define okay." I lean back in my chair. "Because right now I'm hovering somewhere between 'burn down their empire' and 'send Grant a sympathy card for what's about to happen to him.'"

Matteo snorts. "You know, you always had a mean streak. But this? This is art."

“Thank you. I take pride in my growth.”

“And your violence.”

“And my violence.”

He hums. “Listen, don’t do anything stupid, okay? Pops would be pissed, and you don’t want to fuck up anything—”

“Sure. No problem. Wouldn’t dream of doing anything,” I lie through my teeth. Of course, I’m going to do something, but the something I’m going to do . . . he and his father will never know about because they’ll never approve.

“Good talk.” Matteo laughs.

I hang up, letting the silence settle again. Except now, it’s not hollow. It’s sharp.

Alive.

My blood is steady. Focused. I have a purpose. And the purpose . . .

Well, obviously, I’m going to burn down her world—piece by piece.

If she wanted a war, she should’ve picked someone weaker.

Because now?

This is personal.

And I don’t lose.

Ever.

CHAPTER 23

Lorenzo

THE SCREAMING GETS ANNOYING AFTER THE SECOND HOUR. Not the volume . . . I don't mind that. It's the tone. Fuck, this guy is whiny. Too many "please" and not enough "I'm sorry for stealing."

I pinch the bridge of my nose as the sound bounces around the warehouse, ricocheting off rusted beams and oil-stained concrete.

"Jesus." I lean back in the metal chair I dragged from the corner. "Do you have to scream like that? I'm honestly embarrassed for you. You sound like a feral cat."

The man tied to the post is in his mid-forties, stocky with greasy hair plastered to his forehead.

He gasps, and it sounds wet. Maybe he's choking on his own vomit?

Can't have that happen. I need to torture him for a lot longer before I put him out of his misery. If he dies now, his punishment will feel weak. I mean, sure, he'll be dead, but Uncle will demand his pound of flesh.

His right eye is swollen shut, and his lip hangs open. He's missing a tooth I knocked out forty minutes ago.

"You—you're insane," he chokes.

I brighten. "See, that's a compliment. Much better than the

crying. Good job. Gold star." I pat his cheek with the back of my fingers. The same hand still holding the pair of pliers.

He flinches like I slapped him.

"Relax." I sigh, twirling the pliers and making a real show of how unhinged I am. "I'm pacing myself. Torture is an art form. Like tasting a fine wine. You don't just chug it down. You savor it."

"Please—"

"There it is." I groan very dramatically. All part of the show. "We're making progress." I stand, stretching my arms overhead until my spine cracks. Time to get back to work.

Today's victim, let's call him Travis because he looks like a Travis, works for Danforth Steel. Middle management. Probably has a wife who hates him, kids who ignore him, and a drinking problem that gave him courage he absolutely did not deserve.

Unfortunately for him, that courage led him to agree to sell insider info to Rafe, only to back out at the last minute because he "got scared."

Bad move, fella. I have no patience. And I'm definitely in the wrong fucking mood for this bullshit.

I walk around him. "I'll be honest, Travis"—I tap the pliers against my palm—"I'm in a terrible mood today. Someone pissed me off." I bend down so we're eye level. "And when I'm pissed off, I get . . . creative."

"I don't know anything, I swear," he whimpers.

"There it is again. Everyone swears. If I had a dollar for every man who swore on his life while actively shitting himself, I'd own five more warehouses." I grab the chair beside him, flip it around, and sit with the backrest pressed against my chest. "Let's talk about Danforth Steel."

His chin trembles.

Fear. My favorite emotion.

"They're planning on finally going through with the Jameson merger, right?" *Only took five years . . .* I don't say that bit, but I always wondered why it didn't happen years ago. College. That's why. She probably agreed to the marriage after she got her diploma, which she got a few months ago. "Expanding the shipping arm? Moving certain assets off the books?" I tilt my head. "You're the guy who signs half the internal memos. Don't play dumb."

"I-I can't—"

"Oh my god," I snap, dropping my head back. "If you say 'I can't' one more time, I will get my scalpel real quick and personally peel your skin off your face."

He sobs.

"Okay, okay." I sigh and pat his knee. "Let's take a step back. Breathe. Try again. How about I help you help me? You can give me the access code to get into their computers and records, right?"

His nostrils flare. *Bingo.*

"I don't—"

"Don't do that." I lift the pliers. "You do know, Travis. And you know why I know this? Because you're the guy who hands out the employee badges when they get reprogrammed."

I tilt my head to the side, grinning like a fool.

"And if you don't give me what I want, I'm going to find a new use for these. Starting with your fingers. Maybe toes. Maybe something else entirely, depending on how flexible you are."

"You're crazy," he whispers.

"Finally." I grin. "Someone who gets me."

I lean forward, gripping his wrist. Hard. He squirms, gasping through clenched teeth. "Last chance, Trav. Give me something useful."

He crumbles fast.

"They—they have a shipment, just came in," he blurts. "South docks. It's raw steel."

My blood hums.

"There we go." I squeeze his wrist like I'm proud of him. "See? I like this. I think we can be friends."

"There's more." His voice shakes. "There's a board meeting coming up. They're going to announce new equity partners. Jameson's son—he—"

"Grant?" I cut in with a tilt of my head.

His eyes widen, shocked I know his name.

"Y-yes. He's taking a larger role. He's—they plan to marry him into—"

"Oh, I know." I wave a hand. "Trust me. That part? I'm painfully up to date."

He swallows. "I told you everything. Please, I-I have children—"

"That sounds like a you problem."

His face blanches.

"And now," I add cheerfully, "you get to be useful one more time."

His relief lasts half a second.

Until I squeeze the pliers around his index finger.

He screams. The sound echoes beautifully through the warehouse. "Aw, don't be dramatic," I taunt, twisting. "We're barely past the appetizer."

"Please—please stop—"

"Buddy"—I chuckle—"you should be grateful I'm doing this by hand. Rafe wanted to use a drill."

He screams again. This time much louder.

"Christ," I groan, "I'm going to get a noise complaint. And this doesn't have a neighbor for miles."

I twist the pliers one more time.

His finger snaps off, blood spraying.

"Tsk. Tsk, I hate making a mess." I turn to look over at Rafe. "Think that will come out?" I point at the puddle of blood now staining my shirt. Rafe shrugs.

Travis sobs, his head hanging down. I drop the broken digit on the floor and lean back, blowing out a breath.

"You know," I muse aloud, "this really helped. I feel lighter. Refreshed. This is basically therapy."

He gurgles something. Probably a request for death. It's cute. Adorable. Maybe I'll throw him a bone . . . or just remove another. That works too.

"Fine." I sigh, standing. "I'll speed it up. But only because I have a meeting in an hour and my shirt has blood on it."

I pull the knife from the small of my back. He tries to shrink away.

"Relax." I drag the blade against his cheek. "Anyone ever tell you that you're very tense?"

And then I open his throat with my blade. He slumps instantly. Blood spills down his shirt.

I step back before it hits my boots. "See, Rafe. Like I said . . . therapeutic." I wipe the blade on the back of his shirt and toss it on the table. Rafe bellows out a laugh.

The warehouse door creaks. Vin (one of my uncle's men) steps in. He's got no idea what I wanted with this fool, but luckily for me, Vin isn't the sharpest tool in the shed and won't ask any questions other than where to bury it. "Body?"

"Recycling." I shrug. "Or compost. I'm not picky."

Vin snorts. "Anything useful?"

"Everything useful," I answer, grabbing my phone. "Rafe and I have some personal business, so see to it that he gets disposed of."

Vin nods sharply. "Got it."

He disappears again. I pull up Matteo's name and hit call. He answers on the second ring.

"My favorite cousin," Matteo drawls. "What're you up to?"

"A whole lot of nothing," I snap.

"Sounds about right, you are pretty useless."

I roll my eyes. "Shut up and listen. I'm going dark for a bit. Need to get my dick sucked." We're really moving on Danforth

Steel, but he doesn't need to know that. Let him think I need to blow off some steam.

"Seriously?"

"Yes, seriously, my ex is getting fucking married, which means my cock will be in some whore's mouth before the end of the night. You got a problem with that? Because you know as well as I do, you'd be doing the same thing in my position."

"Fair. I got your back."

Thank fuck for that because honestly, I don't know what I'd do if he didn't. I do hate lying to him, though, but this is one secret I'll have to take to the grave. If my uncle ever finds out what I have planned for Victoria, he'd kill me. And while I'm not afraid of death, the Grim Reaper can't make an appearance until I've gotten my pound of flesh, courtesy of my revenge plot.

I hang up the phone, and the moment I do, Rafe whistles. "Can't believe you just lied to Matteo, and I can't believe he bought it."

"Fuck off, Rafe."

"What's the plan?"

"Oh, nothing major," I say lightly, flipping a bloodstained coin between my fingers. "Just dismantling their company piece by piece. Starting with blowing up the steel arm of their empire."

"Subtle." Rafe laughs. "Anyone tell you you've become quite cruel?"

"I'm not cruel." I scoff. "I just know what I want."

Rafe hums. "And what do you want?"

I smile. It's a slow and feral kind. "I want to ruin them," I say. "Strip them of everything."

His laugh is sharp. "Love that for you. Orders?" he asks.

"Simple," I say, stepping farther away from the body on my way to the door. "We hit the Danforth Steel plant. Tonight. Don't destroy it. That's too obvious. Can't have them figuring out it's me yet. How about a fire? Cripple production. Make them scramble."

His tone darkens with anticipation. “Understood.” He nods before he walks out of the room to put my plan in place.

The warehouse feels quieter now. Heavy in a different way. I walk into the office, shutting the door behind me with a click. The desk is clean except for one thing.

The photo.

Her photo.

Victoria in white, smiling at a man whose hand shouldn’t be there. I drag my thumb across her image—slow, almost tender.

Then I lean back in my chair. “She’ll come back to me.” My jaw tightens. “One way or another. And then she will pay.”

This is war.

And I’ve already won.

CHAPTER 24

Victoria

I WALK THROUGH THE HALLWAY OF DANFORTH STEEL headquarters, tablet pressed to my chest, hoping I don't see my father when his yell echoes from behind the closed door to his office.

I freeze.

What the hell is going on?

And why is he so mad?

I inch closer, not wanting to be seen but needing to find out what's happening at the same time.

"If you weren't so damn busy trying to marry my damn daughter, none of this would have happened."

"What the hell does that mean? I have nothing to do with this."

"Sure, you do. If you had just agreed to the merger . . ."

"Victoria or nothing," Grant Jameson fires back.

My stomach drops so fast I nearly sway.

"It's not my problem you couldn't seal the deal, Grant."

"Well, she shouldn't have been a problem. She was promised to me years ago." There is a low growl, clipped by irritation.

Promised.

I grip the tablet harder.

"It's not my fault she's stubborn."

"You could have forced her—"

I don't wait for the rest. I shove the door open so hard it slams into the wall. Papers jump on the desk. Both men freeze like I just pulled a gun.

"Forced me?" I snap, stepping inside with the kind of righteous fury I didn't know I still had. "News flash, gentlemen—I couldn't have been forced to do anything."

My father's face tightens. Grant's eyes narrow with that calculating, smug tilt I've hated since I was seventeen.

I walk in farther, heels clicking against the marble. "And while we're making declarations, I already lost everything. The one thing I cared about was taken away. So did you really think I'd marry Grant because you said so?"

Grant adjusts his cufflinks, his smirk sharpening. "It wasn't exactly a suggestion, sweetheart." He tilts his head like he's analyzing something. "It's happening. It's still the plan."

My jaw locks so tight I could crack teeth. "You can take your plan," I say, voice soft like silk, "and choke on it."

My father slams his hand on the desk, rattling the pen set. "Enough. None of this matters right now."

"Oh?" I lift a brow. "Forgive me for interrupting this riveting misogyny seminar—"

"If we don't stop arguing," he cuts in sharply, "we won't be able to figure out what went wrong."

That stops me.

The anger doesn't leave, it just rises differently, colder, more alert. "What do you mean?" I ask, stepping closer.

My father scrubs a hand down his face. He looks older and tired. "Have you seen the news?"

I blink. "No."

He gestures toward the wall-mounted TV. Grant grabs the remote and flicks it on.

The headline hits first.

FIRE AT DANFORTH STEEL FACILITY. BUILDING LOST. INVESTIGATION UNDERWAY.

My breath catches, and my pulse spikes as I watch the flames swallow the building.

"Is everyone okay?" I step forward until the images burn into my eyes. "What happened?" I whisper.

My father exhales like the air itself weighs too much. "Arson. Or negligence. Or a goddamn curse. I don't know yet."

"First things first, was anyone hurt?" I ask, and my father shakes his head.

"Okay, good. Objects can be replaced. People can't."

"We lost the whole facility, Victoria." My father scoffs.

"I know, and it's awful, but we have insurance. I'm sure everything will be okay."

Grant's laugh comes soft and smug. "Ah. See, that's the problem."

My father glares at him, then looks at me. "The policy on that building lapsed."

My mouth falls open. "We let our insurance lapse on an entire facility?"

"It was supposed to be temporary." He's pacing now. "We were shifting assets during the merger with the Jamesons, and someone fucked up the paperwork. We didn't catch it. And now—"

I swallow, the dread sinking deeper. "Now we're liable."

Grant taps the TV remote against his palm, eyes gleaming like he enjoys the drama. "Not just liable. Exposed. Vulnerable. Investors will panic. Rivals will circle. The competitors—"

"Enough," my father snaps.

I cross my arms to steady myself. "What's the plan? How do we fix it?"

"We don't know yet," my father admits, sliding his hands into his pockets. It's the first honest thing I've heard him say in years. "We'll weather the storm. We've done it before. Just have to tighten the reins. Cut nonessential spending. Delay a few expansions. We'll get through it."

Grant leans back casually against the edge of the desk. "Assuming it was just a fire." His voice dipped in suspicion. "And not someone making a point."

A chill spikes at the base of my spine. But I shove it down.

"No one is targeting us," I say, too quickly.

Both men look at me. I glance away. Because the truth is—I don't know. A fire starting on its own seems unlikely.

I don't know anything anymore.

My father clears his throat. "Victoria, we need to be united. Image is everything right now."

My laugh comes out rough and humorless. If a laugh could sound bitter, this one would be that. "United? You and Grant were just arguing about whose fault I was."

My father stiffens. "We were discussing logistics."

Grant's lips curl. "Darling, you're always a logistic challenge."

I whip toward him. "Say one more word like that, and I'll show you a logistic challenge."

His smirk flickers. Just barely.

Good.

My father pinches the bridge of his nose. "This isn't the time for dramatics."

"Your definition of dramatics," I say quietly, "is my definition of survival."

Silence. Brief and heavy.

Grant pushes off the desk with a sigh. "Whether you like me or not doesn't change anything. The merger is still standing. The market's watching. Our names are tied together publicly. We need to make us official. We need to get married."

"There is no us," I hiss.

My father hits the desk with his hand. "Enough. We need to project stability until we get more information." He turns to Grant. "While I agree we need to go public with your relationship—"

"We don't have a relationship," I grit out through clenched teeth.

"That's where you're wrong, Victoria. We do. I've waited five years for you to finish college, and don't think I don't know you stalled. So this is happening. Your family needs me more than ever, so don't piss me off."

"Grant, I agree, and appreciate your family's help . . ." My father turns to me. "I won't hear another objection from you. You've always known what's expected." His words land in my belly like a punch. I'll find a way out of this arrangement, but for now, I need to bide my time to come up with a plan.

I blow out a breath. "Fine." I start to pace. The room suddenly feels too small. "But no more talking about a wedding. We have more important things to deal with. Like the burning buildings."

"For now," Grant adds. I want to punch his smug face, but instead, I turn to my father, who is kneading his temples.

My father's jaw tics. "It was just one plant."

"Just one plant," I repeat, staring at the flaming building on the screen. "But what if it isn't the last?"

No one answers, because there is no answer. There's only tension. And fear.

My father rounds his desk. "We'll figure out what went wrong," he says firmly. "We always do."

"And until then?" I ask.

"We stay quiet," he replies. "We stay composed. And we stay in control."

Grant nods like this is all a business seminar. "We'll handle the PR. You handle being cooperative."

I stiffen. "I'm not your puppet."

Grant's eyes gleam. "Oh, sweetheart. That's where you're wrong."

My father gives him a sharp look. But not sharp enough. I inhale slowly, pushing the air deep into my chest.

If I speak now, I'll explode.

So I don't respond.

I turn and walk out.

Close the office door softly behind me, even though I want to rip it off the hinges.

Once I'm in the hallway, the breath I've been holding slips out in a tremor.

The fire. The insurance lapse. The fear in my father's voice . . . How is this the same man who once bragged he could buy God if the price was right?

Something is wrong. I don't know what, but I can feel that a change is coming, and I'm not sure what that means.

I force myself to breathe, then for my legs to move, and as I head down the hallway, I try to silence my thoughts.

But as I walk through the steel corridors of my family's empire—shaking, pretending not to be afraid—one truth curls cold and certain in my chest.

If this is just the beginning . . .

We are not ready for the storm that's coming.

CHAPTER 25

Lorenzo

THE REPORT HITS MY DESK WITH A THUD.

I don't look up at first. Because if I do, and it has anything to do with Victoria, I might put someone through the drywall.

Then Dom, the head of my private household security, clears his throat.

My jaw tightens. "If you're coughing like that, you'd better be dying."

Dom shifts his weight. "You need to see this."

He slides the file closer. I flip it open. The first page is a still image from a security camera—time-stamped ten minutes ago. It's taken inside Danforth Steel's executive conference room.

And there she is.

Victoria.

Standing at the end of a long conference table like she's made of glass and fury. Hair twisted back. Jacket thrown over one arm. The look on her face? Pure steel.

The look I remember.

The look that ruined me the first time.

My pulse spikes in my throat.

She's talking. Arguing probably. Her father's across from her, looking like he swallowed a grenade. Grant Jameson sits beside him wearing that smug, oily confidence I'd like to beat off his face with a chair.

I flip the page so hard it tears.

Another angle.

Another shot of her.

Eyes sharp. Chin up. Tension in every line of her body like she's holding herself together with sheer force of will. Something hot and ugly twists in my chest.

He shifts again, carefully keeping his distance. "She was at the office today. From my intel, they were discussing the fire. Thought you'd want to know."

I tap two fingers on the photo, slow, controlled . . . deadly. "She looks tired."

Dom stays quiet.

Smart man.

I slam the file shut. "Get me every detail from that meeting. Verbatim. I want the audio. I want the minutes. I don't care who you have to blow to get it, get it."

"Already on it," Dom replies before heading out.

Smart move since I'm clearly unhinged with my obsession.

The moment the door clicks shut, I stand so fast my chair skids back.

She looks tired.

Good.

Let her feel a fraction—a sliver—of what I felt when I woke up one morning to find her gone, replaced by a note.

Fuck.

Even now, five years later, it still feels like I've been stabbed in the chest.

I push the file aside and grab the next stack waiting for me.

Financial analysis.

Market reports.

Risk evaluations.

The kind of data you could build a war out of, and I will.

I drag my finger down the first column.

Danforth cash flow.

Bleeding.

Hard.

Laughing under my breath, I flip another page. A graph shows a sharp downward drop. The kind that ends careers. The kind that destroys dynasties.

"Oh, sweetheart." I trace the line. "Your castle is cracking."

The fire at the steel plant was the first domino.

And now the reports show exactly what I expected.

They are hemorrhaging money, and the investors are panicking.

The downfall will be delicious.

I take my time reading every page, savoring the numbers, and when the door bursts open without a knock, I don't flinch. I know who it is. Only one person in this house would enter without permission.

Rafe strolls in like he owns the place.

He glances around the room, eyes landing on the open bottle of tequila, then the half-shredded report on the floor.

"Jesus." Rafe whistles, leaning against the doorframe. "Did you lose a fight with your office again, or is this part of the aesthetic you're curating? I thought you only destroyed the warehouse, but this is making me think you need anger management classes."

"Get out," I mutter, not bothering to look up.

He ignores me.

"Rude," he says, stepping farther inside and helping himself to the whiskey on my shelf. "Is this about business or the girl?"

My jaw flexes.

I keep reading.

He raises a brow. "Ah. So it's both."

I slam the file shut. "Why are you always here? Don't you have a life?"

He downs the whiskey in one swallow. "Not really. My ex is

trying to kill me all the time, so I'm much happier being here, when you only threaten to kill me half the time."

"Glad I could provide emotional support," I flip another document.

Rafe walks up behind me and looks over my shoulder. "What's this? Oh. Their numbers dropped harder than you fell for that girl."

My eye twitches.

This fucker thinks he's funny . . .

Let's see how funny he is when he's facing me?

I turn and catch him grinning.

"Too soon?" he asks.

I toss a pen at his head. He dodges, laughing as it clatters across the floor.

"Look," Rafe says, hands up like he's surrendering, "I'm just saying—Danforth Steel bleeding out isn't going to magically fix what happened between you two."

I smile.

Slow.

Sharp.

"What's funny." He backs up a step, "is nothing about that smile is normal."

"She shouldn't have been in that meeting," I say, voice low. Controlled. "She shouldn't be anywhere near the fallout."

"She's part of the company," Rafe reminds me, pacing to the window. "She was always going to be dragged into this."

"She's not built for war."

"Well"—he shrugs—"she'll have to be."

I turn the page violently, ripping the corner without meaning to. "I'll handle this." I shove the next file open, then grab my phone off the desk and dial Dom. I don't wait for him to talk before I start barking orders.

"Order the remaining inventory hijacked," I say, while punching in a message to my logistics crew. "Every truck leaving Danforth Steel gets detoured. I don't care how. Make it disappear."

"On it," Dom responds and waits for me to continue.

"Wow," he says quietly. "You're really doing it?"

"Oh, I'm just warming up." I flip a page. "Next are the partners. Pull them out. Quietly. Bribe some. Threaten others. Make it look like financial instability. Just enough to get the board nervous."

Rafe's jaw drops. "You're dismantling a billion-dollar company."

"Brick by brick," I reply.

"And for what? Revenge? Or because you're still in love with her and want her to come crawling—"

"Back off," I snap, whipping my gaze at him.

He raises both palms. "I'm not judging."

"You are."

"A little."

"Well, don't."

Rafe sighs and grabs a second glass from the shelf. "You know, you've always been unhinged, but recently, this past week? It's like watching a Greek tragedy, yet I'm not even sure if you're the hero or the villain."

"Villain obviously," I respond, reading another report. "And thanks."

"Not a compliment."

"Didn't ask."

He sets the glass down and plants his hands on my desk. "Lorenzo. Seriously. You can't keep doing this. She made her choice."

A hot pulse flashes through me.

"Shut up," I growl, standing slowly.

"You need to move on," Rafe says softly.

I stare at him.

He stares back.

The silence crackles.

Then I laugh.

"Move on?" I repeat. "You really want to do this? You really want to piss me off?"

He hesitates.

Exactly. Then rolls his eyes. "You're a dick."

"Go home," I say, dismissing him with a flick of my fingers. "But don't forget to get me what I asked for."

He lingers for a moment, searching my face.

Then he sighs, grabbing his coat. "Fine. But, Lorenzo . . . be careful. When you blow up someone else's empire, make sure you don't take yourself down with it."

I grin. "Oh. . . that's the fun part."

He shakes his head and walks out, muttering something about therapy. The moment he's gone, I pick up the file again. Victoria's face stares back at me.

My chest tightens.

I brush my thumb over the image.

"You shouldn't have fucked with me," I whisper.

But she did.

So now?

Now I escalate.

Now I end this.

I reach for my phone.

"Dom, you still on the line?"

"Yes, boss."

"Tank their reputation. Anonymous leaks. Fake scandals. Use the press like a weapon."

"Yes, sir."

"And, Dom?"

"Yes?"

"Make them bleed."

I hang up.

Then sit back in my chair, staring at the grainy photo again.

The girl who once read to me in an abandoned boathouse.

The girl who once kissed me like I was her whole world. The girl who left without a trace.

My voice comes out low.

Certain.

"I'm coming, Little Bird."

I tap the picture, right over her face with one finger.

"And when the smoke clears . . ." My eyes narrow. "You'll come back to me."

A dark smile curls across my lips. "One way or another."

CHAPTER 26

Victoria

I'M SITTING AT MY KITCHEN ISLAND, SPOON HALFWAY TO MY mouth, when my phone lights up with my mother's name.

She never calls me unless she needs something, and usually that something isn't good.

Usually, a dress code is involved, which is something I really don't want to deal with right now.

I swipe to answer. "Mom?"

"Victoria, you need to come home." Her voice cracks.

I shift in my seat. "What happened?"

"Not over the phone." She doesn't sound right. Something is off. "Just come. Right away."

My stomach knots. "Mom—"

"Victoria." Even the way she says my name is different. It sounds flat and broken. I open my mouth to say more, but before I can, the line is dead.

She hung up without giving me an explanation or even clarity.

I stare at the screen for three seconds, then shove my chair back so hard it screams against the wood.

Where are my keys?

Jacket?

I need my purse, too.

Everything is moving too fast in my brain. Endless possibilities of what can be wrong play out in my mind.

I feel like I'm drowning in thoughts of what-ifs. But regardless of what it could be, I'm out the door before my brain finishes the scenarios.

This is bad.

The drive to the estate feels tedious. When I finally arrive, my chest feels so tight it burns.

I hate this place.

Sure, I've been here a million times over the years, and yes, I always feel like I'm suffocating when I arrive, but today feels different.

Once the house is in view, I inhale deeply, pushing down the bile that crawls up my throat.

It's fine.

Everything is fine.

I throw the car in Park, then step out . . . and like every time I come here, I'm bombarded with memories. This time, instead of walking straight inside, my feet betray me, turning left.

Not toward the house, but toward the old boathouse.

In all the times I've been here since I left, I never could bring myself to go back there. Too many memories, but now, for some reason, I can't stop myself. I must be a masochist.

The stone path has tiny cracks now. Time has a way of doing that.

I follow it without thinking, as if it's muscle memory. As if I'm seventeen again, racing down this same trail.

The roses are wild now.

Untamed and beautiful.

I step past the roses and keep walking until the boathouse comes into view. While it was abandoned for as long as I can remember, it is now completely overgrown and unloved.

For a moment, I almost expect to see him leaning there like

he never left. Lounging against the doorframe while pretending to fix something as an excuse to spend time with me.

But the doorway is empty.

I keep moving, cracking open the door.

It feels like I can't breathe as I step inside. This place holds memories that are now carved into me like scars.

I lower my gaze to the worn floorboards. In my mind, I can still see every moment from that summer.

Every kiss.

Every touch.

Every little glance.

And I still can't think about it without feeling something collapse behind my ribs.

I force myself to step back.

The need to run back to the main house wraps around me. I'm not here for a past long since forgotten. I'm here for my parents.

I take one last breath and turn, heading toward the main house.

Once inside, everything feels wrong. Especially when I walk into the sitting room and see my mother already there, standing. I freeze in place.

Why does she look so frail?

The better question is, why does she look the way she does? Hair slightly frizzed. Makeup smudged. Sweater slouching and off one shoulder.

Who is this woman?

This is not my mother, or at least, this is not a version of her I've ever seen before.

"Took you long enough." She sighs.

I shouldn't have come. This is a big mistake. I thought for a second she needed me, but it's obvious that she has no plans to ask nicely.

"Mom, what's going on?"

Before she can answer, the sound of a slammed door echoes down the hallway.

Heavy footsteps that sound erratic. Is someone pacing?

Then my father strides into the room, and I don't recognize him either.

It's almost like I'm in an altered reality. Because if my mother's appearance is shocking, his is worse. His tie is crooked, and his shirt is untucked.

Don't get me started on his hair. It's a complete mess.

Rounding out the look are bloodshot eyes that are glassy and wild, darting around the room like an addict searching for his next hit.

He doesn't see me at first. The man is too busy muttering to himself, running his hands through his hair. "Years of work—sabotage—what do they want? Why now?"

"Dad?" I step forward. "Dad."

He whips around. "Victoria." His voice is rough like he didn't sleep. "Do you know what's happening?"

"No," I say carefully. "Mom called. What's going on?"

He lets out a laugh—the brittle, unhinged kind you only see in thriller movies. "What's going on? Everything is going on!"

My mother squeezes my arm. "He hasn't slept."

No surprise there. His hair was a dead giveaway.

My father continues pacing. "Someone is dismantling this company," he spits. "They're destroying us."

I blink. What the hell is he talking about? "Destroying? Dad—"

He slams his fist against the wall, and the sound is so loud, I'm surprised the plaster doesn't crack. "Someone is intentionally trying to destroy Danforth Steel."

His words make no sense. Who would do this and why?

"At first, we thought it was the fire," he continues, pacing. "But it's so much more than the fire."

My mother sinks into the couch. "Much more."

My throat tightens. "What happened?"

He grabs a paper and thrusts it at me. I have no idea what I'm looking at. "Three shipments of steel are now missing. If that weren't bad enough, clients are pulling orders. Partners are backing out. Investors are withdrawing funding. Our entire operation is on hold." He drops the page. "And it all happened in hours . . ."

I stare.

But I can't even form words, because that's a lot to wrap my head around.

"And PR?" he snarls. "A nightmare. Anonymous leaks. False scandal. Someone feeding the press garbage that looks just true enough to stick."

"Who would do that?" I whisper.

"That's the fucking problem," he roars, gripping his hair. "I don't know."

My heart jumps. "Dad, calm down—"

"Calm down? Calm down?" He throws up his hands. "We're bleeding. Someone is gutting us from the inside out."

Mom rubs her temples. "We're going to have to sell assets."

My father whirls toward her. "We will do no such thing—"

"We have to," she snaps, voice shaking. "Unless a miracle drops from the sky, we don't have a choice."

He slams his fist against the mantel. "We are not selling pieces of what I built!"

I step forward. "Dad . . . do we have enemies?"

He goes still. Then lets out a harsh breath. "Everyone has enemies. But not any who would do this."

"Could it be hackers? It could be a cyber attack."

"This isn't a cyber attack," he fires back as though my suggestion is ridiculous.

I hesitate. Just a breath. A tiny fracture in my composure. It smells like corporate warfare, but why?

I breathe out slowly. "So what do we do now?"

My father sinks onto the leather sofa. "We'll tighten operations.

Cut spending." He buries his head in his hands. "Fuck. I don't even know."

I take a slow breath, looking at him and then looking at my mother, who is currently rubbing her temples.

After a few more seconds of silence, my father lifts his head and meets my stare. "We will find the son of a bitch who did this to us, and we will end it." He leans back, exhausted. "We'll regroup tomorrow."

My mother nods. "We'll figure it out."

But the silence afterward says none of us believes that.

She turns to me. "You should stay the night. Just in case we need you."

"Yeah. Okay," I answer, before I slip out of the room and head outside. I need some air after all of that.

I step into the garden without thinking. Once there, a tight breath leaves my chest.

This is why I hate coming home. This is why I stay away.

Because the second I'm on this property, it's all about them, and what I can do for *them*.

I wrap my arms around myself. Everything will be okay.

It has to be.

CHAPTER 27

Lorenzo

THE DANFORTH ESTATE LOOKS SMALLER. NOT PHYSICALLY. Physically, it's still a monstrosity of money and arrogance.

But now it's different.

This place used to feel like a prison.

Now it feels like a means to an end.

I'm going to burn it all to the ground. And the beautiful part of my plan, is how long I'm going to drag it out.

The gravel crunches under my boots as I walk up the drive. My steps are slow and deliberate.

I savor every step. This is my moment.

A full circle.

I died here, yet was born here too.

The house looms ahead, and while I was intimidated the first time I saw it, now it does nothing of the sort.

How could it?

I've gutted men.

Watched them gurgle on their own blood.

This shit is child's play.

As I make my way up to the front door, I wipe my boots on their pristine marble step just to be petty.

A second later, a butler who looks like he's two missed

paychecks away from selling his organs opens the door. His eyes drag over me, hesitant, confused, and then terrified.

Does he recognize me?

If he does he doesn't say. But by the way he steps back quickly, spine snapping straight, I think he does.

Because he looks terrified.

Good.

Fear makes people polite.

I step inside.

The smell hits me first, and I'm instantly transported to when I worked here.

Just the thought of working for these assholes has me wanting to rip out their skulls.

Okay, Lorenzo, there will be none of that.

Carving a hole in their head won't give me the revenge I want.

I make my way down the hall.

Her father's office is exactly where I remember it.

I don't knock.

I push the door open and step inside like I own the place.

Her father jolts to his feet, eyes bulging when he sees me.

He's aged, and badly.

Sweat stains circle his collar. His hand twitches toward his phone like he's debating whether to call for help.

Cute.

Help isn't coming.

You let the devil into your house through the front door.

"You've been busy," I say, strolling farther in, nodding at the stacks of paperwork scattered across his desk. "I'd congratulate you, but everything you're working on is already dead. So this feels like watching a man perform CPR on a corpse."

He stiffens. "Who the hell are you?"

I smile, slow, sharp. "The man holding your leash."

"If this is about the fire, we—"

"Oh," I interrupt, waving a lazy hand. "The fire was adorable. But no. I'm here about the rest of it."

He blinks. "The rest?"

"Yes." I lean in, tapping a finger against a framed photo of his family. "The part where I burn your whole world to the ground."

His mouth opens, but before he can speak, the office door swings wider.

Her mother steps in, and she freezes right away, hand flying to her mouth. "Lorenzo?"

He whips toward her. "You know him?"

Her gaze never leaves me. "He . . . he worked here. Years ago. The summer Victoria—"

I tilt my head. "Good to know I made a lasting impression."

Mr. Danforth stares, expression shifting from confusion . . . to recognition . . . to something close to horror. "You're the boy who—"

"Don't say it like that." I cut in with a laugh. "You'll hurt my feelings. Actually—" I pretend to think, tapping my chin. "No. Feelings require a soul. Mine's been on vacation for a while."

He narrows his eyes. "What do you want?"

I step forward until I'm in his space.

Let him see the boy he destroyed, who was reborn into a monster.

"Everything."

His jaw clenches. "Why?"

A slight sound slips from the mother's lips. "Is this because we sent you away?"

I grin, slow and unhinged. "Sending me away was the best thing you ever did to me." They both freeze. "Because that boy you threw out like trash? He's gone. Dead. Buried. And in his place is the man whose sole purpose is to ruin you."

Color drains from their faces so fast I almost clap.

"That's right." I lean back on my heels. "You didn't just piss off a teenager. You pissed off a psycho."

Silence suffocates the room. I savor it.

"Let me clear up a few things . . . " I chuckle. "I took everything from you." I pace the office. "Let's recap, shall we? Your steel plant? Ashes. Your inventory shipments? Missing. Your overseas accounts? Gone."

I turn and grin.

"Oh. And the house?" I gesture around the room. "It's technically mine now. Paperwork was surprisingly easy."

Her father stumbles backward until he hits the bookshelf.

"You're lying."

I hold up a set of folded documents between two fingers. Inside are his bank reports, his asset liquidation notices, and his bankruptcy projections.

I place it down in front of him. "Read it. This will be fun," I purr.

Her mother sinks into the nearest chair, her face ghost-white. "Is this because of Victoria?"

"In part, but it's also because of my mother. You treated her like she was beneath you. Mocked her often. And then there's me, what you did to me . . . " I reply, pocketing the papers again.

Her mother's eyes narrow. "You still love her?"

I laugh so violently it echoes off the walls. "Love?" I repeat, pretending to wipe a tear from my eye. "No. No, Mrs. Danforth. I don't love your daughter."

I step close enough that she will feel the heat of the threat behind every syllable.

"I hate her. And I plan to spend the rest of my very long and violent life making sure she regrets ever walking away from me."

Her husband coughs. Hard. "What is this? What do you want? You've already taken everything."

"Not everything," I correct.

I stroll to the desk and drop a thick envelope onto the polished wood. It lands with the weight of a guillotine blade.

Inside is a contract.

A proposal. An ultimatum.

"I'm offering you salvation," I say. "A bailout. Complete erasure of your debts, a restoration of your company, and protection under my organization."

Her father stares at the envelope like it's ticking. "What's the condition?"

I smile. Like a wolf circling its prey. "I marry your daughter."

He pales. Mrs. Danforth opens her mouth, but nothing comes out. She's in shock, apparently.

It's Victoria's father who finds his words first. "That's impossible, she's already marrying Grant."

"Nothing is impossible. Where there's a will, there's a way. And I can be very convincing, as I'm sure you've noticed already . . ."

"Victoria would never marry you," the asshole grits out.

"She doesn't have a choice—"

"You can't be serious," his wife shrieks.

I lift a hand. "You don't want to fuck with me. I haven't even started to show you what I'm capable of."

"Fine." Her father straightens his jacket, swallowing hard. "If this is the only way—if this saves the company—"

Her mother jerks to him. "You can't be serious? You can't let her marry *him*," she bellows.

"It's better than ruin," he snaps, voice breaking. He turns back to me. "You have a deal."

I nod slowly, savoring the moment he signs his soul away with words.

"Good, I'll draw up the final paperwork. We'll do it legally. Privately, though. No one can know. Do you understand?"

This part is imperative. If my uncle ever finds out what I'm doing, he'll kill me.

Her mother's eyes narrow.

"Don't worry," I coo. "I won't hurt her." Not that she cares. "Not physically." I turn toward the door. "Tell your daughter," I say softly, "the wedding will be soon."

"She won't agree."

I pause, then glance back at the vile woman. "You'd be surprised what people agree to when they realize I've left them no other choice."

With that done, I walk out of the office and down the hallway.

The last time I was here, I was a boy . . .

Now I'm not.

Now . . .

I'm their worst nightmare.

CHAPTER 28

Victoria

THE PHONE RINGS WHILE I'M HALFWAY THROUGH A SAD excuse of a sandwich—gluten-free bread, wilted greens, and the most pathetic piece of turkey I've ever seen—when my mother's name flashes across the screen.

Shit.

Why is she calling?

I freeze.

She never calls twice in two days. She barely calls twice in two months.

I can't handle any more of this shit. For a moment, I consider not answering. With all the shit going on with my family, though, I don't have the luxury of denial. I need to know what she wants.

I swipe to answer. "Hi, Mom?"

"Victoria, you need to come home. Now."

Hello to you too.

Would it kill the woman to show a little emotion toward me?

"What happened? Did something else go wrong at the company?"

"Don't ask questions. Just come home."

"What's going on?" Silence crackles on the other end. "Mom?"

"I can't say it over the phone . . . just come."

Something in me goes very, very still. "Okay," I breathe. "I'm coming."

The estate sits two hours outside the city.

With every mile, my heartbeat climbs higher into my throat. This is the second time they've dragged me back this week.

The moment the wrought-iron gates appear, I swear I might pass out. Which won't bode well for me since I'm driving. The guards open them automatically.

The house looks the same as it did a few days ago, so I know it didn't burn down like our factory. It's still too big and way too perfect, but it's standing, so at least we have that going for us.

I park, then step out and head inside.

Once I've entered, I head through the foyer without a word, searching for my mother or father. I find them in the dining room.

My mother and father sit stiffly at the far end of the long table, dressed like they're attending their own funeral. The table is set for dinner—polished silver, crystal glasses, candlelight flickering.

Four place settings.

I stop. "Who else is coming?"

No one answers.

My father doesn't even look at me. He gestures stiffly toward the seat across from them. "Sit."

"I'm not sitting until someone tells me—"

"Sit," he repeats, voice clipped and strained.

My pulse kicks into a sprint. Something is wrong. Very wrong.

I take one step toward the table—

And the dining room door opens behind me.

I turn.

My heart stops.

Holy shit . . .

It can't be.

But it is.

My mouth opens and shuts as I try to find words, but my

throat feels extra dry as the man who's haunted my dreams for years enters. Lorenzo walks in.

No.

No, not walks. He storms in but then in a complete contrast to his entrance, he closes the door with a soft click that makes my skin prickle.

He's older now. With broad shoulders, and a defined jaw.

This is not the boy from the boathouse.

This man . . . This is someone else.

My breath stumbles out of me. "Lorenzo?"

His eyes flick to mine. No warmth. No softness. No recognition of the girl who loved him.

Just hatred wrapped in ice.

I take a small step forward. "Where have you—?"

He lifts a hand.

Just a single, silent gesture.

My words die immediately.

He walks past me, slow and deliberate, every step echoing with power and danger. He sits at the empty place setting, smoothing the tablecloth with gloved fingers as if he's straightening a throne.

His presence fills the room. All-consuming.

My father swallows hard and my mother grips her napkin so tightly that it tears.

"Let's begin." Lorenzo's voice slices through the air.

My chest tightens. "Begin what?"

He doesn't look at me when he answers. "Your parents have been . . . very busy."

My father clears his throat, attempting something like authority. "The company has suffered recent—"

Lorenzo slams his palm down on the table.

Everyone jumps.

"Do not speak," he growls, eyes pinning my father like a knife on display. "I told you to let me handle this."

My mother trembles.

I stare at them. What the hell is going on? "Dad?"

Lorenzo leans back in his chair, eyes glittering darkly. "Your parents"—he gestures lazily toward them—"have lost everything."

My father opens his mouth, but Lorenzo slowly turns his head, and the look he gives him is enough to silence a hurricane.

My father deflates in his seat.

Lorenzo continues, tone almost bored. "Your wealth. Gone. Your investments. Drained. Your factories. Sabotaged. Your offshore accounts. Frozen."

My mother's lips part in a soundless gasp.

My father's face reddens with humiliation. "Because of Vict—"

Lorenzo lifts a hand sharply.

"Say her name," he snaps, "and I will personally string you up by your intestines and turn you into my own art project."

My body locks. I'm not the only one scared. I peer over where my father has gone rigid, and my mother makes a choked noise, reaching for his arm.

Words are hard to find, but when I do, I stutter. "Wh-what is happening?"

Lorenzo finally looks at me.

And when his eyes meet mine, everything inside me goes silent.

"Your family," he says softly, "has been ruined. Completely."

A cold tremor runs down my spine. "Why?"

He tilts his head, eyes narrowing with something like bitter amusement. "You'll understand soon."

I can hardly breathe. "Lorenzo, what do you want?"

His lips curl into a smile that is not a smile at all. "You."

The air leaves my lungs. "Me?" I whisper. "What does that mean?"

Lorenzo steeples his fingers, elbows resting on the table. "It means your parents have agreed to give me what I want."

My heart free-falls. "What did you do?" I breathe.

"We had no choice, Victoria. He made us an offer. To fix everything," my father tells me, as if that explains anything.

Breathe.

Fucking breathe.

I need to pull my shit together and figure out what the hell he's talking about.

My fingers dig into the back of a chair. "An offer that involves me?"

"Victoria—" My mother speaks, but I have no interest in hearing anything she has to say right now.

"No," I snap, staring at them both. "You sold me? You sold me off like inventory?"

Lorenzo chuckles, a low, vicious sound. "Inventory?" He taps the table with one gloved finger. "No, sweetheart. Inventory is replaceable."

My blood runs cold.

"You," His eyes devour my fear, "were the price."

I stumble backward like he physically struck me. "My god."

Lorenzo watches me fall apart with calm fascination. Something tells me he's waited a long time for this moment.

"What kind of monster are you?" I whisper.

He smiles. Cold and violent. Beautiful in a way that makes my skin crawl.

"The one you created."

"I-I didn't—"

He raises a brow. "You broke me once. I'm simply returning the favor."

I want to scream. I want to run. I want to crawl across the table and claw his eyes out. I want to cry for the boy I loved and strangle the man he's become. Maybe I can do both? Something tells me I wouldn't make it an inch before a gun is pointed at my head.

Neither is an option. "You can't do this," I manage to choke out.

"Oh, I can," he answers, rising slowly from his seat. "And I already have." He buttons his jacket with a smooth, practiced motion. "The arrangements are made. The deal is sealed. Your parents traded your future for their lives."

I stare at them. It can't be true. It can't be . . . but when I see my mother's face and that of my father's, I know it is. "You agreed to marry me off without even asking me?"

I don't know why I'm surprised, but I am. I never thought they would stoop this low. All my life, I've known they only cared about themselves, but if I harbored any belief that maybe they could change, be less selfish, now I know the answer . . .

No.

"It was better than ruin," the man who raised me mutters under his breath. This man is no father. He's a weak, disgusting person who only cares about his status.

Lorenzo smiles with teeth. "Your family is saved, Victoria. And you should be grateful. Very few people get to be the solution to a centuries-old empire collapsing."

"And why would I ever do this?"

"You have to, Victoria," my mother pleads.

"Why? What more can he do? He's already taken everything. What more can he threaten us with?"

"Violence. Death," my father hisses.

"What?"

"Do you not know who your little boyfriend became?" My father scoffs.

"What the hell are you talking about?"

"Well, apparently, he wasn't at all what you thought he was. Your old friend is part of the Amante crime family . . ."

"What the—"

"Which is exactly why you will go along with this plan, Little Bird."

The moniker sends chills down my spine. His words are clear. I'm a bird in a cage, and there is no way out because he holds the key.

My pulse pounds in my ears. "You're insane."

He shrugs casually. "Probably."

He then turns toward the door, and something in me snaps. "Lorenzo," I rasp. "Don't walk away from me."

He pauses.

I storm around the table, closing the distance between us until I'm right in front of him.

His cologne hits me—dark, smoky, expensive, sinful—and it's so unfair how familiar it feels.

I glare up at him, trembling. "Tell me the truth. Why are you doing this?"

His eyes soften for a fraction of a second, like a dying star flickering before the explosion. Then the softness is gone. He leans down, lips brushing the shell of my ear.

"You left me," he whispers. "So now I'm going to show you what that feels like."

He pulls back.

"And, Little Bird?" His smile slices into me like a blade. "I'm just getting started."

He walks out of the dining room without another word. The door shuts behind him, and the world that I thought couldn't possibly fall apart any further . . . collapses completely.

CHAPTER 29

Lorenzo

THREE . . .

Two . . .

One . . .

"Lorenzo?" She says it so quietly I almost don't hear her. "I'll marry you."

As I suspected, the moment I walked out of the room, she followed me, and I'm happy to be right.

This is exactly where I want her. Not broken. Not hysterical. Not begging. Just resigned to her new future.

But I'm fully aware she's not finished with me yet. Here it comes . . .

"With conditions."

My lips twitch. "Conditions?"

She nods once, chin trembling even as she tries to hold it high. "No intimacy. You won't touch me. You won't try to own me. And you won't—"

I laugh.

It's not polite, nor is it light. It's also clearly not amused.

Instead, my laugh comes out like a man who's spent years sharpening the edges of a blade and just cut himself open with it. *Clearly there is something very wrong with me.*

Unhinged would be a good word to use.

I am unhinged.

And I love it.

This feeling.

Her hatred.

It's all the aphrodisiac I need.

Her eyes flash. "What is so funny?"

I drag my thumb across the corner of my mouth, trying to tame the grin. "Little Bird . . . you're adorable. You think you're negotiating."

Her shoulders stiffen. "If you want me, those are the terms."

"If?" I echo, stepping closer. "That's cute too."

She swallows, throat bobbing. "You said you wanted me. I'm giving you parameters."

"Parameters." The word rolls off my tongue like a joke. Only the punchline will come later, when she least expects it.

I let the silence stretch, savoring the panic building behind her wide eyes.

Finally, I shrug, casual as sin. "Fine."

She blinks. "Fine?"

"Fine," I repeat, smirking. "I'll agree to your little list."

The relief that floods her face nearly makes me laugh again. She's still so sweet and innocent. Her relief is comical. *It's also delusional.*

But what she doesn't realize is that none of her conditions matter. Not a single one. The moment she said yes? The moment her parents sold her future for a bailout, her rules would never matter.

I turn toward the door. "Lovely chat. I'll go finish arranging your new cage."

She stiffens. "Lorenzo, I'm serious."

"So am I." I glance back at her over my shoulder. "Always."

I don't give her time to push. I don't give myself time to feel. Instead, I head toward the front of the house to leave.

I pull out my phone and call the one person who's been there for me since my life changed.

Matteo answers with a tired growl. "You better not be calling to say you've murdered someone. Again."

I stare toward the doors. "Relax. If someone dies, I'll send you a postcard."

He sighs so loudly it rattles the speaker. "What the hell are you up to, Lorenzo?"

A slow smile cuts across my face. "I'm taking a short sabbatical."

"A short sabbatical? What do you think, this is a nine-to-five where you punch out and get lunch breaks?"

"I need a little time to handle something."

"Elaborate."

"No can do, Cuz."

"And you expect me to be okay with that answer?"

"I do, because you love me," I tease.

"Are you in trouble?"

I smirk to myself. "Define trouble."

"Fuck, Lorenzo. That is not the answer I want." He sounds pissed, but he'll get over it. That is as long as he never finds out the truth.

"I'm fine. Just a personal matter I want to deal with. Don't worry, no one will die."

He exhales. "Do you need help?"

"You know me, I never do."

"Which is why I'm worried."

"You need a life, Matteo. Then you might get out of mine." I laugh.

"Go to hell," he taunts back, but I know he's not pissed.

"I'll send you a postcard from there, too." I hang up before he can say anything else.

I step outside. Evening has fallen across the sky. I scroll to another number. Rafe picks up before the first ring even finishes.

"Well, well. How are the future in-laws? Are they welcoming their favorite harbinger of doom into the family with open arms?"

"Like I give a fuck," I retort.

"What's the problem tonight?" he asks.

"The usual. I need you to find me a priest."

He coughs out a choking sound. *Wasn't expecting my comment, obviously.* "Is someone getting married?"

"Fuck off."

"Who's the lucky lady?"

"As I said before . . . fuck off."

"And you think this will get me to help you?"

I laugh. "Hi Rafe, how was your day today?"

He hums. "Much better."

"Good, now get me a priest. Someone who won't ask questions and make sure no one outside the house finds out."

"On it. I'm very efficient when I want to be."

I end the call and slip the phone into my pocket as the front door creaks open behind me.

Her scent hits me first. Soft. Familiar. Still my favorite smell, but I digress.

She steps out slowly, barefoot on the marble like she's afraid someone might hear her as she sneaks around the house tonight.

"So we're really doing this?" she whispers.

I turn to look at her over my shoulder. "We are."

She wraps her arms around herself. "You agreed to my terms."

"I did."

"You'll honor them?"

She looks fragile and fierce and heartbreakingly naive, all at once.

"I'll honor them," I tell her.

She exhales shakily, nodding. "Okay." She walks back inside, and I don't stop her.

Because she doesn't need to know that her terms were bullshit.

The second she said yes, she gave me everything I wanted. That whatever cage she thought she built?

It's mine now.

And she will live in it. Forever.

She disappears behind the door, leaving me alone with my dark thoughts.

"You have no idea what you agreed to, Little Bird," I whisper, letting the monster inside me stretch.

"No idea at all."

CHAPTER 30

Victoria

I'M STILL HALF ASLEEP WHEN MY PEACEFUL MORNING COMES to a screeching halt when a vision of Lorenzo plays behind my lids.

Shit.

I hate the man, yet he still haunts my dreams. It's been years since I've seen him, but he's only gotten more beautiful.

Life is truly unfair, and it's especially cruel how devastatingly handsome he's become.

I roll over in bed, hair shoved across my face, reach blindly for my phone on the nightstand, and check the time.

Instead, I see a text.

I freeze so hard my breath cuts out.

Lorenzo: Hope you slept well. You have a long day ahead of you.

My hand goes numb, and my phone almost slips through my fingers.

How does he have my number, but worse . . . how is his number programmed into my phone?

I sit up so fast the duvet tangles around my legs, all while my heart slams into my ribs like it's trying to break out of me.

I stare at the words again, like maybe they'll rearrange into something sane.

But they don't. They sharpen.

What does he think I'm doing today?

"Oh my god, I can't believe this is happening," I whisper into my empty room, voice cracking.

My palms begin to sweat, and my stomach churns.

I hit the call button for my mother.

She answers in one second—too fast, like she's been pacing the phone for hours.

"Victoria . . . we have a long day. I need you ready—"

I stand, pacing the edge of my room with the phone pressed to my ear. "I know, Mother. Don't you think this is crazy? I can't do it. Don't make me . . . "

I stop mid-step when she doesn't say anything. Did she hang up? "Mom?"

Her exhale comes out broken. "Come downstairs."

"Mom—"

"Come now." She hangs up.

My legs nearly give out. She dismissed me without an explanation. Why should this be surprising? It's basically the story of my life.

Do this, Victoria.

We expect this, Victoria.

For my whole life, I've been bossed around and moved around like a pawn. Why should this be any different?

I throw on the first clothes I find in my old closet, a sweater with a stretched neckline and jeans that don't fit right. I shove my hair into a claw clip with shaking hands.

My mother will loooove my appearance . . .

Within a few minutes, I know today is going to suck. Because before I leave the room, I step toward a window and see the staff rushing across the back lawn carrying white roses and a giant arch made of more flowers.

What the hell is happening?

I move away from the window and head to find my mother.

I'm not even down the hallway when a staff member spots me and gestures wildly. "Miss Victoria, this way."

"I don't—wait—" My voice cracks as he shepherds me like a stray cat. "I don't understand what is happening."

He doesn't answer. He just escorts me down the hall and pushes open the door to the study.

My mother is inside.

She looks like a mess, which doesn't at all match her outfit of silk. Her hair is frizzy, her makeup is smudged, and her eyes are swollen.

Tired. She looks utterly exhausted.

"What—what is going on?" I blurt, stumbling backward.

"We're preparing for a wedding, Victoria."

The word punches me straight in the chest.

I stand there frozen, trying not to hyperventilate. "I-I didn't approve any of this."

Her eyebrows lift like she finds that adorable. Ice slides through my veins.

She presses her fingers to her temples, and I continue to stare at her.

"Mom." My voice cracks. "Tell me you didn't actually agree to this. I know the other day, Father said yes, but I thought—" What the hell did I think? I knew Lorenzo meant business. "I thought you would put him off, stretch it out until we could figure out another way."

She stiffens, and my throat tightens. Her eyes close for a second and then reopen. "We had no choice."

The words hit like a blade. This is really happening.

I step back. "There is always a choice."

"Not anymore." Her voice breaks. "Your father tried, but Lorenzo—he has everything. Believe me, your father was up all night. He's tried everything. But Lorenzo didn't leave us any other choice. If we don't do this—"

"If *we* don't?" My breath catches. "Don't you mean if *I* don't?"

She flinches.

I want to scream. Or cry. Or tear wallpaper off the walls.

But instead, I inhale through my teeth and whisper, "You sold me off."

She reaches for me, pretending like she cares, but I know it's a lie. She just needs me to fall into line.

A knock interrupts us.

A middle-aged woman walks in, carrying a few dress bags.

She beams at me. "Hello, time for gown fittings."

I want to vomit.

"Come on, sweetheart. Let's make you a princess."

I can't move at first. Then I do.

I'm numb to the world and currently being dragged to God knows where to try on gowns. *How is this my life?*

I follow her to a parlor room converted into an impromptu fitting room.

She unzips bag after bag.

Lace, satin, silk, beading, tulle, column gowns, ball gowns, mermaid cuts.

I can't even keep up.

Fabric is everywhere.

My heart hammers, throat raw.

"I don't—" My voice breaks. "I don't even know what I'm doing."

The woman gives me a small, sympathetic smile as she helps me step into a gown. "You're finding the perfect dress."

"I don't want to."

Her expression dims. "Some weddings aren't about want, honey. They're about need."

The room tilts.

I think I might pass out.

A mirror sits in front of me, and I find myself staring at my reflection.

White lace hugs my body, but my face is pale. I look like a ghost.

More like a sacrifice.

"I can't do this," I whisper.

In the blink of an eye, I'm naked again, and then it's a different dress, and another fitting. Another reflection I don't recognize.

My mother appears behind me. "This will do."

I glare at her through the mirror.

Her jaw tightens. "You have to do this."

"No." My voice trembles. "I don't."

"Yes. You do."

I turn to face her fully, ready to scream, to unleash everything I'm holding inside . . .

"Breathe."

I try.

I fail.

But I follow her out anyway, because everything is moving whether I want it to or not.

Because the wedding is happening. This engagement is real.

And somehow, I'm yet again the pawn.

CHAPTER 31

Victoria

BY THE TIME THE GRANDFATHER CLOCK IN THE HALL CHIMES, indicating it's seven, I've already changed outfits three times and fantasized about faking my own death twice.

Apparently, neither plan is acceptable.

Which sucks.

Unlike Juliet, I have no way of making it look believable, and with my luck, I'd one hundred percent accidentally kill myself for real.

Running away is another option.

If I jumped out my window, it's a straight shot to the backyard. I bet I could be miles away before anyone realizes I'm gone.

Who am I kidding? This place is probably locked down like Fort Knox. I won't be able to make it out of my bedroom, let alone the house.

Take my mother right now . . .

She currently stands right in front of me, fussing with the sleeves of a black silk dress I don't remember owning. "Stop slouching," she smooths a wrinkle that doesn't exist. "He'll be here any minute."

"He," I echo, catching her gaze in the mirror. "You mean the monster who bought my life like he went online and ordered a bride?"

Her fingers pause. "Victoria, please."

I arch a brow. "Which part am I supposed to be polite about? The financial collapse or the arranged marriage?"

Her mouth flattens in displeasure. *Sorry, I don't feel bad for you, Mom.* "We need this dinner to go well. Lorenzo insisted it be . . . civil."

I snort. "His version of civil involves arson and threats. Or did you forget he apparently works for the Mafia now?"

A hollow laugh escapes her. "And that is why you have to play nice."

This is all too much.

I'm pissed and angry, yet I can't do anything about it.

Not unless I want my fiancé to put out a hit on my parents.

Well . . .

No. I don't want that. Even if they suck as parents, I'd never wish them harm, nor would I sell them, but I digress.

With a shaky breath, I stare at my reflection in the mirror.

I might look pretty, but I want to gag. Even though I recognize the girl in the mirror, she's not me.

A knock sounds at the bedroom door.

Helen's voice floats through, tight and formal. "Miss Victoria. They've arrived."

They. Who the hell is they? Did he bring the rest of the mob? I hope not. I'm not sure I can handle that. One criminal is enough for me.

My mother grabs my shoulders. "Remember your manners."

I shrug her hands off. "He ruined us. You sold me. What's the etiquette for that, exactly? Do I curtsy?"

Her jaw clenches, but she doesn't respond.

Good.

I follow her down the hallway, my heels clicking with each step. The house smells fantastic. It appears father is trying hard to impress Lorenzo because he pulled out all the stops.

Speaking of the asshole . . . when we reach the dining room, my father stands right outside the doors, hand clamped around a decanter of scotch.

That's great, Dad. Perfect time to get sloshed.

But why should today be any different? Just because we have a Mafia guy in our house who wants to kill us.

Yes, please . . . Let's continue with business as usual.

He looks like shit. His collar is too stiff, as is his tie, but it's his bloodshot eyes that really give him away.

"You're late." He glances at me and then looks away just as fast.

I fold my arms across my chest. "You scheduled a family dinner to celebrate selling me. Forgive me if I didn't rush."

His jaw flexes. "This arrangement will save us."

"At my expense."

"That's enough," my mother hisses. "Please. Don't do this here."

"Where then?" I ask, voice low. "Or better yet, when? During the vows?"

Before anyone can answer, the dining room door opens, and one of the members of the staff bows slightly. "The room is ready."

It's now or never.

We step inside.

The dining table is set like a stage, with crystals gleaming and candles flickering.

Oxygen explodes from my lungs as I see the room isn't empty.

At the far end, in my father's usual chair, sits the man who stole everything from me.

Lorenzo wears a black shirt open at the throat, tattoos teasing his collar.

His rings catch the candlelight as he lifts a glass, the metal glinting.

If I think there's a chance I'll be able to walk in without catching his attention, I'm instantly proved wrong. Because as soon as I step inside the room, his gaze finds me instantly. For a moment, everything goes quiet.

He rakes his eyes over me slowly—not hungry, not soft. Assessing. Cataloging the girl he once knew against the woman he now owns.

His mouth curves, and it's not in a smile that forms on his full lips. It's something colder.

Shit.

This is not good.

The room begins to spin.

Get it together, Victoria.

Don't fall on your face. You can't appear weak.

"Little Bird." Lorenzo's voice is as smooth as an expensive whiskey. "You clean up nicely."

I lift my chin, forcing my feet to move, each step measured. "You're in my father's chair."

He leans back, casual and powerful. "Oh, princess. I'm in everyone's chair."

The man beside Lorenzo snorts under his breath, swirling his drink. Who is this asshole? One of his hired goons?

My father clears his throat like he wants to reclaim some authority he hasn't possessed in weeks. "Please. Sit, Victoria."

I slide into the chair opposite Lorenzo, my parents flanking me. The candles flicker between us, casting shadows across his face. If this weren't bad enough, now he looks downright deadly.

Great, *I love this for me.*

A server pours wine, and another brings plates, but Lorenzo . . . he just watches me.

The asshole sitting beside Lorenzo, and whose name I still haven't gotten, breaks the tension first, lifting his glass toward my parents with a lazy half smile. "Thank you for hosting us. It's not every day I get to attend a secret wedding."

Secret wedding?

Why is it a secret?

And by secret . . . what does that mean?

My mother's laugh comes out brittle. "We're . . . honored to have you."

Lorenzo taps his fork against his plate, the metallic ring slicing through the room. "Relax. I only commit arson when it's necessary. So have no fear, now that I'm getting what I want, you're perfectly safe . . . well, unless Victoria chooses to disobey."

My father chokes on his wine.

"And we should believe you?" I stare at him across the table. "You burned down our factory, and don't even get me started on the rest of what you did."

Lorenzo's gaze slides to mine, amused. "Allegedly."

"Allegedly? You admitted to it." My fingers tighten around my fork. "You called it leverage."

He shrugs, unbothered. "Semantics."

Dessert forks clatter softly as the staff reset the table between courses. No one has touched the food yet.

Who could possibly have an appetite right now? His friend, that's who. He's currently lifting his fork to his mouth.

My father clears his throat. "We should discuss logistics. The wedding is . . . in a few days. The guest list, the ceremony, press control—"

"As I've said before. This is private. No guests," Lorenzo slices into his steak with calm brutality.

"Will your mother be attending?" I ask.

"My mother is dead." The rough baritone of his voice leaves no room for questions. I want to ask more, but I don't dare.

"As I was saying . . . no press. Priest is already booked . . . someone I can trust. Other than that, not a word."

My mother blinks. "I thought—"

He smirks. "You thought what? That I was going to make a big announcement."

My stomach twists. "Well, you did go out of your way to strong-arm me into the sham of a marriage, so why is it a secret?"

He spears a piece of meat and lifts it. "You agreed to marry me."

"Cut the shit, we both know I didn't really agree to shit."

He chews, slow and deliberate, eyes locked on mine. "Little Bird, I don't like your attitude."

"Stop calling me that."

"Why? It's so fitting after all, even more so today than five years ago."

"You need therapy."

Lorenzo flashes me a grin edged in ice. "I am therapy."

His friend lets out a bellow of a laugh. "You're something, that's for sure."

"Who are you?" I scoff. "A name would be nice."

"Oh, this is Rafe . . . but you don't need to concern yourself with him. He's here to make sure you all stay in line."

A.k.a. he's a crazier motherfucker than Lorenzo . . .

My father dabs at his mouth with a napkin, trying to steer the conversation back to something he understands. "Our reputations have taken a hit with all the . . . recent events. Maybe we should announce the marriage."

"No," Lorenzo replies, resting his knife on the edge of his plate. "We will do no such thing. If you want to keep your house and not lose everything, you will obey my rules."

My mother's fingers tremble against her wineglass. "We will. We're grateful for your help, Lorenzo."

His head tips slightly. "You should be. I don't usually save the people I dismantle."

Her face goes pale.

I slice into my own steak just to have something to do with my hands. "And what do you get out of this, aside from new toys to break?"

He smiles slowly. "I get you."

The words land like a slap.

Heat floods my cheeks, equal parts anger and something I don't want to name.

"You can't own a person," I hiss, setting my fork down a little too hard.

He lifts his glass, eyes dark. "That's adorable. Wrong but adorable."

Rafe's gaze flicks between us, measuring the distance and most likely the danger of me stabbing his friend with a knife. "Maybe we steer away from the 'owning people' part of the discussion while we're all armed with cutlery."

"What will you do to stabilize the public opinion of my company?" Always business with my father.

"A few puff pieces." Lorenzo rests his chin on his knuckles. "Don't worry, I'll make you look like a saint so fast your head will spin. Profits will be back to normal in no time."

My fork nearly snaps in my hand.

My mother gives me a warning look. "Victoria . . ."

I force a smile that feels like it might shatter my face. "Oh, don't worry. I won't be a problem. Even if I hate him, and you basically sold me off like cattle . . ."

Lorenzo's eyes flash with something sharp and fleeting. "Careful, Victoria. You might hurt my feelings."

"You don't have feelings," I whisper.

He leans in, elbows on the table, voice dropping low. "No. I had them. Once. I donated them to a cause."

My throat tightens. "Which cause?"

He smiles, small and vicious. "You."

Rafe shifts uncomfortably, clearing his throat. "How about we talk about something that doesn't sound like the setup to a murder-suicide?"

"Oh, relax," Lorenzo reaches for his wine again. "If I kill anyone tonight, it'll be metaphorical."

My father drains his glass, the crystal clinking against his teeth.

The main course is cleared. Dessert arrives. No one looks particularly thrilled about the soufflé.

My mother picks at hers. "We were thinking of hosting the wedding in the garden, near the fountain. It photographs beautifully."

"No pictures. And there is no need for a big wedding . . ." Lorenzo says. "The location is ideal, though. We aren't too close to the ocean. That way, no one will accidentally drown." He lifts a brow, almost in challenge.

"You mean when you throw someone in," I mumble under my breath, but he still hears.

His lips twitch. "Accidents do happen."

I stare at him across the table, nausea rising. "Why are you doing this?"

His expression doesn't change. "I told you. Consequences."

"For falling in love with you?" I whisper.

His gaze sharpens. "For walking away."

The words slice me open.

I look down at my dessert, breath shaky. "You think ruining my family, forcing me into a marriage, taking away my freedom . . . evens us out?"

"I don't believe in even," he answers. "I believe in balance."

"That's the same thing."

"No." His eyes darken, voice low. "Even is forgiveness. Balance is knowing someone finally feels the weight you've been carrying for a years."

Silence grips the table.

My mother stares at her plate.

My father drinks even more alcohol.

Rafe studies Lorenzo. There is something in his features I can't read. If I had to guess, it's worry, but maybe loyalty all tangled into one.

I squeeze my hands together under the table. *You'll survive this. You're stronger than you think.*

A tremor runs up my arm. Am I, though?

Lorenzo must see something in my gaze because he flashes me a warning. One that says whatever you're thinking about . . . stop.

Too bad for him, he has no control over my thoughts.

My mother lifts her glass to her lips. "To the new family."

Lorenzo raises his glass. "To mergers."

I stare back at him, throat burning. "To surviving."

We drink.

The meal is agonizing and through it all, Lorenzo watches.

Like he's ten moves ahead in a game the rest of us are still learning the rules to.

When dessert plates are cleared, and coffee poured, he finally pushes his chair back, napkin dropped neatly on the table. "Walk with me," he says, his gaze locking on mine.

It isn't a request.

My spine freezes. "I'm fine here."

His brow arches. "I wasn't asking if you were fine. I'm telling you to walk."

My mother opens her mouth, then closes it again.

I stand.

Because I don't have a choice. Because the whole house knows it.

I follow him out of the dining room, the murmur of my parents' voices fading behind us. He leads the way down the corridor, past portraits of dead Danforths. Ornate frames won't hide the fact that we are new money and pretending to be the opposite, but at this point, I'd pretend to be anything not to have to go ahead with this sham of a wedding.

It's pointless, though. Lorenzo will never let me go.

We reach the end of the hall, the moonlight spilling through the tall glass doors that lead out to the terrace.

"Why are we here? To discuss my cage?"

He steps closer. "You think this is about a cage?" he asks softly.

I meet his gaze, anger bubbling up inside me. "Isn't it?"

His lips curl. "No, Little Bird. This is about a mirror."

"What does that even mean?"

"It means . . . " He brushes a knuckle along the edge of my jaw in a touch that feels more like a threat. "You're finally going to see what you turned me into."

I swallow, refusing to let him see me flinch. "What kind of monster are you, Lorenzo?"

The smile that follows is slow, brutal, devastating. "The kind you made."

He steps back, leaving the ghost of his touch and the echo of his words hanging between us.

The voices from the dining room drift faintly down the hall—my mother and father entertaining our future executioner with small talk.

And me?

I stand in my parents' house, in a dress I didn't choose, promised to a man I used to love and now barely recognize—

And realize I'm not waiting for a rescue.

I'm standing at the beginning of a war.

One I didn't start. One I'm not sure I can win.

But one I'll have to survive.

Because if Lorenzo Amante thinks he's the only one who learned how to weaponize heartbreak—

He's not paying close enough attention.

And that?

Might be the only advantage I have left.

CHAPTER 32

Victoria

THE GOWN HANGS IN FRONT OF THE MIRROR, TAUNTING ME. Silk. Lace. Hand-stitched beading that probably costs more than most people's yearly salary. It's beautiful in the way daggers are beautiful—intricate, polished, designed for one purpose.

Hmm . . .

Not a bad idea.

Death is certainly an option right now.

It would be easier than the road ahead of me, that much is for sure.

Helen, one of the older maids who's been with us for years, stands behind me, fingers smoothing the bodice like she's petting a wild animal she's trying not to spook. "You're shaking." She pulls a loose thread near my shoulder.

"I'm not shaking," I lie, and it's obvious. My voice is way too flat to be telling the truth. "I'm perfectly fine. Just vibrating with happiness."

The corner of her mouth lifts. She knows I'm full of shit. "Of course." Her hands move to the laces at my back, tightening the corset in steady, practiced pulls. "Hold the rail," she adds, nodding toward the post of the old canopy bed. "If you fall, I'm too old to catch you."

I grab the post and exhale as she yanks the laces. "You're not old," I grit through my teeth as she pulls so tight I'm afraid I'll pass out. "You're in your prime. You put up with me and my father. That's got to give you bonus points for a long life."

"Or put me into an early grave." She laughs. "Your father, I mean. You . . . You're the easy one."

I swallow hard. "I used to be easy. Before everything went to hell."

Helen ties off the last knot, fingers lingering against the small of my back like she wants to say more. "Turn." She taps my hip.

I rotate slowly, the dress fluttering around my legs in a cloud of ivory.

A mirror stands in front of me, and I don't recognize the girl in the reflection. It's not that I don't look like myself, but because now I look like a bride. I always thought I'd be excited for this moment, but instead, as the tears fill my eyes, I'm scared.

What will happen to me once I'm his?

Helen steps closer, reaching for the veil draped over the chair. "Ready?" she asks, the word thick.

"No," I answer, not even pretending. "But go ahead."

She lifts the veil slowly, hands careful. Then she adjusts it around my face. "You are so beautiful," she whispers, voice breaking. "They don't deserve to see you like this."

A lump punches the back of my throat. "Then maybe we should just skip it." I force a hollow smile. "You can help me climb out the window. I'll hitchhike to Canada. They have really good healthcare. It can't be that bad."

Her smile falters, grief sliding over her face like a shadow. She presses her lips together, glancing toward the door as if it might sprout ears. "You know we can't." She breathes. "Not now."

"Because he'll find us," I say quietly.

She closes her eyes for a moment, lashes damp. "Because he already has," she answers, and I swear the air feels thinner.

I want to ask her more. I want to say his name and hear what she thinks of him. The boy who fixed our doors and kissed me under the stars. The man who burned down my father's empire and came back with a ring and a cage.

But she's already risking everything by being in this room with me and talking to me about it.

A knock sounds, two sharp raps on the door. My mother's rhythm. I'd recognize it anywhere.

Helen's hands drop instantly, posture straightening. "Are you ready?" she asks again, but this time, it sounds like a script.

"I'm dressed," I answer. "That's as close as we're going to get."

She gives me one quick, fierce look—something like *I'm sorry and be careful and you are stronger than you think* all wrapped into one—and moves to open the door.

My mother slips in, her champagne-colored dress is tailored and elegant. Her eyes find me. "You look very nice, Victoria."

"Thank you." I force a crooked smile under the veil. "In my opinion, I look like a very expensive hostage."

"Victoria," she warns.

"What?" I ask. "Too soon?"

Helen's eyes flick to mine in the mirror, a silent plea to stop. Not make this worse. As much as I love her, I'm not sure I'm able to do that. I'm feeling extra prickly today.

I exhale slowly, lungs pressing my corset. "Is he here?"

My mother hesitates a moment too long.

My heart drops. "He is," I answer myself, the words flat. "Of course he is. God forbid he ditch me at the altar. I'd happily welcome that."

Her jaw tightens. "Your father is waiting in the hall," she says instead. "We should go. The priest . . . he doesn't want to be kept waiting."

Of course, he doesn't. Poor man probably didn't expect to risk his soul over a private Mafia-adjacent hostage wedding when he woke up this morning.

Helen steps back, smoothing invisible wrinkles from my skirt. "Walk slow. The dress is heavy."

"The dress is the least heavy thing in this room," I mumble, before my mother hooks her arm through, pretending to be the perfect mother.

Too little, too late, woman. No one in this house is fooled by your act.

We move toward the door, then head out into the hallway. We keep walking until we see my father. He's waiting at the end, near the side entrance that leads toward the backyard, where my mother wants the ceremony to take place.

While Lorenzo has been clear that this wedding will be a secret—why, I have no clue—my father still dresses the part despite the lack of cameras to document it.

He's in his black tux, shoulders rigid, expression carefully arranged into something neutral and proud. But his eyes are . . . off. Too bright. Too sharp.

He looks at me, mouth opening to speak. *Here it comes.* "You're late." He checks his watch purely to be an asshole.

"I'm worth waiting for," I answer, my chin lifting.

He huffs through his nose. "Let's not keep him," he says, holding out his arm. "The sooner this is done, the sooner—"

"We can start pretending this wasn't your idea?" I finish, sliding my hand into the crook of his elbow.

His jaw flexes. "It was this or ruin."

I look straight ahead. "You chose you," I say quietly. "It's fine. I expect it by now."

He goes stiff beside me.

Neither of us speaks as we continue to walk down the side corridor.

We pass the garden. My peripheral vision catches a flash of the weathered building all the way by the water.

The boathouse.

For a second, my mind plays out a picture, but I shake my head.

Not today, Satan.

I look away and continue toward the fountain. Once there, my father stops, adjusts his sleeves for no reason, and finally looks at me properly. "Whatever you feel, you cannot let it show. Not to him."

"That's the funny thing." I lift a brow. "He already knows exactly how I feel. He's counting on it."

The muscle in his cheek jumps. "Smile."

The air already feels thicker as I take in the makeshift canopy that's supposed to be an altar.

The priest stands there, fingers tangled together.

Rafe stands near the front, his suit black, tie loosened, as if this is mildly annoying. His gaze slides over us, assessing, as if he's checking off a mental list.

And at the altar across from the priest is—

Lorenzo.

He turns toward us.

Then he takes me in.

A dark look spreads across his features.

He's in a black tailored suit, dark shirt, no tie, top button undone. There's a small cut on his lip, already healing, and a faint bruise under one eye. How did he manage to get into a fight on the one day I haven't seen him, and what does the person he fought with look like? Something tells me worse than him.

He looks me up and down, and heat crawls up my spine. Not the good kind.

My father's arm tightens under my hand. "Head up."

I lift my chin, my gaze still locked with Lorenzo's as we walk. His mouth curves, lazy and lethal.

Not a smile. A promise.

My heart pounds harder with every step, and I swear my palms are sweating. The dress rustles around my legs.

We stop in front of him.

My father's fingers tense around my hand, then pry it off his arm. He turns toward Lorenzo, jaw clenched. "She's yours," he forces out.

Lorenzo's brows tic. "She's mine," he agrees softly, reaching out.

His hand closes around mine. It's warm, firm, and most importantly . . . unyielding.

A flash of memory hits me—his fingers on my skin. Touching softly. *Lovingly.*

This is none of those things.

The priest clears his throat. "We are . . . gathered here today," he begins, looking around at the five of us, "to join this man and this woman in holy matrimony."

Rafe snorts under his breath, low enough that only the three of us at the front hear.

Lorenzo's mouth twitches.

My fingers tighten in his instinctively.

"Victoria Danforth," the priest continues, clinging to the script like a lifeline, "do you take Lorenzo Amante to be your lawfully wedded husband, to have and to hold, in—"

"I do," I cut in, voice calm and flat.

The priest blinks. My mother chokes, and Rafe glances away like he's hiding a grin.

Lorenzo's eyes flash, dark amusement sparking. "Impatient, Little Bird? Can't wait to sign your soul away?"

I keep my gaze on the priest. "I'd like to be done before the Stockholm syndrome kicks in," I reply, sweet and deadly.

A huff of laughter catches in his chest. "You always were impatient."

The priest flounders for a moment, then stumbles forward. "And . . . and you, Lorenzo Amante," he tries again, "do you take Victoria Danforth to be your lawfully wedded wife, to have and to hold, in sickness and in health—"

"I do," Lorenzo answers, eyes never leaving my face. "Obviously."

The word wraps around me like a noose.

The priest's gaze flicks between us, sweaty and panicked. "Do you have vows prepared?" he asks hopefully, like maybe someone will start talking about love and save him from this nightmare.

"I think we've said enough," Lorenzo deadpans.

"Yes," I add, pressing a smile that shows too many teeth. "I wouldn't want to lie in front of a priest. Something tells me that won't help my bid to get into heaven."

My father winces.

The priest swallows hard. "Then . . . umm . . . we will proceed with the rings."

Rafe steps forward, pulling a small velvet box from his jacket with a resigned little shrug, like even he can't believe he's playing ring bearer in this particular tragedy.

He flips it open and offers it to Lorenzo.

Lorenzo takes the first band, cool metal glinting between his fingers. He grasps my hand, turning it palm down, his thumb stroking along my knuckles once in a touch that doesn't match his eyes at all.

"Look at me," he orders.

I don't want to, but I do anyway. *Show no fear.*

He slides the ring onto my finger slowly, deliberately, like he's carving his name into my bones.

"This belongs to me now," he says, voice low.

"My hand?" I whisper, throat tight.

His gaze doesn't flicker. "We both know the answer."

My lungs forget how to function for a beat.

I pick up his ring from the box. My fingers don't feel like they're attached to my body. I feel like I'm stuck in a nightmare, and I can't shake myself awake.

I grab his left hand and shove the ring down his finger with a little more force than necessary.

It still slides on smoothly.

He smirks. "Easy, Little Bird," he drawls. "I know you want to maim me, but we haven't taken pictures yet."

"I thought you said there are no pictures," I bite out.

"You're right." He smirks. "We'll have memories. Those last longer."

The priest's voice drones on. I can't even hear the words. All I hear is *husband and wife.*

That's all I need to hear for my knees to buckle. Lorenzo doesn't wait for me to right myself before he tugs me toward him, one hand clamping around my waist, the other curling possessively at the back of my neck.

His mouth crashes onto mine.

It's not gentle.

It's not tender.

It's not anything a wedding kiss is supposed to be.

He kisses me like a punishment.

He's telling me he owns me.

That I'm a possession.

He's reclaiming every breath I took without him for the past five years.

His lips move against mine, not giving me room to fake this.

Despite my internal resistance, my body betrays me, a shiver sliding down my spine, as my damn traitorous fingers curl in his jacket.

Fury mixes in my chest.

I don't want this. Then why do I feel so hot all of a sudden?

Head in the game. *Stop this insanity.* We do not enjoy kissing the enemy.

As if he can read my mind, Lorenzo deepens the kiss, and like the idiot I am, my pulse spikes.

I swear a sound slips from my mouth, and I want to die of embarrassment. Then, as if the moment can't get any worse, it does. Because he pulls back first. His lips graze the corner of my mouth. "To your cage."

Great. Just great.

My hand snaps up until my fingers grasp his lapel. "I hate you," I whisper, breath shaking as I push him away.

His eyes flare, but I know that look, and it's not shock . . .

It's satisfaction.

Asshole.

"Good," he murmurs. "You'll need the energy."

I turn my head toward the priest. Maybe it's not too late for him to step in and say this isn't right. He looks like he might faint.

He won't be helpful.

My mother wears her blank stare, and my father continues to stare straight ahead. It's like if he doesn't acknowledge this, it's not really happening.

Rafe, on the other hand, is having the time of his life. His huge grin is only cut off by his lips puckering to blow out a low whistle.

Lorenzo releases my waist but keeps hold of my hand, turning us toward the side door. "Time to go, Mrs. Amante," he says, voice smooth. "We have a long night of pretending not to kill each other ahead of us."

I lift my chin and let him lead me back toward the house, the train of my gown trailing me as I march my way to my metaphorical prison cell.

He thinks he built me a cage.

He doesn't realize I plan on testing the bars.

CHAPTER 33

Victoria

THE CAR DOOR SHUTS, AND IT FEELS LIKE THERE IS NO OXYGEN. Lorenzo slides into the seat beside me without looking at me.

He's pissed. I'm not sure what he's got to complain about since I'm the one being held hostage. But his jaw is locked so tight that it looks like it might crack.

The driver begins to drive us away from my childhood home.

I keep my hands clasped in my lap as we head to God knows where. Silence presses between us so hard I swear it would be comical if anyone else was sitting beside me.

I stare straight ahead, breathing in the floral scent of my bouquet that is still clutched in my hands. My wedding bouquet. I'm shocked I was even allowed one. This whole wedding was a sham. I should throw it out the window, or better yet, wait until we get to his house and then set it on fire.

I should shove it down his throat.

Unfortunately, that's not an option, so instead, I break before the silence does.

"So . . . this is it?" I fix my eyes on the back of the driver's seat, not wanting to look at Lorenzo. "You won. You got what you wanted."

Lorenzo's rough chuckle echoes through the space. It sounds

low and amused. "Don't be dramatic, Little Bird. If I wanted to win, I'd be happier."

His fingers start to drum against his knee. *Bored with me already?*

Too bad. I'm just getting started with my questions. "What do you want from me? Why are you doing this?"

From the corner of my eye, I can see Lorenzo turning his head in my direction, so I follow suit until our gazes lock. His eyes gleam in the dark of the limo, studying me.

"Because you left," he says.

Blunt. Cruel. Too honest. I'm shocked that he's admitting this to me.

My breath catches. "I—what? When? We were kids—"

"And I never did," he cuts in. "Not really."

My throat tightens. "That doesn't explain anything."

He leans back in his seat, expression unreadable. "Then don't ask questions you aren't ready for answers to."

"Try me."

His jaw tics once. "You wouldn't like the truth."

"Tell me anyway."

That earns a quiet laugh, dark and sharp. It sends a cold shiver down my spine.

"You think you want the truth? You think you can handle the version of me you created?"

"I didn't create anything," I snap.

He tilts his head. "Didn't you?"

The car fills again with silence. But this silence isn't empty. Nor is it peaceful. It's suffocating.

I turn toward the window, watching the world slide by in expensive blurs of light.

It feels like forever, but eventually, a new estate emerges through the trees.

It's not as large as my parents', but it's still very much

intimidating. A massive iron gate opens without the car slowing. Armed men step aside silently.

Armed men . . . what the fuck is happening?

Where is he taking me?

"Welcome home."

My stomach drops. "*You* live here?" I whisper, unable to stop myself.

Lorenzo looks out at the mansion like it's just another tool. "I own *here*."

The car glides up the circular driveway. Stone lions flank the stairs. Windows stretch wide across the facade. It looks like a palace built for a king with an anger management problem.

We pull to a stop.

I stay frozen. Lorenzo doesn't.

He opens his door and climbs out, then leans back in, eyes glinting with amusement.

"Come on." He gestures to the estate. "It's time to see your new home."

There's that word again . . . It feels like a punch to the gut.

I step out on shaking legs.

Lorenzo stands beside me, shoulders broad. He's watching me take in the estate. Is he enjoying this? It's hard to tell, but my guess is yes.

Fear curls low in my stomach, but I don't let any emotions play out over my features, even though I feel like I've been thrown into the ocean and can't swim.

His brows furrow as he studies my face. "What are you thinking?"

"That's none of your business," I fire back, and the bastard smirks.

"Everything you think is my business."

I cross my hands in front of my chest. "I'm not yours."

"You keep saying that like it matters."

"I mean it."

He steps closer; his steps are slow and deliberate.

A predator bored enough to toy with its prey.

"Lorenzo—stop."

He pauses and tilts his head. But it's his smile that shakes me to the core. He's enjoying this.

Finally, after he appraises me for a few more moments, he gestures toward the mansion doors. "Inside."

The air shifts as we walk in, and he leads me through the front hall. My breath actually leaves my body when I look around. This place is incredible. With vaulted ceilings and marble floors. It must have cost a fortune. How can he afford this?

Memories slam into me in waves of the boy Lorenzo used to be. Then the vision fades and morphs into the man Lorenzo is now.

Scary as hell.

I stop at the base of the staircase. "We're not sharing a room."

He glances down at me, one brow lifting. "Of course not."

Relief hits so fast it's dizzying.

But he steps closer again, lowering his voice. "I have no interest in forcing a woman to fuck me." His hand reaches out, pushing a piece of my hair off my face.

"You promised no touching."

"I promised no touching," he retorts. "But it's a conditional agreement."

"Conditional on what?"

"Your obedience."

I go still. "I'm not your pet."

"No," he says softly. "Pets get affection."

I want to slap him. Maybe kill him. I definitely want to run. But I'm smarter than that, so I do none of those things.

I lift my chin. "Separate bedrooms. No touching. No . . . anything."

"Anything?" he echoes, amused.

"Yes. Anything."

He studies my face a moment too long. "You're shaking."

"I'm exhausted."

"You're scared."

I glare. "Shut up."

He steps closer, lips curling. "Adorable."

Anger flares bright in my chest. "Why are you doing this to me? Why did you want to marry me?"

He leans in, mouth brushing my temple—a ghost of a touch that feels nothing like affection.

"This isn't a marriage," he whispers. "It's a reckoning."

My chest tightens. "You hate me that much?"

"Oh, Little Bird," he taunts, "you have no idea."

His fingers close lightly around my wrist, not hard, not tender, just deliberate. He guides me up the stairs and down a shadowed hallway lined with dark wood.

He stops before a door and then swings it open.

A bedroom comes into view. One with soft lighting, cream bedding, and huge windows overlooking the forest. It's beautiful. *At least it's a pretty cage.*

"This is yours," he says.

I take a shaky breath. "And yours?"

"Down the hall."

I nod slowly, tension bleeding from my shoulders. "Good."

He watches the relief wash over me, and something shifts in his expression. In the past, I would have been able to read his expressions, but I don't know this version of Lorenzo.

He steps into the room with me. "What are you doing?"

He touches the edge of the vanity, fingers brushing the wood. "Setting expectations."

I swallow. "I already told you, no touching. No closeness. No—"

"No husbandly duties?" he interrupts.

I nod.

He wets his lower lip with a quiet, humorless laugh. “Relax. For the hundredth time, I don’t want you in my bed.”

The words sting more than they should. I turn away. “Good. Great. Perfect.”

“Victoria.”

I stop, but don’t look back.

“You sleep here,” he says quietly. “You breathe here. You stay here. You belong here.”

My stomach twists. “You don’t own me.”

“I own your future,” he replies. “That’s enough.”

The words hit like ice poured down my spine. I grip the back of the chair so tightly my knuckles ache. “Get out.”

“As you wish.”

He steps past me, his shoulder brushing mine as he pauses at the doorway.

For a moment, I think he has more to say, but then I hear the door click shut.

I stand there, shaking. “I can do this.” At least we aren’t sharing a room.

But something tells me his revenge plan is only getting started.

My knees nearly give out at the thought.

Because for the first time since seeing him again . . .

I realize my life really will never be the same.

CHAPTER 34

Lorenzo

An hour has passed since I placed her in her new room and left her.

It's too quiet.

Not the usual silence that happens in the dead of night, when my men do their rounds.

No. This is different.

It's because of her.

I stand outside her bedroom door with a glass of whiskey in one hand and my phone in the other, staring at the carved wood, waiting for an invitation.

It will never happen. Not that I would want her. She's not here for that. She's here for my amusement, for her to be as miserable as I've been.

It also helps that I got to fuck over her parents. Those bastards treated my mother and me like shit.

Ever since she died, I've wanted revenge. While they might not have killed her, I still blamed them. This plan killed two birds with one stone.

I continue to watch and listen for anything coming from her room.

My wife.

The word tastes good and wrong and addictive.

I take a slow drink, the burn settling low in my chest, when my phone buzzes.

Matteo.

Perfect.

The last person I want to speak to right now. I'm not sure what my plan is, but keeping a bride locked up in my house won't go over well with him, so for now, I have no plan.

I slide my thumb across the screen. "If you're calling to discuss your feelings." I lean against the wall with a lazy slouch, "please lose my number."

"Where the hell are you?" Matteo asks, the sound of engine noise behind him. "I've been at the estate waiting for you for thirty minutes."

"Well . . ." I examine my reflection in the whiskey glass. "That sounds like a *you* problem."

"You sound drunk, which I obviously don't care about, but you said you'd meet me. My father wants you here now. He's losing his mind."

"Uncle losing his mind is not breaking news." I laugh. "That's a typical Tuesday."

"Lorenzo. Just come."

I sigh dramatically, pushing off the wall. "Fine. I'm out running an errand. I'll be there in twenty."

"What errand?" he asks.

I smirk. "The kind you don't get to ask about," I say in a mocking tone, so he thinks I'm joking. Hopefully, he doesn't call my bluff.

Matteo sighs. "Just get here."

"I'm touched by your concern," I respond before hanging up.

I finish my whiskey and glance at her door.

I should feel powerful. Victorious. She's in my bed, wearing my ring, tethered to my world whether she wants it or not.

Instead, something sharp sits in the center of my ribs.

I shove it down and walk to the landing where two of my hired private guards stand watch. They straighten the second they see me, hands clasped behind their backs.

"She stays put," I adjust my cuffs as if that's the most natural command in the world. "She doesn't step outside this hall. If she does, you call me. If someone comes to the property, you call me. If she sneezes suspiciously, you call me."

One nods. "Yes, sir. Understood."

"Good." I head toward the stairs. "Because she's the one thing in this house more dangerous than me."

Their eyes widen, but neither asks for clarification.

Smart men.

I head outside and approach my car, sliding into the driver's seat. Then I'm peeling down the long driveway.

My estate sits in the middle of nowhere. It's private and fortified like a fortress.

I bought it the second I turned twenty-one. My salary wasn't enough to afford this beast of a house.

Neither was saving every penny.

Nope, it was the inheritance I received from my father's passing, with interest, that sealed the deal. Because, as it so happened, when I turned twenty-one, my uncle told me about the money he had put aside for me, my father's portion of the family business.

I drive fast, one hand on the wheel, jaw tight. The road lines blur beneath my headlights. My brain is a fucking mess.

I shouldn't have married her because every time I look at her, the eighteen-year-old version of me—the boy I killed to survive—tries to claw his way out of the grave.

And I don't have space for him.

Not anymore.

It's not long before the Amante estate comes into view.

Iron gates open by the time I reach them, and guards nod me through.

I pull into the courtyard, step out of the car, and straighten my jacket before striding toward the entrance.

Inside, Matteo waits beside the staircase, arms crossed. His dark hair is a mess from running his hands through it. "You certainly took your time."

I make a show of looking at my watch. "It took me less than an hour to get here."

"Where have you been the past few days?"

"I was busy," I reply.

"With what?"

"Not killing someone," I say, shrugging. "Barely managed."

"Great," Matteo sighs, rubbing his temples. "Just what the family needs. A Lorenzo mid-spiral moment."

"You love my spirals." I grin, but it's empty.

He snorts. "Let's get this over with."

We walk down the hall to my uncle's office. Two guards open the doors the moment they see us.

My uncle stands behind his desk. He's a large and scary man, despite being in his fifties.

He doesn't smile. "Lorenzo." He extends a hand. "Good. You're here."

I shake it, my expression neutral. "I was told it was urgent."

"It is." He gestures toward a map laid out across the table. "Someone is making a move against us."

"Yes, Father." Matteo steps forward. "We already confirmed the skimming—"

"This is more than skimming," my uncle interrupts, slamming his palm on the map. "One of our warehouses was hit. Cash went missing. Product, too."

"What kind of product?" I ask even though I'm pretty sure I already know.

"The kind we don't discuss outside these walls," he snaps.

Rafe stands in the corner with his arms crossed and a hard face. He meets my eyes with a slight nod.

My uncle points at the map again. "This is coordinated.

Someone wants a piece of our territory. Someone young. Reckless. Hungry."

"So we kill them." I shrug.

My uncle's gaze sharpens. "That's what I need you for."

Silence settles.

Matteo turns toward me, brows lifting. "He wants you to run point."

"I want you and Rafe," my uncle clarifies, stepping around the desk. His hand lands on my shoulder, heavy and with purpose. "You have an instinct for threats. You see war coming before the rest of us."

He squeezes once.

"Your father would be proud."

It lands like a punch.

My throat tightens for half a second before I crush the feeling beneath my heel. My father wouldn't be proud. I don't remember him, but I know what he stood for, and my father would kill me if he knew what I did tonight.

Because his son just married a woman he abducted through paperwork. And if my uncle finds out? He'll kill me himself.

Matteo bumps my arm lightly with his elbow. "You good?"

"Peachy." I step back so my uncle's hand falls. "We'll handle it."

"I know you will," my uncle says, returning to his chair. "Find out who's coming for us, Lorenzo. And end them."

A simple order.

A deadly one.

And exactly what I need right now.

I nod once, the predator in me waking. "As you wish."

My uncle studies me carefully, almost too carefully. "You've been . . . distracted lately, nephew."

I school my expression into bored annoyance. "I've been busy."

"With what?"

I smile. "Errands."

He doesn't push. Matteo doesn't question.

Good.

The fewer people who know where I go at night, the fewer who know who shares my last name now, which means there is a chance this secret will remain safe.

"I'll give you updates," I tell my uncle, turning toward the exit.

Matteo taps my shoulder as I'm leaving. "Hey, listen, whatever it is, you can tell me."

"I'm fine."

He nods once. "Don't disappear again. My father gets twitchy."

"You're the emotional support son," I remind him, smirking. "Not me."

"Yeah, well, I can only do so much. Your brooding brings balance."

"Glad to be of service."

He stops me just before I reach the door. "Lorenzo."

I turn.

"You sure you're okay?" he asks quietly, eyes searching my face with that too-perceptive Amante intuition.

For a second, I almost answer. I almost tell him the truth: that I forced Victoria to marry me. That she's technically a prisoner.

My prisoner.

Instead, I grin. "I'm always okay."

Matteo might not believe me, but he respects me enough not to ask.

I walk out before he can press.

Outside, the night feels heavier. The weight of the lie sits between my shoulders like an invisible blade. I slide into my car and check my phone automatically.

A camera feed shows Victoria still asleep. Silk sheets are tangled around her body. She tosses and turns, a hand reaching out frantically. It's like she's fighting demons in her dreams.

Probably me.

Good.

She should fear me. She should hate me, and hopefully, that will keep her exactly where I put her.

Because if she runs, if she leaves me again—

This time, I won't survive it.

I start the car, the engine rumbling like a threat, and pull out of the estate.

War is coming. I can feel it.

And I'll burn down all of Boston before I let anyone take another thing from me.

Especially her.

Even if she never wanted to be mine.

CHAPTER 35

Victoria

I WAKE UP WITH A START.

It feels like I'm choking.

My eyes blink against the bright sunlight streaking across my room, and apparently my face.

Wait. Something feels wrong . . .

Where the hell am I?

My brain scrambles to place the room: the towering ceilings, the carved moldings, the unfamiliar silk sheets tangled around my legs.

Then it hits me like a fist to the sternum.

The wedding.

I close my lids, my hands lifting to my eyes, and I rub frantically. This has to be a dream. Scratch that, I mean nightmare.

But with my lids shut, an image plays out in my mind of Lorenzo's mouth on mine.

My lungs seize. I sit up so fast the room tilts.

I'm married to a man who hates me.

Great. Just fucking great.

The man looks at me like he wants to kill me. Seeing as he works for the Mafia, something tells me it would be an easy task for him.

I slide out of the bed, my legs shaky. Thinking of my death is not how I want to spend my day. I need to come up with a plan and start.

The cold floor shocks me as I make my way across the room to grab clothes.

Last night it was fully stocked with things for me to wear, so this is a good place to start.

I yank open the wardrobe and grab the first thing I see—a soft gray sweater, fitted black pants, and flats.

Easy, neutral, *forgettable.*

Maybe if I stay far away from him, he'll forget that I exist, and maybe hell would have to freeze over for that to happen.

Then something else captures my gaze.

A pebble.

It looks just like the ones he used to leave for me, but he wouldn't do that now, right?

My hand reaches out and my fingers touches it.

No. It's just a coincidence.

With a shake of my head, I step back and get to work of getting dressed. I have no time for the past.

Once I'm fully dressed, I brush my hair until it looks like it belongs to someone whose life hasn't imploded. But the moment I step into the hallway, the panic returns. It creeps up my spine.

Even though I saw the place last night, I'm not prepared for what I'm seeing in the fresh light of the day.

This mansion is enormous.

Gorgeous too.

I walk past room after room, each one somehow colder than the last.

A formal sitting room full of furniture no one will ever sit on. A music room with an untouched grand piano. A sunroom drowning in light, and a library with shelves that stretch so high that I'm happy a ladder hangs from one of the shelves.

Every door that I've opened is another reminder that this is now my life.

I try to breathe. *I really do.*

But then I push open the next door, and my blood freezes.

What is this place?

I squint my eyes, taking in what I'm seeing and trying to understand it all at the same time.

Floor-to-ceiling TV monitors line the walls, all buzzing with live feeds. The estate gates. The perimeter. The hallways I just walked down. The bedroom I slept in.

This is a security room.

What the hell?

Who needs a security room?

The nephew of a Mafia boss, apparently.

Two armed guards sit at a long desk, eyes flicking between screens, hands near their comms.

Watching everything.

Including me?

I step back, heart hammering so loudly I hear it in my teeth.

And then a breath grazes my neck, and before I can see who's there, a hand wraps slowly around my waist.

And I know.

I jolt so hard I hit his chest.

"What are you looking for, Little Bird?"

I don't need to turn around to know Lorenzo stands behind me, towering over me. I still do, though.

He's still in a crisp black shirt rolled up at the forearms. His eyes drag down me, slow and assessing, like he's deciding what to do with me.

A smirk twists his mouth, lazy and lethal.

Shit.

I don't like that look.

It's sex. Pure and simple.

Or I should say *sinful.*

I don't answer his question because I can't. My tongue feels like it's made of sandpaper.

He brushes my hair off my shoulder. His touch is gentle, but for some reason, his soft touch feels crueler than if he grabbed me. Lorenzo guides me out of the room with one hand pressed to the small of my back. Possessive. Cold.

When he closes the door behind us, the guards don't even look our way. They don't need to.

Everyone here already knows who owns me.

We head down a wide hallway toward the dining room, and the whole time, he never moves his hand. It's pressed hard enough that it feels like a brand.

"Relax." His tone drips with a mock concern that makes my skin crawl. "You look like you're walking to your execution."

"That's certainly how it feels," I answer quickly, trying to sound sharper than I feel.

He huffs a dark laugh. "If I wanted to kill you, Little Bird, I'd do it somewhere prettier."

"Comforting," I mutter.

He pushes open the dining room door. A long table sits in the center, set with white china and silver cutlery. An obscene amount of elegance for two people who could barely stand to breathe the same air last night.

He gestures to a chair. "Sit."

I don't want to, but I do.

He sits across from me, lounging back like this is a casual brunch and not the breakfast from hell.

A server enters, places a plate of food in front of each of us, and vanishes like a ghost.

Lorenzo picks up his fork and spins it in his hand with a bored flick. "Let's talk rules."

My stomach tightens. "Rules?"

He gives me a slow, almost amused look. "You didn't think marriage came without terms, did you?"

I glare at him, refusing to let him see how much my hand shakes when I lift my water glass.

"What do you expect me to do?" I ask, voice tight. "You blew up my life. My job. My future. What now? Am I supposed to sit around like some . . . decorative hostage?"

He leans in slightly, shadows slicing across his cheekbones. "You hated working for your father."

My throat closes. "That doesn't mean I wanted you to take that from me."

His mouth curves in a slow, vicious smile. "I didn't take anything you weren't already desperate to escape."

"That's not true."

"It is." He taps the table once with two fingers. "But don't worry. You won't be working anymore."

My spine snaps straight. "Excuse me?"

"You heard me." He cuts into his food with surgical precision. "You don't need a job."

"I need a life," I fire back.

"You have one," he says with a shrug that's pure sin. "This one."

"So my only job is to be a prisoner?"

"You're my wife."

"That's not better."

"It wasn't meant to be."

The air goes razor-sharp between us.

His eyes drop to my untouched plate, then back to me. "Eat."

"I'm not hungry."

"You haven't eaten since yesterday."

"I'll eat when I'm not nauseous with dread."

He chuckles, low and dark. "Your stomach will adjust."

I want to throw the plate at his head.

Instead, I fold my hands in my lap and glare at him, my jaw aching from how hard I'm clenching it.

"What am I supposed to do all day," I ask, "if I'm not allowed to work, leave, or function as a human being?"

He lifts his glass of coffee and takes a slow sip. "Take up a hobby."

I laugh once, sharp and humorless. "A hobby?"

"Knitting, perhaps," he deadpans. "Or gardening. Or pottery. Something domestic? Maybe something . . . soothing."

"You're insane."

He shrugs. "Occupational hazard."

"Be serious."

"I am." His gaze pins me. "If you need inspiration . . . maybe read."

"Read what?"

He cocks his head, pretending to think. "Oh, I don't know. Maybe finish *Wuthering Heights*."

My mouth goes dry.

His smirk widens. "See how it turned out for Cathy."

I shove my chair back so hard that when it skids across the floor, the legs screech against polished wood.

Lorenzo watches me stand, completely unfazed or bothered.

It's infuriating.

"You're a monster," I whisper.

His smile turns soft, and now I'm scared. I riled the beast. He's like a wolf lowering its head before the kill. "Maybe. But you aren't much better."

I shake my head, confused.

"You still haven't taken responsibility for what I've become."

The room feels too hot. I reach the door before I realize my hands are trembling. As I grab the handle, his voice slides across the room.

"Breakfast is at eight every morning. Try not to be late tomorrow."

I don't look back.

Not because I'm strong.

But because I'm terrified of what I'll see if I do.

CHAPTER 36

Lorenzo

Victoria's footsteps echo down the hall. Her retreat should make me happy, but instead, the farther she gets, the more it pisses me off. Every click of her shoes feels like I'm being stabbed.

When she turns the corner and disappears out of sight, I want to demand that she comes back. But something tells me that even if I ordered her to return, she'd tell me to fuck off.

It's a bit of a turn-on if I'm being honest.

Her defiance.

Her strength.

It makes my dick hard.

As I stand there, staring at the empty doorway like she might walk back in, I have to adjust myself.

She doesn't.

Obviously.

I drag a hand over my jaw and laugh.

"I'm pathetic."

Thank fuck, no one is here to hear me.

It's the one benefit of having an estate no one even knows about. Well, my armed guards are here, but none of them answer me or acknowledge if they even heard me. Having them here is necessary because I'm not allowed to have weaknesses. Not when my uncle is the one wearing the crown, and he would murder me if he knew what I have hidden here—namely, Victoria.

The hard part is keeping Matteo out of the loop. Matteo is a brother to me, but I just can't risk it.

Fuck. Even thinking of lying to him makes me want to murder someone.

Speaking of killing someone, I need a distraction, and that would be the perfect one.

Something that bleeds or screams or begs for mercy. Preferably, all three will help my mood.

I pull out my phone and dial Rafe.

He answers on the second ring with a groan. "What now?"

"You find the rat yet?" I cut in.

Rafe exhales hard, like he's debating whether he should hang up on me or keep talking. "Good morning to you, too."

"I don't do mornings." I pace toward the balcony doors. "I do results."

A sigh hisses across the line. "We have a lead."

"Is he breathing?"

"For now—"

"Bring him to the warehouse." My teeth grind around the words. "Whole body. I need him to talk. I'm not in the mood for bullshit today."

"Rough time with the missus?"

I ignore his question. "Bring him."

"I know you want him breathing, but do you want him conscious?"

"That's how interrogations usually work," I snap. "Unless you know something I don't about corpses. If so, call the Vatican."

"I'll bring him."

"Good." I hang up without another word.

I don't say goodbye. That's for people who aren't planning to beat answers out of someone before lunch.

I slip a gun into my waistband and head down the staircase toward my garage.

If I stay in this house another second, I'll lose the last shred of control I pretend to have.

Time to hurt someone.

The warehouse, as usual, smells like death.

Which is perfect for what I have in mind.

The guy Rafe dragged in sits zip-tied to a steel chair in the center of the concrete floor. He's already breathing like he ran here. Chest jerking and throat working overtime.

His eyes flick from me to the door, like he's trying to find an escape route in my face.

Spoiler: there isn't one.

His lip is split, and one eye is swollen shut.

The sight soothes me more than the best drugs could.

Rafe stands off to the side, arms crossed, expression carefully blank. If he looks too amused, it encourages me. *It encourages me anyway.*

I circle the rat slowly, boots echoing across the concrete, and then I trail a finger along the back of his chair.

I like toying with my prey.

"You know," I muse, voice almost light, "I actually woke up today in a bad mood."

Rafe makes a sound that might be a laugh.

The guy in front of me, however, stares at me with his one good eye, like I'm speaking another language.

"Long night," I continue, letting my smile sharpen. "No sleep. Lots of . . . personal problems." My gaze drifts over his trembling hands. "And then I found out you existed."

His breath catches.

"And suddenly, I felt happy. Soon, I got this itch."

"What kind?" Rafe asks, rubbing his jaw comically. He's clearly enjoying this.

"The urge to pull someone's spine out of their throat type of itch."

Rafe's mouth twitches. "Is that even possible?"

"Not sure, but I'd like to find out," I say pleasantly, then crouch in front of my prisoner so he can see exactly how calm I am. "And you? You're the perfect specimen."

"I didn't do anything," he stammers. "I swear, I wasn't—I didn't—"

"Please," I interrupt, tone dripping with fake sympathy. "Don't lie. I'm already traumatized enough for the week."

His throat bobs. His one eye shines wet.

Good. Fear is motivation.

I tilt my head like I'm considering him as a concept. "Let's not beat around the bush. Tell me what I want to know."

"N-no—"

"Don't insult me," I snap, tapping his cheek—lightly, almost affectionately, the way you'd pat a child before you punish them. "I'm already in therapy." I lean closer, voice dropping. "It's going terribly."

"You're not in therapy," Rafe retorts.

"Exactly," I reply without looking at him. "Imagine how much worse it could get."

I turn back to the moron in front of me, a smile returning. "You going to talk?"

He clamps his jaw shut.

Ah. A bold stance.

I stand and drag the chair backward across the floor. The legs screech like tortured violin strings. He winces at the sound, like it hurts more than the bruises.

"You know," I continue conversationally, "the last guy who fucked with me had the courtesy to confess to all sins right away." I pause, considering. "Saved everyone a lot of time."

Silence.

I sigh like I'm inconvenienced. "Fine. Have it your way."

Rafe steps forward and slides a folding blade into my hand like he's passing a pen to sign paperwork. The man knows my moods.

I flip it open, admiring the glint under the fluorescent lights. "Last chance. Who are you working for?"

The rat's voice cracks. "If I talk, they'll kill me."

I grin, bright and terrible. "Then we have something in common."

His eyes widen.

I drag the blade lightly along the collar of his shirt—not cutting, just enough to make him feel the difference between mercy and choice.

"We can do this easily," I offer, almost kindly, "or we can do this creatively."

He stays silent.

Creativity, it is.

I drag the chair sideways until he's under the harshest spotlight. His sweat glistens.

My pulse slows in that familiar, pleasurable way. Violence is the only thing in the world that can calm my rage, and today I'm raging.

"Talk," I whisper.

He trembles.

My blade taps his cheek. "Talk."

Nothing.

I drive the knife into his upper arm, taking careful measures not to hit any major arteries. A tortured scream escapes his mouth as he jerks so hard the chair skids.

"You know what I hate?" I ask, standing tall and spreading my hands like I'm hosting a seminar. "Wasted potential." My gaze drops to him. "And wasted time."

Rafe shifts, gaze scanning the door out of habit. "We can do this without killing him."

I blink slowly. "That's adorable."

The rat makes a choking sound, yet he still doesn't talk. I turn to Rafe behind me and reach out my hand.

Rafe is already smiling and prepared as he hands me a set of pliers.

Returning my attention to my guest, I grab his hand and rip off one of his nails. "Last chance," I say again, voice soft now. "Who? Or do I need to rip off each one . . ."

After a long, ragged pause, he croaks, "It wasn't supposed to go this far."

My brows lift. "Oh? So there is a 'far.'" I lean in, voice velvet over steel. "Keep going."

"I-I can't."

I bring my mouth close to his ear, the words sliding in like poison. "You will."

He opens his mouth—finally about to do something intelligent—

And passes out.

I stare at his limp body.

"Unbelievable," I mutter. "I only stabbed him once. What the fuck."

Rafe shrugs. "He's breathing at least. Better luck next time?"

"But you know how much I hate waiting."

Rafe gestures toward a bucket of water sitting nearby. He came prepared for my personality. "You want us to wake him?"

"No," I decide, straightening and rolling my shoulders. "Not yet." I flick a look at the rat. "Let him dream. Maybe his subconscious is braver than he is."

Rafe's eyes narrow. "There's more . . ."

I glance over.

He steps closer, voice dropping into business—into war. "The skimming wasn't isolated. Money's being funneled offshore. Multiple accounts. Layers and proxies."

"Someone's making a play." The familiar edge of war sharpens inside me, bright and clean. Better than lust. Better than regret.

Rafe nods once. "Someone with reach."

I smile slowly. "Good. I've been bored."

Two men drag the unconscious idiot away, boots scraping, chains clinking.

I stand alone for a moment, breathing in the cold warehouse air, letting the violence settle under my skin like ink.

And because life enjoys humiliating me, Victoria's face flashes behind my eyes anyway.

Her voice. Her rage.

I shove it down viciously.

Not now.

War first.

I need my uncle on my side and busy; that way he won't interfere with my marital bliss. Solid plan. Hopefully, we can find out who put the scumbag up to stealing from us.

I walk toward the steel exit door, my boots echoing like a countdown to someone's funeral.

"Find me names," I warn, not looking back. "Not theories. Names."

"You'll get them," Rafe replies.

"Good. Because I'm in the mood to kill someone."

And God help whoever it ends up being.

CHAPTER 37

Victoria

DINNER FEELS LIKE A HOSTAGE NEGOTIATION.

I'm currently sitting across from him, which isn't saying much, because this room certainly isn't intimate.

It's huge.

This place doesn't fit the man I know . . . knew.

I don't know him now.

The table is long enough to seat a small nation, and Lorenzo, like the asshole he is, sits at the head like he was born into royalty.

And now that I know that his uncle runs the Amante crime family . . . I guess he is.

Despite everything, the man is gorgeous. He looks like he's carved from stone. With broad shoulders and a squared jaw, it's unfair he's this handsome. Don't even get me started on his deep brown eyes.

It should be criminal how much, even after all these years, I'm still attracted to him. And of course, I'm stuck sitting across from him.

Front row to my own personal nightmare.

There's no one else here but us. It's odd. Why does he pick to eat here if the rest of the spots are empty?

As if he can hear my inner thoughts, Rafe steps into the room.

Good. At least with him here, I won't have to make small talk with Lorenzo.

He leans against the doorway, deciding whether he's going to come sit or just stare. His gaze flicks over me.

Come on . . . join us.

Please.

"What are you waiting for? Sit or leave," Lorenzo barks out, and if I could, I'd throw my fork and stab him with it.

Rafe, on the other hand, doesn't seem put off by Lorenzo's attitude and chuckles.

"Wasn't sure if you lovebirds wanted company."

"We do." The words slip out of my mouth before I can stop them, and Rafe can't help but smirk.

"That's what I thought," he adds, before strolling toward the spot next to Lorenzo and then plopping down into the chair.

A member of the staff glides in, eyes down, hands steady, and sets a plate in front of me. I want to tell the young woman, I'm not like Lorenzo. She can make eye contact, and I won't bite, but she's already turned her back to me.

I can't even identify what's being served, but man, it smells good. My stomach growls. My lack of food today is now showing its face. In my defense, I couldn't eat.

One: I didn't want to bump into Lorenzo.

Two: Actually, it was just number one. I didn't want to see him. Even now, I don't want. But I wasn't given a choice.

The air in this room feels heavy, and an awkward silence fills the space.

Lorenzo lifts his glass first. "To new beginnings." He swirls the wine.

Rafe clears his throat and raises his own glass. "To . . . health."

Why didn't he mention me? Or our marriage? And then I remember what he said at my parents' house . . .

The marriage is a secret.

Maybe it has to do with Lorenzo's uncle, the man who sits on the family throne . . . Maybe if he found out, he would kill me? Shit. Is that it?

Maybe he sees marriage to me as a liability, a weakness.

Which means for the time being, or maybe forever, I'll be the sin Lorenzo committed in secret.

I don't toast back. I stare at my plate and then stab a piece of lettuce.

Lorenzo watches me, like he always does.

The silence stretches for so long that it starts to feel intentional.

The bastard is waiting for me to break first.

I try to refuse on principle, but eventually I crack.

"Is dinner always like this?" I scrap the edge of my plate with my fork.

"Like what?" Rafe leans forward, clearly excited for whatever answer I'm about to give.

"A riveting bundle of joy."

Lorenzo tilts his head. "Careful, Little Bird." His voice is as smooth as silk. "You keep talking like that, and I'll start thinking you missed me."

"Yeah. No. Can't say that I'd ever miss this version of you . . . You know the version who probably carves people up in his spare time."

His mouth curves, and while he might look handsome, the smile is also lethal. "You always had a talent for melodrama."

I lean forward just slightly because if I sit back, I'll look smaller, and I refuse to be small in front of him. "And you always had a talent for pretending you aren't the problem."

Rafe shifts, flicking his gaze between us like he's watching a tennis match.

Lorenzo sets his glass down with a soft clink. The sound is delicate, the threat beneath it is not.

"Look at you"—he folds his hands like a man about to sign paperwork—"trying so hard to pretend you're not terrified."

"I'm not terrified."

Lie.

Huge lie.

Enormous lie.

He nods toward my hands without moving anything but his eyes. "Then why are you gripping your fork like you plan to stab me with it?"

"Cause I do."

Rafe actually snorts.

Lorenzo's brow lifts, amused. "Don't stop on my behalf."

"Please stab him," Rafe adds.

"Ugh. You're so annoying." I glare across the table, then look at Rafe next. "You too."

"What did I do?" Rafe asks, shaking his head. "I think I miss when you were single," Rafe says to Lorenzo.

Lorenzo doesn't even look at him.

I push food around my plate, refusing to give him the satisfaction of me eating. After a second, I realize that's exactly what he wants, and that doesn't sit well with me. There's no way that he deserves the satisfaction of my not eating. Eventually, I compromise by taking one bite.

Lorenzo eats with a maddening calmness. Every movement is controlled. He looks like he's about to perform surgery. If he's going to be so miserable in my company, why doesn't he invite someone more entertaining over?

Halfway through the meal, the truth lands in me.

He can't.

This dinner isn't small because he wants romance. He kept it small because secrecy is survival.

The whole secret marriage thing.

I'm going to need to figure out why. Maybe I can use it to my advantage. Knowledge is power, after all.

After a few more minutes, Lorenzo finally stands.

My spine goes stiff when he moves closer to me, and I'm practically shaking when he steps behind my chair.

Lorenzo lowers his mouth to my ear. "I like the act. But both of us know none of it's true."

I have no idea what he's talking about, and I open my mouth to speak, but he cuts me off before I can.

"Meet me in ten minutes in my study," he says to Rafe, who nods, and then Rafe stands up from his chair and heads out of the room.

The door closes behind him, leaving Lorenzo and me alone.

"Come on. Let's go."

He leads me to his study, which is dimly lit but warm. It has mahogany shelves and leather chairs that look comfy. It smells like whiskey and Lorenzo.

I hate that I like the smell.

He shuts the doors with a soft click, and the sound seals me inside with him.

"That went well," he drawls, drifting toward his desk all while my hands shake.

"Define well." I cross my arms so he can't see my pulse jumping in my throat.

He glances at me over his shoulder, a lazy smile on his face. "You didn't try to run. I consider that growth."

"I'm not running," I grind out. "I'm enduring."

His laugh is dark, low, delighted. "You always were stubborn."

"You always were unbearable."

"How sweet," he coos, turning fully now. "You're being nostalgic."

I clench my fists. "What do you want?"

He picks up a velvet box from his desk and approaches slowly. "A gift."

"I don't want anything from you."

"You're getting it anyway." He flips open the lid. A necklace sits nestled in black velvet. Diamonds.

Intricate and dazzling.

But I know what this is . . . while it might look like jewelry, it's nothing more than a shackle.

"A wedding gift." He lifts it delicately between his fingers.

"A nice gift would be an annulment," I fire back.

"That would be a gift for you," he counters. "This is for me."

I take a step back. "I said no."

He takes a step forward. "I didn't ask."

His hand goes to the back of my neck, and he draws me close, the clasp clicking into place like a lock.

The metal is cold against my skin, and a shiver runs down my back.

It's from the necklace . . .

Oh, who am I kidding? It's from him.

His breath drags along my shoulder blade as he leans in. "Now," he whispers, thumb brushing the frantic beat in my throat, "you'll remember what you are. Mine."

My whole body goes rigid.

I shove his hand away and lift my chin in defiance. "You don't own me."

His smile sharpens. "I bought your silence. Your family's stability. Your future." He tilts his head, eyes cutting. "Call it whatever you must."

"You're disgusting."

"And you're glowing in diamonds. My diamonds." His low timbre makes my knees wobble. "I'd say the arrangement is working."

"I hate you."

He shrugs, the movement casual, almost bored. "Hatred looks good on you."

I want to rip the necklace off and throw it in his face.

Instead, I walk out without another word, because if I open my mouth again, I'll either scream or cry, and I refuse to give him either as a gift.

I can feel his gaze between my shoulder blades as I go, like a blade sliding down my spine.

The necklace digs into my skin like a chain.

Once I'm back in the hallway, I yank it off with both hands, the clasp snapping open with a tiny, violent pop.

I stare at the diamonds in my palm.

I should smash it.

Throw it out the window.

Drop it down a drain.

Instead . . .

I head to my room, and when inside, I open the nightstand drawer, dropping it inside. Then slam the drawer shut so hard the wood rattles.

What the hell am I going to do?

I sit on the edge of the bed, shaking, angry, and most of all, humiliated. I'm sick of the fact that my heart is doing something it has no right to do.

He married me to ruin me.

And somewhere deep inside my ribs . . . in the place I swore was dead . . . my heart aches in a way I hate.

Not because I miss him.

Because I miss the version of him I loved so much, it almost killed me.

I bury my face in my hands, breath cracking against my palms.

The marriage may be a cage.

But the worst part?

Some broken part of me still remembers how it felt to love him.

And that part hurts most of all.

CHAPTER 38

Lorenzo

THE REPORT HITS MY DESK.

When I look up, I see it's Rafe who dropped the folder in front of me. His jaw is tight, and his eyes are darker than usual.

I'm not going to like whatever is inside.

"Start talking," I spin my pen between my fingers while I stare at the closed file.

Rafe drags a hand over his face and leans on the edge of the desk. "You remember how you asked me to find out who our little accounting genius was working for?"

"I remember asking for a head in a bag," I correct, letting my mouth twitch. "But sure, let's go with what you're saying instead."

He exhales through his nose. "We've been hearing rumblings. A new outfit is moving through the East Coast. Young guys. They're trying to make a name for themselves."

"Great," I snort. "Adorable. Do they have a mission statement?"

"There's chatter they're tied to a Boston family, and that there is someone who knows our inside workings," Rafe continues, ignoring me. "Nothing fully confirmed yet, but all of what I'm hearing makes sense."

I flip the file open with my thumb. Photos, reports, transaction logs.

My pen stills. "Which one?" My voice drops.

Rafe jerks his chin toward the photo. "Southside. We found the place hit last night. Doors blown. Our guys knocked out cold, but alive."

"And the product?"

He hesitates.

I look up slowly. "Rafe."

He grimaces. "Gone. Every brick. Cleaned out."

A laugh slips out before I can stop it. It's not a nice sound.

"So," I say, closing the file with a soft thud, "not only are they stealing from our books, they're now hitting our warehouses and walking out with our product."

Rafe straightens. "We're treating it as an act of war."

"Oh, it's worse than war." I stand and then button my jacket. "It's disrespect. I need to tell my uncle."

Rafe's gaze sharpens. "You want to pay our guest another visit first?"

I smile, all teeth. "He and I do have some unfinished quality time scheduled."

I step away from the desk, feeling the old, familiar heat of violence rise.

This is going to be fun. Last time, I had nothing to lead with. Now I do . . .

I jerk my chin toward the door. "Let's go see if our friend has found a sense of self-preservation yet."

Rafe falls into step beside me as we head down the hall.

"Just a reminder," he mumbles, half under his breath, "you told Vin you'd try not to kill him before he talks."

"I recall making no such promise," I answer, amused. "But I'll do my best. Think of this as . . . anger management."

"You should try yoga," Rafe grunts.

"I prefer hobbies that make my blood pressure rise."

Together, we head to my car and leave for the warehouse.

When we arrive thirty minutes later, we step out of the car and walk toward the building.

We push through the metal door, and the moment we do, the air changes to that familiar cocktail of concrete and blood.

In the back room, our little problem is still zip-tied to a chair. He looks like shit with a swollen eye and split lip. The arm of his shirt is still red with the blood from my stabbing.

I'm surprised he hasn't died yet, but alas . . . soon.

He blinks when he sees me, then swallows. He knows his days are numbered.

"Look who's awake," I croon, strolling in. "I was starting to worry you'd sleep through all the fun."

His breathing picks up. Good. I enjoy his panic. It brings me joy.

Rafe takes up a position against the wall, arms crossed, watching like a man at the movies.

I circle the chair once, slow, boots echoing on the concrete. The man's shoulders tense with every step I take behind him.

"Bad news," I say lightly. "The situation has escalated."

His body trembles. "I told you everything I know."

"You told me nothing," I correct, stopping in front of him. "You passed out, which is frankly rude when someone is taking such an interest in you."

This time, he flinches.

I tilt my head, studying his face. "See, I was willing to believe you were just an idiot with a death wish. But it turns out you're part of something bigger."

He shakes his head, breathing rough. "I don't know what you're talking about."

I glance at Rafe. "You hear that? He doesn't know."

Rafe lifts a shoulder. "Maybe he suffers from memory loss. Get a concussion recently?"

I plant my hands on the back of the chair and lean forward.

"One of our warehouses was hit," I tell him. "Product stolen. The funny thing is that it happened at the same time, you've been skimming from our accounts. That doesn't seem like a coincidence, does it?"

He squeezes his eyes shut. "I'm just middle. I swear. I'm nobody."

"Then give me somebody," I reply, fingers digging just a little into the chair. "Give me a name and walk out of here with all your limbs intact."

He licks his lips. "They'll kill me."

"They," I echo. "There is a 'they.' Progress."

"I can't," he whispers.

I straighten, sighing dramatically. "I always appreciate when people make bad choices. It keeps my hobbies funded."

I nod at Vin, who's standing by a workbench.

Vin moves forward and drops a small bag of tools on the floor beside me. The clatter makes the man jolt so hard he nearly tips the chair.

He stares at the bag like it's a live grenade.

"Relax," I say, crouching to unzip it. "I'm not going to do anything too terrible. Yet." I glance up at him. "I mean, relatively speaking. It'll be horrible for you, obviously. Perspective is everything."

I pull out a length of rubber hose and slap it lightly against my palm, considering.

Rafe groans quietly. "Not the hose."

"You have a better idea?" I lift a brow.

"Not really." He shrugs.

"You're no help." I step around the chair, and the guy tries to twist away, like there's anywhere to go.

"Okay. Let's try this again." I swirl the hose. "Who are you working for?"

He clamps his jaw shut.

Disappointing.

And also, very predictable.

Boring . . .

The first strike lands across his thighs, jarring his whole body with a crack that bounces off the concrete. He cries out, more from shock than pain.

That swing was mild at best.

A warning of sorts.

The next time, he won't be as lucky.

I wait a beat for him to speak, but he doesn't.

This will be fun.

The second blow catches his upper arm. He sucks in a sharp breath, biting down hard, eyes bright with panic.

I'm careful where I aim and how hard I hit. I want pain, not unconsciousness. I want fear, but I also want him awake enough to regret every decision that led him to this chair.

After a few more strikes, his breathing turns ragged. Sweat runs down his forehead as his arms strain against the zip ties.

It's cute that he thinks he can escape.

"See . . ." I step in front of him again, still calm. "This can stop any time. You aren't built for this. You fold. It's who you are. So how about you be useful?"

He wheezes. "You're insane."

"Objectively," I agree. "And you still decided to test me. Whose fault is that?"

His head drops down, and I know I've got him. I lift my arm, more for show but just high enough to scare him.

"Fine. Stop. There's a new crew," he rasps finally, words scraped raw out of his throat.

"I know that," I say. "Try not to bore me."

"They wanted access," he coughs. "Said if I skimmed a little, covered some shipments, they'd cut me in. Said Antonio Amante was . . . comfortable. Told me you were his nephew, and that you were lazy. That you wouldn't notice."

I smile slowly. "People say the wildest things when they've never met me."

"They paid me well," he rushes. "Said they had backing, that no one would dare—"

"Who?" My patience snaps, the word cracking like a whip. "Which crew?"

He sucks in a breath like it's acid.

"This is where lying would be a very exciting choice for you," I say. "I'd love to see how far you think you can push my mood today."

"They're . . . they're connected to Boston," he chokes out. "At least that's what I heard. A young guy. Trying to prove himself. Said his uncle runs half the port. He handles the rest."

Boston. We already knew this. I need more before I can bring this to my uncle.

I take a breath, roll my shoulders, and let that settle into place.

"Name," I say.

He shakes his head frantically. "If I say it, I'm dead."

"If you don't say it," I counter, voice very soft, "you're dead now. I'm offering you the possibility of later."

His eyes flutter shut. His chest heaves.

"Connor," he whispers. "Connor Gallagher."

I stare at him.

Rafe goes still by the wall.

"Gallagher," I repeat, voice flat. "As in—"

"His uncle," the man blurts, panic tipping him into honesty. "Declan. The old man runs the Boston family. Connor's his nephew. New school. Wants expansion. Wanted to . . . wanted to prove he could cut into Amante's business without . . . without anyone—said he has someone who knows Amante business."

He trails off under the weight of my stare.

"Who does he have that knows my family's business?" I narrow my eyes. This is information I need to know.

His shoulders start to shake. "I don't know. I swear."

"What do you know?" I hit him again.

"Only what I was told," he cries out.

"And that is?"

"They said to hit the warehouse you ran for your uncle, that you were distracted and busy with other problems. Said it was the perfect time to test your borders."

Rafe growls, "Stupid fucking bastards."

I toss the hose back into the bag and grip the edge of the chair, leaning down until I'm eye level with the rat.

"So let me get this straight . . ." I grab a knife from the table. "A kid in Boston wants to impress his uncle. He skims our money through you, hits our warehouse, steals our product, and thinks he can spread rumors that I'm too distracted to notice." I stab his thigh, all while smiling. "Do I look distracted?"

The man shakes his head so fast he looks dizzy. "I didn't hit the warehouse. I didn't touch your men. I just—"

I tap the knife against his cheek, silencing him. "Sadly for you, I don't grade on a curve."

"Please," he croaks. "I told you what you wanted."

"If this is genuinely all you know," I cut in, "then you aren't very useful, are you?"

I straighten, rolling the tension out of my neck.

Rafe watches me carefully. "What do you want to do with him?"

I consider the man. He's shaking so hard the chair vibrates.

"There's a certain mercy," I say, "in making sure he doesn't end up back with the Gallaghers."

His eyes go impossibly wider. "No—please—"

I look at Rafe. "Get whatever else you can out of him. Cross-check what he said. If it all lines up . . ." I glance back at him. "Make it quick. He did talk, after all, so no reason to torture him . . . too much."

Relief and terror cross his face in the same breath.

Rafe nods once. "You got it."

I step away, dropping the knife on the table before wiping my hands on my jeans.

As I reach the door to leave, the man croaks, "You're going after them."

I pause, looking back. "What do you think?" I ask.

His throat works. "They're not ready for you."

I grin, dark and sharp. "No one ever is."

I step into the hall with Rafe right behind me.

He stays quiet until we clear the threshold into the main warehouse. "You want to loop Matteo in?"

The question hits like a warning shot.

Matteo's my brother in everything but blood. My closest thing to a conscience. Also, and most importantly, the son of the man who would put a bullet in my skull if he ever learned what secrets I'm keeping.

"No," I say flatly. "He'll want to question him, and I'm not sure what this idiot knows. He said he knows I'm distracted . . ."

"That could mean anything."

"It could also mean they know everything." I don't say anything about Victoria, but by the way Rafe's eyes narrow just slightly, he understands what I mean.

"Then we keep it clean," he says.

"We kill him fast," I correct, stepping toward the light spilling from the open door.

Rafe huffs a laugh. "Want to handle Boston on our own? Quietly."

"Yeah, I'll tell my uncle I want to spread my wings and handle this. Then we're going to fuck shit up."

Rafe snorts. "You planning to kill them all?"

I slide my sunglasses on and smile. "Not all at once," I answer. "I'm not greedy."

Rafe turns to walk in the opposite direction to start making calls.

"Rafe?"

"Yeah?"

"Get me everything on the Gallaghers," I order. "Ports, fronts, lieutenants, accountants, girlfriends, enemies. Including when they shit and what type of toilet paper is used."

Rafe's smirk turns wicked. "This should be fun."

I open the steel door to leave. "Everything."

A few moments later, I'm in my car, hands on the wheel.

Connor Gallagher wants to be a problem.

I know exactly how to solve problems.

Permanently.

CHAPTER 39

Victoria

I FIND THE ASSHOLE IN THE FOYER, PUTTING ON A BLACK JACKET. Guess he's going somewhere today . . . again.

It's not that I want to be near him, but I don't like being alone.

At least when he's here, my brain is busy thinking of ways to murder him. If he's gone, I'm just bored.

Lorenzo doesn't notice me at first, or more likely, he does, but chooses to ignore me.

Asshole.

"Where are you going?" The question comes out ruder than I intend because apparently, my self-preservation has left the building.

He is still mid-button. Slowly, he turns his head.

Lorenzo's gaze slides over me. It moves from my head to my feet, then trails back up. It feels like he's cataloging me, for what? I don't know . . . maybe to measure my casket?

"Business."

Wow. He's a man of many words.

"That's not an answer."

"That's all you get." His mouth twitches.

I step closer, because standing back feels like surrender. "I'm your wife. I think that earns me more than a single syllable."

He walks past me. "If you were looking for transparency, Little Bird, you married the wrong man."

"I didn't choose anything," I hiss. His brows lift, but he doesn't respond. "And what am I supposed to do while you're gone?" I follow him to the door, anger filling my body.

He pauses with his hand on the handle, then looks over his shoulder like he's considering whether to toss me a bone. "Stay put and behave."

"Behave?" The word comes out bitter. "I'm not a pet."

"No . . ." His lip tips up. "Pets are wanted."

The sentence shouldn't hurt. It does anyway. It hits some old bruise I didn't know was still there.

He turns back to the door, and I feel like I've been punched.

"Don't test the perimeter. My guards won't take it well."

"Are you serious?" I demand.

He opens the door, and the morning light slices across the foyer, bright and stupidly cheerful. It doesn't belong in this house, especially right now. "Deadly."

Then he's gone.

A heavy final thud echoes through the cavernous space. The silence that follows feels eery.

Like if I step out of line . . . Well, I don't want to think about what that means. His warning hangs in the air, heavy and suffocating.

My teeth grind and my heart pounds. I want to throw something . . . something expensive. Instead, I take one long breath. Then I turn and walk straight toward the nearest exit.

Because if Lorenzo Amante wants obedience, he should have married someone else.

I push open the back entrance and step outside. It's chilly today. I probably shouldn't be out here without a jacket, but I can't find it in me to care. Because for one perfect second, the world feels normal. Like I'm just a normal woman stepping outside to breathe in the fall air.

Then all my illusions are smashed to the ground when two guards step into my path.

And by step, I mean materialize from the shadows.

"Mrs. Amante." One of them dips his chin, voice low, polite, empty.

The title makes my stomach clench.

"I'm going for a walk." I keep my tone light.

"No." The answer comes clean and immediate.

The second guard folds his arms. "You were instructed to remain indoors."

I blink at him. "You can't be serious."

"We are." No apology. No smiles. Just an order, and a hidden threat beneath it.

A laugh bubbles out of me. "So that's it? I'm trapped in my own home?"

The first guard's eyes meet mine. "This isn't your *home*."

"I'm allowed outside." I lift my chin. "I'm not trying to escape."

"You're not allowed outside *alone*."

"Oh my god." I drag a hand down my face. "If I bring a chaperone and a permission slip—"

"Mrs. Amante." The second guard straightens. "Please return inside. Don't make this difficult."

I stare at them. I can push . . .

I can even scream.

Hell, the world is my oyster with the shit show I can create, but instead, I turn sharply and walk back inside, fury coiling in my spine.

Fine, I won't go outside, but I'll find freedom somewhere else, and I know exactly the spot . . .

The library feels like stepping into a different century. Floor-to-ceiling shelves stuffed with leather-bound books. Tall arched windows spilling gold light across the floor.

I trail my fingers along the spines, letting the texture ground me. Nothing beats this feeling.

My gaze skates over the titles, and I'm not surprised that half the collection is violent in some way. *The Art of War*, *The Iliad*, *War and Peace*. I mean, what did I expect from Lorenzo's library? Jane Austen?

I pull out a volume at random.

The Count of Monte Cristo

Of course.

I shove it back like it burned me and keep wandering. Toward the back wall, behind a half-open cabinet, something catches my eye.

A frame.

Face down.

Which, in Lorenzo's world, might as well be a neon sign that says don't touch.

My fingers slide it out gently anyway because being told no has never been my kink.

I flip it over—

And forget how to breathe.

It's him.

Young him.

Maybe sixteen. Maybe seventeen. Wild hair. A grin that's reckless and real.

He's standing in front of a rusted chain-link fence, shoulders relaxed, eyes soft. Looking at this makes my throat tighten painfully. Because I knew that boy.

And that boy didn't survive.

My thumb drifts along the edge of the frame, slow and stupidly tender. He doesn't smile like this anymore. He barely smiles at all unless it's sharp enough to cut someone. *This is the way he used to smile at me.*

He used to be human.

I swallow hard and set the frame down with careful precision, like if I handle it wrong, I'll shatter something inside me.

My eyes fill with tears, and I know I'm close to breaking. I need to get out of here, to go home . . . because the guard is right, this place isn't my home. It's not his either. It's a museum of what he became. And now it's supposed to be my cage.

Fantastic.

I start to walk back out of the room to find somewhere else to hide away with my depressed thoughts.

A corner desk sits beneath the windows, and while that's not anything special, what's sitting on top of it is.

A phone.

Perfect.

Ever since Lorenzo took my phone away after the wedding, I've missed having a line of communication to the world.

I'm not a big texter, and social media is not my thing, but I like having it. But I guess in Lorenzo's mind, prisoners don't get to make calls after all.

I grab the receiver and dial my parents.

"This number is temporarily unavailable."

I frown and dial again. Same response. I try my mother's direct line. My father's office. The estate. Every number, and every time I dial, I get the same thing . . . Nothing.

Just that same calm, automated voice, saying, "This number is temporarily unavailable."

"Seriously? They can't all be unavailable."

A throat clears behind me.

I jump and spin, heart slamming like it's trying to break out.

A man stands in the doorway. He's in his mid-thirties, tall, dark hair trimmed neat to his face, tattoos crawling down both arms. He's handsome, but not like Lorenzo. *Lorenzo is something else entirely.*

"Sorry." He lifts his hands slightly, palms open. "Didn't mean to scare you."

"You didn't," I lie automatically.

His gaze flicks to the receiver still clutched in my hand. "Lines are blocked."

My throat tightens. “Blocked?”

He nods once, like this is normal. “Boss’s orders.”

The word boss lands heavy. Lorenzo might work for his uncle, but this scary man works for Lorenzo . . .

I steady my breathing. “So I’m cut off from the world.”

He shrugs, a small movement that reads like resignation. “That’s one way to phrase it.”

“And your way would be . . .?”

“Safe.” He says it like a rehearsed line. Then his expression shifts. “I’m Nico.”

He steps forward a half pace, then hesitates. What is he doing? Then his hand reaches into his jacket, and my whole body tenses. This is when it happens . . . I’m going to die. Lorenzo told him to kill me if I try anything.

But instead of a gun, I’m met with a small phone. I’ve seen enough movies to know it’s a burner. He holds it out discreetly, palm flat, like he’s offering contraband in church.

I stare at it like it might explode. “Why are you helping me?”

Nico’s jaw flexes, eyes flicking toward the hall. “Because everybody needs someone. Even in situations like yours.”

He doesn’t say prisoner. There’s no need to.

“I’m not—” My voice catches on the lie before it can form.

Nico tilts his head slightly. “Aren’t you?”

My stomach drops.

“Use it when you need it.” His voice lowers. “Not now. Cameras don’t cover the west hall bathroom. Bad wiring. Use that spot.”

My pulse spikes. “If Lorenzo finds out—”

“He won’t.” Nico’s mouth tightens. “And if he does, you didn’t get it from me.”

He steps back into the hall, already retreating like he knows staying longer makes him a target.

At the doorway, he pauses, eyes on mine. “Mrs. Amante.”

The title again—soft, cautious.

Then he's gone.

I stand frozen with the burner in my hand, feeling the weight of it like a weapon I don't know how to use.

A lifeline.

A trap.

A test.

I slip it into my pocket and force my legs to move, carrying myself upstairs like I'm not trembling under my skin.

My room is too big, too perfect, too wrong. Sunlight spills across the bedspread. Everything looks peaceful, but it's a lie.

Nothing about this place is a paradise.

Blocked phone lines. Stopped at the doors. Eyes everywhere.

I don't care what anyone says . . . this is my cage. Like my nickname, *Little Bird*.

The funny thing is that he thinks he can control me.

That he can keep the world from me.

But he doesn't get to keep me from myself. I straighten slowly, making my spine harden.

He wants me contained.

He wants me compliant.

He wants me broken.

"No," I whisper.

If Lorenzo Amante thinks he can trap me in this house, choke off my world, and call it protection—

He's forgotten who he married.

I'm not eighteen anymore.

I'm not fragile.

I'm not blindly in love with him.

And I will not break the way he wants me to.

Not now.

Not ever.

Let him wage his war.

I'll quietly start mine.

CHAPTER 40

Lorenzo

STEEL SCREECHES AGAINST STONE.

The knife doesn't need sharpening, but it always relaxes me to do it. Something about the sound scrapes my brain and halts all my thoughts.

I love it.

Rafe stands across the table, arms folded, watching the blade. Vin's to my left, flipping through a folder thick enough to qualify as a novel.

"Again, from the top." I drag the knife along the whetstone.

Vin taps the photo clipped to the front page. "We still can't get a location on the nephew. Connor Gallagher stays hidden behind other idiots." He flips the page with a crisp snap. "But we have a friend."

"Everyone does." I test the edge with my thumb. Sharp. Already was. "Who's his?"

"Patrick Murphy." Vin slides the photo to the center of the table. "Mid-level out of Southie. Bookies. Small-time loan sharking. He's been taking bigger risks for the past six months. Lines up with when the money went missing on our end."

Rafe leans forward, squinting at the picture. "He looks like a douche."

Vin doesn't even blink. "Murphy's our bridge. He's handling

local recruitment for Connor's expansion. He's the one funneling the skimming. Launders through three bars and an import business."

I pick up the photo and study Murphy's face. Average. Forgettable.

"What about routes?" I ask. "How are they moving what they stole from us?"

Vin flips to a rough map, finger stabbing inked lines. "Two corridors. One: Providence, reroute near the docks. Two: private trucks, fed into legitimate shipments that end up through Boston Harbor."

"Any overlap with our people?" I ask.

"Not direct," Vin answers, jaw tightening. "They're avoiding our main lines like they know them."

My knife pauses mid-stroke.

"Someone is feeding them our secrets," I growl. "Fantastic. They have someone on the inside."

Rafe drags a chair out with his boot and drops into it. "Yeah. This isn't some kid screwing around with a side hustle. This feels very coordinated. We need to find the rat."

"Agree. But in the meantime, let's concentrate on closing ranks, so no information slips through the cracks, and then find the nephew. He's going to get reckless. He's trying to prove he's a man." I set the blade flat on the stone.

Vin flips another page. "Murphy likes to go to a bar on the edge of Dorchester. The Rusted Crown. Maybe we can find him there."

A faint smile tugs at my mouth. "While that would be fun a bar might be too public for my needs."

My phone buzzes on the table, and I glance down. UNKNOWN CALLER.

Rafe's eyes narrow. "You expecting anyone?"

I shake my head, then hit the button to answer. "Speak."

"Lorenzo." The familiar angry voice says my name like he's already planning my death. "Where are you?"

Shit. My spine goes subtly rigid.

"Running an errand," I answer, trying to say as little as possible.

There's a beat of silence.

"Get to the estate," he says, and the line clicks dead.

I stare at my phone, trying to decipher whether I'll make it home for dinner tonight.

Rafe watches me carefully. "Boss calling?"

I roll my shoulders. "Yep," I answer. "He wants me at his estate."

Vin closes the folder slowly. "Now?"

"He didn't send me a calendar invitation, so yes."

I pull out my phone and open my security app. Rafe's gaze flicks to my hand, trying to see. Image after image pops up on my cell's screen.

All of my house.

The camera shifts. Hallway. Guards. Door.

Victoria's door.

Still closed. Still guarded.

Good.

Only Rafe and the household staff know what's behind that door. Because if my uncle finds out I dragged this girl into my life—

He wouldn't understand.

I push away from the table and stand. "I'm going to see him."

Rafe lifts a brow. "Want backup?"

I snort. "He's my uncle, not a rival crew. If he wants me dead, backup just means more bodies."

Vin's mouth twitches. "We'll keep digging."

"You'll do more than dig." I grab my jacket. "I want a full map of Murphy's life. What he drinks, where he sleeps, who he talks to."

I slide the knife into its sheath with a quiet click. "And I want you to find the rat in our house. We need to shut that shit down now."

Rafe stands, following me so that no one can hear him. "And what about your wife?"

I stop at the door, keys in hand, and glance back at the app on my phone. Victoria's door again.

"She stays asleep," I say flatly, like it's an order to myself as much as anyone else. "She doesn't leave the property. She doesn't touch the perimeter. If she asks questions . . ." I pause, then add, "Be polite while you lie."

Rafe's expression doesn't change, but his tone turns a fraction softer. "Got it."

"Good." I smile, but there is no warmth. Rafe might be a friend, but if he fucks me on this, his blood will spill. "Because if she slips past you, it won't matter that my uncle will kill me. I'll kill you first."

Rafe snorts. "Yeah. Knowing you, you'll come back as a ghost to finish the job."

"Exactly."

I leave the warehouse, get into my car, and drive.

Once I pull through and stop by the entrance, a guard opens my door before I can touch the handle.

"Mr. Amante," he greets, eyes forward, no emotions.

I nod before heading up the stairs and walk inside.

A few seconds later, I'm in the main room, and my uncle sits with two capos, a glass of something dark in his hand. He looks the same as always: calm but brutal.

He's the kind of man who never raises his voice because he doesn't need to.

"Lorenzo." His gaze pins me. "Sit."

I sit—not out of obedience, but because of respect. He took me in and taught me how to be a man.

Also, I might not remember my father, so in truth, he's the only father I know.

One of his men, Tony, slides a file to me. "Another hit on one of our warehouses."

I flip it open, eyes scanning.

"I'll handle it," I respond simply. "Rafe and I got it. We can run point."

"Good." His mouth tilts, not quite a smile. "I know I've already told you this, but your father would've been proud."

A muscle jumps in my jaw as the words land like a fist to my ribs. If he knew what I did, what I'm hiding in my house—

He wouldn't be proud. No, the only emotions I'd get are fury.

And fury from a man like him, or in this case, a man like my uncle, wouldn't end in lectures.

It would end in a funeral.

Mine.

I lean back, feigning ease, making sarcasm do the work guilt tries to do. "Anything else?"

"I'm proud of you too," he says evenly.

I nod once, the motion tight.

Meeting done. Orders given. I walk out feeling like a liar, but at least I walk out . . .

On the drive back, the image of Victoria's door won't leave me.

She's asleep.

My stomach twists.

I'm a scumbag.

Why? Because I'm lying to the one man whose approval I still crave, and if that wasn't bad enough, I'm hiding a marriage and have forced a woman into my life.

When I get back to my property, I don't go inside right away. I stand on the front steps, breathing in the air.

Then I look at the security feed again because apparently, I'm obsessed. Still closed. Good. I drag a hand over my face.

I'm pathetic.

CHAPTER 41

Victoria

I KNOW HE'S HOME BEFORE ANYONE SAYS A WORD.

The door to my room is closed, but even tucked away, I can hear the voices from down below.

For as large a house as this is, it's odd how voices travel.

Right now, I can clearly hear footsteps from downstairs.

Next is a car door slamming.

My nervous system fires into overdrive because I know it's him.

I move to my door and place my ear against the wood. I can hear the low murmur of male voices in the foyer.

Slowly, I open my door. Not dramatically. A small crack, just enough to try to hear.

Unfortunately, my plan sucks, and I can't hear anything.

Before I know what I'm doing, I'm out of my room and on the second-floor landing.

I grip the banister, pulse jumping like I'm about to have a heart attack.

You are not going to hide on the stairwell like some pathetic woman. You are his wife, not his prisoner.

Actually, you're both.

And you're also his secret wife, let's not forget that.

I roll my shoulders back, exhale once, and start down the staircase. Lorenzo steps into the foyer as I reach the bottom.

He looks exhausted, wrecked. He also happens to look devastatingly handsome and deadly. His dark shirt is rumpled, and the sleeves are shoved up. His gorgeous tattoos are on full display.

A part of me wants to ask him to remove his shirt so I can see just how far they go, but I bite back that desire. Nothing good will come from lusting after my asshole of a husband.

My gaze drops down, and I see his knuckles are scraped.

There's also a faint smear of something red on his collar.

Dirt.

I'm sure it's just dirt.

Red dirt . . .

Sure.

I don't know any idiot who would believe that.

With a shake of my head, I lift my gaze. Lorenzo's hair is a mess. It looks like he's raked his fingers through it in an angry rage.

I need to pull my gaze away because looking at him does crazy things to my belly.

Two guards hover near the doorway, speaking in low voices. The moment they see me, their words die in their throats.

Cowards.

Lorenzo's gaze finds me. It drags over me slowly, from the bare soles of my feet, up my leggings, to the oversized sweater slipping off one shoulder.

His mouth curves. "Look at this," he drawls, dropping his keys into a dish on the console. "My dear wife coming down to greet me."

"You should've stayed gone," I shoot back, stepping off the last stair. "Maybe the world would be a better place."

His eyes glitter, amused. "Missing me already?"

"Yes, like I miss food poisoning." I plant myself at the edge of the foyer. "We need to talk."

"Do we?" His voice stays lazy, but the tension in his shoulders tells a different story. He shrugs out of his jacket with the smoothness of a man who knows exactly how he looks when he moves. “I had such a nice drive imagining silence when I got home.”

“You blocked every phone,” I snap, ignoring the bait. “Your men won’t let me outside. I can’t step onto the grass without two human brick walls materializing out of nowhere like I’m a criminal. You cut me off from everyone.”

He drapes the jacket over the stair rail. “You make it sound dramatic.”

“It is dramatic,” I fire back, stepping closer. “You’ve turned my life into a hostage situation.”

His nostrils flare like my choice of words amuses him. “Your life’s been a hostage situation since you were born into that family. I just . . . relocated the leverage.”

“I’m what now?” I demand. “A pet you keep on a leash. A trophy you hide in a box?”

“Trophies get displayed.” He looks me up and down. “You’re on lockdown.”

“Why?” My voice rises despite myself. “Who am I going to run to? You’ve destroyed everything.”

“Exactly,” he replies as calmly as a man discussing the weather. “Which makes containment efficient.”

My jaw tightens so hard it aches. “You can’t just cut me off from my parents. From my friends. From my job—”

He barks a humorless laugh, and it ricochets off the marble like a gunshot disguised as amusement. “Your job? The one you hate. Your parents? You hate them too. And don’t say friends . . . We both know you don’t have any. I did you a favor.”

“You don’t get to decide what’s good for me.” Heat climbs my throat, turning my words sharp. “You don’t get to put guards on me like I’m a thing you’re afraid of misplacing.”

“I am afraid of misplacing you.” His eyes narrow. “I worked very hard to acquire you.”

Acquire.

The word makes my skin crawl. It also makes my stomach drop.

I take another step toward him, anger buzzing like a live wire. “You’re isolating me.”

“I’m protecting what I own,” he corrects, head tilting. “Two different words. Same result.”

“Seriously?”

He shrugs. “You married into my world.”

“I. Didn’t. Have. A. Choice. Or did you forget?”

“What was your other option? Your father was one deal away from selling you to the Jameson spawn.”

The memory of Grant Jameson’s dead eyes flickers through me. Lorenzo was not wrong. I’d managed to push back the relationship as far as I could, but it was only a matter of time.

“Don’t,” I grit out. “Don’t act like you’re some upgrade. You broke into my life like a wrecking ball, and now you’re standing in the rubble like you own the land.”

“I do own it,” he replies, completely unbothered. “Metaphorically. Legally. Financially.” His eyes flick to mine. “Emotionally, we can debate.”

Something in me snaps so loud I’m surprised no one hears it.

I shove him. Two hands flat against his chest, pushing hard.

He rocks back half a step, more surprised than moved.

He’s solid as stone.

Was he always this strong?

His brows lift like I’ve offered him a gift. Then slow amusement unfurls across his face.

“Well.” He glances down at my hands. “Look at you. Violence. I’m touched.”

“Don’t you dare laugh at me,” I spit, yanking my hands away. “You don’t get to joke.”

He chuckles low, and the sound curls around my spine. “You’re adorable when you think you have options.”

I shove him again. Harder. He lets me this time. Moves with it.

He's acting like I'm a child throwing a tantrum, and he's humoring me so I can tire myself out. The humiliation burns hot behind my eyes.

"Stop that," I snarl.

"Stop what?" He spreads his arms, smirking. "Letting you touch me?"

"Stop acting like this is funny," I fire back. "Like my life is some game you're playing to entertain yourself."

His gaze sharpens. Slowly, he steps into my space, crowding me backward. I stumble, my back hitting the wall. He plants one hand beside my head, close enough to trap me without actually touching me.

Then the other hand comes up to cage me in.

My heart beats so fast I think I might pass out.

We're close. Too close. His breath brushes my cheek. It feels warm, but it also feels like it's edged with something darker underneath.

His eyes are fixed on mine, unblinking.

"Funny"—he leans in a fraction—"is not the word I'd use for you."

My fingers curl against my side.

I should be terrified.

I am terrified.

But that's not the only thing cracking under my skin, and I hate myself for it.

My pulse is hammering everywhere: my throat, chest, low in my stomach. The air between us hums, charged, like the second before lightning strikes.

"Let me go," I whisper, hating how thin it sounds. "You're crowding me."

"I'm barely touching you." His eyes dip to my mouth and back up. "If you think this is crowded, you're out of practice."

Heat floods my cheeks. Anger. Shame. And shit . . . something else. Something worse.

"Move," I rasp.

"Or what?" His voice drops into a low rumble. "You'll shove me again? Scratch me this time? Maybe you'll scream? Do you want me to make you scream?" The innuendo isn't lost on me.

My lips part, and a thousand memories slam into me like waves.

The boathouse.

His hands on me.

The way he used to kiss me.

I hate my body for remembering, but I hate it more for wanting it. *Wanting him.*

Please don't notice . . . but of course, I'm not that lucky because I know without any measure of doubt he notices. Of course he does.

His gaze flicks down for the barest second, taking in my flushed cheeks, the way my breathing isn't steady, and the way my throat bobs when I swallow.

His smile comes slow.

It's dark and knowing.

"Careful, Little Bird. You're looking at me like you did before you realized I was bad for you."

"You were always bad for me," I whisper.

"Yet," he hums, leaning closer, "here we are. Again. You pinned between me and a wall. History has a sick sense of humor."

I can't think. His presence fills the space, thick and suffocating.

Addictive.

He's always been my weakness.

Time hasn't changed anything.

He might be bigger now and more dangerous than the boy I knew, but he still has the same eyes.

The same mouth.

The same scent.

"Why are you doing this?" I breathe, but his expression doesn't change.

"Because you left," he answers, steady and lethal. "And I never did."

His words don't make sense. He did leave . . .

"What?" My voice cracks.

He watches my face. "You took the easy exit. Schools. College. All those pretty opportunities your last name buys." His mouth twitches. "Meanwhile, I was left behind."

"I didn't know," I choke out. "I asked. They told me you were gone—"

"They told you what they needed you to believe," he responds.

Pain lances through my chest. "I tried—"

"Stop." His eyes narrow. "You didn't do anything. You left. Plain and simple."

"I-I was trapped," I whisper.

"And now you're shocked you ended up in another locked room?" His voice is soft, but I know the truth. It's deadly. *He's deadly*. "At least this one is free of your parents."

Anger flares inside me. "And this is your payback. Great. You wreck my family's world, drag me into your house, because you want to watch me suffer."

His mouth curves. "You make it sound romantic."

"I hate you," I spit.

"I know." He watches me, studies really, then a smirk. "But you're also doing an awful job of hiding what else you feel."

I stiffen.

"Don't," I whisper because I don't know what I'm asking him not to do—touch me, look at me.

His voice dips, quiet and cruel. "Don't confuse my restraint with weakness."

My breath catches.

"If I wanted to take what I want," he continues, eyes locked on mine, "I would."

My spine chills.

Then I force my chin up anyway because fear is not obedience, and I refuse to let him mistake it for surrender.

"Don't confuse my fear with obedience." I swallow hard.

His hand lifts slowly, like he's going to touch my face, and my skin tingles in anticipation and horror.

Just when I think he will, he stops himself.

Footsteps pass down the hall.

"Car's still outside. Vin's waiting on a callback." Rafe's voice drifts around us.

Lorenzo doesn't look away from me as he answers, voice flat. "Tell him to keep waiting."

Rafe keeps moving without pausing.

Once the hall goes quiet again, Lorenzo steps back.

"Go to bed," he orders, voice rougher now. "Find a hobby. Read something depressing. Don't test the guards."

"Or what?" I can't stop pushing, and apparently, fear makes me reckless. "You'll lock me in a tower? Take away my books? Chain me to the bed?"

"Careful," he says. "Keep talking like that, and you'll confuse us both."

Heat flashes through me, mortifying and hot.

Luckily, he turns before he notices. I'm sure he would torture me with the fact that I'm clearly not myself right now.

"I have work to do," he throws over his shoulder as he walks toward his study. "Try not to break anything while I'm gone." Then he disappears.

I stay pressed to the wall for a long moment, lungs trying to remember how to work.

My hands are shaking. My heart is racing. I'm furious.

But most of all . . . I'm turned on.

I drag a hand down my face, cursing him silently. Cursing myself harder.

"Fantastic." I push away from the wall. "Welcome to hell, Victoria. Population: you and your terrible taste in men."

I stalk back up the stairs toward my room, each step a fight between my brain and my body.

He wants me contained.

He wants me quiet.

I slip into my room, shut the door, and lean against it, chest heaving.

That's when I see it . . .

From across the space it sits on the dresser, taunting me . . .

A tiny pebble.

I stalk over, grab it and throw his damn rock across the room.

He thinks this cage will break me.

He thinks time and silence and locked doors will wear me down.

Maybe it would've years ago.

But not now. Not after everything.

Not after him.

CHAPTER 42

Victoria

As my bare feet hit the marble, I spot one of Lorenzo's men standing at the end of the corridor. For the past week, ever since our showdown in the foyer, I've had a constant shadow.

He's not blocking anything, and surprisingly, he's not standing in a way that signifies that he'll be a threat. He's just . . . there. Hands loose at his sides, his weight balanced on the balls of his feet.

He's trying to blend.

He doesn't.

I have no desire to speak to him.

Maybe he won't look at me. As if he hears my thoughts, his eyes flick to mine, then away.

Good, we have one professional, not an asshole, in this place. He reminds me of the guards at Buckingham Palace.

I stop, eyes narrowing.

"Do you ever blink?" I adjust my grip on the book. "Or is that part of the training?"

His shoulders tense. Just a fraction.

"Mrs. Amante." His voice is steady, respectful. "You should head back to your room."

I tilt my head. "That sounded rehearsed."

"It's an instruction."

"From him," I say. Not a question.

A pause.

"Yes."

I take a step closer. Not invading his space, just enough to exist inside his peripheral vision. I smell soap and coffee.

"You're very quiet. Does that come naturally, or did someone break you in properly?"

His jaw tightens. "Please don't."

That's when I know. Not from the words. From the fact that he doesn't look at me when he says them.

"Don't what?" I ask, softer now.

He exhales through his nose. "Don't make this difficult."

I smile.

"Oh," I say. "I'm excellent at difficult."

A sound echoes behind us. Boots. Slow and measured. *Shit.*

I'm not sure how it's possible, but the air feels like it shifts.

I don't have to turn to know who's there.

Lorenzo's presence fills the space like gravity, bending everything toward him whether it wants to or not.

"Victoria."

My name lands low. I haven't seen him yet today, and somehow my very existence has already irritated him.

I glance over my shoulder.

He stands at the far end of the hall, dark shirt open at the collar, sleeves shoved up like he's been scrubbing something off his hands.

His gaze cuts to the man beside me first, then back to me.

It's sharp and makes a shiver run down my spine. "Go upstairs, Little Bird."

That damn name again. All those years ago, it was endearing, but now, in my current predicament, it feels like a chain tethered to me, reminding me I can't escape.

I look back at the guard and then at Lorenzo. "No."

The word is quiet, but it's clear enough to show him I won't back down.

His jaw tightens. "That wasn't an invitation."

I step closer to the guard instead, close enough that I can see the pulse jumping at the poor guy's throat.

"Hi, Nico." I smile at him.

There is no question that I'm playing with fire. But sometimes it's fun to get burned.

The guard's eyes narrow. "Mrs. Amante."

"It's good seeing you again," I say, and behind me, Lorenzo exhales. It's slow and drawn out, and I can tell right away he's pissed.

Good. I hope I piss you the fuck off.

"That's enough."

I pivot my body so I'm staring at him now, book still tucked against my side. "I'm just talking."

Lorenzo takes one step forward, moving closer to me like a panther stalking its prey.

"You're not subtle," Lorenzo grits out through clenched teeth.

My lips spread into a smirk. "I'm not trying to be."

Another step. "Upstairs. Now."

I glance at Nico again. Smile faintly. "Thank you for keeping me safe."

His throat works, and his shoulders are noticeably stiff.

I turn and walk away before either of them can stop me. I don't rush. And I don't look back.

I slip into the sitting room and close the door, not fully, just enough to dull the sound without killing it. I lean my shoulder against the frame. And wait . . .

Silence.

Then I hear him, Lorenzo's voice, closer now. "What do you think you're doing?"

"Standing my post," Nico answers carefully.

"You call that standing your post?" he asks. "You let my wife step into your space."

"She initiated conversation."

"I have cameras."

A beat.

"And I have expectations."

Another pause.

"If you so much as look at her like she's an option," Lorenzo continues, "I'll make sure you don't look at anything ever again."

My stomach tightens.

"Understood."

"And Nico?"

"Yes," he answers.

"She touched you because she wanted me to see."

Silence stretches, and I swear I'm crawling out of my skin to see what happens next. I'm scared for the poor guy. I shouldn't have poked the beast. Now Nico's blood will be on my hands.

"That makes her clever," Lorenzo adds. "And makes you disposable if you help her."

Footsteps. *Please don't come here.*

The door opens.

I straighten.

Lorenzo steps into the room, closing the door behind him with controlled force. His eyes snap to mine immediately.

"What are you doing?"

"Relaxing." I shrug.

"Stop."

"No."

We stand there, facing off across a few feet of polished wood.

"You don't get to threaten people because I speak to them," I say.

His mouth curves slightly. "I don't threaten. I clarify."

"You clarified very loudly."

Now a full-fledged smirk greets me. "Only for you."

I step closer. "You're jealous."

The grin drops from his face. "I don't get jealous," he scoffs.

I cock a brow. “You threatened to blind someone.”

“Efficient communication.” Lorenzo shrugs.

I shake my head. “I don’t understand this obsession.”

Something flickers in his expression. Not anger. Exposure. “You think you were temporary,” he says quietly. “One summer . . .” I don’t move. “You weren’t. You were never the middle. You were it.”

The words settle heavily in my chest. “That’s not love,” I whisper.

“No,” he agrees. “It’s worse.”

Silence hums between us, tight and volatile. I’m not sure what he will do. Maybe step closer, or perhaps that’s just wishful thinking from a place deep inside me. Instead, he steps back.

“Go upstairs,” he says. “And stop flirting with my men.”

“Or what?”

His eyes darken. “Or I’ll stop pretending I have restraint.”

He turns and walks away, and I stay where I am, heart pounding, breath shallow.

Because I didn’t flirt for attention, I flirted to test a theory, and now I know . . .

He can cage my body. Control the house. Hell, he can even threaten my world.

But he can’t control what he wants.

And what he wants is me.

CHAPTER 43

Lorenzo

I'm spiraling. As much as I'd like to pretend I'm not, I'm about to murder every person in this fucking mansion because they breathed the same air in as Victoria. If that doesn't mean I've lost my mind, I don't know what does.

I don't bother announcing my departure and don't even look back. I don't trust myself not to take out my gun and start shooting.

The front door slams behind me with a crash. A guard standing outside by the front door flinches. Good. If they're startled, they're paying attention. If they're paying attention, they're not letting anyone in.

I stride down the steps, my fingers already curling into fists.

Once outside, the night air hits me in the face, calming me for exactly half a second before my damn phone buzzes.

I grab it out of my pocket and check the message.

Still nothing from Boston. Of course.

I slide into the car and slam the door. Tonight, I'm not driving, so instead, I bark directions to my driver. A second later, tires peel out of the drive, gravel spitting behind us.

I press my thumb against my jaw, hard enough to hurt.

She did that on purpose.

Not the flirting. That was amateur hour. The timing. The look she gave me was not coy, not innocent, not even defiant. It was curious.

She was testing how close her fingers could get to the metaphorical blade without getting cut.

I should have shut it down. If I were smarter, I would have ordered her upstairs and locked the door myself. Instead, I threatened my own man and let her see it.

Stupid.

I roll my neck once, twice. "Fucking hell."

Twenty minutes later, the warehouse comes into view. The car barely stops before I'm out, my boots hitting pavement hard enough to echo.

The sooner I get in there, the sooner I can get back to making sure Victoria is keeping out of trouble.

I hate that every thought leads to her.

Maybe I didn't think this plan through properly.

With a shake of my head, I stride inside. Rafe looks up from a table scattered with folders and phones, eyes sharpening the second he sees my face.

"Well," he drawls, pushing off the table, "you look like someone just pissed in your dinner."

I ignore him. "I need updates," I snap, stripping off my jacket and tossing it aside. "Now."

Vin straightens from a crate, tablet in hand. "Boston's still quiet."

"I figured, but I'm going to need you to define quiet."

"No new hits. No movement on the docks. No chatter on the usual channels."

I pace. Fast. Aggressive. Too tight. "That's not quiet. That's waiting."

Rafe watches me like he's deciding whether to stay put or duck.

"You're wound pretty tight," he says carefully. "Something happen at the house?"

I stop, slowly turning to face him head-on. My lips part, but the smile doesn't reach my eyes. "Unless Boston developed the ability to walk into my living room and piss me off," I reply, "I'd say no."

Vin glances back and forth between us. He doesn't understand what's going on, but he's wise enough to keep his mouth shut.

Rafe raises a brow. "You want to stab something, maybe kill someone?"

"Both," I say immediately.

"Good," he mutters. "We're aligned."

I grab a bottle off the table, twist the cap, and take a long pull without tasting it.

"Anything on Connor?" I ask.

Vin scrolls. "We picked up some noise through Providence. One of his runners missed a payment window. Might be sloppy. Might be bait."

"Let's see if we can bring him in," I say.

Rafe tilts his head. "Alive?"

I consider it. "Preferably," I answer. "But I'm flexible."

Rafe studies me. "Something else bothering you?" He lifts his brow, and I glare at him. Like the idiot that he is, he doesn't look away.

One day, I might kill this motherfucker, but it won't be today. I like him too much.

I turn back to the table and grab a knife. "Vin, out. I want to speak to Rafe alone."

Vin looks at me, then at the blade in my hand. He thinks his friend is about to die, but is smart enough not to object, choosing to scurry out of the room instead.

Once we are alone, I look at Rafe. "She smiled."

Rafe blinks. "Who? I'm confused."

I drag the blade across the tabletop once. "She smiled," I repeat, "at one of my guards."

"Oh." Rafe sighs. "You let her get under your skin."

"I didn't let her do shit," I snap.

"Sure, buddy," he deadpans. "Not sure what you want me to

do. You married her." Rafe folds his arms. "You going to punish the guard?"

"I threatened him."

"You threatened him, but did you punish him?" he says flatly.

I glare.

"Exactly. That's not punishment."

I bare my teeth. "Careful."

He doesn't back down. "Interesting how you don't spiral over territory. Yet you're spiraling over a guard."

I slam the knife into the table, and the wood cracks. Rafe doesn't even flinch. The silence in the room stretches thick and heavy.

Finally, I straighten. "Find me Patrick's location."

"I said I'm on it."

"Work harder," I snap. "I want an address asap."

Rafe nods once. "And when we find him?"

I hesitate for a fraction, then turn away. "I guess only time will tell."

Since there's nothing useful to kill here, I leave. That was a giant waste of my time. Unfortunately, these things sometimes take time.

I'm back at the estate. It's quieter now. I don't ask where she is. I don't need to. I already know. I move through the halls without direction, steps guided by instinct I don't want to examine too closely.

The sitting room is empty. No surprise there. The library lights are on. Bingo. I stop outside the doorway, but I don't enter.

She's in there, curled into one of the chairs with her legs tucked beneath her, book in hand. She looks . . . calm. Hair loose. Face intent. Lips moving faintly as she reads.

I stay in the shadows and watch. She turns a page, frowns at something, then mutters under her breath. I can't hear the words, but her expression tells me everything I need to know. She's annoyed.

Good.

I want her annoyed. I can deal with her more easily when she's like that.

I shift my weight, and the floor creaks.

Her head lifts instantly, eyes snapping to the doorway. For half a second, she looks like she expects a fight. Her spine straightens, and her chin lifts in defiance.

I've got to hand it to her, it's impressive. There is no fear. Just a challenge.

We are at a standstill. She's waiting for me to step inside, but I don't.

I also don't speak. I just watch.

Her gaze flicks over me, and she smirks.

Just a little.

Like the victory is hers. Something ugly coils in my chest. I turn away before she can say anything. Before I do something I can't undo. I walk back down the hall, my pulse loud in my ears.

This is a problem.

Her.

Because after everything, I shouldn't want to know what she's reading, what she's doing, and certainly not what she's thinking. But I do.

I shouldn't feel this restless need to go back and finish something that hasn't even started. I step into my study and shut the door, then lean my palms against the desk.

Breathe. "Get a grip."

The reflection in the window stares back. Hard eyes. Tight jaw. A man who used to be in control but now isn't.

I straighten slowly.

Fine. If she wants to play games—

I'll let her.

But I won't be the one who loses.

I reach for my phone. The war in Boston will need to wait. Because the more important one has already started . . .

In my house.

CHAPTER 44

Victoria

I'M HALFWAY DOWN THE HALLWAY WITH THE STOLEN BURNER when I hear a noise.

What is that? It's not a doorbell, and I'm pretty sure it's not a phone either. It sounds . . . I'm not even sure how to describe it, maybe like a metal door opening?

I stop so fast my bare feet squeak against the polished wood.

A second later, the security panel near the stairwell flashes once. A red blink that makes my stomach tighten.

Shit.

Somehow, I know he's coming . . .

Then I hear him.

Well, I hear heavy steps, most likely from boots. But I'm sure it's Lorenzo.

My pulse spikes because my body is stupid. I'm going to need to do something about my reactions to him.

As if he can hear my inner ramblings, Lorenzo appears at the end of the hall.

His phone is pressed to his ear, voice carrying low and sharp. "Sure." He strolls toward the stairs without looking at me. "I'll handle it. I'd hate for you to strain yourself by doing your job."

He pauses at the top of the staircase, eyes flicking down to the foyer. There's a moment of silence. I wait for him to do something, but no words come, only his lips curving up.

"Yeah." His fingers tighten around the railing. "I'm aware it's a problem. I'm also aware problems can stop existing." He listens again, jaw ticking.

Then a strange laugh escapes his mouth.

It's quiet and ugly and makes a chill run down my spine.

"Don't worry," he adds, voice smooth. "I won't leave a mess. I know how much you hate a mess."

My stomach flips. I make my way closer. An idiot moth to a flame . . .

I deserve to be burned.

Lorenzo's gaze snaps up and locks on me instantly.

The phone stays at his ear, but his attention is now on me.

Great. Just fucking great. Why am I so stupid sometimes.

I'm a glutton for punishment, that's why.

"Mmm," he hums, eyes never leaving mine. "I'll call you back."

He ends the call and pockets the phone.

I stand frozen in time, waiting for him to ask me why I'm here, but he doesn't.

His mouth twitches. He looks amused.

Glad I'm here to entertain him.

He starts down the stairs.

"Who were you talking to?" I ask, stopping only a few feet away from him.

"Business." He adjusts his watch.

"That's not an answer," I push, stepping closer. "That's an answer people use when they don't want to tell you the truth."

"Not true."

"Whatever . . . I get it. Whatever you're talking about, I'm sure it's a crime." I roll my eyes.

A faint smile spreads across his face. "Crime is such an ugly word. I prefer problem-solving."

"You're allergic to honesty," I shoot back, pointing toward

his phone with a small, furious flick of my hand. "Let me guess, someone annoyed your uncle?"

The moment the word uncle leaves my mouth, the smile drops from his face.

Lorenzo's eyes flicker with warning.

"Careful." He steps into my space. "You're not allowed to say certain names in this house."

I hold my ground even as my pulse does something traitorous.

"Why?" I whisper, forcing the question out through my teeth. "Because secrets make you feel powerful?"

"No," he answers, voice dropping. "Because secrets keep people alive."

For a second, it looks like he wants to say more, but then it's gone.

I'm about to open my mouth and say something when the front door beneath us opens.

I move closer to the railing and peer down as Rafe steps inside. He doesn't glance up at me right away. He clocks Lorenzo first, then his gaze drifts, and he catches my gaze.

Lorenzo starts heading toward the stairs, and I trail him.

This seems important, and I want to know . . . curiosity killed the cat after all.

Rafe pauses beside the console table, dropping a slim folder onto it.

"Movement again." Rafe rolls his shoulders. "And it's not subtle."

Lorenzo makes his way over to where he is, and I follow closely.

Rafe's gaze flicks toward me, then his gaze finds Lorenzo again. "We need to talk."

"Sounds good. Can't wait to hear," I cut in, pointing at myself dramatically. "I give great advice. It's kind of my thing now."

Rafe's mouth tightens as if he's choosing between lying and dying. Lorenzo decides for him.

"Go back upstairs," Lorenzo orders. "Now."

My spine stiffens. "No."

Lorenzo's eyes lift. The silence that follows is a blade. Each second that follows is more deadly than the last.

"You want to hear?" Lorenzo asks, voice almost gentle. He takes one step closer. "Fine. Here's the part you get to hear."

He turns slightly, angling his body so Rafe can still speak without appearing to speak to me.

Rafe clears his throat, voice lower. "One of our secondary routes got hit."

Lorenzo continues to watch me even though I'm not part of the conversation. "And?" he asks.

Rafe flips the folder open, thumb pinning down a sheet as he speaks. "We traced Doyle back to a building on the outskirts of town."

"We got eyes on it?"

"Yep."

Lorenzo exhales slowly. "Good. I want to know everything before we attack. No surprises."

My stomach turns, not because of the words, but because of how casually they sit in his mouth.

Rafe keeps going, voice careful. "We've also got the name of the guy who's acting as the bridge between Gallagher and Doyle. If we pick him up, we can squeeze him for more details. Maybe we can find out where he lives. Hit him where it really hurts."

Lorenzo's gaze doesn't leave my face. "Good. Get me everything before we act."

Rafe's mouth twitches like he wants to smile. "On it."

Lorenzo's eyes narrow slightly. "Also, once you grab him, I want to question him."

Rafe nods once, then hesitates. "That could be a problem."

"How so?" Lorenzo tips his head back.

Rafe gestures with the papers. "If we move on him tonight, we risk drawing attention."

Lorenzo's laugh is quiet. "Attention from who? Let them find out. I have zero fucks to give."

"Good to know. And your uncle?"

At the mention of his uncle, Lorenzo's back stiffens. I can't figure that one out. From what I've heard, he loves his cousin, but for some reason, he's scared of his uncle.

"I'll handle it," he answers.

Rafe nods quickly, relief flickering. "Got it."

I step forward, anger rushing up like a wave I can't stop. "What does that even mean?"

Lorenzo's eyes slide back to me, expression bland. "It means you're about to go upstairs."

"No," I snap, voice cracking with a fury I refuse to apologize for. "I want to know what's going to happen. I'm sick of you hiding things."

Lorenzo's mouth curves. "No can do. Now go to bed."

"No can do," I parrot.

Rafe laughs.

Lorenzo doesn't.

"Listen." He lifts his finger to catch a loose strand of my hair and tucks it behind my ear. My heart rattles in my chest at how tender his touch is. "You're not part of this."

I slap his hand away, my palm stinging from the contact. "I'm part of whatever you dragged me into."

His eyes flash with irritation, something darker under it. *Heat?*

"You're part of what happens in this house," he corrects, voice sharpening. "Not what happens out there."

"Why?" I demand, breath shaking. "Because you don't trust me? Because you think I'll run?"

His gaze holds mine, unblinking. "Because if you know too much, you become leverage."

My throat tightens.

Rafe clears his throat, shifting like he's trying to remind Lorenzo there are witnesses. "We should go."

Lorenzo's eyes flick toward Rafe. "Get the car."

Rafe doesn't argue. He just turns and leaves with the brisk efficiency of a man used to taking orders.

Lorenzo pivots back to me, his expression smoothing into something colder.

"Go upstairs," he repeats, voice quieter now. "Stay in your room."

I plant my feet. "Make me."

His eyes narrow, but then he smiles.

"Oh . . ." He leans in so close his mouth brushes the shell of my ear without quite touching. "Don't tempt me, Little Bird. I'm trying very hard to keep you alive."

My stomach drops.

He pulls back, gaze dragging over my face. Then he turns on his heel and heads for the door like the conversation is finished.

I stand there, breathing hard, watching him.

He pauses at the threshold, one hand on the door, and glances back over his shoulder.

"Don't test the guards tonight. I won't be here to stop them from being stupid."

Then he's gone.

The front door shuts, and I realize I've been holding my breath like I expected something else to happen.

I'm still standing in the foyer when I hear footsteps, then hushed voices. A maid passes with a tray in trembling hands. Her gaze meets mine for a split second, and in that glance, there's fear so raw it makes my stomach churn. Not fear of me. *Fear of him.* Maybe I should be scared of Lorenzo, too.

I'm not, though, and that should be alarming.

Despite what I was ordered, I don't go upstairs right away.

Instead, I drift through the hallways like I'm mapping the mansion.

Eventually, I find my way back upstairs, then slip back into my room and close the door quietly.

I wonder when Lorenzo will be home.

Home.

What a funny word.

This isn't my home, yet despite being caged here, I do feel safe, so maybe it is.

Because Lorenzo is protecting me. While he's currently planning a war, he still thinks of my safety.

I should feel scared, but ironically, I trust Lorenzo to keep me safe. And while I might want to fight him, I know that whatever is happening outside these walls . . .

It's bigger than me.

And for the first time since the wedding, the fear in my chest isn't just about what Lorenzo might do to me.

It's about what someone might do to him.

And I hate myself for that.

CHAPTER 45

Victoria

THE LIBRARY IS THE ONLY ROOM IN THIS HOUSE THAT DOESN'T make me feel like I'm suffocating.

It's exactly what I need . . .

It smells like paper and dust and the amazing fragrance of old leather.

Also, from what I can tell, no security monitors stare at me in here. Unless they are hidden, which I wouldn't put past Lorenzo, but at least I don't have to see them.

Nothing is worse than seeing the damn blinking red light. Every day, in every room, it torments me.

I slip inside and close the door behind me.

"Okay," I press my palm to my chest. "One minute. Just one."

I love how quiet it is.

My fingers graze the spines of the books.

My eyes going wide when I notice a certain spine sitting on the bookshelf.

Of course, he has it.

My heart beat picks up, it feels like I'm punched in the gut.

Wuthering Heights.

I take a step closer, reaching my hand out until my fingers hover beside it.

For a second, I'm back in the boathouse, laughing too loudly, thinking nothing bad could ever happen to me.

How wrong I was.

Because now, at twenty-three, I'm married to that boy, and he's using our past against me.

I pull the book out carefully. It's not going to bite, but I'm still scared of it.

Once it's in my hands, I take it in.

My brow furrows.

It looks well-read. The cover is worn, with faded letters and yellowing pages.

My throat tightens.

I flip it open.

This is very old. *A first edition?*

My breath catches. "No," I whisper, because it feels like the only word my brain can manage.

It can't be.

Or . . .

I've seen first editions behind museum glass, and it looks exactly like that.

Would Lorenzo really have one sitting here like it's a casual thing? Like it's just another knife in his collection.

Yes.

Yes, he would.

I turn the page gently.

A thin pencil line runs along a passage. My eyes snag on the words.

Whatever our souls are made of, his and mine are the same.

Like whoever underlined it hated how true it was.

My mouth goes dry. I trace the line with my fingertip, skin prickling.

"Of course," I huff. "This is the passage that would be underlined."

A floorboard creaks behind me, and my whole body stiffens. The book is still in my hands when I turn.

Lorenzo stands in the doorway. His expression is blank, but his eyes latch onto the book immediately, and something sharp flickers there. Recognition.

I don't move, and neither does he.

The silence stretches, thick and uncomfortable.

"How do you always sneak up on me?" I clutch the book tighter. "Is this a talent of yours?"

Lorenzo eases the door shut behind him, and the soft click echoes through the space.

As he strolls over to me, his gaze doesn't leave the book. Something about the look in his eyes seems predatory. Dangerous.

"Natural talent . . ." He stops a few feet away. His eyes drag up from the book to my face. "But you're the one who looks guilty."

I blink. "Guilty? For what? Reading? I think you're projecting."

His mouth curves, but only barely. A hint of amusement plays on his lips. "For touching my things."

I hold up the book, fingers splayed around the worn leather. "It's a book, Lorenzo. Not a gun."

He takes a step closer, and I flash to the open book. His eyes dip to the underlined words, and something changes in his face so quickly I almost miss it.

A micro-flinch. A crack. Then his expression smooths again.

"Sometimes books are worse." His voice is low enough to make me shiver.

And man, does my pulse do something stupid.

I hate my pulse.

I shift my grip, forcing myself to focus on the object instead of the man. "This is a first edition."

His shoulders rise in a careless shrug as he drifts toward the nearest chair, lowering himself into it. One ankle rests over his knee.

"You're observant," he drawls.

My laugh comes out sharp. "That's one way to phrase it. The other way would be . . . why do you have this just sitting here like it's a paperback you found in a little free library?"

His gaze lifts again, slow and lazy. "Because I can."

"Of course." I flip the book closed and then reopen it, unable to stop myself. "Of course, the answer is because you can."

Lorenzo's eyes track every movement of my hands. "You're looking at it like you're planning on stealing it."

"Not a bad idea. You need security," I shoot back.

His mouth twitches. "I think I have plenty of that."

I glare up at him, not finding his joke funny at all. "Have you finished it?"

The question slips out before I can stop it. All those years ago, we never did finish it.

For a second, I expect him to mock me. To make a joke. To turn it into something cruel and clever.

Instead, his gaze drops to the book again, and the air in the room shifts.

He leans back in the chair, fingers steepling for a moment like he's deciding what version of himself he's willing to show me. Then his jaw tightens.

"Many times," he mutters under his breath.

I blink.

He's showing a part of himself to me.

The most ordinary thing he's offered me since the wedding, and my brain doesn't know what to do with it.

"How many?" I ask, slower now, voice softer despite myself.

Lorenzo's eyes lift—sharp, direct—and hold mine.

"Too many to count."

The words hang in the room like a large weight.

A raw admission that he doesn't dress up or pretend is something else.

It lands.

Hard.

Right in my chest.

My throat tightens in a way I hate. "That's . . . depressing."

His mouth curves, but it isn't amused this time. It's bitter. Almost tired.

"Depressing is the point." He taps two fingers on the arm of the chair. "It's a love story about obsession. Ruin. People who mistake destruction for devotion."

My fingers curl around the pages. "You read it for fun?"

His gaze slides over me, slow and assessing. "I read it because it's honest."

I swallow. "Honest?"

Lorenzo's eyes flick down to the book again, then back up. His voice stays quiet, but there's steel underneath it . . . something personal.

"It doesn't pretend love is gentle," he tells me. "It doesn't pretend that longing makes you noble. It admits what people really do when they want something they can't have."

A shiver runs down my spine.

All these years ago, we joked about the book and us, but now more than ever, it feels real. No longer a coincidence.

I try to smother it with sarcasm. "Do you keep it around as inspiration?"

His eyes narrow slightly. "Inspiration?" he repeats. "No. It's a reminder."

My heartbeat stutters. I hate that I hear the edge in that sentence. I hate that I know who he's aiming it at.

I lift my chin. "You're implying I'm Catherine."

Lorenzo's gaze drags over my face, and his mouth curves again, but this time, it's wicked. "You're not Catherine."

I bristle. "Oh? Thank you for the character assessment."

His eyes flick to my mouth and linger for a fraction too long. "You married me after all."

My stomach drops.

"Yet you still consider yourself Heathcliff," I say, voice sharper than necessary. "Brooding. Unhinged. Ruined by love. Out for revenge."

Lorenzo's laugh is low, dangerous, amused in the way a predator is amused by prey that tries to bite.

He rises from the chair with slow grace, crossing the room toward me.

"I might have been ruined by love." He's close enough that I can smell him. "But I also think I'm improved by it."

I swallow hard. "That's the most horrifying sentence you've ever said to me, and you literally threatened to cage me."

His eyes glitter. "The cage is a metaphor."

"Not in my experience," I deadpan.

He leans slightly closer, and I can feel the heat of him without him touching me. The space between us is as thin as paper.

"Are you enjoying my library?" he asks, making my head spin from the change of subject.

I blink, thrown. "Am I . . . what?"

He gestures toward the book in my hands, then toward the shelves around us. "You've been in here more than once."

My fingers tighten instinctively. "I'm allowed to be in here."

"You're allowed to be wherever I decide you're allowed."

The cruelty is back, and let's not forget the control.

My anger flares hot enough to burn through the softness his earlier admission created.

I lift my chin and force my voice steady. "Then why are you here?"

His eyes flick down, and his brow furrows. Then his expression smooths, and his mouth curves. "Because you took my book."

I scoff, but the sound comes out too thin. "I didn't take it. I touched it."

"Yet you're still holding it."

My chest tightens, and I hate that he notices everything.

I try to cut the moment with sarcasm. "It's rare to find a first edition that isn't locked behind glass. I'm appreciating it."

"Appreciating," he repeats, voice low. "It's a pretty fucked-up book if you ask me."

"I didn't ask."

His eyes lift to mine, sharp. "No, you didn't."

The air between us feels charged. My pulse bangs against my throat like a warning.

I hate that my voice softens anyway. "Why do you read it so much?"

His jaw tightens, and for a moment, I think he'll snap. Mock. Deflect. Turn it into something vile. Instead, he exhales slowly.

"Because it touches on something most don't get."

My breath catches. "What don't most people get?"

Lorenzo's lips tip up, but there's no humor in the way they move. Instead, it feels bitter. Broken. "Wanting someone, and realizing wanting isn't the same as being wanted back."

My throat tightens so hard it hurts.

I stare at him, stunned by the honesty. By the fact that it's slipping out of him. I don't know what to do with it. So I do what I always do . . . I go for the throat.

"You're not a victim," I whisper, forcing steel into my voice. "Don't talk like you are."

His gaze hardens. All the softness is gone instantly, replaced by something cold and lethal.

"Victim?" He steps closer, forcing me to tilt my head back to keep eye contact. "No, Little Bird. I'm the consequence."

My stomach flips. I tighten my grip on the book like I can anchor myself with paper and ink.

"What happened to you?"

Lorenzo's mouth curves into a smile that is all teeth and darkness. "Now that's a story for a different day."

"I don't want to hear any of it," I fire back. "All that matters is that you're not the boy who used to—"

"Don't." His voice is as sharp as glass. His fingers lift again, hovering near my jaw, then curling into a fist at the last second like he's strangling the impulse. "Don't talk about him. *He* was weak."

My breath stutters.

He takes a step back, just barely, giving me air again.

"Have you read it recently?" he asks, voice low.

I blink, thrown by the reversal. "Yes."

His eyes flick up. "How recently?"

My mouth twists. "Once a year."

He leans back against the shelf behind him, one shoulder resting against the wood as if he belongs there. "At least you have insight into why you're here."

My pulse spikes, but I force my voice steady. "I don't need to read a book to know that you brought me here to punish me."

Lorenzo's jaw flexes. "That's what you think this is?"

"What else would it be?" I whisper, my throat tight, my hands shaking.

His eyes hold mine, and something in them looks almost tired. His obsession costs him a part of himself.

"You were never a phase . . ." My breath catches. His gaze doesn't waver.

The room tilts.

For a second, my brain goes silent.

No anger. No sarcasm. No clever retort. Just the raw weight of that sentence, crushing and intimate and awful. I don't know how to hold it.

I don't know how to survive it.

My fingers loosen slightly on the book, and my throat hurts from the emotions I'm choking on. "That's not—"

"It is." His voice is rougher now, like the honesty scraped his throat on the way out. "You don't get to rewrite it into something smaller so you can stomach it."

My chest burns, and I want to sob. "I didn't know."

His mouth curves, but it isn't humor. It's pain wearing a smile. "Does it change anything?"

I swallow hard. "Why would you—why would you do all of this over—over a summer?"

His eyes flash, and for a moment, the monster returns, furious and sharp.

"A summer," he repeats, voice dropping. "That's what you call it?"

I flinch.

He sees it and exhales, long and controlled, as if he's forcing himself not to snap.

"You were the only part of my life that ever felt like I wasn't drowning." His voice comes out quieter, almost raw. "And then you vanished. And I had to learn how to breathe underwater."

My chest aches so sharply it makes me dizzy.

I hate it.

I hate that some part of me wants to reach for him, to fix it, to undo it.

I hate that I can't because I'm still angry. Still trapped. Still wearing his ring like a brand.

My voice comes out brittle. "So you decided to drown me too."

"I decided you don't get to walk away clean."

I choke on a laugh that isn't really a laugh. "You're—" I swallow. "You're insane."

His smile returns, slow and wicked. "Yes."

"And what am I supposed to do with that? With . . . whatever this is?"

"I guess you can read." He shrugs. "Learn how stories like ours end."

I lift my chin, forcing steel back into my voice even as my heart trembles like a traitor.

"And if I don't like the ending?"

Lorenzo's eyes glitter. "Then change it. But don't pretend you can escape it."

The air between us hums.

We're so close now, I can feel the heat off his body. So close that if I lifted onto my tiptoes, our lips could touch . . .

A muscle jumps in his jaw.

He steps back suddenly like he's pulled away from something that might burn him.

His voice turns sharper, more controlled. "Put it back."

I blink.

"Put the book back where you found it."

My anger flares again, grateful for something easier to hold than sadness.

"You're telling me what to do with a book now?" I snap.

His mouth curves. "I'm telling you what to do with my things."

I lift the book slightly. "What, afraid I'll steal it?"

His eyes flash. "Afraid you'll bleed on it."

The sentence hits wrong—too intimate, too knowing.

I freeze.

Lorenzo holds my gaze for a beat, then turns away like he's done with this moment.

He walks toward the door, hand on the handle, shoulders tight.

Pausing, he turns his head slightly, not looking at me, but not leaving either. "Don't make me regret letting you into this room."

He exits, closing the door behind him with a quiet click that feels like a lock.

I stand there alone, book trembling in my hands, heart pounding so hard it aches.

The library feels different now.

It's no longer safe.

I shove the book back onto the shelf.

Then I take a breath, slow and shaky.

Because if Lorenzo Amante is right—

If I was never a phase for him . . .

Then what does that make me?

The prize?

A punishment?

Something else entirely?

CHAPTER 46

Lorenzo

TIME TO GET MY HEAD OUT OF MY ASS AND GET BACK TO work.

I've been dicking around at home for too long, and I'm about to get gutted if I don't give my uncle some useful intel.

The good news is these idiots out of Boston aren't as slick as they think they are.

It's actually adorable.

While I haven't been able to find Connor, *yet*. I'm sure one of these idiots will lead me in the right direction.

The good news is Rafe came through and we have tracked Patrick Murphy to a location where he's been running a little gambling scheme out of the back office of a laundromat.

I stand across the street from the building, hands in my coat pockets, watching. It's after midnight and everything is dark.

To the outside world it appears no one is inside, but I know better.

Rafe steps up beside me, chewing gum. If he's trying to walk in there with the element of surprise, he's doing a piss poor job.

I turn to look at him. "First off, spit out your gum."

Rafe laughs before spitting it out. "Tough crowd."

"You take the side door." I point to it for emphasis. "And stay quiet."

"And you?"

A smile spreads across my face. "I'll knock."

"God, I love when you knock."

I step off the curb before he can say anything else.

As I approach the door my pulse is steady. This part never rattles me. It's simple . . . either they die right away, or I let them live long enough to talk.

Not much to worry about.

Since obviously, I'm not going to knock, I make my way to the door, and very quietly pick the lock.

Rafe is already inside and has me covered just in case we get any unexpected guests.

I take the steps slowly, making sure that the floorboards don't squeak as I approach the door to the office in the back.

Then without any preamble, I kick it open. Patrick Murphy is sitting behind a table, his eyes wide, cash still in his hands.

He doesn't even get a full breath in before I cross the room and slam him face-first into the table.

His nose breaks with a soft crunch.

The sound is glorious.

Blood spills down his face.

One asshole sitting across the room rushes toward me, swinging wildly.

I duck. Then he's back, lunging at me. I grab him throwing him to the floor and kicking him in the rib.

Behind me, I hear footsteps and then another set.

Fuck.

There were more men than I expected.

I turn over my shoulder and see that Rafe has the other guy handled.

But the distraction is enough that the asshole on the ground has time to reach for his weapon.

He's fast, I'll give him that. Because next thing I know, a silver blade is swiping out as I pivot to avoid it.

The blade slices before I can fully turn.

Heat rips along my side.

Sharp. Immediate.

I hiss through my teeth as the knife drags just beneath my ribs, shallow but enough to bite.

I grab his wrist, pushing him back to the floor, and then with a smile on my face, I break it.

He screams out in pain as the knife clatters to the floor.

I don't give him time to process the pain. I grab his collar and slam his head into the wall once. Twice. Three times. By the third, he goes limp.

Behind me, there's a crash and a grunt. Rafe is obviously having fun.

Rafe drags the one guy by his collar, across the floor to where I've laid out the other one. Then I walk back to the broken nose fool at the table.

I smile at him.

"Hi," I say, as I move to zip tie his hands. Rafe works on securing the other idiots.

Now that they are secure, I remember the pain at my side. I press my palm against my ribs, my hand touching moisture. I wince as I pull my hand away.

"How bad?" Rafe asks.

"It's nothing."

He takes a step closer. "It's bleeding through your shirt."

I glance down. The fabric is darkening. Fuck. I look around the room to see if there is anything I can use to stop the bleeding. It's not deep but still hurts like a bitch.

"Put him in the car." I point with my free hand to the guy at the table.

We load him into the back of the SUV and head off to the warehouse.

Luckily there's no traffic at this time of night, so we make it back in record time, and once inside we tie him to a metal chair that's bolted to the floor. Then we duct tape his ankles to the chair.

Now that he's settled, I lift my shirt up and off my body. The fabric pulls away from the cut slowly, and as the wound comes into focus, Rafe whistles.

He shakes his head. "That's uglier than I thought."

I shrug. "It's shallow."

I look down to see what he sees. The cut is a shallow slice that sits alongside my ribs, and while it may be bleeding and inflamed, it's not enough to kill.

From beside me, I see Rafe grabbing the medical kit we keep in the warehouse.

"This is why you shouldn't play with knives," Rafe says as he hands me a bottle of whiskey he also grabbed. "Drink this."

I take a swig. "What are you waiting for, stitch me up."

He cleans the wound fast and then he's threading a needle. Once he's done, he moves in closer to my side. "Hold still."

I do as he says, and he pushes the needle through skin.

Pain radiates along my side, but I grin and bear it, inhaling slowly through my nose.

Looking down the stitches aren't pretty at all. It's almost like he's trying to be a dick. Wouldn't put it past Rafe to want to give me the ugliest scar ever.

I incline my head down toward where he's working. "Think you can try a little harder to keep it even? It looks like a two-year-old stitched me."

"I think it adds character."

He ties off the final knot.

I glance back down, not pretty but at least I won't bleed out.

I pick my shirt back up but don't put it on yet as I head back to Patrick.

"You know why you're here?" I ask.

He shakes his head frantically.

"I need to find your boss." I grab a metal chair and drag it across the concrete floor. Hurts like a bitch, but I push down the pain. Can't show any weakness.

I sit in front of him.

Rafe stands beside my chair, arms folded, enjoying the show.

"I don't know anything."

I lean forward slightly. "You know where Doyle is . . . "

He shakes his head. "I don't know—"

I backhand him.

Not hard enough to knock him out, just hard enough to make him reconsider lying to me.

"Try again."

He coughs blood onto his shirt. "I don't know—" he gasps.

I nod to Rafe, and then my gaze meets the pliers on the small cart he's rolled in. If Patrick is going to play games, I'm all in.

Rafe hands me the pliers, and I step forward slowly just to be an asshole, then pull of his thumbnail.

Patrick lets out a scream.

The sound is music to my ears as I reach for his pointer. Then pull that one off.

By the time I'm done with his whole right hand, he's shaking so hard I think if the chair wasn't screwed to the floor, it would topple over.

"You want to ship him back in pieces or send a message?" Rafe asks from beside me, eliciting another scream from our guest.

With that settled, I stand slowly. My side throbs. "Pieces."

Rafe nods.

"Doyle. Doyle will lead you to him," Patrick shouts as if his answer will save him. It won't.

I smile faintly. "Good. Now kill him."

"No—"

Rafe is quick to shut him up with a slice to the throat.

All in a day's work.

CHAPTER 47

Victoria

ONE SNOWFLAKE.

Then another.

Next thing I know, it's handfuls swirling in the darkness.

It hardly looks real.

It almost feels like I'm in a movie. Where giant fake flakes float down from the sky, blanketing the ground with artificial fluff.

But this is real.

I stand at the living room window with my arms wrapped around myself, watching the world turn white in a matter of minutes. The driveway disappears first, then the stone steps.

It's almost insane how fast it's coming down now.

But at least it's beautiful.

Behind me, the fireplace pops, sending orange light across the hardwood floor.

Despite how big Lorenzo's place is, right now it reminds me of a Christmas cottage in a movie. The air even smells like pine trees and burning leaves. I love it. Not that I'd let him know it.

"Enjoying the apocalypse?" Speak of the devil.

I don't turn right away. Nope.

I plan to play it cool, so I make myself count to three first.

When I finally pivot, he's leaning against the archway with a calm look on his face.

Damn, this man is handsome.

It's actually infuriating.

Everything about him is perfect, even when he doesn't try.

Right now, his hair is slightly damp, like he's been outside, yet he looks dashing. I'd look like a hot mess. It's not fair.

Rafe stands farther back in the hall, half his body in the shadows. Even though I can't see all of him, I can see that his coat is on and that he has a phone pressed to his ear.

His eyes flick over me once before he turns away again, muttering into the call.

Lorenzo tilts his glass toward the window, eyes glinting in the firelight. "How's this for a honeymoon? A little late, but better late than never."

My laugh comes out sharp and bitter. "I wouldn't call this anything."

The wind howls outside.

Rafe's voice drifts in from the hall, strained. "Road's closed. County says we are getting a shit ton of snow, but the plows won't come up until morning."

Lorenzo doesn't even look at him. He lifts his glass, takes a slow sip, then lets the silence stretch.

Rafe clears his throat. "Power's stable for now. Generator's full. We've got food for . . . plenty."

"Plenty," I echo, forcing a smile. "Wonderful. I'm thrilled to be trapped in a snow globe with my husband."

Lorenzo's eyes flick to my mouth, then back up. "Try not to sound too excited."

Rafe shifts, gaze dropping to the floor. "I'll check the perimeter," he tells Lorenzo before disappearing down the hall.

I lift my chin, meeting Lorenzo's gaze head-on. "This was planned."

His brow arches. "You think I control the weather now?"

"I think you control everything you can," I shoot back,

stepping around the coffee table like I'm circling a predator. "And when you can't control something, you pretend it's a coincidence."

He watches me move with slow interest. "You're giving me a lot of credit."

"You like getting credit for things." I stop near the mantel. "Must be your love language."

His eyes glint. "You're still talking. That must be yours."

I inhale slowly, forcing my body to unclench.

He sets his glass down on the sideboard, then rolls his shoulders. "Drink?"

I stare at the second glass he's already poured . . . red wine, dark enough that it almost looks like blood.

"I'm not drinking with you," I hiss.

His head tilts. "Scared you'll start enjoying it?"

"Scared you'll poison me," I retort.

A low sound vibrates out of him. A laugh, and it's a genuine one, and I hate that I like the sound. "There she is."

I don't move toward the wine. Instead, I move to leave because I need space.

Distance will do me some good right now. If I stay, I might forget why I don't like him.

I take one step, but my feet halt when I see something that looks like pain flicker across Lorenzo's face.

I watch him for a beat as he shifts his weight. I wonder what's bothering him, but then his hand goes to his side, and it looks like he winces.

"Are you—?" The words catch in my throat, unwanted. "Are you hurt?"

His eyes lift, sharp. "No."

My gaze continues to look at his hand, eyes narrowing. Something is on his sweater. It almost looks like a faint stain near his rib. It's dark . . .

Blood.

My pulse jumps, and he catches me noticing.

His jaw tightens. "It's nothing."

"It's bleeding," I snap.

He takes a slow breath. "It's handled."

I point at the stain. "Handled by what? Or better question, by who? Your ego?"

The corner of his mouth lifts. "Have you always talked so much?"

"Yep. What about you? Have you always been this dumb?" I fire back, taking a step closer despite myself. "Where's Rafe?"

"Checking the perimeter," he responds.

"And you're just . . . bleeding out for fun?"

His gaze holds mine for a beat before he turns away without answering and walks toward the hallway.

For some reason, I find myself following him . . . *I hate my body.*

After a few more seconds, he stops and pushes open a door. It's dim inside, and I can't see much before he shuts the door behind us, making it even darker.

A shiver runs up my spine.

Lorenzo moves to a cabinet, opens it, and pulls out a clean cloth, antiseptic, and gauze. He acts like it's just another day, but what kind of man stores this stuff in a cabinet in a study?

A bad man who needs to . . .

I try to swallow down that thought as he moves.

"I can—" I start and then stop. Do I offer to help or not? I'm at a loss. "You don't have to . . ."

Lorenzo's eyes flick up. "Don't start."

"I wasn't starting," I lie, stepping closer anyway. "I was . . ."

His mouth twitches. "You were what?" He peels his sweater up and off his head, and all words die on my tongue.

I suck in a breath.

A shallow slice sits alongside his ribs. It's angry and red and stitched poorly. A bruise is blossoming around it.

My stomach turns, and my mind does something traitorous.

It imagines my hands there.

Bandaging.

Touching.

Helping.

I clamp down on the thought so hard it feels like biting my own tongue.

Lorenzo presses the cloth to the wound, jaw flexing. He doesn't flinch and doesn't even make a sound. But of course, he doesn't. The man is barely human.

"You're going to reopen it," I mutter, voice tight.

"Are you offering medical advice?"

"I'm offering basic logic." I step closer, then stop, because closing the distance feels dangerous in a way I can't name.

He reaches for the antiseptic. His fingers are steady, but there's a faint tension in his wrist. Maybe it does hurt . . . and he's just refusing to admit it.

My throat tightens around something I don't want to feel. "Who did this?" I ask before I can stop myself.

His gaze goes flat. "Business."

"That's not an answer," I snap, the same line I've used on him before. It tastes familiar. Bitter.

Lorenzo's mouth curves faintly. "It's the only one you get."

I exhale sharply. "Anyone ever tell you that you're very annoying?"

He drags the gauze across his skin, then tapes it down, movements precise. "A few times. But not for long . . ."

I ignore his comment, knowing very well that he's trying to bait me into a conversation I don't want to get into right now.

Instead, I continue watching him take care of himself. Something about his movements makes my chest ache.

I don't want to know this version of him. Knowing will make me vulnerable, and I can't afford vulnerability.

Lorenzo finishes taping the gauze, then places his sweater back on and straightens it.

For a second, he just stands there, breathing slowly, eyes locked on mine. It's almost like he's waiting for me to say something stupid. Which, in all fairness, will probably happen. I keep my mouth shut despite my heart banging against my ribs.

I force a laugh that comes out too thin. "Congratulations. You're not dying."

"Disappointed?"

I huff out a bitter laugh. "Don't flatter yourself."

He takes a step closer, but I don't move. I hold my ground. It feels like heat rolls off him. My skin pricks at his proximity.

"You look shaken." His voice is low.

My chin lifts. "You wish."

His gaze flickers with amusement. "I don't need to wish. If I want something, I can just take it."

My breath hitches.

Is the room getting warmer?

"This is . . . ridiculous." I back up.

Lorenzo follows that movement like a predator following his prey. "What is?"

"This." I gesture vaguely between us, my hand trembling. "Me . . . standing here. Caring. Wondering if you're hurt. Wondering if this means something."

His eyes soften, and it scares me.

"It does mean something."

My throat tightens. "It shouldn't."

His hand lifts slowly, like he's going to touch my cheek.

I freeze.

Shit.

Is he going to touch me?

Do I want him to?

Shit. Shit. Shit.

I can barely think and now he's so close . . .

"You still remember?" His voice is low and hoarse.

"Remember what?" My voice cracks. *I hate that it does.*

His gaze drops to my mouth. "How it feels when we were together."

I do remember.

I remember everything . . . The boathouse. The summer air. The way he used to hold me.

I should be disgusted by him now. But for some reason, I'm not.

I swallow hard. "Of course, I do," I force the words out. "But that means nothing now."

He leans closer, head tilting, as he watches me with those eyes . . . those relentless, knowing eyes.

"I was seventeen. I'm not the same girl."

"Yeah, you are." Lorenzo's gaze sharpens. "You're still you."

My chest tightens so hard it hurts. "I'm not."

He moves until there is no space between us.

His hand finally cups my jaw.

I go still.

His thumb drags lightly along my cheekbone, slow and possessive.

"You pull away like you're scared of me."

"I am scared," I admit, hating myself for it. "Because you're the boy I once loved and now . . ."

His jaw flexes. "And now that boy is dead." The words are blunt. Final.

My throat tightens. "Is he?"

Lorenzo's eyes flash. Something raw pushes up behind them, then gets shoved back down.

His voice comes out rough. "Don't."

"Why?" I ask, the question spilling out. "Why do you look at me like I ruined you when you're the one—"

His hand tightens slightly on my jaw, not hurting but a warning. "Because you left."

The words hit.

Again.

Always that.

My voice cracks. "You don't know what I—what they did—what they told me—I thought—"

"I don't care what they told you. I care what you did."

My heart pounds so hard it hurts. He's so close I can feel his breath. His mouth hovers near mine, just a fraction away. I can't tell if he's going to kiss me or devour me.

My body leans in without permission.

My mind screams . . . *no.*

I jerk back like I've touched a live wire, and his hand falls from my face.

There is a beat of silence.

I wrap my arms around myself.

"I can't," I whisper, voice shaking. "I can't let my head get messed up. Not here. Not with you. Not when—when everything is a lie, and you're—"

Lorenzo's jaw flexes. "You think this is your head being messed up?"

I glare at him through heavy lashes. "Yes."

He steps closer again, but stops himself. His hands clench at his sides.

"It's not Stockholm, Little Bird."

My pulse accelerates. "What is it, then?" I ask.

His gaze pins me. "It's you."

The simplicity of his answer guts me.

My throat tightens. "You don't get to—"

"I don't get to what?" His voice rises, sharp for the first time. He catches himself, breathes once, then lowers it again. "Tell you the truth you're choking on?"

My eyes sting.

I hate that.

I hate that he can still do this, make me feel things I don't want.

I back toward the door, fingers fumbling for the handle without looking. "I need to go."

Lorenzo's gaze follows the movement like a knife tracking skin. "Run to your room."

"It's not running," I snap, voice breaking. "It's . . . choosing not to drown."

His mouth curves. "You were always dramatic."

"And you were always selfish," I retort, yanking the door open.

I step out, then pause just long enough to look back at him.

He's standing in the study, eyes dark. He acts as if nothing can hurt him, but that's a lie.

I slam the door before I do something stupid, then head down the hall.

I reach my room and shut the door, pressing my back against it like it can hold the world out.

My hands tremble.

My chest aches.

I hate him.

I hate this house.

I hate the part of me that still remembers what it felt like to love him.

I close my eyes, swallowing down the panic.

"It's just this house, this space . . ." I whisper to myself, like a mantra. "It's survival. It's nothing."

Sure, it is . . .

Or it's something. Something that won't change even if a million miles separates us.

CHAPTER 48

Victoria

I SIT AT THE LONG TABLE WITH MY ARMS CROSSED. I'M STILL wearing yesterday's sweater, and if I'm being honest, I'm also still in a bad mood.

My foot bounces under the table.

I feel like I'm going to crawl out of my skin. There's no reason for me to be worked up, but I am.

Across from me, Lorenzo reads something on his phone. It's infuriating how calm he is. He's got his damn elbow on the table, and untouched coffee in front of him, and hair still damp from a recent shower.

The kicker . . .

He hasn't looked at me once.

Not once.

Which somehow makes everything worse.

I clear my throat loudly.

Nothing.

I shove my plate away; the porcelain scraping against the wood. The jarring sound gets his attention.

Despite everything, he takes his time acknowledging my existence. His gaze lifts so damn slow, I want to punch him. He's trying to piss me off. I know he is. It doesn't take a rocket scientist to know that Lorenzo is baiting me for a fight.

Insufferable asshole.

"Something wrong with your eggs?" His smooth voice is conversational, as though he didn't almost kiss me last night while simultaneously egging me on for a battle.

Did I mention I hate him?

I lean forward, palms flat on the table. "I need to leave."

One brow lifts. "You just got here. You've barely touched your breakfast." He gestures toward my plate.

I bite the inside of my cheeks while counting to five slowly in my head so I don't throw something at him, most likely my plate.

"My parents' house," I clarify. "I need to go to my parents' house."

Silence stretches. Long and tedious.

Lorenzo sets his phone down. "No."

My jaw tightens. "I wasn't asking."

"Yeah, so that's not how this works." He folds his hands. "I decide what you do, Little Bird."

"No." I push back from the table and stand. "I've been trapped in this house. I need to get out of here. I need to be able to talk to someone who isn't you."

His eyes sharpen. "There's staff."

"I can't talk to them," I fire back. "They report to you."

"Well, technically, they report to the house manager," he corrects coolly. "There's a difference."

"Not to someone who's locked in," I shoot back.

He rises slowly, the chair scratching the wood.

"You're not locked in," he responds. "You're protected."

I laugh, but the sound holds no humor. "That's a cute. Did you practice it in the mirror?"

"Don't forget, the roads are closed."

"Then fly me out," I snap. "I really don't care how you do it. Just get me out of here."

"Absolutely not. Can't risk it."

My chest tightens. "Yes, you can. I want my mother. I want my father. I want someone who's not you."

His jaw flexes. Good. That hit a nerve.

He knows how much I hate them and yet I still prefer them to him.

I hope he's pissed.

If he's mad at me, there is less chance he will talk to me, and then I won't do something stupid like kiss his smug face.

"I'm a hostage," I say, voice shaking despite my best efforts.

He moves faster than I expect.

In two strides, he's around the table, closing the distance until I have to tilt my head back to look at him.

"Watch your mouth," he commands.

I lift my chin. "Make me."

The air between us snaps tight. I know I should stop taunting him, but I can't bring myself to quit. Instead, for a second, I close my eyes and imagine what it would be like if he took away my choice and just kissed me.

A soft sigh falls from my lips. Against my lips, I can almost feel the ghost of something touching my skin.

My lids flutter open, and my gaze collides with Lorenzo's. His pupils are huge and dark. The depth and longing appear endless. He looks like he might devour me.

I step back, heart racing.

Get yourself together.

I take a deep breath and rein in my emotions. Remembering what I was trying to say before I got sidetracked by need and want.

"I never did anything to you." The words spill out of my mouth with a raw intensity I don't normally show. "I didn't deserve this. I didn't deserve to have my life ripped apart because you decided to punish me."

His eyes darken. "You left."

"I was a kid. I did what I was told. I didn't know—"

"Enough. This is how things have to be."

"Why?" I demand. "Because it's easier for you? Because you don't know how to let go of a grudge without turning it into a war?"

His hand curls at his side. "Because letting you walk back into your old life as if nothing happened isn't an option."

I step into his space, fury buzzing under my skin. "You don't get to decide that."

"I already did."

The slap happens before my brain catches up to what I'm doing. My hand reaches up and connects with his cheek, the sound loud in the quiet room. A sharp crack that echoes all around us.

My breath catches as his head turns slightly with the impact.

For one terrifying second, the room goes utterly still.

Then his hand closes around my wrist. His touch is not crushing, but it's not gentle either.

He steps in, forcing me back until my spine hits the wall beside the window. One arm cages me in, palm braced against the wall just inches from my head.

His voice drops, low and lethal. "Don't."

My pulse screams to run, but I don't. "Let go of me."

"Don't hit me." His eyes lock on mine. "Ever."

"You don't get to do this to me," I counter, chest heaving. "You don't get to isolate me."

His grip tightens. It doesn't hurt, but I know he's there.

"I never did anything to you," I repeat. "I didn't betray you. I didn't ruin you. I don't deserve to be locked away from my family."

For a moment, something flickers across his face.

I can't place it, but it doesn't feel like anger. It looks like pain, but that doesn't make sense.

Before I can overanalyze it, the look slips from his face.

"This is the way things have to be." His voice is quieter now. "You're safer here."

"From what?"

His gaze searches my face, jaw clenched. "From anything or anyone that would lead you to hurt me."

The words land heavy.

"But the thing is, you don't get to make that choice for me."

His gaze doesn't waver as he stares at me.

The room feels too small.

I can feel his breath on my skin.

The tension inside of me coils tighter with every second he doesn't move away.

I can barely think with him this close to me.

Especially with my wrist is still trapped in his hand, and my body pressed against his. And if this all weren't bad enough, of course my heart beats faster. My damn treacherous heart . . .

This is the danger.

Not the guards.

Not the snow.

This.

I swallow, needing to pull myself together. "Let go."

His jaw flexes, and for a heartbeat, I don't think he will, but then his hand releases my wrist. He steps back abruptly, making his arm drop from the wall.

I watch him as he drags his hand through his hair. It almost looks like he wants to say something but is refraining.

"You want to go to your parents' house?" he says, voice rough. "We'll discuss it when the roads open."

"That's not an answer."

"It's the only one you're getting." He grabs his jacket from the chair and turns to walk away. "I'm done with this conversation."

"You're running," I accuse.

He pauses at the doorway, shoulders tense. "I'm exercising restraint."

He doesn't look back.

The door shuts behind him with a solid finality that echoes through the room.

I slide down the wall slowly, legs giving out as adrenaline drains from my system. My hand trembles where he held it. My cheek burns with the ghost of his presence.

I press my forehead to my knees, breathing hard. Shaken. That's what I am. By him. By myself.

By the way my body reacted when he crowded me.

I hate him, hate this.

And most of all, I hate that I leaned in instead of pulling away.

CHAPTER 49

Lorenzo

WE ALL TAKE POSITIONS AT THE WAREHOUSE.

Two of my uncle's men are stationed at the front door. One stands in the back of the building, and another looks bored while his hand rests on his gun.

I sit at a folding table with a scale and a ledger. Rafe hovers two feet to my right, jacket open, also with a hand on a gun.

Matteo, who's leading the charge, stands front and center in the warehouse. Waiting. Arms crossed. Gaze sharp.

A truck rumbles outside. I can hear the tires crunching over the gravel before it rolls to a stop.

"Positions," Matteo orders.

Rafe's hand drifts casually to his gun as he waits.

"Hopefully, this goes smoothly." Matteo cracks his knuckles.

"Smooth, doubtful. Does anything ever go smoothly?" I answer, watching through the window as the first SUV door opens.

"Have you always been so pessimistic?" Matteo laughs.

"Yep."

The buyer steps out. He's got to be in his mid-thirties. Hair gelled; he's really giving off the stereotypical made man vibe. I swear I'm in an old 1990s mafia movie.

His men spill out behind him. Three men, to be exact.

The guard at the door swings it open, and the buyer and his men walk inside.

As soon as they do, they spot Matteo and me.

The greasy one walks forward with a smile.

"Matteo," he calls, stopping a respectable distance away before acknowledging me next with a nod.

We let silence do the greeting.

His smile falters, then recovers. "Appreciate you both meeting us in person."

"Appreciate you showing up," Matteo replies, voice mild.

The buyer gestures behind him, and one of his guys drags a duffel toward the table. He drops it with a thud.

Rafe drifts over, fingers hooking the zipper, opening it.

So far, so good.

From where I'm sitting, I can clearly see the stacks of cash stuffed to the brim in the bag.

The buyer's nostrils flare. "That's the full amount."

Rafe lifts a stack, thumbing the bills. "Relax. Nobody's accusing you of anything . . . yet."

The buyer forces a laugh. "We're good for it."

"Good," I rest my fingertips on the table. "Because being bad for it ruins my mood and his." I gesture to Matteo. "And when our mood gets ruined, people start losing things they need."

I let my gaze slide to the buyer's hands.

Then his throat.

Then back to his eyes.

He swallows.

Matteo shifts beside me, rolling his shoulders like he's getting comfortable in the tension. "You two want to sing love songs, or are we doing business?"

The buyer's eyes flick back to Matteo, confused, then to me, like he's trying to figure out if this is my "friendly cousin" or my "loose cannon cousin."

Both.

Rafe nods toward the crates. "Product's ready."

Vin snaps his fingers, and two of our men crack open a crate. One of the buyer's men steps closer, reaching for a brick of cocaine.

Vin's knife points at him in a warning.

The buyer's guy freezes. Vin tilts his head, smiles sweet. "Ask first."

The buyer lifts a hand, palm out. "Easy. We're just verifying quality."

"I'm going to need you to verify with your eyes." Matteo strolls around the table. "I'm a man of my word. By touching it, you're saying you don't trust me . . . So what is it? Do you trust me?"

"Of course." The buyer chuckles nervously.

"Good, that means we don't need to take any fingers." Matteo grins, looking sadistic.

Rafe's mouth twitches.

I smile too.

"Matteo likes fingers. I like to take the whole hand," I add. "We might be cousins, but we have different personalities."

The buyer's laugh dies in his throat. He nods quickly. "Right. Understood."

Vin gestures at the product with a bored tilt of his chin. "Look all you want."

The buyer leans in, peers, and nods like he has any idea what he's looking at. "We're good," he announces, straightening.

"Fantastic," I wave at the cash.

"Count it. Load your car. Then leave," Matteo adds.

His men move fast after that. The money gets counted, and the product gets carried out.

When the last bag disappears into the SUV, the buyer pauses at the door. He glances at Matteo again, then at me. "Pleasure doing business." He leaves in a hurry.

Matteo stays where he is, watching the car drive away before turning to me. He steps closer to where I'm sitting. "You're off."

My jaw tightens. "I'm fine."

"Your face is doing that thing." He taps his jaw. "The one where it looks like you're deciding whether to kill someone, or well, I don't know what else. You just look like you want to kill someone."

"I'm not making a face."

Matteo's mouth lifts, amused. "Yeah, you are. You're practically my brother. Trust me, I know you're making a face."

I reach for the ledger and flip it open. Matteo steps up beside me and closes it again. Matteo holds my gaze without flinching. He's the only person on earth allowed to do this without getting killed.

"You can talk to me," he says, quieter now.

I stare at him for a second. His concern is clear as day on his face. He's right, he's a brother to me, but I still can't tell him what's wrong.

My chest tightens.

"You want me to talk?" I stand and step around him. "Or you want me to entertain you with feelings?"

Matteo follows easily, matching my pace. "I want you to stop walking around like this."

"I'm busy," I reply, gesturing at the warehouse. "Your dad wouldn't be happy if I didn't work."

He leans closer, lowering his voice. "This isn't about work or my father."

That's where he's wrong. This has everything to do with his father.

I can't lose the only family I have, and if they find out what I've done, I will.

I laugh once, sharply.

Matteo's eyes narrow. "You're not sleeping."

"Sleep is overrated," I counter.

"You're not eating."

"Not true. I eat all the time." I shake my head. "Did you come here to mother me?"

"Someone has to."

I snort despite myself. It lasts half a second. Matteo catches it like a win.

"There it is." He smiles, satisfied. "Still human. Barely." I hate that he reads me so well.

I walk toward the office. Once inside, I head over to where a bottle of whiskey sits on a shelf. I grab it, twisting the cap with one hand.

Matteo is only a step behind but makes fast work of grabbing two chipped tumblers from a cabinet.

I pour.

Amber liquid splashes into the glass.

Matteo lifts his glass, clinking it lightly against mine. "To no issues today."

"To small miracles." I take a sip.

The whiskey bites, but it also steadies me. Something I need while I lie to him.

Matteo watches me over the rim of his glass, then drops it to his side with a sigh. "You need to blow off steam."

"I have steam. It's simmering. It's fine."

"That's not steam," he counters, leaning his hip against the desk. "That's a volcano ready to erupt."

I take another sip. "Maybe that's how I have to be to get the job done."

Matteo laughs, low and warm. "Peace might be nice . . ."

"Peace is boring." I swallow the whiskey and let the burn distract me.

"You want advice?" I ask.

Matteo's brows lift. "Do I?"

"Worry about someone else. I'm fine."

Matteo's eyes narrow. He's suspicious. He's also loyal enough to let me hide if he thinks I need it. "I was going to suggest you find a woman," he says, as if testing the waters.

I choke on a laugh. "A woman?"

"Yeah." He shrugs. "Someone to take the edge off. Someone warm. Breathing. Preferably not armed."

I wipe my mouth with the back of my hand. "You think sex will fix my attitude?"

Matteo's smile turns wicked. "It fixes a lot of things."

"Sex won't fix that. I want to kill everyone."

"That's true," he agrees readily.

"But I'll think about it."

Matteo's eyes brighten like he's pleased with himself. "Look at you. Growth."

"Don't get excited," I warn, sipping again. "My growth is mostly cancerous."

He grins. "So what's the plan tonight?"

I glance at the clock, as if time is something I can still control. "Poker game."

Matteo perks up. "At Cyrus's?"

I nod once.

Matteo's grin widens. "Perfect. I'll go with you."

I freeze mid-sip.

Matteo catches it immediately. "What? You afraid I'll embarrass you?"

My jaw flexes. "You're a walking embarrassment."

"Aw." He clinks his glass against mine again. "You love me. You do remember he was my friend first, right?"

"Fuck off. And I don't love you."

"You do."

I push past him, heading for the exit. "Get in the car."

Matteo follows.

The drive to Cyrus's doesn't take that long.

Matteo talks the whole way. Trying to figure out the shit with Boston. I let him fill the silence because if he doesn't, my mind drifts to Victoria.

When I'm busy, I'm able to distract myself, but now that I'm not actively torturing or doing a deal, she's all I can think about.

Her mouth.

Her eyes.

The way she looks at me, like she hates me and wants me in the same breath.

I focus on the road, on the snow, on anything but the fact that I'm not with her.

Luckily for me, Cyrus Reed's mansion appears in the distance.

Warm light glows behind the huge glass windows as I pull up the driveway, passing the security gate that's opened for us.

Matteo whistles low. "I'll never get over how nice this place is."

"Well, he does collect power and money," I respond, pulling into the circular drive.

Matteo grins. "That he does."

I cut the engine and glance at him. "Don't lose all your money, like last time. Your dad will kill me."

Matteo laughs as we step out into the cold. Snow crunches under our shoes with each step we take until we are finally inside.

Inside, we are instantly met with the smell of smoke and expensive liquor.

Cyrus stands in the main lounge, a glass of scotch in hand, sleeves rolled up. His gaze slides to me before flicking to Matteo.

"Matteo, fucking finally." He looks over at me next. "Lorenzo."

"That's it? Where's my love?" I joke.

"I see you every week, idiot."

Matteo laughs at Cyrus's words.

Cyrus's attention swings back to me. His eyes drag over my face. Then he lifts his glass. "You look like you've been chewing glass."

"Dinner." I walk past him toward the bar. "My favorite meal."

Cyrus chuckles softly.

Matteo drifts toward the poker table, already talking casually to the men sitting behind it.

I pour myself a drink, moving closer to where Cyrus stands.

Cyrus leans in so only I can hear. "How did it go?"

I don't look at him. I swirl the scotch, watching the amber move.

"Fine," I reply.

Cyrus's mouth curves. "That's not an answer you give when things go fine."

I take a sip, letting it burn. "I got the desired results."

His gaze is steady, calm, and intelligent. "Nothing more?"

I let silence hang.

Cyrus doesn't press. That's why I trust him with exactly what I trust him with—very little, very carefully measured.

He lifts his glass slightly. "Then congratulations. You got . . . whatever you wanted."

I clink mine against his with a soft, controlled tap. "You don't even know what I won, so don't sound so proud."

Cyrus's smile sharpens. "Pride is my best quality."

Across the room, laughter rises from the men seated at the table. Matteo catches my eye and jerks his chin, telling me to come over. I should go. I should lose myself in the game. That's what I'm here for after all.

Instead, my mind drifts, unwanted again back to her . . .

Back to the way she looked when she almost kissed me.

Cyrus's voice cuts through the fog. "You're distracted."

I glance at him.

His eyes are unreadable, but his tone is casual, almost kind. "Try not to be," he adds. "Distraction gets men killed."

Matteo calls from the table, waving a card. "Lorenzo. Get over here before I take all your money out of spite."

I force my mouth into a smirk and walk over, sliding into a seat with the weight of my mood dragging behind me.

The poker game starts.

Chips and cards are handed out, and the scotch flows.

Matteo needles everyone within reach, and for a while, I almost forget the storm in my head.

Almost.

But between hands, and between the laughter and the banter . . . my mind returns to Victoria.

The dealer slides me a hand, and I glance at my cards.

Five three of hearts.

Of course.

Across the table, Matteo grins like he can smell a win. "You look happier. That's terrifying."

I fold. "I'm not happy."

"You're something," he counters, taking a sip of scotch. "I just can't tell if it's homicidal or something else."

My jaw tightens. It's something else all right. The need to get home and see my wife.

Matteo's grin widens. "Now that's an interesting reaction."

I lean back, spinning a chip between my fingers. "Play your cards, cousin."

Matteo's eyes narrow, amused and suspicious in equal measure. "One day you're going to tell me what's going on with you."

"One day," I agree, voice smooth.

Matteo lifts his glass. "Liar."

I clink mine against his. "Idiot."

The game continues, yet my brain won't shut up.

My fingers tighten around the chip until it bites my skin.

I don't like caring.

I don't like the way it makes me hesitate.

I don't like that she still has the power to make my choices feel like they matter.

Across the table, Matteo laughs at something Cyrus says.

I force my attention back to the game.

But the thought of her doesn't die.

When the hand is over, new cards are dealt.

And this one doesn't suck.

I push a stack of chips forward, eyes fixed on the center of the table. "All in."

And somehow, those words feel like I'm talking about something else.

Someone else.

CHAPTER 50

Victoria

I SWING MY LEGS OVER THE EDGE OF THE BED, AND MY BARE feet hit the cold floor, making a chill run up my spine.

Socks would be nice right now. Where did they go? I could have sworn I fell asleep in them . . .

As I start to search the bed, a knock sounds against the wooden door.

It's not him.

That much I know for sure.

The knock is too soft. It's almost polite. Probably a staff member, most likely female.

My suspicions are proven correct as I cross the room, pull the door open, and see Marta, one of the maids, staring at me.

Her gaze flicks over my face, searching, then she offers a slight nod toward the hallway.

"You're wanted downstairs." Her fingers twist the edge of her apron.

My throat tightens. "Who wants me?" It doesn't take a rocket scientist to figure out who is beckoning me, but I still ask.

Marta's lips transform into a straight line. "By . . . him."

"I'll be right down. I need to freshen up."

She bows her head in understanding before stepping back.

With that done, I head into the bathroom and go about making myself presentable. Using the toilet and then brushing my teeth. After I'm decent, I step out into the hallway and head to where he is.

For some reason, the staircase feels longer today, and don't even get me started on the stairs.

Time seems to stand still as I move, and my heart beats so fast, I fear it might explode.

Once downstairs, the foyer is dim, and it takes a second for my eyes to adjust, but then I see him.

Lorenzo stands by the front doors. Ominous as always, but he's not alone. His dumb friend Rafe is with him.

Rafe stands with his shoulder against the wall, eyes tracking everything with a bored look. Typical.

On the other side of the foyer is Nico. He's probably the only guard who's done anything remotely nice for me. So at least his presence doesn't piss me off even more.

Lorenzo's gaze snaps to mine the second I step off the last stair. It's like his body is wired to my existence.

His eyes drag down my body, starting at my feet, then up my sweatpants, until they lift back to my face.

"You look comfy." He adjusts his cuff, like we're discussing the weather.

I stop at the edge of the foyer, letting my spine go straight. "I look like I just woke up, which I did."

Rafe's mouth twitches. He wants to smile so badly, but probably doesn't because his friend might kill him. Nico's expression stays neutral, but his gaze flicks to Lorenzo.

Lorenzo takes a step closer, and the space between us shrinks in a way that makes my pulse climb my throat.

"You're adorable," he deadpans.

"Call me adorable again," I snap, folding my arms tight over my chest, "and I'll bite you."

Lorenzo's mouth curves, slow and sharp. "Promises before breakfast. I'm blessed."

I force myself to breathe. "Why are all the guards here? Planning on killing someone?"

Lorenzo glances toward Nico without turning his head fully. "Because I'm taking you somewhere."

I freeze so hard my ribs ache.

Somewhere.

"Like outside?"

Lorenzo nods, not giving anything up until he's ready to, or at least until I ask the right question.

"Where?"

Lorenzo's gaze holds mine. It's steady and unblinking. "Your parents'."

My brain actually stutters. Like short-circuits completely.

Did he just say he's taking me to my parents' house?

My mouth opens, and nothing comes out.

Rafe shifts, clearing his throat, probably reminding me that I'm standing in the foyer with my mouth open.

I swallow hard. "Why?"

Lorenzo's shoulders lift in a lazy shrug that doesn't match the sharpness in his eyes. "Because you've been throwing a tantrum, and it's getting annoying."

My fingers curl into a fist. "So this is, what? A treat? You're taking me for a walk like a dog?"

"Of course not . . ." His mouth parts into a smirk. "Dogs are loyal."

I flinch without meaning to, and Lorenzo, the fucker, watches the flinch and loves it.

Then he steps back, as if granting me air is a privilege. "Get dressed. Something more suitable for the public, but also something you can run in if you decide to be stupid."

My jaw tightens. "Are you threatening me or giving fashion advice?"

His mouth kicks up. "Both."

Rafe laughs but tries unsuccessfully to cover it up with a cough.

I glance at Nico because my brain wants an ally, even when it knows better. "And him?"

Lorenzo follows my look, voice turning colder. "Nico escorts you. You don't leave his sight. You don't talk about where you've been. You don't say my name at all."

My teeth grind together. "As if I'd ever willingly talk about you."

Lorenzo's eyes gleam. "If you behave, maybe this won't be your last excursion."

I stare at him for another beat, then spin on my heel and head back up the stairs before I do something that ends with me bleeding on marble.

In my room, I dress fast in jeans, boots, and a sweater. I drag my hair into a knot and stare at my reflection. *Not bad.*

A knock comes again, and like before, it's soft.

Not Lorenzo . . . thank God.

I open the door to find Marta holding my coat. Her fingers are trembling as she offers it to me.

"You're going out?" she whispers.

I take the coat and pull it on slowly. "Apparently, I've been granted a day pass from jail."

Marta's lips part, then close again. She wants to say something.

"Don't. It's fine." I give her a small smile before I walk past her into the hallway.

Once downstairs, the air feels colder and heavier. Lorenzo stands by the door.

His gaze drifts over me, then stops on my face with something like satisfaction.

Why? No clue. But something tells me he's going to tell me.

"Good," he drawls, opening the door. "You listened."

"As if I had a choice," I snap, stepping past him into the winter bite. Outside, Nico stands by the car.

"Ready?" Nico asks Lorenzo.

"I'm ready," I say as if I have a say.

No one here listens to anyone other than Lorenzo.

"Don't make this harder than it has to be," Nico says under his breath as I walk past him. He follows me and opens the door. "Get in the car, Victoria."

He uses my name like he's warning me, and right now, I don't want to know why.

I slide into the back seat, and Nico takes the seat beside me. The driver pulls out, and when the estate gates open, we are gone.

Neither of us speaks as we drive off. Soon, the mansion disappears behind us, and the road curves through trees dusted with old snow. I stare out the window and pretend my chest doesn't hurt.

"You're quiet," Nico says as he checks his watch.

I don't look at him. "I'm practicing for the rest of my life."

He snorts, then smothers it into a cough-like laughter. "Don't do anything reckless."

I turn my head slowly, letting my eyes meet his. "Define reckless."

Nico's stare goes flat. "Running."

"I haven't run from anything in years." I regret the honesty instantly, but at least Lorenzo isn't here to hear it.

"Just . . . don't speak," Nico responds.

Thirty minutes later, the Danforth estate is before us. The gates open before we even stop.

My stomach twists. Because that means they're expecting me, and I don't know how I feel about it. A month has passed since I've seen them last, and from what I can tell, neither has tried to contact me . . . so do I even want to be here?

The SUV rolls up the drive. My mother is already on the steps, wrapped in an expensive-looking, useless coat. Her hair is pulled back too tightly, and she looks frail. My father stands behind her, hands clasped, jaw rigid.

Now, he's trying to look like a man in control.

Spoiler alert, Dad: You're not.

The car stops, and my door is opened. Cold air hits my lungs, but I welcome it anyway because it's real. Like freedom, even if it's short-lived.

My mother takes a step forward but doesn't approach.

Gee, thanks, Mom. Missed you too. "Victoria."

My father steps closer, gaze flicking past me, landing straight on Nico. His nostrils flare.

"Who is that?" my father bites out, voice low.

Nico remains two steps behind me, posture neutral, eyes scanning him before looking around the property. He doesn't speak.

Smart man. I answer for him, keeping my tone light because that's the only way this will work. My mother will be too dramatic if I tell her the truth. "Security."

My father's mouth tightens. "Security for what?"

I tilt my head, letting my smile sharpen. "For me."

My mother gestures to the door. "Come inside, I'm cold." Some things never change. She's still the most selfish person I've ever met. "You look . . ." She narrows her eyes, trying to find the word she wants to use. It's usually an insult, so I help her with it.

"Tired?" I walk past her toward the doors. "That's just my face now. It's a trend."

She rolls her eyes. She's never found me funny. I guess almost losing everything and selling your daughter to a mafia man didn't help her get a sense of humor.

Fine by me. I have no intention of ending this line of jokes. She deserves to know I'm miserable. She did sell me like cattle, after all.

Once inside the house, we move into the front sitting room. Nico stays by the doorway.

My father notices immediately. "Does he have to stand there?" he snaps, gesturing toward Nico.

Nico's eyes slide to my father, expression calm in a way that makes my spine prickle.

I beat him to it. "Yes."

My mother flinches. "Victoria—"

I lift a hand, cutting her off without raising my voice. "Let's not pretend we get to make rules today."

Silence drops hard.

My father's jaw clenches like he's chewing glass, and my mother's hands flutter at her chest.

Then she tries again, softer. "What brings you here today?"

I look at her. Really look. Her makeup is done, but her eyes are swollen. Her lips are pale beneath the lipstick, and her hands shake when she reaches for the tea service.

Guilt?

Or sadness.

Most likely neither. Never can tell with this woman, but what I can tell is she isn't happy, and I'm certain it has nothing to do with me.

"Is that your way of asking if I'm okay?" I settle into a chair without taking my coat off.

My mother doesn't speak, so I answer my own question anyway. "I'm alive."

My father's laugh is harsh and bitter. "Cute, Victoria."

I angle my head toward him. "I do what I can."

His face goes red. "Stop with the attitude, young lady."

I lean forward, elbows on my knees. "Aw, do you not like me reminding you of what you did? Treating me like an asset?"

My father goes still.

Nico shifts slightly in the doorway, the tiniest adjustment.

My mother sets a teacup down, and the porcelain clinks at the movement. "I will not have this in my house," she whispers, as if Nico can't hear.

"Then where?" I shoot back, letting my voice sharpen. "How do you want it, Mom? You want me to smile and say thank you? You want me to pretend this is fine because the alternative is admitting what you did?"

Her eyes harden. "We didn't have a choice."

I laugh once, short and ugly. "Funny. That's what everyone keeps saying, but you kind of did."

My father's hands curl into fists. "Enough. You wanted to visit, so we allowed it. If you don't want to be here, why are you?"

"Good question, Dad."

His mouth opens to say something, but before he can, the door to the adjoining study opens.

And in walks Grant Jameson.

Fabulous. Of course my dad and him were having a meeting the day Lorenzo lets me come for a visit. Just my luck.

This is exactly what I need to make this day worse.

I know I said I wanted to get away, but maybe this wasn't a well-thought-out plan.

Always so damn perfect. Too bad what's inside is rotten to the core.

Perfect suit. Perfect hair. Perfect smile built for cameras and boardrooms.

Barf.

His gaze lands on me and brightens too quickly. "Victoria," he breathes, stepping forward.

My stomach drops, less from fear, and more from irritation so sharp it feels like nausea.

Like I said . . . *barf.*

Grant's eyes sweep over me, down my body, then flick up to my face.

"I'm glad you're okay," he adds, voice smooth, concerned in a very fake way. Someone get this guy an acting class because he needs it.

My mother stiffens, gaze snapping to him like she forgot he was here.

My father's posture tightens, jaw locked.

I stand slowly because sitting feels like surrender. "Grant."

Grant moves closer, then pauses like he senses the tension—like he senses the invisible trip wire of what he doesn't know.

His eyes flick toward Nico at the doorway.

Nico doesn't move.

Grant's smile tightens. "I came by as soon as I heard you were . . . back."

Back.

Not married. Not taken. Not locked away. He doesn't know.

Lorenzo said no one can know, but I didn't realize my parents would obey.

Not to protect me, at least. But it isn't to protect me, it's to protect themselves. They can't tell him without risking everything.

Grant lifts his hands in a placating gesture, eyes on me. "Where have you been?"

My mother inhales sharply, and my father goes rigid. They have nothing to worry about. I know the rules.

I tip my head, forcing my mouth into something that resembles a smile. "Out."

Grant's brows lift. "Out where?"

I take a slow step toward him, letting my tone turn sweet the way my mother taught me—polite enough to pass as civil, sharp enough to cut. "What is this, Grant? An inquisition?"

His jaw flexes. "You vanished. No one could reach you."

My father's gaze drills into me like he's begging me not to say the wrong thing.

Nico's presence, on the other hand, dares me to.

I meet Grant's eyes. "I wasn't available."

Grant lets out a small laugh, forced. "That's not funny."

"I'm not trying to be funny," I reply, the softness in my voice a lie. "I'm trying to be clear."

His gaze narrows, suspicion creeping in. "Who is that man?" He points at Nico.

"A guard." I roll my eyes. "My father suddenly cares about my safety."

Grant's eyes flick to my father, then to my mother, then back to me. He reads the room and doesn't like what he sees.

"Victoria." He lowers his voice in a caring way. I'm not stupid. He's an even worse option than Lorenzo. "If you're in trouble—"

My laugh comes out too sharp. "You don't get to play hero.

Not after years of hovering around my life like a vulture in a designer suit."

His expression hardens, the mask beginning to slip. "I'm trying to help you."

"Are you? Or are you trying to help yourself get me?"

"You're being difficult."

"I'm always difficult." I tilt my head. "It's the only language I know."

Grant steps closer, voice lower, eyes intent. "Tell me where you've been?"

I feel it then: the pressure behind his questions. The interest. The calculation.

He isn't asking because he cares.

He's asking because information is power, and Grant has always believed power belongs to him. He wants power to find a way to control me, and that thought alone scares me.

I glance at my parents. I could end this right now and just tell him. I'd finally be away from Lorenzo. But I don't tell him. Not because Lorenzo told me not to but because I refuse to give Grant anything. Because some ugly, complicated part of me won't hurt Lorenzo.

The realization tastes bitter on my tongue.

His nostrils flare. "You're protecting someone."

I hold his stare, heartbeat steady. "I'm protecting myself."

Grant studies me for a beat too long.

Then his gaze flicks past me to Nico, and something shifts in his expression.

He forces a smile back onto his face, turning toward my parents like he's remembering decorum. "I should go," he says, voice tight. "But Victoria and I will talk soon."

My father's voice is strained. "Grant—"

Grant cuts him off with a smooth nod, already backing toward the hall. "I'll be in touch."

His eyes slide to me one last time, and then he leaves. The front door clicks shut, and silence descends quickly upon us.

My mother exhales shakily, pressing a hand to her chest.

"Why is he here?" my father barks out. "Who told him you were here?"

My mouth twists. "My guess is he has friends on your staff. It makes him feel important."

I stare at the spot where Grant stood.

"It's time to leave," Niko cuts in.

It's weird. I thought I'd feel safe here, but I don't. I feel hollow.

Nico gestures toward the door. I turn to leave, but instead, I pause in the doorway, my back to them, throat tight. I thought that if I came here, I'd feel something different. Love . . .

But the only time I ever felt love here was with Lorenzo.

I don't turn around. I just walk out.

As we pull away, I stare at the estate shrinking behind us and think about Grant. How his eyes sharpened when I refused to answer. He was frustrated, but there was something else. Something I can't put my finger on.

"You did good." Nico's low voice breaks the silence in the car.

I blink, turning my head. "Good at what?"

He shrugs one shoulder, his gaze forward. "Not talking."

I let out a bitter laugh. "It's funny. Everyone keeps complimenting me on being quiet."

"Quiet keeps you alive." Nico doesn't smile.

I stare out the window again, watching the trees blur, as my chest aches with everything I didn't say.

With everything I can't.

I didn't tell Grant.

I protected Lorenzo.

I don't know what that makes me.

But I'm scared to find out.

CHAPTER 51

Victoria

THE HOUSE FEELS DIFFERENT WHEN I COME BACK.

I'm not sure why, but it is. Hell, I can't even put my finger on what's different about it.

Maybe it's me. Maybe I'm different.

I step inside, the front door shutting behind me with a soft click. Surprisingly, Nico doesn't follow me this time. "You're back *home*."

The man is so weird.

Sometimes I think he feels bad for me, and other times, I think he's just plain annoyed.

I peel off my coat and hang it in the foyer closet. "Try not to sound so disappointed."

Nico's mouth twitches. "Rafe texted that your *husband* is in his study."

The way he says husband makes me pause. Almost like a reminder to me that he, too, covered for Lorenzo, or maybe it's something else . . . I'm not sure.

"Did Rafe mention if he's in a mood?"

"From what I've gathered, yes."

"Charming." I adjust my sweater, needing something to do with my hands.

Nico lifts a brow. "Don't wander around."

I glance at him, letting my smile sharpen. "Wouldn't dare."

He huffs a quiet laugh, then takes a step outside.

I nod, but as soon as the door closes, I do the opposite of what he tells me. One place is calling my name, and even though I probably shouldn't go there, I find myself standing outside the door to the study.

My hand reaches out and rests on the wood. Should I? I pull back, hovering now, deciding whether I dare. What about Lorenzo makes me so damn confused?

I should hate him, and I shouldn't be seeking him out, yet . . . I push the door open anyway.

Lorenzo is stretched on the couch, one ankle propped on his opposite knee, scotch in hand.

He looks . . . wrecked.

Yet dangerous all at the same time.

It's scary.

His dark shirt is half unbuttoned, his tan skin peeking out, and his sleeves are shoved up to his forearms.

His hair is slightly out of place, the way it looks when he rakes his fingers through it because he's pissed. And if I weren't sure of his attitude, his jaw seals the deal. It looks like it's been clenched for hours.

I stand in the doorway for a few seconds, and he doesn't look up. Just continues to swirl the scotch in his glass slowly.

"You're home." He finally breaks the silence with a voice deep and rough.

I step farther inside and shut the door. "Don't sound so thrilled."

His gaze finally lifts, finding me with that intensity that always makes my skin feel like it's under a spotlight. He drags it over me, then settles back like he didn't just make my whole body tingle.

"How was it?" he asks, the words casual.

I blink once, forcing my mouth into something neutral. "Wonderful."

The corner of his mouth lifts. "You don't look like you believe that."

I walk deeper into the room, heels silent on the rug. "Doesn't matter."

He takes a slow sip, eyes never leaving mine. "Your parents behave?"

I shrug. "They made tea."

"Enlightening. And you," he prompts, rolling the glass between his fingers. "Did you behave?"

I scoff, stopping near the coffee table. "Don't I always?"

His expression shifts, almost amused. "Debatable."

"Can't you just stop already?" I shoot back, then stop myself from saying more. I don't want a fight right now.

Not when I'm still unnerved by Grant.

I exhale and then tilt my chin up. "It was . . . fine."

His eyes narrow slightly. He knows I'm leaving something out.

I keep my face still.

He stares one beat too long, then leans back into the couch like he's letting it go. Not because he believes me, but because he doesn't want to be bothered right now. He really must have had a bad day.

"Good."

I should turn and leave. The smart thing to do would be to go upstairs and lock myself in my room, but instead, my gaze drops.

To his hands.

I squint.

His knuckles are bruised, and they are not old bruises. These marks are fresh. Purple and red. The skin looks swollen.

He was in a fight. My stomach twists, and before I can stop myself, my body moves until I'm so close I'm able to reach out. My fingers hover over his bruises, hesitating.

"Are you okay?" I whisper, concern evident in my voice.

Lorenzo's mouth curves. There is something sinister in the way he looks right now. Almost bitter.

He shifts his hand away slightly, not fully withdrawing, just enough to keep control of the situation. "That . . . is nothing."

I swallow, my hand pulling back like I've been burned. "Nothing doesn't look like that."

"You should see the wall."

I blink. "You punched a wall."

He makes a small, dismissive gesture with his bruised hand. "In my defense, the wall started it."

"That's a lie," I chide.

Lorenzo's gaze lifts to mine, and a flicker of something is there. If I had to guess, it looks like a mixture of humor and pain. A nostalgic moment, which I know he will shut down as fast as I saw it.

"You're staring." He narrows his eyes, and it feels like a curtain is dropping on a show I've been watching.

"I'm assessing you, if you want to know the truth." I smile.

"Assess this," he replies.

Slowly, he turns his forearm outward, and I'm met with a long scar running up the length.

It's not a thin white line. No, this one looks like it cut to the bone.

It's jagged, thick, and pale against his skin. It disappears beneath his sleeve, but I can tell it goes higher. Farther.

My breath catches hard enough that my chest aches, then my eyes snap up to his face. "What is—"

Lorenzo watches me, expression unreadable. "That's a scar."

"I know it's a scar." My throat tightens. "But how are you—"

"Alive?" he supplies, leaning back like the story is entertaining. "Stubbornness. Spite. Excellent medical care. Take your pick."

I stare at the scar like it might start bleeding in front of me.

Because all I can see is Lorenzo. This new Lorenzo. The violent one, with scars and wounds I can't even see.

What happened to this man?

"Tell me," I whisper, then immediately want to slap myself for wanting to know so badly.

Lorenzo's gaze drags over my face, catching on my eyes. "No."

My stomach drops. Then he exhales slowly, like he's tired of being like this to me. Or maybe that's wishful thinking on my part.

His fingers tap the rim of his scotch glass once. Twice. "Sit." He nods to the couch beside him. It isn't a request, and it certainly isn't gentle. But it also isn't a command, either. It's . . . something else. And I'm not sure what that something else is.

I hesitate, then lower myself onto the couch, keeping space between us because I don't know what will happen if I don't. My hands clasp in my lap, fingers twisting tight.

Lorenzo shifts, angling toward me just enough that I feel his heat without him touching me.

"A few years back," he says, voice low. "I was running a collection."

My brows lift. "You make that sound like you were selling coupons and not collecting money from bad people."

His mouth twitches. "Don't be impressed. I was a glorified errand boy."

I stare at him. "You?"

He rolls his eyes, letting out a short breath that might be a laugh if he didn't look so exhausted. "Yes, me. Believe it or not, I didn't wake up one day with a god complex."

I snort before I can stop myself. "Debatable."

His gaze flicks to mine, sharp, then the corner of his mouth lifts like he likes that I still fight. "Anyway. I was sent to collect from a crew who thought they could . . . restructure their payments."

I tilt my head, watching him. "By restructure, you mean refuse?"

"By restructure," he replies, picking up the scotch and swirling it, "they meant 'ambush.'"

My stomach twists again.

Lorenzo's eyes drop to his scar as if he's seeing it happen all over again.

He doesn't flinch.

He just talks.

"They picked a dock warehouse," he continues, voice steady. "Late. Cold. Definitely dangerous."

I press my fingers into my knee, grounding myself.

"I walked in thinking it was going to be simple." Lorenzo shrugs. "Some threats. Some broken fingers. The usual."

I stare. "That's your version of normal."

His gaze slides to mine, deadpan. "Don't pretend you're surprised."

I swallow hard. "Go on."

Lorenzo leans his head back against the couch, eyes on the ceiling.

"There were more of them than there should have been," he says. "That was my first clue. Second clue was when one of them smiled at me like he was envisioning gutting me . . . spoiler alert, he was."

My stomach is in knots.

Lorenzo takes a sip, then sets the glass down again.

"They came at me fast," he continues. "Not amateurs. Not drunk idiots. These were men trained to hurt someone and keep them alive just long enough so that they could enjoy it."

My throat tightens. "Lorenzo—"

His gaze snaps to me, eyes bright with something dark. "It gets worse, Little Bird. Don't interrupt the show."

Heat flickers under my skin at the nickname, even now, even here.

I hate it.

Oh, who am I kidding . . . no, I don't.

Lorenzo's hand lifts, palm facing up. "I managed to put two of them down," he says, voice almost bored. "One tried to take my gun. That was . . . impolite."

"Did you—" I stop myself because I don't want details. I don't want images in my head.

Lorenzo's mouth curves. "Yes, Victoria. I did. Turns out, I'm a violent man. I know, shocking development."

I glare at him. "I'm trying not to picture it."

He leans closer a fraction, eyes narrowing. "Then stop asking questions you don't want me to answer."

"Fine. I won't," I say before clamping my mouth shut.

"One of them caught my arm," he says. "Blade."

My stomach turns.

Lorenzo lifts his scarred forearm slightly, fingers tracing the jagged line. "Went deep," he mumbles. "I remember thinking . . . that's a lot of blood. They stabbed me a few more times before leaving me to bleed out and die."

My breath catches, and I hate that my eyes sting.

Lorenzo notices immediately. His gaze flicks up, sharp.

"Don't," he warns, voice quiet. "Don't look at me like that."

"Like what?" I whisper, my voice rough.

"Like I'm human," he replies, the words bitter.

I swallow hard. "You are."

Lorenzo's laugh is low and unpleasant. "That's generous."

I lean forward slightly, hands gripping each other tighter. "How did you survive?"

He shrugs. "I didn't feel like dying."

"That's not—"

"That's exactly it. I dragged myself out. Used my belt for a tourniquet. Bad knot. Worse pain. But it did the deed."

I stare at him, horrified.

"And then," he adds, lips curling, "since I had fucked up by going without Matteo and backup, I called Rafe."

My brows lift. "And?"

Lorenzo's eyes gleam with dark amusement. "He answered like I was interrupting his beauty sleep."

Despite myself, a laugh escapes. "No way."

Lorenzo's mouth lifts, the closest thing to real humor I've seen from him since the wedding. "He thought I was joking. Told me to 'stop being dramatic.'"

"That sounds like him."

"He showed up, but he wasn't alone. He brought Matteo,"

Lorenzo continues, voice rougher now. "Both of them took one look at me and went white, which was satisfying.

"I remember both of them so clearly despite being delusional from blood loss," Lorenzo says, quieter. "Rafe was trying to hold pressure. Matteo kept telling me not to close my eyes."

My chest aches. "And then?"

"I lived, obviously. But I told him if I died, he owed me a drink."

I blink. "That's what you said?"

He shrugs one shoulder. "I was trying to motivate him."

"That's not motivation."

"It worked," he replies.

Silence settles between us. I stare at the scar again, then at his bruised knuckles, then at his face. Something shifts in me.

Understanding.

Because monsters aren't born. They're made.

I swallow hard. "Does it hurt?"

His gaze flicks up, surprised.

"Still," I clarify, gesturing helplessly at his scar. "Does it still hurt?"

"Sometimes," he admits, the word reluctant. "When it rains. When it's cold. When I'm tired."

My throat tightens. "So basically always."

His mouth curves faintly. "Basically."

I stare at him, and my voice comes out before I can stop it. "Why show me?"

Lorenzo's eyes sharpen, and he looks at me like I just asked him to confess to a crime he didn't commit.

Then he shrugs. It's small, almost careless. "You asked. And you were looking at me like you wanted to know."

My cheeks heat. "I was looking because I was shocked."

"Sure," he replies, gaze dropping to my mouth briefly, then back to my eyes. "Shocked."

My pulse stutters, furious at my body for responding.

I force my tone back into something safer. "You keep scars like trophies."

Lorenzo's lips twitch. "They're reminders."

"Of what?" I challenge.

His eyes go cold. "That I don't get to be naive."

The words hit harder than they should. Because I remember him as naive. I remember him laughing in the boathouse like the world hadn't taught him cruelty yet.

And now here he is, older, sharper, full of violence, carrying wounds that will haunt him for life.

I take a slow breath. "I didn't know."

He shakes his head. "Don't start."

"I didn't know anything," I whisper, the sentence heavy with everything I can't say.

Lorenzo's jaw flexes. "You didn't know because you didn't stay."

Pain flashes in his eyes, too quick to be anything but real.

I flinch, and he sees it. Of course he does.

His hand lifts, fingers reaching toward my face, then stops. For a second, he just hovers there, knuckles inches from my cheek.

Then, slowly, his hand moves and brushes a loose strand of hair back behind my ear.

His touch is careful, like he's handling something easily breakable.

Lorenzo's thumb grazes my cheekbone once, a ghost of contact, and his eyes hold mine as my breath catches.

"Stop looking at me like I'm salvageable."

I swallow hard. "Stop acting like you're not."

"You think you can fix me?"

"I think you're more than this," I whisper, then immediately want to take it back because it makes me feel vulnerable.

Lorenzo's gaze drops to my lips again, and the air changes.

It reminds me of the moment right before a storm breaks. My pulse starts racing, and I can't tell if it's fear or something worse.

Lorenzo leans in a fraction, and my whole body braces. A

weird feeling of electricity rushes through my body, and that terrifies me more than anything.

His breath warms my mouth. "Careful."

I don't move. I can't. I'm frozen in place, and the room feels too small for both of us.

I expect him to cross the space . . .

Please cross it.

But he doesn't. Instead, he pulls back, not far, just enough to keep some semblance of control.

I blink, trying to breathe like a normal person. I should leave. I should run upstairs, lock my door, and pretend I didn't almost melt when I thought he might kiss me.

Instead, I stay.

I'm tired of running.

I clear my throat, voice rough, needing to change the narrative of the moment. "I saw Grant."

"What?"

"I . . . didn't tell him anything."

His eyes snap to mine, cold and sharp. "Grant was there? Nico didn't mention that . . ."

I regret telling him instantly. I should have kept it to myself. But it's out now, hanging between us, making my stomach tighten in fear.

"Yes, he was there." I lift my chin. "At my parents' house. Asking questions."

Lorenzo's jaw tightens, and the room feels like it drops ten degrees.

"And you told him what?"

I swallow hard. "As I said before, I didn't tell him anything."

His gaze searches my face like he's looking for a lie. I hold still because he won't find anything.

"Why not?" he asks, voice low.

"Because I didn't want you to—" I whisper.

"To what?"

"Get hurt."

He leans back slowly, like he needs distance from that confession, and drags a hand down his face.

"Christ. You really are going to ruin me twice."

My chest tightens. "I didn't do anything."

"You don't even realize you're holding the knife."

My throat bobs. "Then take it away."

Lorenzo's mouth curves, dark and bitter. "I can't." The word hangs there.

Heavy.

Too honest.

I stare at him, my voice barely a breath. "Why?"

His eyes lock onto mine, unblinking, and for a second, the cruelty peels back far enough that I can see the raw thing underneath. He shifts closer, not touching, but close enough that I feel him.

"You want the truth?"

My pulse jumps. "No."

His mouth twitches. "Liar."

I swallow hard. "Fine. Yes."

"You were never a phase." His voice is rough. Filled with emotion. "You were always the end."

The words hit like a punch. Not because they're romantic. Because they're terrifying.

Because an ending isn't gentle.

An ending is final.

My mouth opens, but nothing comes out.

I don't know what to do with that kind of confession from a man who turns love into a weapon.

Lorenzo watches me struggle with it, eyes dark, and then his mouth curls.

He walks over to where he placed his glass, lifting it slightly in a mock salute. "Congratulations. You've successfully traumatized me, again."

I blink, breathing again. "That's . . . not the reaction I was expecting."

He takes a slow sip, gaze never leaving mine. "I aim to disappoint."

My heart races, and I still tingle from where his fingers touched my hair.

I'm frightened.

But I'm not even sure why.

The fear lodges under my ribs like a thorn.

I move toward the door.

I need to leave.

If I stay, I might do something stupid. Like reach for him again. Or forget I'm supposed to hate him.

Lorenzo's gaze tracks me, slow and heavy. "Running."

"Breathing," I snap, turning toward the door. "There's a difference."

"Barely."

I take a step and then stop. "Thank you for telling me . . ."

About the past. About its scars.

"Don't mistake honesty for softness, Little Bird."

I glance back, meeting his eyes for one beat. "Don't mistake my concern for forgiveness," I retort.

His smile is small. Dangerous. Almost proud.

I leave before either of us can say something worse.

Once I'm upstairs, I feel safe again.

Even though I shouldn't.

Because tonight, for the first time, I saw the wound beneath the surface. Which means I'm in even more danger than I thought. Because the moment you see the truth in the monster . . .

You start wondering if the monster can see the truth in you, too.

CHAPTER 52

Lorenzo

I STAND IN FRONT OF THE SECURITY MONITORS, WATCHING surveillance footage that Dom hacked into.

Eventually, we will find this fucker.

Connor might be good at hiding, but I'm better at tracking.

"Back it up," I say, signaling to the video currently playing in front of me.

Dom taps the keyboard, and the footage rewinds. The video is from a street camera outside of a nightclub.

My gaze narrows as Dom replays the clip. I narrow my eyes and focus on the figure stepping out of the door.

It looks like Connor.

The man slips through the crowd standing out front of the club.

"Zoom in," I order.

The image tightens. He turns just enough for the camera to catch his profile. My jaw sets. Yep. It's him.

"Okay. Now that we know it's him, let's zoom and focus on where he goes."

We watch as Connor exits through the door. The timestamp says it's 2:17 a.m. The camera outside catches him lighting a cigarette, then he heads toward the street.

"There," I say. "Freeze it."

The car pulls into frame. It's a black SUV. He opens the passenger door and gets inside.

"Enhance the plate."

Dom does what I ask, and I jot down the license plate number on my phone.

Got you.

Now I can use my connections to find him.

"Run the plates," I order. "Find out everything you can, and let's see if we can track the bastard."

"No problem, Boss," Dom answers.

I step away from the screens and pull my phone from my pocket, already dialing. Matteo picks up on the second ring.

"You find him?" my cousin asks, cutting right to the chase.

"I have a lead," I say. "We have him on video leaving a nightclub. Clear image of the plate too."

"Good work. Need help? I'm handling something for my pops now, but I can meet you at the warehouse tonight to go over a plan?"

"Nah, all good."

"You sure?" he asks.

"Yep."

"Cool. Thanks, man. Appreciate you taking point on this."

"Of course. Talk later."

I hang up and slide the phone back into my pocket before heading out of the security room and back upstairs.

I turn toward Victoria's room without thinking. When I get there, her bedroom door is open, but the room is empty. I step inside and glance around. Her bed is neatly made, but other than that, there is no sign of her, or that she was ever there.

I stand in the middle of the room, jaw clenched. Where is she?

Unease settles in my gut.

Could she have left?

No.

There's no way.

But . . .

Nope.

She's got to be somewhere, and I'll find her.

I turn on my heel and head back the way I came, down the stairs, and straight back into the security room.

"Dom." At the sound of my voice, he turns his head and meets my stare.

"Yeah?"

"Pull interior and exterior feeds," I order. "Last twenty minutes. I want eyes on Victoria."

No questions asked. Dom reaches forward, and his fingers type furiously on the keyboard.

He checks every angle of the estate. Inside and out. There's no way she could have escaped, but I just don't like not knowing where she is.

Which is a huge problem in itself . . . but I can't think about that now. The need to find her is stronger than my need to evaluate my obsession with my wife.

"There," Dom says, freezing the video and pointing.

Victoria appears on the screen, moving through the hall.

Something is off about her.

She seems slower than usual. And one of her hands skims the wall. Almost like she's bracing herself.

Then she turns left.

"The library."

I'm already gone before Dom can say anything else, sprinting down the hall until I reach the library. The doors are open when I reach them. I step inside and see that she's standing near the shelves, one hand braced against a ladder, the other holding a book she hasn't opened.

She looks up when I enter but doesn't speak. Something is off with her.

"What are you doing?" I ask.

She turns fully, and my chest tightens.

Her skin is pale. Too pale. The sharpness I'm used to, the fire in her eyes, is dulled.

"I couldn't sleep," she says. "I have a headache. Thought I'd grab a book before lying down."

There's no rude rebuttal. No sarcasm. And her tone . . .

I narrow my eyes.

"You hate reading when you're tired," I say, remembering her years ago saying that when she's tired, her eyes hurt.

She huffs. "Congratulations. You know your wife."

A little better. More like her normally hostile personality, but still, it's weak.

I take a step toward her. "Are you okay?"

She rolls her eyes. "Yes. It's just a headache, Lorenzo."

Just when I'm about to believe her, she shifts her weight and wobbles.

I grab her automatically, one arm wrapping around her waist to steady her.

She feels warm.

I lift my free hand and press my palm to her forehead.

"Shit. You're burning up."

She frowns, blinking at me. "I'm fine."

"You're not," I say flatly.

Before she can protest, I bend and scoop her up, one arm under her knees, the other braced across her back. She gasps, startled.

"What are you doing?" she demands, voice sharper now, but there's no real bite behind it.

"You're sick." I turn toward the door. "And you're going to bed."

"I can walk—"

"No."

She glares up at me, stubborn even when she has a fever. "You don't get to—"

"I absolutely do." I carry her out of the library. "Because you're about five seconds from passing out, and I'm not letting that happen."

She exhales, head tipping briefly against my shoulder. "You're being dramatic."

"And you're sick."

CHAPTER 53

Victoria

I WAKE UP CHOKING ON HEAT.

And not the warm and cozy kind of heat. This is different. I feel like I'm suffocating. Like there is a fire under my skin, yet it feels like my bones are brittle and made of ice. It makes no sense.

I try to pry my eyes open, but nothing happens at first. When I finally get them open, my lids hurt from the effort. Hell, my whole body does.

Now up, I take a moment to evaluate the situation, quickly realizing that my sheets are damp, and my hair is sticking to my neck.

I try to sit up, but the room tilts, making me sway.

"Don't," a deep voice snaps at me.

A hand presses gently into my shoulder, anchoring me back to the bed. The touch is cool against my overheated skin.

"Easy," the voice adds, lower now. "You'll pass out."

I blink. Once. Twice.

Lorenzo swims in and out of focus.

"You're . . . loud," I mumble.

His mouth twitches despite himself. "You're delirious. Don't flirt. It's unbecoming."

"I flirt beautifully," I say before I cough so hard my chest burns.

He swears under his breath and reaches for a glass on the nightstand. Then he does something I don't expect. He slides an arm behind my shoulders, lifts me to a seated position, and presses the rim to my lips.

"Drink," he orders.

I do. Because I'm too tired to protest, and in truth, I know my body needs it. Cool water spills down my throat, and I moan without meaning to.

Lorenzo's grip tightens around me. "Jesus." He makes a weird grumbling sound in his chest. "Try not to sound like that unless you're fully conscious."

I glare at him . . . which is hard to do in my current state, and I instantly regret it. "You're disgusting."

"You married me," he replies, easing me back down.

My vision swims again, and if I weren't already lying down, I'm sure I'd have fallen.

This is awful.

I feel like shit.

My skin feels too tight, like it doesn't even belong to me.

"I feel . . . like I'm dying." I groan, and even that hurts.

"Unfortunately," he agrees. "That's usually how illness works."

I scowl, or at least try to. I'm pretty sure I look like a wounded animal that someone should take pity on.

I expect Lorenzo to leave, but surprisingly, he doesn't leave. Instead, he reaches for my wrist, and his fingers press lightly against my pulse.

His brows knit. "How bad?" I ask, my voice slurring around the edges.

"You'll live," he answers.

I huff weakly. "Wonderful."

My eyes start to shut, and I swear I hear him whisper that he won't let anything happen to me as I drift off to sleep.

Time ceases to exist.

I'm in and out of consciousness for hours.

Eventually, I wake to a cool cloth being laid on my forehead.

At some point, my stomach rebels, and I barely register being lifted and held steady as I sip soup.

"Slowly," Lorenzo orders, not gentle but not cruel either. "You don't want to get sick."

I follow his orders, and when I'm done, he wipes my mouth.

And because I'm delirious, when he moves, I grab his wrist.

"Don't leave," I whisper, the words slipping out before I can stop them.

His body stills. "I'm not," he says after a moment, voice lower. "Go back to sleep."

I do.

When I wake again, it's morning.

Pale light filters through the curtains. My body feels wrung out, but I do feel different. Better, maybe.

I turn my head slowly and freeze when I notice I'm not alone. Lorenzo is asleep in a chair beside my bed.

His head is tipped back slightly, jaw slack in a way I haven't seen in years.

My chest tightens.

A thought springs to life in my head.

In another life, this could have been normal. Sick days and shared beds and someone staying up all night because that's what you do when you love someone.

As if he can hear my thoughts, Lorenzo stirs.

His eyes open slowly and land on me instantly. "Good, you're still alive." His words don't match his actions, and I know he's full of shit when he says them. But I'll play along.

"Disappointed?"

"Deeply . . ." He rubs a hand down his face. "I had plans."

I smile. Regardless of our words, we are both full of it.

"You stayed," I say quietly.

"I did." He stands and rolls his shoulders. "You did ask."

"True, but that didn't mean you had to sleep there." I point at the chair.

"Where else was I supposed to sleep?"

My cheeks warm as it hits me that the only other place he could have slept is next to me.

"Drink this." His words cut through my thoughts as he gives me a glass of water. "And don't move."

"You know I don't like to follow orders."

"Yeah, I know, Little Bird. That's why if you do, I'll just chain you to the bed." He smirks.

"Don't threaten a girl with a good time."

That makes him laugh. "Glad to see the fever broke and you have your personality back."

I open my mouth to respond, but can't think of anything to say, so I finally say what's in my chest, which makes it hard to understand why he's still here.

"I thought you hated me," I say softly.

He looks at me then. Really looks.

"I don't," he answers without hesitation, before he turns to go.

"Lorenzo," I say. He pauses without facing me. "Thank you," I add, quieter. "For . . . last night."

He nods but still leaves.

The door shuts softly behind him.

I lie back against the pillows, staring at the ceiling. My body is still weak, and my heart is doing something reckless and stupid and entirely on its own.

Is this how we could have been if the world hadn't stepped in and tore us apart?

CHAPTER 54

Lorenzo

I'VE TRIED TO KEEP AWAY. BUT SHIT, IT'S MUCH FUCKING HARDER than I anticipated.

It's been three days since I slept in her room for the first time. Yep, I've camped out there every night since.

I'm fucking pathetic.

But in my defense . . . there is no defense. I just can't keep away.

Even now, as I'm halfway down the hall, I can hear her, a soft, muffled gasp filtering past the closed door to her room.

Then another.

I take a deep breath.

Don't check on her.

She's okay.

Another sound. This time, it sounds like a cough.

Shit.

My hand stops on the banister, fingers tightening.

She's been sick for days, but she no longer has a fever, so she's recovering.

Yet something about the sound of her in pain has me wanting to turn around and go to her.

I should keep walking, but my feet move before I can stop them. I'm at her bedroom door in three strides, and I'm pushing it open before I can stop myself.

Her room is dim, but I can still see her. She's twisted in the sheets, hair fanned across the pillow. Her face is pinched with lips parted.

"No," she whispers.

The word isn't loud, but my jaw still tightens.

I step closer.

Her body jerks again, a tremor running through her body. "I didn't—" she breathes, voice cracking. "I didn't . . . I'm sorry . . . I'm sorry . . ."

My throat goes tight. She might not say it, but deep in my gut, I know exactly who she's apologizing to.

And that someone is me.

I stop at the edge of her bed, staring down at her.

She chokes on a breath. "Please—"

I don't think. I just sit on the edge of the mattress and gently grab her wrist.

"Victoria. Wake up."

Her eyes snap open, and for a split second, it's like she doesn't see me.

She looks like she did when she was seventeen, and her father caught her sneaking out.

Like the world is about to hurt her, and she knows it.

Then her gaze locks onto mine, and she freezes.

"Lorenzo," she whispers.

I let my hand stay on her wrist.

"You're having a nightmare."

Her eyes search my face. The expression on her face looks like she expects me to vanish.

"I—" Her voice breaks. "I thought—"

"I know." My mouth twists. "You always think too much."

She makes a sound that might be a laugh. Her hand tightens around mine suddenly, fingers cold. And that's when I realize . . . she's *reaching* for me.

My chest aches in a way I don't have a name for.

"Don't look at me like that," I grit out.

Her eyes flash. "Like what?"

"Like you're relieved I'm here." The words come out sharper than I mean.

Her lips part, but she doesn't speak. She just stares at me. Her gaze is raw and confused.

Her mouth trembles again, and her gaze drops to our hands like it's the first time she's realizing she's holding me. *She's going to let go.* She doesn't.

Instead, her fingers slide up, touching my knuckles. My freshly scarred knuckles.

She notices.

Of course, she notices.

"There's more." Her brows pinch. "What happened to your hand?"

I pull away automatically. "Nothing."

She follows the motion, sitting up farther, hair falling over her shoulder. She looks smaller now, wrapped in white sheets, face still flushed.

"You have new scars?"

"It's fine." I flex my hand, as if proving it's nothing.

Her lips twitch faintly, and tears fill her eyes. And they are real.

Her jaw tightens. Then a tear slips down her cheek, and she turns her face away from me like she's ashamed of her feelings.

Something inside me snaps. Not in a violent way. In the other way.

The way I hate.

I reach out and cup her jaw, forcing her face back toward mine.

Her breath catches, and her eyes flare. "Don't."

"Don't cry," I correct softly, thumb brushing the tear off her skin with a slow stroke. "Not for me."

A small laugh escapes her, but her chin still trembles.

She stares at me for a long moment, like she's trying to decide what to do.

Then she reaches up, and her fingers slide into my hair.

I go still. "Victoria," I warn.

Her hand trembles in my hair. "I can't—" she whispers, voice breaking. "I can't do this anymore."

"Do what?"

"Hate you." The words sound pained, and I feel the pang in my own chest. "I don't—I don't hate—"

"Stop." My voice comes out harsh, and I regret the tone immediately when she flinches.

I lean in closer, lowering my voice, forcing control back into my bones. "Stop. You don't have to speak. Just breathe."

She leans forward, lips parting. I expect her to say something, but she doesn't. Instead, her lips find mine. She kisses me.

Slow.

A surrender.

And my mind blanks.

For one stunned second, I don't move. I don't respond. Hell, I don't even breathe.

Because I've imagined this a thousand times.

But in every version, I'm the one taking.

But this isn't me . . .

This is her.

All her.

Thank fuck.

My hands lift slowly, hovering near her face, until I gradually grab her behind the neck, deepening the kiss.

She trembles as our mouths collide. Her fingers tighten in my hair like she's afraid I'll vanish if she loosens her grip.

I hear her breathe, a shaky exhale against my mouth, and something in me breaks open.

Soon, the kiss grows hotter, less gentle.

I'm a starved man, desperate for her.

It feels like I've been held underwater for too long and can finally breathe.

She makes a soft and surprised sound, then after one more swipe of our tongues, she breaks the kiss.

I peer down at her.

Her eyes are wide, her lips swollen, and her breathing ragged.

Her fingers press to my chest, but she's not pushing me away. She's just touching me.

"This is . . ." Her voice shakes. "This is wrong?" It raises a question. I shake my head.

"Almost everything in my life is wrong." I brush my thumb across her cheek. "But this isn't."

I pull back slightly.

My voice comes out softer. "Tell me to stop, and I will."

Her breath catches, and her eyes search mine.

She didn't object . . . so I kiss her again.

Slower this time.

Deeper.

My hands slide down her back, feeling every shiver, every tremble. She arches into me.

This isn't just a kiss. Nor is it lust. It's so much more.

It's grief.

It's history.

It's years of longing for each other despite never admitting it.

I move her back, guiding her into the pillows, my body hovering over hers, careful not to crush.

This time, she pulls me down until her lips find mine again. She kisses me urgently.

Needy.

"Lorenzo." My name on her lips, like a prayer . . . It wrecks me.

"Don't say my name like that," I brush my mouth over hers. "I'll start believing I deserve it."

"You don't," she whispers.

I smile against her lips. "I know."

This moment feels inevitable.

Like we've been moving toward this since the day she walked back into my life . . . or I stormed into hers.

I keep my mouth on hers, keeping my hands steady.

Victoria lies beside me, curled toward my chest as her body moves there without asking her permission. Her hair is a mess across the pillow.

"I hate you," she whispers, voice barely there.

I kiss her forehead. "I know."

Her fingers curl into my shirt. "But I don't. . ." She chokes. "Not really."

I hold her tighter, my jaw clenched, throat burning. "Neither do I," I admit quietly.

She just buries her face in my chest and breathes me in. Eventually, her fingers loosen on my shirt, and her head sinks into the hollow of my shoulder.

She's asleep, and I stay awake.

Staring at the ceiling. Listening to the storm outside.

Feeling the weight of her in my arms.

I should feel triumphant.

Maybe even satisfied.

I should feel like I won.

Instead, I feel terrified.

Because I wanted her to suffer.

And now I've tasted something that feels dangerously like forgiveness.

Or worse—love.

I press my mouth to her hair, breathing her in. "Sleep, Little Bird, I've got you."

And the most horrifying part?

I mean it.

CHAPTER 55

Victoria

I BLINK AT THE CEILING.

Is it warm in here?

I turn my head toward the window. The curtains are half drawn, and bright morning light streams in through the gaps in the blinds.

Clips of last night filter through my brain.

His mouth.

His hands.

His voice.

The moment I kissed him . . .

I sit up too fast; the sheets slipping down my shoulder. Cold air bites my skin, and I suck in a breath, scanning the room.

Empty.

Unlike when I was sick, he's not propped in the chair, fighting for rest.

I wrap the blanket around myself and swing my legs over the side of the bed.

I feel . . . strange.

It's almost like my heart got shocked back to life. My ribs ache with it.

I stand from the bed and then stumble into the bathroom.

Once the faucet is on, I splash cold water on my face and stare at myself in the mirror.

Did yesterday really happen?

Yes, idiot. I've already established it wasn't a dream.

I touch my damp fingers to my lips, which still feel swollen.

Is this what it looks like to be kissed until you barely know your name? Forget my name; I look like a woman who got kissed until she forgot how to breathe.

Once my hands are dry and my teeth are brushed, I head back into the bedroom and grab a change of clothes.

I change quickly into leggings and a thick sweater.

Once I'm ready, I open the bedroom door.

The hallway is quiet.

Guards stand at a distance, pretending not to watch me.

I take a step. Then another. As I walk, I realize something unsettling . . . no one is looking at me.

Well, that's not true, but they're looking at me like I'm supposed to be here. Like I'm not a prisoner.

I reach the staircase and start down, each step echoing as I descend. I'm almost at the bottom when I smell something baking.

I follow the smell like I'm starving, until I step into the kitchen.

Lorenzo.

He stands at the stove wearing black sweatpants and a dark Henley, sleeves shoved up to his forearms, with hair still damp, like he showered.

He's concentrating on the stove, a pan in one hand, a spatula in the other. Something sizzles in the background. I cock my head and take a peek. He's making eggs and bacon.

My brain short-circuits at the sight before me. There is something so sexy about Lorenzo being domestic. I swear my ovaries just exploded on the spot.

Get a grip, Victoria.

The chance of my being able to control my thoughts is lost the moment he turns slightly, glancing over his shoulder and looking right at me.

For a second, his eyes go unreadable. Then his gaze drops—to my mouth. My entire body reacts before I can stop myself.

My whole body is warm. Shit, do I have a fever again? It's not my fault, really . . .

The man is practically undressing me with his eyes.

My pulse flutters as my face is now officially on fire, or at least it feels like it is.

And to pour salt in my wounds, his mouth curves. Damn. He's not playing fair. Being this sexy should be illegal. And the way he's enjoying my reaction? Also not fair.

"You're alive." He flips something in the pan with effortless skill.

I blink once, trying to right my thoughts, and not think of last night's kiss. "Morning." I step farther into the kitchen, arms crossing over my chest. "What are you doing?"

He slides food onto a plate, then sets it on the island like he's presenting something sacred. "Cooking."

"I can see that." I eye the eggs as if they might bite. "Why?"

His brows lift slightly, like he expected me to ask a different question. "Because you've barely eaten the past few days."

My pulse jumps, and I clear my throat in a half-assed attempt not to seem so affected by his concern. "You have staff."

"I do," he agrees, grabbing another plate. "But I wanted to do this for you."

"You did?" I stare at him, then look at the eggs, then back at him.

His mouth twitches. "I did."

He sets his plate down, like nothing happened, like he didn't just shake my world. Sure, we kissed last night, but a part of me thought that was a fluke.

But now, in the bright morning light of a new day, while Lorenzo strolls to the coffeepot to pour me a cup, I don't even know how to react, because it's obvious something has changed between us, and I can't help the butterflies flying in my stomach at the idea.

I take a seat at the table, in front of the breakfast he cooked me, as he slides over a hot mug. Then he leans his hip against the counter, watching me. "Eat, Victoria."

My brows lift. "Is that an order?"

"Yep. Don't ruin it." His voice is light and playful, reminding me of the Lorenzo I once knew.

I blink again, and then I stare at the eggs, not knowing what to do with myself. I guess I'll eat.

I take a bite, and it's good. Of course, it is. Because Lorenzo excels at everything he does.

I take another bite, then stare at him as I watch him watch me.

His mouth tilts. "Like what you see?"

"You're the one staring," I retort.

"Or maybe it's you, and I'm just following suit."

"What else am I supposed to do? You're acting all husbandly."

He arches a brow. "Because I cooked you breakfast?"

"Yes."

"Careful . . . I'll buy a minivan next."

A laugh bubbles out of my mouth, and his eyes lock onto the movement. His face shifts, his features softening as he watches me.

"So . . ." He taps his fingers lightly against the counter. "I want to take you somewhere."

My fork pauses midair. "Where?" I ask.

His gaze comes back to mine, steady. "Outside."

I blink. "I thought I wasn't allowed outside . . ." The moment the words slip out, I regret it. He just offered me something I want, pissing him off by being snippy isn't a smart idea. I don't want Lorenzo to go back to being an asshole.

"That's a rule I made." His voice softens. "I can change it."

"Why would you do that?"

"Because you've been staring out the windows like a caged animal, and I don't like it."

My mouth opens and shuts, and he smiles at the movement.

He leans forward slightly. "Finish eating, Little Bird."

My stomach flips at the nickname, but I shrug it off and still, for some reason, try to pretend I'm not affected by it.

I roll my eyes. "I'm not your Little Bird anymore."

He watches me for a beat too long. "That's where you're wrong. You always were. And nothing will change that."

I don't answer.

Because I don't know what to do with that. The kitchen goes quiet again, but it isn't hostile for the first time since I've moved into this house, it's . . . something else.

When I finish eating, Lorenzo stands, walks to the pantry, and returns with a thick coat, handing it to me with a smile.

It's heavy black wool, warm.

I look down at it, then up at him. "You planned this?"

His eyes gleam. "I plan everything."

My heart rate picks up again. Damn my treacherous body. And if it weren't bad enough that I'm losing a war within myself to not be affected by this man, he grabs the gloves off the counter and pulls them on with slow precision.

The sight is obscene.

A man shouldn't look so hot putting on damn gloves.

I have it bad for my husband.

This isn't good.

Together, we move through the hallway until we are at the door to leave the house.

Lorenzo pauses, his gaze flickering to the nearest guard. The guard straightens.

"Stay where you are," Lorenzo orders, voice low, controlled.

He opens the door then, and together we step outside. No security, just us.

Cold air slams into my face, crisp and sharp.

Lorenzo walks beside me, hands in his pockets, coat collar turned up. His expression is unreadable, eyes scanning the property like he's watching for threats I can't see.

We walk down a path lined with snow-covered hedges. My breath clouds in front of me.

We go farther than I expected.

The house falls behind us, shrinking through the trees. The path curves toward the back edge of the property, where the land slopes gently downward.

I can hear something.

Not the guards. Not Lorenzo. Something rhythmic. A hush, then a low crash.

My steps slow, and then my breath catches. Because as soon as the trees thin, I see it . . .

Water.

A wide, sprawling view of the ocean.

I stop walking, and my heart thuds in my chest because across the water is a familiar shape on the opposite shoreline.

A massive estate.

With a small building set against the shoreline . . .

A boathouse.

My boathouse.

"That . . ." My voice comes out thin. "That's . . ."

Lorenzo's gaze stays fixed on the horizon. His hands remain in his pockets, and his posture is too still.

"Yes. It is."

I turn sharply toward him. "That's my parents' house. Why?"

He looks at me with those dark eyes.

"Why?" I ask again. "Why would you—"

"Because I could." His mouth twitches. "And because I wanted to . . ."

His words hang in the air. The meaning of them, though, is a bit more complex . . .

My head spins with what it could mean, but no matter how

much my brain circles around the words, it always comes back to the same thought: he wanted me close.

He wasn't over me.

He's still not.

My heart beats rapidly in my chest.

I gesture wildly at the view. "You bought an estate across from my parents just to—what? Stare at them? Torture yourself?"

His eyes flicker. Something dark passes behind them. He looks out at the water again.

"I bought this place with my father's inheritance." Lorenzo's voice is softer than I expected. "The one my uncle gave me when my father died."

My throat tightens.

"I'd been saving for years," he adds, looking down at the snow under his boots. "Every paycheck. Every scrap. Every dime. I didn't buy much. Didn't go out. Didn't waste money."

I stare at him, stunned.

He glances back at me. "Don't look at me like I'm noble. I'm not. I'm obsessive."

My voice cracks. "You were . . . here?"

His jaw flexes once as the question hits him somewhere unpleasant.

"Yes. I was . . . always here."

My chest feels too tight. I swallow. "That's insane."

A faint smile tugs at his mouth. "Yes."

I stare at the estate across the water. The boathouse is visible from here. A small structure, white and gray. A speck at this distance.

But my brain fills in the details anyway. I turn back to him. "You watched me?"

His gaze locks on mine.

It's dark.

Unflinching.

"I watched the house," he corrects, voice low. "I watched the shoreline. I watched the world that took you away from me."

My throat burns.

"And you didn't—" I choke, trying to force the words out. "You didn't come back."

His eyes narrow, and a muscle jumps in his jaw. "I did. In every way that mattered."

My breath catches in my chest, and suddenly I feel like I'm standing on unstable ground.

And it terrifies me.

"I don't understand."

His gaze drags down my face, slow. "You never did." He steps closer. Close enough that his presence fills my air.

"Last night," he says, voice low, and rough, "you kissed me."

My pulse spikes, and I swallow hard. He watches my throat move like he's cataloging it.

"Do you regret it?" he asks, quietly.

My heart pounds so hard I feel it in my teeth. I lift my chin, defiance instinctive. "I don't know."

His mouth curves faintly. "Honest?"

My breath shakes. "No. I don't regret it." I look out at the water again, then back at him.

"You're . . . not who you were," I whisper.

"Neither are you."

Silence stretches.

Wind whips around us as his hands touch my shoulder and then turn me to face him. Then he brushes a strand of hair off my cheek.

My skin tingles where he touches.

"Come here," he orders.

I don't move. Because if I move, I might fall. He steps closer anyway, closing the distance.

Lorenzo wraps his arms around me and pulls me closer.

His gaze drops to my mouth.

I whisper, "This is insane."

"Yes," he agrees, and then he kisses me.

Not devouring.

Not punishing.

Not taking.

This kiss is slow.

Careful.

Almost timid, like he's afraid the wrong pressure will shatter whatever fragile truce exists between us.

My hands lift, trembling. They rest against his chest, and I feel his heart beneath my touch. Steady. Strong.

He deepens the kiss gradually, mouth warm, breath steady, and I respond.

And for a second, it feels like we're back in the summer when everything still felt possible. When we were stupid enough to believe we could outrun our families.

He pulls back slightly, forehead resting against mine, breath mingling with mine.

"It was always you." His voice drops to a whisper. "*Always.*"

CHAPTER 56

Lorenzo

Victoria's hand is in mine, and the surprising part . . .

Is this an accident? No, this is deliberate. She's already decided where this is going.

Thank fuck.

Because I don't know what I'd do if it doesn't.

I need this fucking woman so much I can barely breathe.

Her thumb brushes the inside of my palm, an unconscious motion that hits me harder than it should. Muscle memory. Or maybe it's proof that some things never change.

We walk back toward the house together in silence.

The only sound is the gravel crunching beneath our feet. My large estate looms ahead, almost taunting me with the distance.

"I used to think," she says, voice low and measured, "that loving you was something I could outgrow."

I glance at her, but she's staring straight ahead.

"And now?" I ask.

Her fingers tighten around mine. "You can't outgrow something engraved in your soul."

That lands deep, the kind of deep men like me pretend doesn't exist because it would make us weak.

"I never stopped loving you," I admit, because there's no point lying now. Not when she's still here. Not when she hasn't let me go either. "I just got better at pretending I had."

She looks at me then, her eyes shining in the low light with the look she used to give me all those years ago.

"You were everywhere," she whispers. "Every version of my life still had you in it. I just . . . hated myself for that."

I stop walking. She does too, turning toward me automatically.

"You don't get to hate yourself for loving me," I say quietly. "That's my job."

Her lips tremble, but it's not a smile. Something softer. "I don't want to fight it anymore, Lorenzo."

"Me either," I say, lifting her hand and pressing my mouth to her knuckles.

She leans into me, her body molding to mine.

"I never got over you," I tell her, lips resting against her forehead. "I just learned how to survive without you."

She lets out a broken laugh. "You're not supposed to say things like that."

"Well, it was awful if it makes you feel any better."

We both grow silent, and for a long moment, we stand there. Then she squeezes my hand once.

"Take me inside," she says.

I don't hesitate. I do.

We barely make it to the bedroom before all restraint is out the window.

The moment we are alone in my bedroom, the air around us shifts.

"Hi," she whispers, her voice barely audible. It's almost like she is suddenly nervous.

I step closer to her. "Hi."

"You're staring."

"Of course, I am. You're gorgeous, and I need you."

Victoria's mouth opens, and I know she's going to say something, but I don't let her.

Instead, I close the distance between us, lean in, and seal my mouth to hers.

The kiss is soft at first.

I don't want to go too fast.

It's been years since we were last together like this.

I'm in no rush . . .

But soon she presses closer, and then when her hands reach for me, tangling in my shirt, I lose my shit, and cup her face in my hands.

"Need you," I groan against her mouth.

Her fingers curl into my chest at my words. "Need you too."

At her words, I pull her tighter. The kiss grows more frantic and desperate.

I've waited too long for this moment.

She tugs at my shirt, pulling the material up until her nails scratch my skin.

The feeling of her hands on me is almost too much right now. I want to devour her. Consume her.

I should take it slow, but fuck it, I can't.

I grip her tighter.

Pull her closer.

I want to savor every second of this moment. Her lips on mine. Her skin beneath my palms.

"Everything off," I order as I pull my shirt off, finishing the job she started.

Next, I kick off my pants.

My cock juts forward, ready.

She follows suit, stripping down slowly.

It's slow and seductive, and the tiny smirk on her face tells me she's doing it on purpose.

"You trying to kill me?"

"I am."

"With you like this . . . I'd happily die right now."

"Stop talking and kiss me." And then we're crashing back together.

Lips touching. Kissing.

Her hands roam down my chest until they find my cock.

When her hand grips the base, I groan. "Fuck." She tugs upward. "Just like that, Little Bird. Touch me. I love how you make me feel."

She continues her ministrations, working my dick with her hand.

She runs her hand from root to tip. Nothing has ever felt this good.

"On the bed."

Victoria drops her hand and lies down on the edge of the bed. I step between her parted legs. I run my hands over her thighs until my fingers settle on her pussy.

She's drenched, and it makes me smirk.

"Someone's excited." I slide a finger inside her, and she moans as her head rolls back.

I thrust another inside her. Fucking her with my hand. Getting her nice and ready for my cock.

"You like that?" I ask, as I curl my finger up to hit her G-spot. She wiggles her hips in answer, a moan slipping through her parted lips.

Her walls start to quiver, so I pull my fingers out. "I want to feel you come on my cock."

I quickly replace my hand with my cock.

"Hurry up," she groans, making me laugh.

I line myself up, but don't push in. "Patience is a virtue."

"Stop talking."

"Do you want me to fuck you?"

"You know I do."

"Beg . . ."

"Fuck off or fuck me," Victoria orders.

"Whatever you want, wife."

I push forward until the tip of my dick slips inside her.

"Move."

"Are you always so bossy?"

"I've waited five years for this, so yes."

"Good answer, wife." I reward her by feeding her pussy more of my cock.

I hold for a beat, until she lifts her hips, slipping another inch inside her, but when I can't take it anymore, I drive in, thrusting my whole length inside her greedy cunt.

I start to move my hips faster, harder, deeper.

"So good." Her walls tighten around my dick, and the feeling is sublime.

I drive into her again.

"Oh god," she moans, so I pick up my pace.

My movements are now punishing as I reach forward and start to furiously rub her clit.

She feels like heaven. This is heaven.

Pure fucking bliss.

Picking up my pace, I feel my balls tightening. I'm close, but I can't come without her.

As if she can hear my thoughts, she quivers around my cock.

"I'm coming," she pants as her pussy tightens.

"That's right, Little Bird, come all over my cock." And she does. Her pussy tightens to the point of exquisite pain.

"Fuck," I groan as my balls tighten, and I follow her over the edge.

After a minute, my breath finally regulates, and I drop down on top of her.

"Lorenzo." Her voice sounds winded. I move up, and she follows me, placing her head on my chest, her fingers slowly moving on my chest. "You really don't hate me," she says softly.

I close my eyes.

"As I said before, Little Bird, I never hated you," I admit. "I hated that the only place I ever felt human was with you."

She goes still. “Is that really so bad?”

“No. You ruined my life beautifully. But I wouldn’t have it any other way.”

Her eyes shine.

“And I’d let you do it again,” I add quietly. “Every time. Just to have you look at me like this.”

“What happens now?” she asks.

I brush my thumb beneath her eye before the moisture can fall.

“Now,” I say softly, “I stop pretending you’re not the only thing that ever mattered. And we do this . . .”

“Do what?”

“The whole forever thing . . . for real.”

“Okay.”

Just as I’m about to say more, the phone rings on the nightstand.

Reality crashes back into the room.

She grips my arm. “Don’t answer it.”

I already know who it is, so there’s no other choice. “I have to,” I tell her and myself.

Standing from the bed, I head out the door and step into the hall. “Talk,” I answer.

“We’ve got movement,” Rafe says.

My spine goes cold. “Where?”

“Boston.”

Bingo. I pinch the bridge of my nose. “Let’s head out.”

“Now?”

I look back toward the door and see where Victoria is. There isn’t even a decision made. “No. I have something I need to take care of first.”

“Something? Or someone?”

“Shut the fuck up.”

“I’m happy for you, man.”

“Thanks . . . I’m happy for myself.” With that, I hang up and go back to my wife.

CHAPTER 57

Lorenzo

AFTER A LAZY MORNING IN BED, I KNOW THERE IS ONE PLACE I need to take Victoria.

I don't tell her where we are going, but in all fairness, it's obvious.

Normally, when I step foot on her parents' property, I'm brimming with anger, but today, I'm not.

Hand in hand we walk together in silence, but the silence isn't an uncomfortable kind. It doesn't beg to be filled.

She doesn't ask where we're going as I lead her down the path. She just follows me with no questions, a soft look on her face.

The boathouse comes into view, and I tighten my grip on her fingers.

"This is where it ends," I say quietly.

She looks at me then, searching my face. "Ends?"

I nod. "The versions of us that didn't survive. The children who didn't know how to fight for each other yet."

We step inside together.

She turns slowly, taking it in. The walls. The floor. The place where everything began before it shattered. I know we have both been back since that summer. Her numerous times, I'm sure, but right now it feels different. Like we are both finally ready to put the past to bed.

"You brought me here to say goodbye to the past?" she asks.

"Yes," I answer. "Then we can start clean."

I release her hand only long enough to reach into my coat and pull out the paper I've brought with me.

The paper is folded and thin. It's been open and closed many times over the years. I don't look at it. I've looked at it enough.

I hand it to her.

Her brow furrows as she unfolds it.

She reads it.

The color drains from her face as realization crashes through her. "No," she whispers, and her hands start to shake. "I didn't write this," she says. "I never wrote this."

Her chest rises sharply as she continues to stare at the tiny piece of paper that cost me everything.

"That isn't my handwriting." She looks up at me, eyes glossy, furious, devastated all at once. "This isn't the letter I gave your mom."

"You gave my mom a letter?"

"I did. Right after my parents told me I had to leave . . ." A tear falls down Victoria's cheek. "Why—didn't she give it to you?"

"I don't know."

And I don't. I don't understand why my mother would let me believe this lie . . . but then again, knowing her, she probably thought she was protecting me.

"I'm so sorry. Lorenzo, I would never say those things to you. You know that, right?"

Something inside me finally loosens. It's not rage; it's grief. Then relief, so sharp it almost drops me to my knees.

"I know," I say quietly. "I know that . . . *now*."

Tears spill down her face, and she presses a hand to her mouth.

"They told me I had to leave," she chokes. "They told me I had no choice . . . They said—"

"What did *they* say?"

"They told me if I didn't leave they would call the people your mother was running from, I left because I thought by leaving I was keeping you safe. They lied . . . " she whispers.

"Yes."

The word feels heavy. Final.

She breaks then . . . really breaks.

Her sobs shake her whole body. Grief and fury pour out from her.

I step into her space and pull her against me without hesitation, her forehead pressing into my chest, her tears soaking my shirt.

"I waited," she sobs. "I waited so long."

"So did I," I whisper into her hair. "I just didn't know what I was waiting for."

Her hands fist my shirt like she's afraid letting go will undo us.

"I don't want to be that naive girl anymore," she whispers.

"You aren't."

My gaze drifts to the shelf along the wall, to the old, battered copy of *Wuthering Heights* that I left here all those years ago. I place a kiss on her forehead and reach out to grab it.

I pick it up.

"For years, I thought I was Heathcliff," I say quietly. "That loving you meant suffering. Becoming something bitter. Dying alone just to prove how deeply I felt."

She looks up at me through tears. "And now?"

I meet her eyes.

"I don't care about the tragedy anymore. I don't want to punish the world for loving you. I just want to love you. Fully. Completely."

I take a step back and reach into my pocket.

"What are you doing?" she asks, but it only takes her a second to realize, her eyes going wide, when I pull the matchbook out. Then I ignite it.

The pages curl. Blacken. Burn.

I drop the burning book into the small metal bin that once held tools.

Together, we watch as the book burns.

"What now?" she asks softly.

"I won't live without you. I choose you—here, now, as my wife."

She takes a step closer, then her hand reaches out until it rests on my chest, right over my heart.

"Do we need to forget the past?" she whispers. "Because some of it was good—"

"We don't have to," I reply. "We just have to stop living in it."

She looks at me for a second, and her lips tip up. "We were always coming back to each other," she says.

"Yes." I nod, a smirk forming on my own face. "Soulmates are inconvenient like that."

Then I cup her face, thumb brushing away the last of her tears. "My Little Bird," I say. "You flew so far just to land back here."

She laughs through her tears.

Then she kisses me, but this time, it's not desperate. This kiss is certain. Absolute. As if to finally acknowledge that we are inevitable . . .

When we finally pull apart, I need her desperately. There's something about being back here, where it all started, that makes me need to lay claim to her in all ways.

I pull back, my lip lifting into a smirk. "Take off your clothes?"

"Here?"

"Yes, here. This is the perfect place."

My very sweet and adorable wife blushes like we've never done this before.

I lift a brow. "Really? Are you nervous?"

"Last time we were here . . ."

"Yes?"

"We were still kids."

"We were eighteen," I remind her.

She laughs. "Barely."

"Just enough."

She shakes her head, but she lifts her shirt off, followed by her pants.

Victoria is fucking exquisite.

"I'll never get enough of you."

"Good 'cause you forced me to marry you, so you're kind of stuck with me now."

"Such a mouth on you . . ."

"Gonna do something about it?"

"Yeah, I am. I know what you can do with it." I point at the ground. "On your knees."

She follows my orders like the good girl she is.

"Unzip me." Her hand reaches for my zipper, pulling it down.

"Why am I naked, but you're not?"

I incline my head down. "Tsk. Tsk. No asking questions." I reach forward and place my finger on her lip. "Take out my cock."

She does.

"Open."

Her perfect lips part, and her tongue juts out, swiping the head of my dick. Licking the drop of cum that has beaded on the tip.

It's official. If I died now, I'd be a happy man. Crazy thought for someone who spends 90 percent of their time murdering people.

The feeling is so sublime as she leans closer, taking me fully in her mouth, that a shiver actually runs down my spine. "Fuck. That feels good." I start to fuck her throat in earnest.

She slides her tongue up and down my shaft, making sure to run it up the vein before swirling it over the crown.

Having Victoria on her knees is probably the hottest sight I've ever seen.

My legs nearly give out from beneath me as she pushes forward, my cock now hitting the back of her throat.

Her eyes meet mine, wide yet playful. She still has my dick in her mouth, so she doesn't answer. "I need to fuck you . . ." I groan as she does a swirl with her tongue. "Okay. I'm going to need to do that now because this feels too damn good."

Victoria actually laughs around my dick, and this time, I swear I almost black out from how amazing I feel.

Death by blow job . . .

Victoria pulls back, my dick popping out of her mouth. She's still on her knees, looking at me expectantly.

"Turn around. Ass in the air."

What I love about Victoria is that she might be feisty in real life, but like this, she's not.

She gets into position.

"Good girl." I move to kneel behind her, then run my cock up and down through her drenched folds.

"I want to watch as you take my cock."

With my hands braced on her hips, I push forward, admiring the view as my dick spreads her pussy lips apart. Then I thrust all the way to the hilt, disappearing inside her completely.

Pulling out, I swirl my dick one more time at her entrance before pushing forward again.

"I love watching myself fuck you."

A moan escapes her, so I pull my dick out, torturing us both.

"Please," she groans.

"What, Little Bird. Tell me what you want?"

"Fuck me."

Finally, when I can't take it anymore, I drive my whole length back in.

Harder.

Faster.

Deeper.

Time stands still as I fuck her. I watch as her greedy pussy is owned by my cock.

My hand reaches around. I flick her clit, and her walls tighten around me. My balls tighten, and my dick jerks as I come.

Both of us tremble, trying to catch our breath. "That was amazing," I breathe out.

"It was. And here. It was perfect."

This moment was always going to happen.

For the first time in my life, love isn't something I survive.

It's something I choose.

And I'm not going to let go.

CHAPTER 58

Victoria

In Lorenzo's arms is my favorite place to be. I could stay here forever, but since this is my parents' house, and I'm pretty sure I hate my parents right now, I can't.

How could they have done this to us?

"What's on your mind, Little Bird?"

I open my mouth to tell him, when his phone vibrates beside us.

Lorenzo stiffens.

"Don't answer," I tell him because I'm not ready for this happy bubble to end.

He glances down at the screen. The light reflects off his eyes, turning them harder. "I wish it worked that way."

The vibration stops. Then starts again. Persistent. Demanding. Not a good sign.

He exhales through his nose and straightens up until he's sitting. "Unfortunately, I have to take this."

Despite everything we just went through, his words hurt. I know he doesn't mean to sound stern, but something old and apparently still sore tightens in my chest.

"Of course you do," I reply lightly.

He stands, readjusting his clothes, and takes a few steps away. His voice drops as he answers. I don't hear the words, but I can see how his back straightens, and it's almost like his invisible armor falls back over him.

I wrap my arms around myself, staring out the window and toward the water.

Remembering.

Back when we were younger and things felt simple.

A few seconds pass before Lorenzo comes back. "I need to leave," he says, already reaching for his coat.

My stomach and throat feel tight at the idea of him leaving. "Now?"

His gaze flicks to me, and his gaze softens. "Work. Unfortunately."

Lorenzo crosses the small space between us and places a kiss on my lips. "I'll make it up to you."

I roll my eyes playfully. "You always say that."

"Actually, I'm not sure I've ever said that," he counters, shrugging into the coat. "Do you want me to take you home?"

"I actually want to talk to my parents."

"Now, that I wish I could see, and actually take part in. But alas, my uncle needs me. Nico will take you home."

"When will you be home?"

"Not sure. Hopefully tonight." He reaches out, fingers brushing my jaw before leaning down and capturing my lips again.

The kiss only lasts a few seconds, and I feel empty when he finally pulls away.

"I'll see you later." He turns and walks away, phone already back at his ear. He doesn't look back.

I hate that it still hurts when he leaves.

I storm into the house.

This is the last place I want to be. If I were smart, I'd just leave with Lorenzo . . .

But I can't.

Not after realizing what my mother did.

It doesn't take me long to find her in the living room.

I storm in.

She looks up from the sofa, surprise flickering across her face. "Victoria—"

"Don't." I hold up a hand.

Her brows knit together. "You look upset?"

I laugh.

Yep. An ugly laugh rips from my mouth.

I sound unhinged.

And truthfully, I might be right now. "Upset. Yes, you can say I'm upset . . . Mother."

I step farther into the room, every inch of me buzzing with anger. "Did you know I spent years believing I was unlovable?" I cross my arms at my chest. "Years thinking the man I loved just never came back for me."

Her shoulders stiffen. She knows where this is going. Good.

"I did what I thought was necessary."

"You make me sick," I snap.

She stands, smoothing her sweater. "Victoria, you were young. He was dangerous. His world—"

"Was never your decision," I cut in. "And you knew that. You knew I would never leave him willingly, so you stole my voice instead."

If I thought she had any remorse over her actions, the way she glares at me is all the confirmation I need that she doesn't have any.

"You let him believe I wrote that letter," I hiss. "You watched him walk away thinking I didn't love him."

"I was protecting you."

"No," I say coldly. "You were protecting yourself. Your image. God forbid your daughter loved someone beneath you."

I take a step closer. My hands are shaking now, but I don't hide them.

"You didn't trust me to choose my own future," I continue. "You chose it for me." She opens her mouth, but I don't let her speak. "I loved him," I say. "I love him. And I will not waste another second of my life letting you mess with Lorenzo or me anymore."

Her face pales. "You don't mean that."

"I absolutely do." My voice doesn't waver. "We're done. I'm out of your life for good. I'm choosing Lorenzo," I add. "And I'm choosing the life we were robbed of. You don't get to touch it."

I step back. "Don't ever reach out to me again. You won't like what happens," I warn.

I turn and walk out before she can say anything.

Nico stands by the car when I finally make my way outside. He opens the door for me with the same careful politeness he always uses, like he's afraid Lorenzo will kill him if he steps out of line and upsets me.

I climb in without comment and buckle my seat belt. A second later, the door shuts, and we pull away.

I watch the ocean disappear behind the trees and think about my family and how much they've hurt me over the years.

There is no coming back from what they did to us.

I must be lost in thought because when I look back outside, nothing looks familiar.

My pulse spikes. "Nico?"

He doesn't answer.

"Where are we going?"

He keeps his eyes on the road, jaw tight. "It's for your own good."

What the hell does that mean?

I reach for the door and try to open the door. While jumping from a moving car isn't going to be fun, I have no idea where he's taking me, and I'm starting to get scared.

Nothing happens.

"What the hell are you doing, Nico?"

"Like I said before, it's for your own good."

"That's what everyone says right before they do something unforgivable."

The road narrows and trees grow denser.

"You don't understand," he says quietly.

I turn toward him fully now. "Then help me. Because from where I'm sitting, you just kidnapped me."

His head bobs, but back here, I can't see his expression. "Boss treats you like shit."

Heat flares in my chest. Defensive, immediate. "You don't get to say that."

"I get to say it because I've watched it." His hands tighten on the wheel. "I've watched him cage you and call it protection."

"You don't know him."

"I know enough."

I shake my head, anger and fear tangling. "Unlock the door."

"I can't."

"You won't."

The distinction hangs between us.

"My mother was taken once," he says suddenly.

The words hit like a slap.

"What?"

"One of the Amante brothers," he continues, voice flat, eyes forward. "Not Lorenzo's father. The other one. The one nobody talks about."

Cold slides down my spine.

"He's dead now," Nico adds. "But what Lorenzo's doing to you? It's the same."

"That's not—" My voice cracks, but I force it steady. "You don't understand. He wouldn't hurt me."

"You sound like my mother"—Nico snaps back—"right before she disappeared."

Silence crashes down.

"Take me back," I whisper.

"No."

"Please." The word slips out before I can stop it. "Nico. Please."

The car keeps moving. "I won't let you become another story they bury," he says softly.

A clearing opens up ahead, and a small cottage sits in front of us.

That's where the car stops.

My heart pounds. "Where are we?"

"Somewhere safe."

The doors unlock with a soft click. I step out into the cold and shiver, but not from the chill in the air. No, I tremble because the door opens, and Grant steps out onto the porch.

He smiles when he sees me. *The bastard.* He thinks this is a happy ending. It's not.

"Victoria," he says, stepping forward. "Thank god. I was starting to think—"

"What is he doing here?" I snap, turning on Nico.

"He's here to help you."

Help.

I laugh, hollow and sharp. "You think this is help?"

Grant looks back and forth between us, confusion creasing his brow. "Of course I'm here to help. He said you weren't safe."

"You have no idea what you're talking about," I shout.

"I needed to help you." Grant takes another step toward me.

I shake my head, backing up. "Stop. Don't come any closer."

His hands lift. "I'm not here to hurt you." The words that leave his mouth don't match the crazed look in his eyes. I'm not safe with him.

I turn to Nico. Maybe I can convince him to change his mind.

And I realize with sick clarity that this man won't help me. And just as I finally got out of one cage, I've moved to a different one. But this one terrifies me.

CHAPTER 59

Lorenzo

The gravel crunches under my shoes as I walk the familiar path.

I haven't been here in months.

It hasn't felt right to visit. Not with everything that's been going on with Victoria . . . and even now, it doesn't, knowing what I now know.

Maybe it will bring me closure.

Her name comes into view, and I stop in front of the headstone.

Angela Rossi

My mother.

I drag a hand through my hair, then lower myself in front of the stone.

"So . . ." My voice sounds rough even to my ears. "This is awkward."

I'm not even sure what to say. What do you tell your dead mother in a situation like this?

The truth, I guess. No reason to bullshit.

"I got married."

The words feel weird as they leave my mouth.

I swallow, jaw tightening, and glance away.

This shouldn't be so hard.

My eyes shut, and I can see the memory of her face.

She's standing in front of me, arms crossed, watching me. Knowing full well I'm up to no good.

"I married Victoria." My fingers curl into the grass, dirt pressing beneath my nails. I don't look at the stone when I say that. I can't. "I hated you for a long time . . . I didn't understand how you could keep my family from me." I take a deep breath. "And then you died. I never even got to speak to you before you did. I had only been gone a month . . . for a long time, I blamed them. Victoria. Her family. Then I blamed you." I laugh once under my breath. It comes out broken.

"I blamed you for everything. For the loneliness. For the way I had to change. For her."

I reach out and brush my finger against the base of the headstone. "That was before I knew the role you played. I know now. I'm not going to lie, what you did was wrong. You took away my choice."

My throat tightens, pressure building there from all the words and emotions I've been holding back for too long.

"I don't understand why you lied," I whisper. "Why did you let me believe that letter was real? Why did you let me think she walked away from me like I meant nothing?"

My chest aches.

"Why didn't you give me her letter?" My voice cracks on the word her. "The real one. The one she gave you. The one that would've saved us years of pain."

I bow my head. "I want to hate you. I want to ask why. But I know the reason."

I lift my gaze back to her name.

"You were trying to protect me," I say quietly. "From my family. From the blood that would be spilled once I found out who I was. And you wanted to protect me from what you thought would ultimately be my undoing . . . *her*."

My mouth twists. "You thought if she walked away, I'd be

free. That I'd stop loving her." I shake my head slowly. "You underestimated her."

My eyes burn now, unshed tears gathering behind my lids.

"She taught me how to forgive," I whisper. "I forgive you. Even though you don't get to hear it. Even though it took me too long to say it . . ."

I scrub a hand over my face, catching a drop of wetness on my cheek.

"I still don't like what you did," I add hoarsely. "I don't think I ever will. But I understand it."

I push myself to my feet and stand over her grave. "I'm trying to be better for her. For the life we're building. I want to become the man she deserves."

The wind picks up again, and it feels cool against my skin.

"I hope wherever you are, you see that."

I take one last look at her name, then step back.

"Goodbye, Mom."

I pull up to the warehouse.

Today has been the longest day ever. After the cemetery, I've followed way too many bad leads.

I just want to get back to my wife.

Wife . . .

For the first time in months, this feels like a real marriage. I'd be lying if I didn't admit to myself that I'm ecstatic about that fact.

Sure, my plan was never for either of us to be happy. I only wanted revenge. To make sure Victoria was as miserable as I was, but now that is the farthest thing from my mind. All I want is to be with her.

Grow old with her.

But instead, I'm here right now.

My uncle wants this guy's head on a platter, which I plan to give him once I find the bitch. Unfortunately for me, the little shit is a slippery little fucker.

Rafe drives with one hand on the wheel and the other resting near his thigh, close to his gun. His jaw stays set, eyes forward, and his expression remains calm.

Me . . . I'm not calm. I'm pissed.

I lean my head back and let my eyes close for half a second.

We almost got him.

It's going to make killing him so satisfying.

I picture it for a second—his face when he realizes he built this whole stunt to impress an uncle, and all he managed to do was piss off the wrong enemies and get himself killed.

My mouth twitches.

Rafe glances at me. "That look again."

I crack my knuckles slowly. "What look?"

"The one that makes me know you're about to have fun gutting someone."

I stare out the window at the passing trees and street signs, my reflection flickering in the glass. "After what this asshole has put us through, I will."

Vin puts down his phone. "Matteo is on."

"Cousin, what's the good word?" I ask him.

"The warehouse my team went to was hit too."

My gaze slides to him. "Fuck."

"They moved three hours before we arrived. Like they knew."

"Of course they knew," I grunt. "Everybody's psychic these days."

"We really need to find the fucking leak," Matteo grunts.

"I'm working on it," I reply, voice calm.

"Good, Cuz, because Pops is pissed." He laughs. "He wants answers."

"Fine. I'll keep them alive long enough to talk . . . for now."

"You do that. Got to go, I need to find someone to kill."

After he hangs up, I nod to Vin.

His brow arches. "We still have the last contact. If he's alive, he'll lead us."

"If he's dead," I add, rolling my shoulder until the joint pops, "I'll still make him lead us. I'll just have to get creative."

"You're a sick fuck." Rafe snorts, but it isn't an amused one. It's a tired one. "Your uncle's going to want an update by sunrise."

The word uncle flicks like a blade across my nerves.

He's the reason I'm currently married in secret.

I turn my head slowly. "Then he'll get one."

Rafe's eyes stay on the road, but his voice lowers, careful. "You've got blood on your collar."

I glance down at the dark smear on the edge of my shirt. Not mine.

"Fashion statement," I retort. "I'm embracing colors this season."

Vin's mouth flickers like he's trying not to smile. "You're going to get shot for sarcasm one day."

"I know," I reply sweetly.

By the time we pull into my estate's gated drive, it's 4:03 a.m. Rafe punches the code, and the gates roll open.

The moment the car stops, I jump out, desperate to see Victoria. My boots crunch on gravel. I throw the front door open, then step inside.

"Where is she?"

The guard blinks. "Sir?"

I stop in the foyer, staring at him. Who the hell does he think I mean? Why is he so fucking confused? "Victoria," I tell him.

The guard swallows. "She was—"

"She was what?"

I don't wait for the guard to finish choking on whatever he's trying to say. Instead, I take the stairs two at a time. I hit the second-floor landing, then stalk down the hall until I reach her room. The door is closed. I throw it open.

The room is empty.

Before I freak out, I decide to check my room. Things are different between us now, so maybe she decided to wait for me in my bed.

I head down the hall, throwing open my door, but I'm met with the same sight. Nothing.

Absolutely nothing.

My gaze snaps to the window.

Still closed.

Locked.

And curtains drawn.

My jaw locks so hard it hurts.

Where the hell is she?

I stalk back to her room and straight into the closet. One drawer is half open. Clothes thrown sloppily around.

Was it always this messy? Or did she grab a few things and leave?

But why would she leave? And where would she go?

I hear footsteps behind me. Rafe stands in the doorway, gaze on the open drawer. His face tightens. "Where is she?"

My head shakes. "Not sure. Where's Nico?"

"Haven't seen him," Rafe responds, while typing into his phone. Most likely texting the security team to see if they know where he is.

When he shakes his head at me, my throat goes dry.

I rip my phone out of my pocket and call him.

Ring.

Ring.

Ring.

No answer.

I call again.

Straight to voicemail.

My hand tightens around the phone until my palm aches.

Rafe watches me like he would watch a ticking time bomb. "Try the staff."

"Try everyone," I snap, already moving out of the room. "Wake everyone. Now."

The next few minutes are a blur.

I swing open doors and throw on the lights. I search high and low for Victoria.

"Where is she?" My voice cuts through the hallway.

A few feet away, the maid's eyes go wide. "S-sir, I—"

"You saw her?" I press, stepping closer until the maid backs into the wall.

The maid shakes her head violently. "She never came home from her parents'."

"What did you say?" Rafe's voice cuts in. "Repeat that."

"She never came home."

"And before that . . . had Nico said anything that could be considered out of the ordinary?"

The maid's lip trembles. "I heard him say that he'd handle her—"

My vision tunnels, and the world tilts.

Panic rises so fast inside me that my body doesn't know where to put it.

I slam my fist into the wall, cracking the plaster.

Rafe is suddenly beside me, hand catching my shoulder. "You need to stay calm."

"I need to find her," I snarl, yanking out of his grip.

"And to do that, you need to breathe and think."

He's right. I know he's right, but it still feels like an impossible task. Taking a deep breath, I start to walk toward the stairs, then head down to the foyer.

"Lorenzo."

"What?" I whip around to see Rafe standing at the landing.

"She didn't leave you."

"I know. That's what scares me."

Things are different now. After everything we've been through, especially after yesterday at her parents', I know without any measure of doubt that Victoria didn't go off on her own free will.

She didn't betray me.

She was taken.

My lungs burn.

I stare at Rafe, the room suddenly too bright, too sharp. "I need to find her."

His mouth tightens. "We will. And Nico is the key. Nico wouldn't disappear unless he planned to."

My stomach turns.

I exhale slowly, forcing air into my lungs like it's a decision. "Get me the cameras. Every feed," I snap, already moving. "Security room. Now."

We descend into the belly of the house, down a hallway, until we're opening the door. The security room glows with monitors, each showing a different area of the house.

In the video, Nico opens the door to her room, and he's got a bag in his hand.

My stomach drops.

Rafe's voice comes from beside me, hard. "He took clothes from her room."

My jaw clenches.

Cold anger slides through me, smooth and lethal.

"Where did he take her?"

I turn away from the screens and walk out of the room.

Rafe follows closely. "Where are we going?"

"Warehouse." My voice is flat. "Car."

He falls into step. "You think Nico handed her to Boston?"

I shove open the front door, the cold air slamming into me. "Boston makes the most sense. They want leverage."

Rafe's jaw tightens. "So . . . he—"

My chest tightens. "He gives them my *wife.* And I'm going to burn the city down until we find her."

CHAPTER 60

Lorenzo

MY CAR ROLLS TO A STOP.

Rafe kills the engine and glances over at me once, his jaw locked tight.

I step out into the night air. Instantly, the cold bites through my clothes and seeps straight into my bones.

"Two on the porch. One patrolling the right side." Rafe's voice stays low and clipped so no one will hear him.

I adjust my gloves. "Roll out."

We move through the trees toward the warehouse.

Two guards linger in front. They aren't paying much attention because they are too busy smoking.

The first guard laughs at something the other guy says, head tipping back for a second like he's offering up his throat to me.

Not one to pass up an opportunity, I take aim.

The shot is quiet. A suppressor will do that, but as the guard drops to the ground, his friend is now aware he's under attack.

The other guy spins, mouth opening to scream, but he never gets a chance to make a sound.

It's his turn to stumble back as the bullet finds him.

With both dead, I step toward the metal door and slide it open.

As I step inside, I notice a shadow moving at the end of the hall . . . and I fire without pausing.

The bullet punches into the wall next to his head. The plaster explodes, freezing him in place.

"Don't move," I order.

He follows my command, face draining when he looks at me.

"You—" His voice cracks. "You weren't supposed to—"

"I know," I interrupt, stepping forward. "I like to do things I'm not supposed to do. Keeps shit interesting."

Rafe steps up beside me, his gun now aimed at this idiot too.

I don't look away from the man.

"You have a woman here?" My voice is steady despite my anger.

The man's throat bobs. "We don't—"

I cock my head, and his lips start to tremble.

"She's not . . . she's not here."

I tilt my head. "Interesting."

The man shakes, frantic. "This isn't—this isn't what you think."

"It never is," I reply, sick of this shit. "Let's search the place," I tell Rafe.

It only takes a few minutes to search this floor, and there is no sign of Victoria.

My jaw tightens.

Rafe watches me carefully, trying to assess if I'm going to kill this guy. "Basement door."

I follow his gaze to a door half-hidden behind a coatrack.

A faint sound can be heard, but it doesn't sound like Victoria. I won't know until we go down to check.

We descend, Rafe holding the man as a shield as we head down to the lower level.

Behind a table that's filled with drugs and a scale sits a man who looks to be in his early twenties.

Fuck.

This is him.

The bastard we've been searching for.

"What the fuck are you doing here?" He drops the razor blade. "You're the Amante bastard."

I raise my gun. "I'm really not in the mood for your shit. We can do this the easy way . . . you tell me where she is, and I shoot you. Or you don't, and I torture you . . . and you tell me where she is anyway."

He flinches.

I lean in. "Where is she?"

His eyes flicker. "Who?"

"Got it. Torture." I move until I'm right beside him, reaching out until the tip of my gun drags down his jaw. "I can easily shoot different places that won't kill you, and then after, I'll take my fucking blade and find each bullet inside you. I like to keep my trophies. Want to try again? Where's Victoria?"

His throat works. "I don't have her."

"As I said before, you're dying anyway. I know you're the one hitting my uncle's inventory, so how are we going to do this?" I reply.

I keep my gaze on the man. "Well?"

"Fuck you." He spits near my boots. "Your uncle's old. I was just trimming fat."

Rafe's mouth quirks. "Trimming fat? Cute."

I gesture for Rafe to back me. He nods before shooting the human shield in his arms and then pinning his gun on Connor.

I slide the gun in my waistband before pulling out my knife.

"Tell me where she is." I crouch closer, keeping my voice low.

"I don't have her."

"The hard way . . . got it." I place the tip of the knife on his neck, then slice down the skin. The cut is deep enough to bleed, but I make sure to miss all the crucial spots.

The man laughs weakly, blood dripping down the path I made. "You think you scare me?"

I tilt my head. "No." This time, I stab the blade into his upper arm, then yank the knife free with a slow pull.

His breath jerks out, and sweat beads at his hairline.

I straighten slightly, letting the silence stretch. "While you were taking swings at my uncle's business, someone took something that is mine."

His eyes flicker, but he doesn't speak.

"Don't pretend you don't know what I'm talking about. A woman went missing."

His mouth opens and then closes.

I crouch again, fingers closing around his chin, forcing his face toward mine. "You know something, just speak, and I won't give you to my uncle."

That makes him swallow. "Fine," he breathes out. "One of my men saw something. While we were following you, one of my men hung back to see who the woman was and if we could use her."

My hand tightens around the handle of my knife. It takes everything inside me to stop my need to slash his throat and let him finish. "Go on," I grit through clenched teeth.

"The man I placed to watch her saw a man drive her out of her parents' house. We followed."

My voice stays even. "Nico isn't working for you?"

The man lets out a shaky laugh. "No."

"He's not the one feeding you intel on my uncle's business?"

"Correct again," the smug bastard responds.

I narrow my gaze. "But he's working for someone?"

He hesitates, then nods.

My fingers tighten on his jaw. "How do you know?"

He swallows hard. "Because he met with someone after. At the cottage."

A chill slides under my skin.

"Let me get this straight. You're telling me you followed Nico and watched him hand her off?"

"Yeah."

I stare at him. "Where?"

He trembles. "I don't know the address."

I laugh softly. "Of course you don't."

I step behind him and tip the chair forward hard. He crashes face-first into the concrete with a strangled grunt. Blood gushes from his now broken nose.

I crouch beside him, knife flat against the back of his neck.

"Try again," I whisper. "And this time, don't make me regret being patient."

He makes one ugly sob.

"Speak."

He swallows. "He took her north. A cottage. The tracker on my guy's car will have the location."

My heart pounds heavy and violent.

Rafe's voice turns sharp. "That enough for you?"

I look over at Rafe and nod, then glance back down at Connor. "You're going to live . . . for now." I decide, voice flat.

His eyes fly open, hope flaring stupidly.

I crouch, close enough that he can feel the heat of my presence. "Not because you deserve it. Because after second thought, my uncle would love to meet you . . . He'd love to know who your source is."

"Just fucking let me go, and I'll tell you."

I cross my arms over my chest. "Speak."

"He's an Amante . . . one of your own, a cousin."

Fuck. I don't need him to tell me which cousin is causing shit. It's got to be Salvatore. He's around Matteo's age, so a few years older than me, but I've never met him. After his father was killed by my uncle, Salvatore was no longer around, or so Matteo told me.

Fuck. This changes everything.

"Kill him," I tell Rafe.

"Wait—you said—" Connor cries.

"Shut up," I yell at Connor. His eyes go wide. That's right, buddy, you're fucked now.

"And the news of Salvatore?" Rafe asks me.

"Let my uncle handle it. Right now, my only priority is my wife."

I stand and turn toward the stairs. "Get that address. Now."

Rafe already has his phone out, voice clipped and lethal as he barks instructions to track the car.

I move up the basement steps and head outside. The cold air slices into my lungs, but I welcome it. I pick up the phone and dial my cousin.

"What's the good word?" Matteo answers.

"I found Connor."

"Fuck."

I walk toward my car. "Yeah, fuck is right. You aren't going to like this. I found out who the rat is."

"Just spit it out. You know how I feel about foreplay."

"It's Salvatore."

A loud whistle cuts through the line. "No shit. Didn't know the little bitch had it in him to betray the family."

"Think he'll be a problem?"

"Nah. He's just a spoiled brat. Nothing to worry about."

"What do you want to do about him?" I ask.

"Leave him to my father. He'll handle it."

"Got it. Call you later." I hang up and get back to my own business. Finding my wife and the place to start is finding Nico.

Fucking hell.

But the more important question . . .

Who is he working for?

CHAPTER 61

Victoria

THE COTTAGE IS WAY TOO QUIET AFTER GRANT LEAVES.

My mind is spinning out of control . . . trying to figure out what to do.

I sit on the edge of the sofa, rocking back and forth.

Pacing is out. When I was previously doing it, Nico kept pulling his gun on me to stop.

I'm not sure how he thinks he's any better than Lorenzo, but I'm not going to tell him that. The man is completely unhinged.

My wrists ache. *Zip ties will do that.*

Yeah, apparently, in his big rescue plan, he's decided that keeping hostages wasn't the same.

This whole thing is insane.

And if all this wasn't bad enough, my hands are numb.

Nico stands near the door with his shoulders squared and his jaw locked.

He doesn't look at me. *Maybe he can't.* Might remind him I'm a person, after all.

"What the hell are you doing, Nico? You know Grant is using you?"

Nico's gaze drifts to the window. He's obviously choosing to ignore me.

"Kidnapping me makes you no better than who you think you're rescuing me from. You do know that, right?"

"I know what I'm doing."

"Do you? Or are you just Grant's lap dog?"

"Better than being an Amante dog."

"'Cause Grant is an angel?" I bite the inside of my cheek and try a different approach. "Why am I here? Other than to save me." I roll my eyes.

Nico's mouth tightens, but he doesn't respond. He's probably under strict orders.

I laugh. "You have no idea what you've done. But it will be fun when you find out."

His eyes finally cut to me. "Do you ever shut up?"

I lean forward. "What's wrong, Nico? Already in over your head?"

Nico holds my gaze now, steady, like he's daring me to keep going.

Okay, I will.

The room tilts.

"Lorenzo's going to kill you . . ."

"Actually, he'll be the one to die."

My mouth opens, but nothing comes out at first. I try again, voice thin and strangled. "What did you just say?"

Nico shifts his weight.

"He forced you to marry him. He deserves to die."

"Do you not see the fucking irony—" My throat tightens so hard it hurts. "You fucking kidnapped me."

"I saved you."

"You're delusional. Lorenzo is my husband. You didn't save me from shit."

Nico's eyes flick toward my bound hands, then away. "He doesn't get to keep you."

"Grant does?" The sarcasm drips from my words.

Nico's nostrils flare. "At least Grant loves you."

I bark a laugh. "You really are stupid. Grant doesn't love me. He loves the idea of me. Grant loves ownership. Grant loves what my last name buys him."

Nico's fingers flex at his side. "He's better than Lorenzo."

I stare at him, and something inside me goes cold. "By tying my hands and keeping me here?" I lift my bound wrists as high as I can. "This is protection to you?"

His throat bobs. "It's temporary."

"Everything is temporary," I whisper, the words shaking. "So is breathing, if you make the wrong choice."

Silence stretches.

I twist again, trying to work the tie until it breaks.

Nico notices the movement and steps forward. "Stop."

"Or what?" I glare up at him. "You'll tighten them?"

"I don't want to hurt you." His lips press together.

"You already are." I grit my teeth and keep sawing at the tie.

Nico makes a frustrated sound and crouches in front of me, voice dropping. "Victoria . . . listen. You don't understand."

"I understand I'm tangled in a situation with two men who think they know what's best for me," I snap. "Spoiler alert: you don't. I want to be with Lorenzo. I love him. Always have. Always will."

"You want to go back to him?" Nico's voice turns rough.

"I want to go *home*."

Nico flinches like the word home hits him in the chest. "That isn't your home."

"You're right, it isn't. He's my *home*," I whisper.

Nico's jaw tightens. "He'll destroy you."

I stare at him. "He already tried, and somehow in doing that, he put me back together."

Nico's eyes narrow. "That's not normal."

"And this is?"

"You're defending him."

"I'm defending myself." I swallow hard.

Nico's shoulders stiffen.

The front door rattles lightly, most likely from a gust of wind.

My hands shake as I resume sawing the zip tie. I need my hands. I need control. I need—

The zip tie doesn't budge. My shoulders sag in pain.

Maybe this is it.

A crash hits.

Sharp.

Loud.

Nico's head jerks up, every muscle snapping taut. His hand goes to his waistband in one fluid motion.

My heart slams against my ribs.

Another sound . . .

This time, it's footsteps. Heavy. Fast.

Nico heads toward the door, gun drawn, eyes hard. "Stay here."

Then the front door explodes.

The entire frame splinters inward with a violent crack that shakes the cottage.

I scream.

Nico's gun lifs—

A figure storms through the broken doorway like the devil himself.

I know exactly who it is.

Lorenzo.

For one second, the world stops.

Nico's gun is pointed at Lorenzo. Lorenzo's gaze locks on Nico. And something in Lorenzo's eyes goes feral.

He moves before Nico can even think to pull the trigger.

Lorenzo slams into Nico, driving him backward like a battering ram. The gun flies from Nico's hand, skittering across the floor. They both crash into the wall. Nico grunts, trying to swing at Lorenzo, but he's too fast. Lorenzo's fist connects with Nico's jaw first, and the hit must have been hard because Nico's head snaps sideways.

Nico stumbles, and Lorenzo catches him by the collar and drives him down to the floor with a savage shove. Then Lorenzo is on him again, this time with a boot to Nico's throat.

My breath tears in my throat. "Lorenzo." My voice cracks, but I don't even care.

That gets his attention, because Lorenzo's head snaps toward me. His gaze finds mine but then drops to my bound wrists.

Something in his expression shifts. Nico is no longer important. I'm the only thing he sees.

He crosses the room in three strides. Then, before I know what's happening, he's kneeling in front of me. His hands hover near my wrists.

His voice comes out low, rough. "He did this to you?"

I stare at him, blinking hard, because my eyes are burning, and my throat is closing, and I don't know if I'm hallucinating.

"Are you—" My voice breaks. "You're here?"

Lorenzo's jaw clenches. His hands close around the zip tie, fingers steady despite the blood on his knuckles. "Of course I am."

He grabs a knife from his pocket, and a moment later, the plastic snaps with a sharp pop.

Relief floods me as my hands regain sensation.

He tosses the broken tie, then takes my wrists gently.

My breath catches on a sob.

Lorenzo's eyes sweep over me. First over my face, then down my body. He's checking for injuries.

I shake my head quickly. "I'm—I'm okay."

My hands tremble as I flex my fingers.

Lorenzo's thumb brushes the red indentations on my skin, and the small tenderness of it nearly breaks me.

"Victoria."

I don't answer with words.

I collapse forward.

My body pitches into him, and his arms wrap around me. He's got me. *Always.*

I sob.

It's ugly and loud.

And I don't care.

Because he has me.

And that is enough.

Behind us, Nico groans, but I don't care. I'm exactly where I need to be right now, in Lorenzo's arms.

Lorenzo's arm tightens around me, protective and possessive. I love it.

Nico coughs out a laugh that sounds pained. "She deserved better."

Lorenzo finally lifts his head, eyes hard as rocks. "And you thought keeping her chained up was better?"

Nico spits blood onto the floor, panting. "I got her away from you."

Lorenzo's mouth curls, ugly. "You kidnapped my wife."

The word hits the air like a gunshot.

His voice booms so loud that my breath catches. Nico's eyes widen, and for one terrifying second, I think he will erupt.

"You were supposed to guard her. Protect her."

Nico's face twists with anger. "You forced her into this."

Lorenzo laughs. "Does it look like I can force her to do anything?"

Nico drags himself farther away from us. "I was trying to protect her."

"Then congratulations, you failed."

He shifts me gently to the side, guiding me back against the cushion.

"Time to go home," he whispers against my lips.

I nod too quickly. "I'm not leaving your side."

"Damn right, you aren't."

He turns back to Nico, crouching down so they're eye level.

"Why did you take her? Who put you up to it?"

It's only then that I realize he doesn't know.

"Grant. It was Grant," I tell him.

Lorenzo turns to Nico, jaw locked tight. "Where is Grant?" he grits out. His voice is so deep and low that a shiver runs up my spine.

Nico's lips press together.

Lorenzo tilts his head. "We can do this nicely."

Nico scoffs. "You don't do nice."

Lorenzo's mouth twitches. "I do nice. I'm doing nice right now. I haven't even broken anything yet."

Nico swallows.

Lorenzo's gaze sharpens. "Where. Is. Grant?"

Nico's eyes dart to me.

Lorenzo follows the glance, and his expression turns darker. "Don't look at her. Look at me. I'm the problem you created."

Nico's voice cracks. "He left. An hour ago. He said he had to make calls. He—"

Lorenzo's laugh is soft, humorless. "Of course he did."

I wipe my face with shaky hands, trying to get air. My throat burns.

"Why did he take her?" Lorenzo asks.

Nico looks over at me. "He said she was his. That she loved him, and that you stole her. That—"

"Shut up," Lorenzo snaps. "I don't need to hear any more of this bullshit."

Lorenzo's gaze holds mine, steadying me without touching. "I'm here. And you're mine. And no one will take you from me again."

"You mean it?" I whisper.

"Of course I do." His voice drops into something raw. "There's no version of this life where I survive without you."

My lips part, but no sound comes out.

"Later," Lorenzo says softly to me. He knows me well enough to know it's all too much right now.

He straightens, rolling his shoulders back before he turns to the door. It's only then that I notice Rafe is there.

Rafe steps farther into the cottage, eyes flicking over me quickly. Relief flashes on his face when he sees I'm fine, then his gaze cuts to Nico with absolute disgust.

"Tie him up," Lorenzo tells Rafe.

"With pleasure."

Nico's eyes widen. "Lorenzo—"

Lorenzo ignores him, already reaching his hand out to help me up, but before I stand, he wipes a tear from my face.

"You okay?" The question comes out rough, but I know he's not angry with me. He's angry at the situation.

I nod once, then shake my head, then nod again because my body can't decide between honesty and survival.

He slides his arm around my back and lifts me like I weigh nothing. I clutch his shoulders, fingers digging into him as he starts toward the door.

I cling to Lorenzo tighter as the night air hits my wet cheeks. "I thought you were going to kill him."

Lorenzo's laugh rumbles under my cheek. "Oh, he's going to die."

"He is?"

He pauses, just for a second, his grip tightening. "He betrayed me. But worse . . . he betrayed you."

"He thought he was protecting me." The words taste wrong, but they're true in the saddest way.

Lorenzo's jaw flexes. "Doesn't matter to me. My only job in life is now to keep you safe. And I will do anything to make sure that happens."

Before I can say another word, he opens the back door of the car and settles me into the seat. Then he climbs in beside me.

He doesn't let go.

Not once.

We wait for a few minutes. And I don't know what happens

inside that cottage, but it doesn't take a rocket scientist to figure it out. It's not long before Rafe steps out of the door and heads to the car. Then he starts to drive.

My head rests on Lorenzo's shoulder, and his hand stays on my thigh, anchoring me to reality. I press closer because the fear hasn't left my bones yet, and his presence is the only thing making the world feel real.

By the time his estate appears, my body is exhausted, and my eyes burn.

Lorenzo lifts me again when we arrive, carrying me inside. He takes me upstairs.

To his room.

He sets me on the bed and crouches in front of me, hands on my knees.

His gaze searches my face. "From now on, you stay with me."

I nod. "I'm not leaving you ever again."

His throat works like he wants to say something else. But instead, he leans in and presses his forehead to mine for one brief second.

Then he pulls back, jaw hard. "Try to sleep," he orders.

My fingers catch his sleeve. "Don't go."

His gaze drops to my hand. It looks like he's waging a war within himself. Can whatever he needs to do wait? He must decide it can because he climbs into the bed beside me.

I curl on my side, watching him through heavy lashes.

He looks wrecked.

"Thank you." Those are the last words I remember saying before my eyes close as my exhaustion pulls me under.

And the last thing I hear, right before sleep takes me, is his voice. "No one takes what's mine."

And somehow . . .

I believe him.

CHAPTER 62

Lorenzo

Victoria shifts in my arms. "What time is it?"

"Around two in the morning."

"Seriously, and you're still here?"

"Yep." I glance down at her, letting my mouth twitch. "Did you really think I was going to leave you? I told you never again."

Her cheeks flush in half indignation, half something that makes my blood heat. "You're insane."

"I've been called worse," I respond.

She lets out a chuckle.

A small piece of hair falls across her face, and I reach out and tuck the strand behind her ear.

"I need pj's," she blurts out, which isn't surprising, seeing as she's still wearing her jeans.

I lift a brow. "You can sleep naked."

"Not happening. But nice try."

"Grab a shirt." I nod toward my dresser. "Something comfortable."

She slides off the bed, moving toward the dresser. She pulls open the top drawer, riffling through my black tees. Then she pauses. She pulls her hand out of the drawer. A small stone sits in her palm.

Her head turns slowly, eyes finding mine. "Why do you have

rocks in your room?" Her brows furrow as she pulls the drawer open fully and looks inside.

Dozens of stones, all different sizes and shapes, are in the drawer.

"Are these from my parents' beach?" she whispers.

I nod once. My throat suddenly too tight for words.

"Why have you been leaving me rocks? You did it years ago too."

I drag a hand over my mouth, half laugh, half exhale. "You really want the answer?"

She stands slowly, stone still in her hand. "I wouldn't have asked if I didn't."

I take the stone from her gently, rolling it between my fingers.

"Penguins," I say.

She blinks. "I'm sorry?"

I huff out a laugh. "When I was young, maybe six or seven, I watched one of those shows on TV. The ones about animals. We were moving around a lot back then . . . now I know why, but at the time, I was confused and sad, and well, I saw this one episode." I stop for a second, and even years later, I can see it clearly in my mind. "This episode was about penguins. Penguins pick a rock. One rock. They search for it. They bring it to their mate." My gaze lifts to hers. "It's how they say 'this is it.'"

Her breath hitches in her chest.

"They keep doing it," I continue, voice lower now. "Every year. Same mate. New rock. Even when it's hard. Even when they lose each other for a while. At the time when I saw it, I knew I wanted that . . . and so, when I met you . . . "

Her eyes shine, and then tears fall.

She doesn't wipe them. She just stands there. Listening. Crying. Seeing what was right in front of her the whole time. My undying love.

"I didn't have words," I admit. "Back then . . . and not when I found you again, so I left evidence."

Her lips tremble with a smile.

"It's always been you. Since the first moment I saw you. And collected my first rock, and then well, I did it when I didn't know how to ask you to stay."

Her gaze locks onto mine. "And now?"

I swallow. "Now I'm asking," I say quietly. "Stay."

She leans in, deliberate. Her mouth meets mine, gentle at first, but then my hands slide around her waist, and the kiss deepens.

"You're terrifying," she whispers, voice muffled against me.

I let my mouth curve, kissing her hair. "Yet."

"Yet," she echoes, and her arms tighten around me like she's anchoring herself.

For the first time in a long time, the violence inside me is quiet.

"Do you ever regret meeting me?" The question lands clean and deep, like she's been carrying it for a decade.

I don't hesitate. "Not for a second."

Her breath stutters.

"Even when it ruined me," I confess. "Even when it nearly killed me. Even when I thought you chose someone else and left me bleeding in hell."

Her eyes glisten, but she doesn't look away.

"Because in the end, I got you."

I reach for her, hand sliding into her hair. She leans into my touch immediately, and I press my forehead to hers, breathing her in.

"You always had me." She laughs.

Her palm settles over my chest, feeling the beat.

I close my eyes.

Finally secure that she will never leave me again.

CHAPTER 63

Victoria

I STAND BAREFOOT OUTSIDE LORENZO'S OFFICE, HAND MID-reach, when I hear his voice.

"We need to find Grant—"

My stomach tightens so fast it almost makes me dizzy.

Grant.

The name hits something inside me. A place I tried to pretend wasn't there yesterday, but today, in the light of a new day, it's there. Fear.

I'm afraid of him.

It's not that I think he could get to me again because I know Lorenzo will protect me. It's just that I'm still afraid of how unhinged he was yesterday.

How close I came to being taken from Lorenzo, maybe forever.

I don't move at first. I just breathe, slow.

Then Lorenzo's voice cuts through again . . .

"Bring Victoria in."

He wants me in his office? He wants to involve me in this. If I needed more confirmation that things are different now, his next statement confirms it. "There are no secrets between us."

My heart practically beats out of my chest at his words.

No secrets . . .

Coming from a man who built an entire life out of secrets.

Wow.

My hand hovers over the knob, and I finally turn it.

I don't knock.

I should, probably. There are men in there, but Lorenzo said bring Victoria in, so ask and you shall receive.

I push the door open and step inside.

Lorenzo looks up from behind his desk, eyes flicking to me instantly.

Rafe stands off to the side with his arms crossed, leaning against the wall. Two other men who I recognize from the security room are there too.

Lorenzo's mouth curves, slow and wicked.

"Were you just standing out there waiting?" he drawls, rolling a pen between his fingers.

I plant myself in the doorway and lift a brow. "Kind of." I shrug. "I never got my invitation to the meeting."

Rafe's mouth twitches.

Lorenzo leans back in his chair, gaze dragging over me. If there weren't men around, I'd think he would have his way with me right now.

"You're my wife." His lip lifts. "You don't need an invite."

My pulse jumps. I like this new version of Lorenzo.

Lorenzo taps the pen against the desk once, twice, then lets it go. "Sit." He gestures toward the chair opposite him.

I don't sit immediately. Instead, I lean my hip against the edge of the desk, folding my arms. "You were talking about Grant."

Lorenzo's jaw flexes once at his name. "I was."

I push off the desk and finally slide into the chair because my legs suddenly don't feel as sturdy.

Lorenzo watches me while I do. He then rests his forearms on the desk, fingers lacing together. "Tell me everything you remember about him," he says quietly. He's not ordering. He's asking.

My brain short-circuits, completely caught off guard by the question.

My fingers curl on the chair arm. "He was careful. He didn't say much."

Lorenzo's brow lifts slightly. "He was careless enough to show up and take you."

"He didn't technically take me," I say automatically, then stop myself because he did.

Rafe's mouth twitches again. "Fair."

Lorenzo's fingers tighten together, knuckles whitening. Then he relaxes.

"Start from the beginning." He sighs. "Tell me everything you remember about him."

I stare at my hands, trying to think of anything that could be relevant.

"Grant came into my life when I was young," I say, forcing the words out. "He was just there. Polished. Approved by my parents." I roll my eyes. "My parents liked that he was the kind of man you could take to a charity dinner without him setting something on fire."

Lorenzo's mouth quirks. "I'd like to point out I've never set anything on fire at a charity dinner."

"Not physically," I quip. "But you would have loved to."

"I would have."

Rafe shrugs. "You still have time. I believe in you."

I can't help but laugh.

"Victoria . . ." Lorenzo starts, making me shake my head, trying to drag my brain back into the room. "He . . . he kept proposing." I swallow. "Claimed I was his."

Lorenzo's eyes darken.

"And he liked," I continue, voice tightening, "that I didn't have any real say in my own life."

Lorenzo doesn't move.

But the air around him changes. It tightens. If Grant were here, he'd no doubt be dead.

I look down at my lap, fingers twisting together. "He has that cottage. But he also has more places. Not all in his name, though."

Lorenzo tilts his head. "How do you know?"

I lift my shoulders in a slight shrug that feels pathetic. "He was talking about it to someone, and I overheard. Something to do with not paying taxes."

Lorenzo's gaze never leaves my face. "What else?"

I think.

Hard.

The past few years blur together like a montage of dinners I never wanted to be at.

"He fishes," I say suddenly.

Lorenzo's brow lifts. "Fishes."

"Yes." I nod, more certain now. "He . . . he loves to fish. He used to talk about it like it was some spiritual thing. Like catching and releasing a fish made him a better person."

Lorenzo's brows knit together. "You think he has a lake house?"

"Yeah, I do. Don't know where it would be, but it makes sense."

Lorenzo slowly taps his fingers against the desk. "Men like him collect properties. A cottage. A lake house. Maybe something farther away for when he wants to disappear."

My spine prickles. "Wait. Yeah, he mentioned a lake house once. He said it was quiet. That no one bothered him there."

Lorenzo's eyes flick to his men.

"Pull property holdings," Lorenzo orders, voice turning crisp. "Anything tied to Grant, his family, his known associates. Shell corps. Trusts. Anything."

The guy with the mustache nods once, already turning to the keyboard. Fingers flying.

My stomach twists as I watch.

The way Lorenzo works and takes charge is impressive. It used to terrify me, but now that I'm not his target, I can't help but be in awe of him. He's like a king sitting on his cruel throne.

It should scare me. But instead, it makes me feel . . . safe.

Lorenzo's gaze returns to me. "Anything else he said about the lake house?"

I close my eyes, searching memories in my brain.

"Something about . . . cedar," I mumble. "He said the air smelled like cedar. And that there was a dock." My eyes snap open. "And he . . . he joked once that his neighbors were all 'too rich to ask questions.'"

Lorenzo's mouth curves, humorless. "That narrows it down to every lake within three states."

"Helpful," I chide.

He leans forward, voice gentler. "Keep going."

My throat tightens at the softness. I hate that it affects me.

"He used to talk about some mom-and-pop bait shop," I say suddenly.

Lorenzo's eyes sharpen. "This is good. It would have to be close to the house for him to frequent it. This gives us a lot to go on."

"I have a list," the security guard says, turning his laptop monitor slightly so Lorenzo can see. "Most of it is normal—condos, an office suite, the cottage was under a trust. But . . ." His finger taps a line. "There's a property holding under a shell corp registered out of Delaware. It's connected to Grant's mother's maiden name."

My pulse spikes. "That could be it."

Lorenzo's chair scrapes back slightly as he stands. "Where?"

The guard reads off an address.

Rafe pushes off the wall, already moving. "I'll get the cars."

Lorenzo's hand lifts, stopping him with the gesture. "Not yet."

Rafe pauses, brows lifting. "What?"

Lorenzo turns toward me.

He steps closer, and the air changes. Softens. "Stay here." His voice is soft and pleading, a sound I never thought I'd hear out of Lorenzo's mouth.

My spine stiffens automatically. "I'm not—"

His hand cups the side of my face, thumb brushing under my eye.

The touch is gentle.

"You're not going with us," he responds, voice tight.

My throat tightens. "Why?"

"Because if you see what I do to him, you'll never sleep again."

I swallow hard. "I don't sleep now."

His mouth twitches, almost sad. "You will."

My heart throbs against my ribs.

Rafe clears his throat loudly. "Not to interrupt the domestic moment, but we're on a clock."

Lorenzo doesn't look away from me. "You'll stay put."

I roll my eyes because if I don't, I'll cry. "You love telling me to stay put."

His gaze darkens with amusement. "It's one of my love languages."

I glare. "You're disgusting."

"And you married me." He leans in, placing his lips on mine.

He kisses me.

Deep.

When he pulls back, his forehead rests against mine for a beat. "I love you."

"I love you too." I breathe in, shaky. "Be careful."

Lorenzo's mouth curves. "I'm always careful."

I lean back just enough to look at him, brows lifting. "That's the biggest lie you've ever told."

Rafe snorts, already heading for the door. "She's not wrong."

Lorenzo flicks him a look. "I'll kill you after."

Rafe flashes a grin over his shoulder. "Put it on my calendar."

Lorenzo's attention returns to me. "You stay here," he repeats. "No wandering."

I tilt my chin up, stubborn. "I'm not helpless."

"I know." He smiles, then he steps back. "I'll be back."

"You better."

"Bossy."

Lorenzo laughs, then turns and strides toward the door.

As he reaches the threshold, he glances back once.

His eyes lock on mine, and for a second, I see something raw beneath his stare.

Then it shudders.

I remain in the chair, my fingers still tingling where he touched me.

He'd better come *home*.

CHAPTER 64

Lorenzo

THE ASSHOLE ISN'T EVEN TRYING TO HIDE.

Nope. He's just sitting . . .

Waiting.

Like he knew I was coming and seems happy I've finally joined him.

With a smile on his face, Grant looks up from the glass of whiskey in his hand.

"Took you long enough." That alone nearly makes me smile. "Well," he drawls, setting the glass down with deliberate calm, "this is dramatic."

My gun comes up without thought. "How fucking dare you kidnap my wife?"

Grant laughs.

Not nervous. Not scared.

Confident.

"She was never yours," he says, pushing up from the chair. His eyes flick once to the gun, then back to my face. "She was always meant to be mine."

Something snaps inside me. "You don't get to talk about her like she's a thing," I reply, stepping closer. "She isn't an object you misplaced. She's not a prize. She's a person. And she's mine."

Grant's mouth curls, sharp and smug. "Says the man who kept her hidden away and forced her to marry him."

The words land.

They don't miss.

But I don't flinch.

"I was wrong," I say, surprising both of us. "And I know it."

Grant's brows lift. "Oh? That's new."

"I thought vengeance was the same thing as justice," I continue, my grip tightening on the gun. "I thought punishment would fix the hole she left behind."

I step closer. He takes one step back.

"But I was always fixing the wrong thing."

Grant scoffs. "You really think that absolves you?"

"No," I say calmly. "It explains me."

His eyes flick again toward the exit.

I don't give him time to try.

The gun fires.

Once.

Grant jerks as the bullet slams into his chest. He hits the floor hard.

I step over him immediately, gun still trained on his body.

"You will never hurt us again," I say.

Grant coughs, and crimson rivulets escape his mouth.

It's only a matter of time. The fucker will be dead in a matter of seconds.

What can I say, I'm a good shot.

My hand lifted to fire again, because why not? He might be dead already, but a few more bullets will make me feel better.

My finger pulls back the trigger, but what I see stops me . . .

A smile twists through the blood on Grant's face. He's smirking at me, like he knows something I don't.

"That's where you're wrong," he gurgles on his own blood that's bubbling out of his mouth.

My pulse slows. "What do you mean?"

Grant wheezes, breath hitching. "You just signed her death warrant."

What the fuck. "Speak," I snap, crouching, pressing the gun closer. "Now."

His eyes glass, but there's something feral still burning behind them.

"If I can't have her," he rasps, "no one can."

"What the hell does that mean?" I demand. My heart is beating so fast now that it might explode from my body.

Grant's gaze locks onto mine, triumphant even as he bleeds out.

"I put a hit on her," he whispers, "through a network."

The world tilts.

"Call it off," I snarl, grabbing his collar. "Call it off now."

Grant's breath stutters. "O-only I-I can," he chokes. "A-and I-I don't feel—"

Rage detonates.

"Call it off," I roar.

Grant smiles. One last smile. Because before I can even yell again, his body goes slack.

Dead.

"Fuck!"

The room erupts in motion.

Rafe begins to swear, but all I hear is the echo of one sentence repeating in my skull like a curse.

If I can't have her, no one can.

Rafe grips my shoulder. "Lorenzo."

I turn slowly.

"If that's true," I say, voice hollow and lethal, "then she'll never be safe."

Rafe swallows. "Not unless—"

"I kill them all," I finish.

No hesitation.

No dramatics.

Just fact.

Rafe nods once. “Then that’s what we do.”

“We start tonight.”

I don’t remember the drive home.

I don’t remember walking inside.

My brain is fuzzy until I see her. But seeing her jump-starts my heart.

She takes one look at my face and freezes. “Lorenzo.”

I cross the room in three strides and cup her face, grounding myself in the fact that she’s breathing. Still alive. Still warm.

She’s safe.

For now.

I pull her into my chest anyway.

“What happened?”

I don’t know what to tell her, but when she places her hands on my jaw and looks me in the eyes, I know there is only one thing I can do. Tell her the truth.

So I do.

I tell her everything, and when I’m done, I think she will break down. But not my beautiful, strong girl.

Instead, she steels her spine. “What are we going to do?”

I exhale slowly, forehead pressing to hers. “I don’t know.”

The honesty costs me something.

“But what I do know,” I continue, “is that I will find the network. And then I will find every person who belongs to it . . .”

Her fingers curl into my shirt. “You’ll kill them.”

“Yes.”

Her voice trembles. “Doesn’t that scare you?”

I lean back just enough to look at her.

“If I have to become a monster to protect you,” I say quietly, “then I will.”

She studies my face like she’s seeing something new. “I love you,” she says softly.

The words hit harder than any bullet could. "I love you too," I reply, voice rough. "But this means . . ."

Her brow furrows. "What?"

"No one can know about you," I say. "Not yet. Not until every single threat is gone."

"No one?"

"No."

"What about"—she swallows—"your family?"

"No. No one. I can't keep you safe if anyone knows. They are all a liability. Someone can use them to fulfill—"

"The hit."

He nods.

The decision is final.

Her eyes search mine. "Can you live with that?"

I don't hesitate.

"If I have to choose between them and you," I say, "I choose you. Every time. You're my reason to breathe. Now . . . can *you* live with it?"

Her breath shudders. "Yes."

"Good. Because I will scorch the earth for you," I whisper, pressing my forehead to hers, "to make sure you're alive. And mine."

She pulls me down into a kiss.

We don't speak after that.

There are no words left that matter.

Instead, I kiss her everywhere. My mouth touches and licks every inch of her body.

First down her neck, across her collarbone, down to her chest. My tongue laps at her pebbled nipple, running circles around it. Swirling over the peak, sucking it into my mouth.

Victoria grasps my hair with her hands, her body trembling beneath mine.

With a pop, I pull off her breast, and press a kiss to her other nipple before continuing to where she wants me most.

Down her navel.

Then I settle between her now parted legs.

My tongue flicks against her clit until she moans with desire.

"You like that?" I say against her wet flesh.

"Yes," she moans as she thrust her hips up. "Don't stop."

I continue my ministrations, driving her insane with want.

"So close. Inside me, please," she pleads.

I pull back, giving us both what we want.

Making quick work, I free my cock from my pants, and then I crawl back up her body.

Victoria parts her thighs and line my cock with her core.

Slowly, I thrust inside her. The feeling is sublime. She feels like heaven.

It feels like I'm coming home.

Time ceases to exist as I move inside of her.

I never want this moment to end.

If I could live here, buried deep within Victoria I would.

We aren't fucking. It's so much more. And it's exactly what we both need as we cling to each other. Victoria's body trembles beneath me, her back arching up as she chases her release.

I thrust. Once. Twice. And on the third time, I follow her over the edge.

Later, with her curled against me, I stare at the ceiling and make myself a promise.

No mercy. No half measures.

If this world wants to take her from me—

I will end it first.

CHAPTER 65

Lorenzo

Four months later . . .

TIME PASSES SLOWLY.

Not every moment is tense . . . or at least to be present when I'm home, but outside the walls of this house it is. For me, at least.

Victoria pretends everything is normal.

But it's not.

It feels like we are constantly holding our breaths, no matter how much I insulate my wife from the danger she is currently in.

Victoria has settled into our estate. She smiles and tries to be a good sport, but I know her too well. I know the exact pitch of her voice and the facial expressions she makes when she's pretending she isn't afraid.

Grant's last gift . . . the hit on Victoria's life hovers over us at all times.

We just don't discuss it.

There's no point.

I'm searching for which network he put the hit in.

Every few weeks, something happens, and we think we get closer to a clue, but so far, nothing has panned out. Which, in turn, makes me violent.

I want to kill someone, which is why Rafe has been doing

most of the digging. I've kept myself busy murdering everyone who has ever wronged my uncle. I've been branded the family lunatic. A name I'll happily wear if it means I can exercise my blood lust without bringing it home to my wife.

Tonight, Rafe walks into my office with a folder and a look that says he might make my day.

He drops the folder onto my desk with a shit-eating smile. "You owe me big."

My fingers tap the wood twice. "If this is another dead-end, I'm going to gut you."

"Easy there, killer. Save it for the real bad guys."

I flip the folder open.

Inside are photos. A name is on a Post-it, attached to a grainy shot of a man. The next piece of paper has an address on it.

I look up slowly, meeting Rafe's gaze. "What is this?"

"If my source is right, he's part of it. One of the assassins. He took a contract to kill someone."

My jaw tightens so hard my teeth ache. "Good. Because that means he might be going after Victoria since her contract is still active."

I sit back and stare at the photos. "Tonight."

Rafe's brows lift. "Just us?"

I stand, shrugging into my jacket. "You want me to bring a parade? Maybe invite my uncle so he can personally execute me when he finds out the mess I got myself and Victoria in?"

Rafe follows me out of the office, boots thudding on the marble floors. "Matteo keeps asking where you keep disappearing to."

I glance sideways at him, expression bored. "If my cousin is worried about me, he can ask me himself."

Rafe snorts as we make our way outside. We don't tell anyone we're leaving. Not the guards. Not the staff. And especially not Victoria. I hate that part the most.

The only people in the world who know she's here are the handpicked staff who have no loyalty to anyone but me.

No one who works for my uncle besides Rafe can know, but he knows the gravity of the situation and to keep his mouth shut, and my wife hidden.

The car ride is quiet, and I check my weapon twice to kill the time.

Rafe finally breaks the silence first. "You sure you're ready to do this?"

My fingers tighten into a fist at the thought. "No. But I have no choice. Nothing can happen to her."

My wife is in danger because of me, and she will only be safe because I'm willing to become worse than the men hunting her.

Because I will do whatever I have to.

Protecting her is my only concern.

Forty-five minutes later, we approach the address on the slip of paper Rafe gave me. We park two blocks away and walk the rest of the way.

The air is cold enough to sting, but I'm so revved up I barely notice. My blood pumps furiously in my veins, begging to kill everyone who will hurt Victoria.

Rafe stops moving, crouching behind a dumpster as he points into the air. "Camera's there."

I slide in beside him, shoulder nearly touching his. "Okay, so we stay close to the wall and cling to the blind spot."

Rafe's mouth twitches. "Sounds like a solid plan."

"It's our only plan, so it better be." I shift my weight, checking all the angles.

Rafe breathes out through his nose. "Let's hope this goes easy. I have a date later tonight."

"You have a date?" I watch the side door.

"Nah, was just trying to see if you were paying attention."

"Fair," I concede, then motion. "Move."

We cross the open stretch fast, low, slipping into shadow. The side entrance is two steps away. We're almost clear. Then it happens.

I hear a faint click.

What the fuck is that?

Rafe freezes, and my blood turns to ice.

Without any warning, a silhouette appears behind us, gun already raised and firing.

A shot echoes through the air.

Before I even know what's happening, Rafe is running toward me, pushing me. Then he jerks beside me, his hand flying to his side. I barely have time to understand what's happening when Rafe falls to the ground.

My lungs seize. It's like I've forgotten how to breathe. Time slows in a way that makes everything crueler. Rafe's mouth opens, but no sound comes out at first.

He saved me.

Rafe inhales sharply, eyes snapping to mine. "Run," he tries to bark, but it comes out like a cough.

I don't run.

I explode.

I sprint straight at the shooter.

All rational thought has left my brain.

The only thing I can think about is death.

The hitman steps back, startled, trying to aim again. I slam into him. The gun goes off, the bullet biting into the wall behind me.

My fist meets his jaw.

Bone crunches.

He staggers.

I grab his wrist and twist hard until the gun hits the ground.

He swings at me, but I duck.

I use the moment of him being distracted to drive my elbow into his ribs.

He wheezes, but I don't stop. I don't think. I just hit.

All the fear I live with pours into rage as I hammer him with my fists.

I drive him backward into the wall. He tries to claw at my jacket to stop me, but now that I have him where I want him, I'm functioning on pure adrenaline.

I slam his head against the concrete.

Once.

Twice.

Blood pours from the back of his head.

"Killing me won't stop it," he rasps, voice rough with amusement.

I snarl, shoving my forearm against his throat. "Who runs the network?"

His eyes glitter. "You think I'd tell you?"

"Tell me," I bite out, shoving harder.

He laughs. Actually, fucking laughs. Rage flashes so hot behind my eyes that my vision goes blurry.

I pull back my fist.

But a shot rings out again.

The hitman's head snaps to the side, his body going slack.

For one stunned second, I just stare at him.

Then I turn and see Rafe with a gun in his hand, and the other hand pressed hard to his bleeding side.

His face is pale now. "Couldn't let him live," he manages, then his body slumps forward.

I'm at him in two strides, grabbing him from the ground.

"Stay with me," I order, but my voice cracks as I haul him upright.

Rafe's breath shakes. "Don't . . . don't do that."

"Do what?" I snap, dragging him toward the car.

"Sound . . . scared."

"I'm not scared."

Lies. I am. I don't know how I'll do this alone.

Rafe coughs, blood speckling his lips. "That's . . . the stupidest lie you've ever told."

"Quit talking. I need to stop the bleeding." My fingers rip his jacket open.

Blood. So much blood. My stomach roils from the sight.

I press my palm to the wound, hard.

Rafe hisses, grabbing my wrist. "Fuc-fucking shit—you trying to kill me?" He coughs, blood bubbling up out of his mouth.

"Shut up, Rafe. I need to concentrate."

Rafe's hand tightens around my wrist, forcing me to look at him.

His eyes are glassy, yet calm.

It terrifies me.

"Find them."

"I can't." My jaw clenches. "He didn't give me anything."

"You-you will," he stutters out.

My throat closes. It feels like a part of me is dying as I watch him struggle to breathe. I lean closer, pressing harder against the wound, panic creeping in like a tide I can't stop. "Don't talk."

Rafe coughs again, then winces. "You—you fix things."

I stare at him, helpless, furious, shaking. "You were supposed to drag me out of hell."

Rafe's gaze softens. "I did."

I swallow hard. "Not like this."

Rafe's breath trembles. "Listen to me."

My eyes lock onto his.

Rafe's voice drops, raw. "You can't . . . you can't kill the whole world alone."

"I can," I snap, tears burning behind my eyes like acid, "and I will."

Rafe's mouth curves faintly. "For her."

"For her," I confirm.

Rafe's eyelids flutter. His hand slips from my wrist.

"No," I bark, grabbing his hand and squeezing hard. "No. Don't you dare."

Rafe's lips part, breathing shallow. "Lorenzo . . ." The way he says my name sounds like an apology, and a tear falls from my eyes.

I press my forehead to his. "Stay."

Rafe exhales, weak. "Tell . . . tell Matteo I died doing something . . . noble."

A broken laugh tears out of me. "I will."

Rafe's mouth twitches, and a silent sob lodges in my throat.

Rafe's eyes drift, unfocused. "I-I'm . . ." he whispers.

"Rafe?" I rasp.

"S-sorry," he breathes out, eyes shutting.

My throat tightens so hard it hurts. "Rafe," I whisper.

He exhales once.

For a second, I don't move.

I just stare at him, waiting for him to inhale again.

It never comes.

I have no idea how much time has passed, but my hands are still shaking.

It feels like my chest has been ripped open.

"Fuck," I whisper, voice breaking. "Fuck."

My palm stays pressed to the wound even though I already know it doesn't matter.

Because letting go feels like admitting it.

Admitting he's gone.

Admitting I'm alone.

I squeeze my eyes shut and take a breath.

By the time I make it home, it's nearly dawn.

The gate opens, and I park before heading into the house.

The guards straighten, and no one speaks because the blood on my shirt does all the talking.

I don't remember walking through the foyer. I just remember Victoria's footsteps rushing toward me.

Her hands catch my arm, fingers digging into my sleeve, as her eyes fly over my face and then down to where the blood is.

"Not mine."

Her mouth opens, but no sound comes out at first.

We stare at each other for a second before she speaks. "Where's Rafe?"

My throat locks.

I can't answer.

The silence can answer for me.

Victoria's body shakes as she takes my hand and guides me down the hall.

"Come on." Her voice is low and careful, like a loud sound might shatter me. "Shower."

My feet move because she makes them.

Next thing I know, the bathroom lights flick on.

Victoria turns the water on.

The sound fills the room, soft and steady. I step into the shower fully dressed.

She follows me in, also fully clothed. Together, we stand under the water as it runs down our bodies, washing away the blood.

The fabric of our clothes clings to us, but we don't move. Hell, I don't even blink. I don't do anything except breathe.

Victoria steps closer, hands hovering, uncertain. Her fingers land on my wrist, gentle. "Lorenzo."

I stare straight ahead.

Her voice softens. "Talk to me."

My mouth opens.

But still, I have no words to say. Nothing comes out. Nothing makes sense.

Her arms wrap around me. Warm. Real. *Alive.*

She's alive.

And Rafe is dead.

My hands finally lift, slow, shaking, closing around her like I'm terrified she'll vanish too.

Her voice vibrates against me. "Is he really . . .?"

The water keeps pouring down on us.

"Yes," I manage, voice rough.

Victoria's arms tighten, as a sound leaves her—small and broken.

Then she pulls back just enough to look up at me, eyes glassy but steady. "Go to Matteo," she whispers. "He'll help you."

I shake my head once.

Victoria frowns. "Why?"

I swallow hard, forcing words out. "I can't risk it," I rasp, voice raw. "Not with the hit . . ."

Victoria's brows knit. "But—"

"I can't let anyone know where you are," I say harsher than I want, but I can't risk her life. "Not until every assassin tied to that network is dead."

Victoria's hand slides up to my jaw, thumb brushing lightly like she's anchoring me. "You can't do this alone."

"I have no choice. To protect you, I will. No matter how long it takes."

She nods as tears fill her eyes. Then she takes a deep breath, shoulders straightening.

"Okay."

My chest aches. "Yeah?"

Victoria nods slowly, her chin lifting. "I believe in you."

"It won't be too long."

Her mouth curves faintly, sad but steady. "I trust you."

The words land like a vow.

Like a lifeline.

And for the first time since I watched Rafe die, I feel something other than rage.

I feel fear. The fear of failing her. Of losing her.

Of becoming the kind of man who burns down the world and still can't protect the one thing he loves.

Victoria presses her lips to my cheek. “You’re not alone,” she whispers. “I’ll always be by your side.”

I hold her tighter under the water, pretending everything will be alright for her sake, but in my head, where the monster lives, a new promise forms . . .

I will find the network.

I will tear it apart.

I will kill them all.

THE PRESENT

CHAPTER 66

Lorenzo

Thirteen Years Later . . .

THE PHONE VIBRATES AGAIN. I DON'T LOOK AT IT YET, BUT when I finally do glance down, the name on the screen tightens something in my chest.

Jaxson Price.

I answer without a greeting. "If this is about the servers being down, I already told you in the group chat that I don't care. It's not my problem."

Jax's voice laughs through the line. "You're an asshole, but you will want to hear this."

"Aw, look at you, Jax. You finally learned to flirt. Lay it on me."

"You might want to sit down . . . I found him."

The room goes very quiet. I swear I stop breathing because I don't need him to tell me who he's talking about. I've waited for this call for years.

I lean forward in my chair. "Say that again."

Jax exhales, like he's been holding it in for years. "The last name. He resurfaced three weeks ago under a different name. But I found him."

My throat tightens. "Where?"

"He's in Cape May. Waterfront rental. Cash paid upfront.

He's alone. And before you ask, I'm sure it's him. I double- and triple-checked."

I close my eyes.

Forty-two.

That's how many names were on the list. Forty-two people were gunning to end my wife's life.

Forty-one are gone.

Jax keeps talking, words tumbling now. "I know you said not to ask, and I didn't, but—Lorenzo—are you ever going to tell me what this was all for? I've been tracking names for years. And lord knows what you do to these names once I give them to you . . . But I know this isn't business. This is—"

"Survival. I'll tell you soon."

I hang up before he can push. I've been friends with the man for years. He's helped us all out of so many tight binds, I don't know why I don't tell him the truth. I can trust him. I can trust all my friends . . .

Yet . . .

After Rafe died, I haven't been able to bring anyone else into my mess.

I can't lose anyone else.

I push off my chair and walk down the hall. Victoria is in the sitting room. She looks up the second I enter.

She always does.

Something in my face gives me away because her smile fades before I say a word.

"What's wrong?"

I don't answer immediately.

Instead, I cross the room and pull her against me, burying my face in her hair. I need her. Need to inhale her. To ground myself in her presence.

She melts into me, fingers fisting in my shirt. "Lorenzo. You're scaring me."

"I found him," I mumble against her neck. "The last one."

Her breath catches.

For years, we've lived with this unspoken countdown ticking between us. Years of pretending nothing was wrong. Nothing except the fact that she's lived years locked behind these gates.

We built a life for ourselves, yet . . . she's never been free.

The thing about Victoria is that she never complained.

Never doubted me.

Always knew I'd protect her.

She pulls back just far enough to look at me. Her eyes shine, already filling with unshed tears. "You found him?"

I nod once.

Her hands slide to my arms, gripping tightly. "I knew this day would come."

"So did I."

Victoria's shoulders begin to tremble.

I pull her back into my grasp and hold her tight.

"It's almost over," I whisper. "I won't let this baby be born in secret."

Her hand drifts unconsciously to her stomach. Soft footsteps interrupt us.

"Why is Mommy crying?"

I look up and see my son standing in the doorway. His dark brown hair is wild with curls, and he's holding a bike helmet in his little hand.

I can't help but laugh, though. Only my kid would want to go for a bike ride but has no shoes on and is missing one sock.

Victoria swipes at her cheeks quickly, forcing a smile that could fool no one but him.

"She's just happy," I say, dropping my voice. "You know Mommy. She has big feelings."

He considers this. "Is it the baby?"

I move away from Victoria and kneel in front of him. "No, buddy. The baby's fine."

He brightens instantly. Crisis averted. "Can we ride bikes?"

I glance up at Victoria, and she nods.

"Go grab your bike," I tell him. "I'll meet you outside in two minutes."

He bolts away, and I stand slowly.

Victoria stands too. "You're going tonight?"

"Yes."

Her jaw tightens. "You don't have to do it alone."

"I do."

She shakes her head, stepping closer. "Tell Matteo."

I hesitate. She sees it. Always does.

"You need him," she presses, voice low but unyielding. Now that she's decided I need to involve him, nothing I can say will change her mind. "No more secrets. Not now."

"This ends if I'm alone," I argue, though my heart isn't in it. "If I bring him in and something goes wrong—"

"Then at least you won't be carrying it alone," she says softly. "You've paid enough in blood."

I close my eyes.

I think of Rafe.

And then I think of my son riding his bike outside, unaware of how close he came to not existing at all.

I nod.

"Okay."

She exhales like she's been holding that breath for years.

Matteo is exactly the same and completely different all at once.

Same grin. Same smart mouth. Same uncanny ability to read a room, yet everything is different in his life.

He's typing on his phone when I walk in.

Probably a dumb joke to the group chat.

Matteo pretends he's too good for our juvenile antics, but he's always the first to respond.

His face drops when he sees my expression.

"Lorenzo," he says carefully. "I wasn't . . . I wasn't expecting you. You good? Because you kind of look like you murdered someone, or like you're about to tell me you got some girl pregnant."

"Both," I reply.

His brow furrows. "The fuck?"

I take a deep breath, then exhale. "I need you to listen."

He gestures to the chair. "Sit. Now."

I don't sit.

Then I tell him everything.

Not clean. Not pretty.

I tell him about the marriage. About the fear. About his father and the bad call I made that changed everything.

Then I tell him about Grant.

About the hit.

About the network.

I tell him about Rafe.

Matteo doesn't interrupt.

When I finish, the silence stretches heavy with tension.

"So," he finally says, voice measured. "Let me get this straight."

Here it comes.

"There was a hit put on the woman you love," he continues, leaning back, eyes sharp, "and at no point did you think to come to me?"

"Your father was in charge," I say quietly. "He notoriously killed his brother for trafficking. You think he would've believed me if I said the marriage was consensual?"

Matteo winces. "Fair. But that maybe should've been your first clue not to force a woman to marry you."

"Really?" I raise a brow. "And how exactly did you get your wife to marry you?"

Matteo snorts. "I didn't force my wife."

"You had a marriage of convenience."

"Tomato, tomah-to."

I almost laugh.

Almost.

I open my mouth to speak, but Matteo holds up a finger.

"But what about after? What about after my father died, and I was in charge?"

"I couldn't risk it. I couldn't risk it getting out."

He nods slowly. "I get it."

"Thank you. I'm sorry." I don't say what I'm sorry for, but he understands, and that's all that matters.

For a moment, Matteo just stares at me. Then his brows furrow together. "You really killed forty-one assassins?"

"Yes."

Matteo nods his head. "It all makes sense now."

"What?"

"Why you're a lunatic. I always wondered."

"You wondered why I was a lunatic?" I narrow my eyes at him.

"Yeah." He shrugs. "We all did, but now knowing what you had to deal with . . . yeah. It makes sense. But now that I know . . . *We* finish this," Matteo says. "Then *we* tell everyone."

"Okay."

He studies me for another long moment. "Anything else you're not telling me?"

I hesitate.

Then—fuck it. Might as well drop the rest of the bomb on his lap.

"You're an uncle." While technically Matteo isn't my brother, he is.

I'm met with silence. Then a smile.

"Fuck. I'm an uncle."

And for the first time in a long time, I feel hope.

Tonight, we end it.

CHAPTER 67

Lorenzo

TONIGHT IS DIFFERENT.

Tonight, Matteo walks beside me.

I haven't seen this version of him since he retired, and I took over. But here he is, the scary motherfucker I need him to be.

"This is fun. We should do this more often."

I glance over, letting my mouth twitch without committing to a smile. "Pretty sure your wife would be pissed if you came out of retirement."

Matteo's gaze scans the area, and he sees my men gathering in the corners to back us up. "Cute. You even brought bodyguards. What happened to the man who insisted on doing everything alone?" Low blow. He's still pissed I didn't tell him. He'll get over it.

"We have kids." I step to the door, ready to bust it down and end this for good. "They're here so we don't do anything stupid. Like die."

"'Bout time you finally got a head on your shoulders." He winks.

I push open the door to the house and silently creep inside.

Hope Jax is right about this spot because it feels abandoned. When I turn the corner, I know he was. There, in an oversized recliner, is a man, and by the way he watches me, he's the man I want.

He's not panicking.

He lifts his chin as I stop in front of him, like he's greeting a business partner instead of the end of his life.

Matteo drifts to my right, snagging a second chair and turning it backward before sitting. He folds his arms across the back, posture casual, expression anything but.

"Alright." Matteo gestures to the man. "Let's meet the last asshole on the list."

The man's mouth twitches.

I let the silence stretch, watching him and letting him feel the weight of my attention. Then I lean in.

"Name," I prompt, voice soft.

He swallows. "You already know it."

I tilt my head. "Humor me."

His gaze lifts again, calculating. "Real name or alias?"

Matteo makes a face. "Seriously, I don't have time for this shit." Matteo turns to me. "You already know his name. Drop it and just kill the fucker."

Marcus's (Because yes, I do in fact know his name) lip curls like he wants to laugh, but he doesn't.

I straighten, slow, and pace a small circle around Marcus's chair. My boots echo across the wood floors in steady beats.

Every time I pass behind him, his shoulders tense like he expects the first strike.

He's not wrong.

I stop directly in front of him again, bending at the waist, lowering my voice.

"You know why I'm here?"

His eyes glitter, dark and stubborn. "Because you're obsessive."

Matteo laughs once. "Oh, he is. You should've seen him when he was twenty. He once hunted a guy for a week because the bastard scratched his car."

Marcus's gaze flicks to Matteo. "That true?"

I don't blink. "It was a nice car."

Matteo points at me like he's presenting evidence in court. "See? He doesn't deny it. Psychopathic behavior."

"I'm not a psychopath," I respond, straightening. "I'm a romantic."

Matteo's brows shoot up. "No. Don't. Don't ruin the word romantic."

I glance back at Marcus. "You know what you people did?"

Marcus's mouth tightens.

"Grant Jacobson put the order out," I continue, letting the name hit the room like a thrown knife. "He thought if he couldn't have her, no one could. But he underestimated me." I take a deep breath.

My throat tightens, but not because it hurts. Because I'm so close to closure.

I grab the bag Matteo is holding and start pulling things out.

Marcus's eyes track the objects one by one, his throat moving as his body finally remembers fear.

Matteo's voice follows the movement. "I hate to break it to you, Marcus, but if you thought your death would be fast, surprise, it won't."

Marcus swallows. "You're really doing this?"

I pick up the rubber tubing, weigh it in my hand, as if I'm deciding whether to use it.

"You're really acting surprised?" I turn back toward him. "Did you think the man who spent years erasing your whole network would rush the last kill?"

Marcus's jaw sets. "I figured you'd want to end it and live happily ever after," he scoffs.

I stop in front of him, letting the words hang between us. Then I nod. "Yeah. That would be smart . . . but no one has ever called me smart."

"Nope. They haven't," Matteo's voice slips in.

I let the tubing tap lightly against my palm.

"Every time Victoria jumped at a knock." *Tap*. "Every time

she couldn't sleep." *Tap.* "Every time she smiled, and I saw fear behind it . . ." *Tap.*

"She was safe. You had her well-guarded, apparently."

"Safe," I repeat, tasting the word. "You think safe means living?"

Marcus's gaze drops, just for a second. That second is the only mercy he gets.

I swing the tubing.

Marcus grunts.

"Here's what's going to happen. I'm going to kill you slowly, and you're going to enjoy it."

His gaze flicks back to me. "Where did you hide Victoria?"

The question comes out of nowhere, like a slap. Matteo's posture goes rigid.

"Don't say her name with your mouth," I hiss. "You haven't earned that privilege."

"Was just wondering how you kept her alive so long."

I know what he's doing.

He wants me to kill him faster.

He wants me to snap.

I won't.

"How about instead of you asking me a question, I ask you one . . .? How does it feel? Being the final loose thread in a noose I've been tightening for years?"

Marcus smiles. It's faint and bitter. "Your revenge turned you into a monster."

I tilt my head, considering. "Yes. It did."

Marcus breathes out, a sound like resignation. "We called you the Shadow."

I still.

Matteo's brows lift. "A nickname. Cute. Can't wait to tell the boys."

Marcus's gaze stays on me. "Because you didn't hit us fast. You stalked. You watched."

My grip tightens on the tubing in my hands.

Marcus's gaze flicks down briefly, then up. "You made it collapse from the inside."

"Good."

He braces, shoulders tensing.

I stare at him for a long second, then I smile. "It's time to end this," I tell him. "I've been washing blood off my hands, then going home to kiss my family for too long."

I walk behind him, lift the tubing to wrap it around his neck, and pull.

He struggles against me, his body jerking, but I'm too strong.

I watch as the life leaves his body. As he ceases to struggle, his legs no longer kick.

When I know he's dead, I let go of the tubing.

"Thought you were going to take it slow?"

"I decided he was right."

"About?"

"Happily ever after and all that shit."

That makes Matteo smile.

And then my own lips tip up.

I'm finally free.

"You realize what this means."

I don't answer.

Matteo smirks. "It means . . . that your secret soap opera can finally end."

I raise a brow, not fully understanding where this is going.

"It's time to tell the boys," he clarifies.

I've put this off for so long, I don't even know how to broach the topic, but no fear because apparently Matteo already has an idea as he's pulling his phone out.

"You're enjoying this." I shake my head in mock annoyance.

"Immensely." He smiles so broadly; I think he might break his jaw. Or maybe I'll do that . . .

Before I can come up with a plot for murdering my cousin, my phone buzzes.

Fuck. I don't even need to look to know what he did, but like the glutton for punishment that I am, I still check.

Matteo: Meeting. Cyrus's place. 30 minutes.

Jaxson: If this is about murdering someone, I'm out. You know I hate that shit.

Trent: Context? I'm a little busy.

Matteo: Shut up, Trent. This is important.

Gideon: Someone better be dying.

Tobias: For someone who retired, you're really fucking annoying.

Alaric: You really are.

Matteo: It's Lorenzo-related.

There's a pause in the texts, and I wonder what they're all thinking and who will break first.

Jaxson: Oh shit.

Cyrus: What did he do now?

Matteo: You'll want to hear this in person.

Gideon: That's ominous.

Tobias: Did he finally snap?

Alaric: I thought that happened years ago.

Matteo: 30 minutes. Cyrus's

Cyrus: Why is this at my house?

Matteo: Because Lorenzo won't host.

Cyrus: I hate all of you.

I put my phone down and look up to see Matteo smiling.

"You find yourself really clever, don't you?"

"I do."

I stare at him.

He grins wider.

Thirty minutes later, we head into Cyrus's estate and straight into the poker room.

While there's no game tonight, everyone is hanging around the bar having a drink.

Jaxson is already halfway through a drink and Tobias looks annoyed that we summoned him.

Gideon leans against the wall, while Trent sits calmly. He's most likely afraid to piss off Matteo again. Alaric and Cyrus stand together in the center of the room, both with drinks in their hands.

"You have exactly one minute," Cyrus says as we enter. "And if this is about some investment—"

"It's not," Matteo cuts him off. Cyrus narrows his eyes but waits for him to continue as do all the other men in the room. "Lorenzo has something to confess."

Every single one of them turns in my direction and looks at me.

"There's something I should've told you a long time ago," I say evenly.

Jaxson squints. "If this is about you secretly reading rom coms, I'm leaving."

"I'm married."

Silence. Complete and utter silence. And shock too. It's so quiet, you'd be able to hear a pin drop.

Cyrus's mouth hangs open then he snaps it shut. "You're . . . what?"

"Married."

Trent stares at me. "To . . . a human?"

"No to an alien." I roll my eyes.

Alaric lowers his phone slowly. "No fucking way."

"Yes." That's all I can say.

"For how long?" Trent asks calmly.

"Yeah, so . . . it's been awhile," I admit.

"How long is awhile?" Cyrus chimes in.

"Over a decade."

The room erupts into chaos.

"Over a decade?" Cyrus shouts.

"How the fuck . . . " Jaxson shake his head.

Gideon sets down his drink. "You're barely a functioning adult. How do you maintain a marriage?"

"I prioritize."

Tobias shakes his head. "Sorry I call bullshit. There's no fucking way."

Cyrus runs both hands through his hair. "You're fucking unhinged. Kill on a dime . . . You make serial killers look tame . . . "

Jaxson's eyes widen slowly. "Holy shit."

"What?" I ask.

"Was this the reason for all cryptic shit?" Jaxson demands. "The list of names?"

"Wait. Years ago, you had me do some shady shit for you . . . "

I look at Cyrus and then at Jax. "Yes."

The silence this time is different. Then Cyrus lets out a sharp laugh. "You bastard."

Jaxson points at me. "We've been running a covert wife op?"

"Yes."

"You told me once," Cyrus's eyes are wide, "that you were handling a 'delicate situation.'"

I shrug. "She is delicate."

Jaxson chokes on his drink. "Oh my god. Every time you said 'personal matter.'"

"You were going home to your wife," Cyrus finishes.

I don't bother answering.

Tobias actually claps slowly. "I'm impressed."

Alaric starts to chuckle. "I'm not going to lie, I'm almost proud."

Cyrus studies me carefully. "Why didn't you tell us?"

I take a deep breath. Doesn't matter that the threat is over, it still pains me to think about it. "There was a hit on her. Through a pretty fucking big assassin group . . . I couldn't risk anyone knowing where she was."

Cyrus's expression tightens. "So . . . you let us think you were some crazy sociopath."

"After killing forty-two assassins for my wife, I kind of am a crazy sociopath."

"That's not the point."

"They're all dead now," Matteo adds quickly. "Every last one."

The weight of that settles in the room.

Jaxson lowers his drink.

Cyrus exhales slowly. Then he steps forward and grips the back of my neck before pulling me into a hug. "You idiot. You should've trusted us."

"I did. I do. Just not with her life," I answer honestly.

He nods once.

Jaxson claps my shoulder. "What's her name?"

"Victoria."

Cyrus smiles. "Victoria."

Tobias tilts his head. "Does she know about you? What you do?"

"Yes."

"And she still stayed?" Trent asks.

"She chose me."

Alaric lifts his glass. "To Victoria."

They all raise their drinks.

"We're happy for you," Cyrus says, serious now. "You deserve happiness."

Jaxson nods. "Yeah, you do. As much as it pains me to admit it."

Gideon smirks. "We expect to meet her."

Matteo folds his arms. "Preferably before Lorenzo locks her back in a vault."

I let out a sigh. "Fuck you, Cuz. I didn't lock her in a vault."

Cyrus arches a brow.

"I didn't."

With that the room fills with laughter again.

I welcome it.

Because for the first time in ten years, Victoria doesn't live in secrecy.

And neither do I.

CHAPTER 68

Victoria

IT'S BEEN A CRAZY FEW DAYS SINCE MY LIFE CHANGED, AND I feel like I haven't seen my husband in days.

I stop just inside the doorway of our room to find Lorenzo waiting for me.

"Before you say anything, I need you to listen."

My fingers curl into the doorframe. "I don't like that sentence."

A corner of his mouth lifts, barely. "I know."

He takes a step closer and reaches into his pocket and pulls out a box before opening it.

Inside is a ring.

It's simple and beautiful, and perfect in every way.

"I already married you." I smile.

"That wasn't the right kind of wedding," he says quietly. "This," he continues, lifting the ring between us, "is me asking. No leverage. No threats. Just love."

Tears well in my eyes. "You do know we already have a kid, and another one actively using my bladder as a trampoline?"

His gaze drops instinctively to my stomach, softening in a way that still wrecks me every time. "I'm aware."

"And we've been married for years."

His mouth curves. "Stop being difficult, Little Bird, and say you'll marry me. Again."

I stare at him.

At the man who burned half the underworld to keep me alive. At the boy who never stopped leaving me rocks. At the father who pretends not to cry when our son falls asleep on his chest.

"Fine," I say. "But you get a ring too."

His brow lifts. "I don't need one."

Then I walk over to the desk and grab my own box.

He stills.

"I had a little help getting this from Marta. Don't be mad. I was going to give it to you after the baby was born," I say, opening it. Inside is a darker band. "This time, I choose it. I choose you."

For a long moment, Lorenzo doesn't speak.

Then he exhales like he's been holding his breath for a decade.

"Christ." He drags a hand down his face. "You're going to kill me."

"Eventually," I promise. "But not today."

EPILOGUE

Victoria

THIS PLACE LOOKS DIFFERENT. MAYBE BECAUSE SO MUCH HAS changed.

My parents are long gone now, living god know where. The moment I found out what they did to Lorenzo and me, I wrote them out of my life. And once Grant passed, it didn't take long for them to lose everything.

I'm no longer the young girl trapped in a cage. I'm now a woman who's no longer afraid.

And married to the love of my life.

My son, who's eight now, tilts his head back to stare at the house. "This is where you lived?" His fingers tighten around mine, a protective gesture he definitely learned from his father.

My daughter is two, and stubborn as sin, lets out a delighted squeal from Lorenzo's arms and points at the vines crawling up the columns.

"Jungle?" she announces.

Lorenzo shifts her higher against his chest.

"It's not a jungle." I laugh.

Lorenzo's mouth curls into a grin. "Just no one took care of it." His eyes sweep the property. "Good thing Mommy likes living in the underworld, or she'd have to clean this mess."

My son blinks. "Dad, what's the underworld?"

Lorenzo's expression doesn't change, but I know he wants to laugh. Good luck coming up with something to say.

"It's where people go when they don't eat their vegetables," he answers with absolute calm.

My son's eyes widen. "That's real?"

"Terrifyingly," Lorenzo confirms, shifting our daughter again as she attempts to gnaw on his jacket zipper. "Eat your broccoli."

My daughter (who is apparently my husband's daughter) chooses violence and bites his shoulder through the fabric.

Lorenzo doesn't even flinch. He just stares down at her with the resigned patience of a man who's survived assassins.

"Ah," he playfully responds, voice thick with fake tragedy. "I've been stabbed."

She giggles. *A future criminal in the making.*

I press my lips together, trying not to smile. It doesn't work. The smile creeps in anyway. These kids will always have me wrapped around their fingers.

We keep walking through the garden until we find what I'm looking for: the boathouse.

Despite everything, it still stands.

It shouldn't.

But somehow, it's weathered all the storms.

Like us.

We open the door and step inside. As soon as I'm inside, I'm transported back through time to earlier days and first kisses.

I walk straight to the wall, reaching my hand out when I find what I'm looking for.

My fingers stop before I even touch it. The carved initials are faded but still visible, a wound that never fully healed.

V + L

Crooked. Messy.

Cut into the wood deep.

To last a lifetime.

My throat tightens as my fingers trace the old cut in the wood.

Memories slam into me so hard I almost stumble.

Seventeen. Barefoot. Laughing too loud.

Lorenzo young and reckless.

Now I stand here with two children and the man he became. The man who buried bodies for me in an attempt to stitch my soul back together.

And he did.

I exhale.

My son tilts his head up. "Is this where you fell in love?"

Lorenzo slowly turns his head toward me, eyes fierce with undying love. "This is where our story started."

My chest aches. This was our place. The beginning. The first chapter.

And now, standing here with the people I love most in the world, this place feels like closure.

Lorenzo steps closer. His free hand wraps around my waist, fingers warm through my shirt. He tilts his head, studying my face like he's memorizing it all over again. "Do you ever regret it?"

My breath catches.

"Do you?" I respond.

We both know what he's asking . . .

What I'm asking.

The estate.

The war.

The fear.

The years in hiding.

The blood on his hands.

I meet his eyes. "Not for a second," I answer.

His brow tightens. "Not even the worst parts? Not even . . . what I did? What I became?"

My chest aches.

I lift my hand and press my palm against his cheek.

I smile. "Especially the worst parts," I whisper. "I'll never regret those parts."

His eyes darken, not with hunger, but with something deeper, something grateful.

He exhales like he's been underwater for years and just surfaced.

We thought love ruined us. Turns out it saved us instead.

Together, we step out of the boathouse.

Our son races ahead as our daughter squirms in Lorenzo's arms, wanting to run after him.

Then I tilt my head toward the ruined estate, then toward the water, and last toward the open sky.

Thankful for every challenge that we had to overcome because without them . . .

We wouldn't be here.

Together.

Forever.

Want to read about the other characters mentioned in this story?

Cyrus and Ivy: *Corrupt Kingdom*

Alaric and Phoenix: *Tarnished Empire*

Matteo and Viviana: *Ruthless Monarch*

Trent and Payton: *Shattered Dynasty*

Tobias and Skye: *Broken Reign*

Gideon and Sasha: *Sinful Crown*

Jax and Willow: *Conceal*

ACKNOWLEDGMENTS

I want to thank my entire family. I love you all so much.

Eric, Blake, and Lexi . . . I love you guys more than anything in the world. You are my whole life. Thank you for always being there for me.

Thank you to the amazing professionals that helped with Cruel Throne
Jenny Sims
Kelly Allenby
Virginia Carey
Champagne Formats
Jill Glass
Kaija Wessel
Hang Le

Thank you to my fabulous agent Kimberly Whalen.
Thank you to all of my friends for being there for me.
Thank you to my AMAZING ARC TEAM! You guys rock!
To the ladies in the Ava Harrison Support Group, I couldn't have done this without your support!
Please consider joining my Facebook reader group Ava Harrison Support Group
Thank you to all the Booktokers, bookstagramers, and bloggers who helped spread the word. Thanks for your excitement and love of books!
Last but certainly not least . . .
Thank you to the readers!
Thank you so much for taking this journey with me.

ABOUT THE AUTHOR

Ava Harrison is a *USA Today* and Amazon bestselling author. When she's not writing, you can find her shopping online, cooking dinner for her family, or curled up on her couch watching a thriller movie with her husband.

ALSO BY AVA HARRISON

Corrupt Kingdom
Tarnished Empire
Ruthless Monarch
Shattered Dynasty
Broken Reign
Sinful Crown
Deceit
Entice
Conceal
The Price Dynasty Box Set
Sweet Collide
Twisted Collide
Beautiful Collide
Tempted
Provoke
Resist
Transference
Absolution
Intention
Clandestine
Sordid
Explicit
The Lancaster Brothers Box Set
Here Lies North
Through Her Eyes
Illicit

Co-write with Vanessa Fewings
The Ravishing

www.ingramcontent.com/pod-product-compliance
Lightning Source LLC
LaVergne TN
LVHW010627110826
845149LV00014B/2793

* 9 7 8 1 9 6 1 8 3 8 1 1 6 *